# RUNNING
# ON
# EMPTY

# RUNNING
# ON
# EMPTY

## A WINE COUNTRY COLD CASE

**KARIN FITZ SANFORD**

LEVEL
BEST BOOKS

First published by Level Best Books 2024

Author Photo Credit: Sterling Mohar Photography

First edition

ISBN: 978-1-68512-615-5

Cover art by Level Best Designs

This book was professionally typeset on Reedsy.
Find out more at reedsy.com

*For my grandchildren: Kai Tierheimer, Maisie Sanford, John Sanford, and Lucas Sanford*

# Praise for Running on Empty

"Full of fun clues, quirky characters and a great sense of place, *Running on Empty* is the perfect visit to California's wine country."—Rhys Bowen, *New York Times* bestselling author of the Royal Spyness and Molly Murphy mysteries, and *The Venice Sketchbook*

"The title of this latest Wine County Cold Case may be "Running on Empty," but the story's certainly not. A full-bodied mystery with depth and bite, and a plot that's meaty and lush. Savory, smoky, and smooth, from the first sip to the last."—J.R. Sanders, Shamus Award-winning author of the Nate Ross mysteries

"With a freight train of a plot worthy of any seasoned crime writer—think Elmore Leonard, Karin Slaughter, and Raymond Chandler—Sanford delivers a timeless thriller and heroine in feisty, brilliant, and flawed ex-FBI agent Anne McCormack, who finds herself entangled (again) in a web of mystery and deception in Northern California's wine country. The setting is but one of this book's plentiful charms. There is a cold case—the decades-old murder of a socialite—and a devastating Ponzi scheme that will have readers turning pages well into the night. Full of zigzagging cliffhangers, *Running on Empty* hooks readers from the first sentence and never lets up—not even when it looks like our heroes have run out of gas. I loved this book."—David Samuel Levinson, author of *Tell Me How This Ends Well*

"In this fast-paced, cold-case whodunit, Karin Fitz Sanford will keep you guessing to the end. Mystery and wine country—a terrific combo."—Vinnie Hansen, author of the Carol Sabala Mystery Series and *One Gun*.

# Prologue

## Santa Rosa, California, Fall 2005

Detective Jack McCormack got the call he'd been waiting a year for at the worst possible time: It was after five o'clock, his shift was over, and his Italian take-out order would be arriving at his house across town in ten minutes.

On the third ring, Jack picked up.

"This one's for you, Mac," said the watch commander.

"I'm on my way out of here, Lieutenant. So unless it's some kind of emergency, try one of the rookies..."

"Nope, the call's coming in on the business line, so it's not an emergency. But you're gonna want this. This one has possibilities."

"In what way?" He was watching the back of his partner Dean Diaz, who was beating him out the door. Second night this week.

"Caller's reporting a dead body, and since that's your specialty, I'm transferring it."

Jack sighed, drumming his fingers on his notepad until the transfer came through. "Detective McCormack here," he said while turning off his computer.

All he heard through the line was labored breathing until, finally, a rush of words. "I found a big mound of dirt by the side of a road. It's covering up a dead body, I'm sure of it." The deep voice was muffled and hurried. "And there's a handbag there, too."

"Slow down. What's your name? How did you find it?"

"Hey, man, stop asking questions! Just come."

"Christ," Jack muttered under his breath, and then asked, "Where is it?"

The directions to the body were inch-perfect: Head to the north edge of town, take the Silverado exit west to Old Corral Road, continue driving until the pavement stops and it turns into a bumpy dirt road. Then drive another 600 feet. "The body is on the left side of the road, three feet from the iron gate leading to someone's private property. Hurry before the coyotes get to it."

"Stay there until—"

The tipster hung up.

Jack knew that backwoods area well. Back in the 1970s, it had been the site of the MoonChild Ranch, a long disbanded, mostly peaceful back-to-the-land commune known for its organic farming innovations, free love, and the sexually transmitted diseases that went with it. As a rookie cop, he'd been called out there a few times for minor offenses, usually around harvest time when they'd be selling bags of their home grown weed out of the back of a pickup truck. Today's residents were mostly former Ranch members who had bought up the land, built yurts and cabins without permits, and cultivated small backyard vineyards. They kept to themselves and didn't welcome outsiders—which told Jack that the body wasn't the casual find of someone out for a stroll on a country road who just happened to come across a shallow grave.

Jack relayed the information to the watch commander, who had the dispatcher send out the nearest patrol unit to secure the scene. Then he phoned Dean in his car and told him to head back to the office.

A half hour later in the fading daylight, the partners arrived at the grave—a digging so recent and shallow that a corner of a red purse protruded out of the unsettled dirt. They called in the city's forensic team and assistant medical examiner to take over the scene, and then watched from the sidelines as the crew, working under bright portable lights, unearthed a partially skeletonized body wrapped loosely in a gray mildewed tarp. The skeletal remains, instead of being positioned in a recognizable human form, appeared to have been haphazardly tossed onto the tarp. Some bones had scratch marks, possibly from a shovel. The techs took photos, re-wrapped the remains in thick plastic and removed them for autopsy. They collected some underlying soil for trace evidence for the lab, and then bagged the red brocade purse and handed it over to the two detectives.

Inside the purse was a driver's license, and if it could be believed, they had finally found Dinah Pardini, the fifty-year-old Santa Rosa resident who had disappeared without a trace almost exactly one year before. The last time she'd been seen, on a mild September evening, she was at her hilltop house waiting for a hired limousine to take her to a charity gala at The Parisian hotel. She never arrived, nor was she ever heard from again—not a word or text to either of her teenage daughters or to her husband.

Now, after a year of waiting for kidnapping ransom notes, monitoring her phone and credit card activity, holding news conferences about reward offers, reviewing closed circuit camera footage, interviewing family, friends, acquaintances and colleagues, they finally had a body.

"But one that came with a red evening purse tossed on top of it," Jack said to Dean. Aside from the driver's license, the purse was empty. No keys, no lipstick, no phone. None of the usual things women carry. "Suspicious," Jack said to his partner.

"You wouldn't catch my wife leaving the house without credit cards. So, suspicious is right," Dean agreed.

The discovery eliminated some theories: Dinah wasn't overseas with a new lover like her husband had hinted was possible (*Never*, swore her women friends), and it wasn't likely that she'd been kidnapped since the family never received a ransom note or a call demanding money. Nor did she take her own life—no one moves their own body.

"Someone went to a hell of a lot of trouble to dig her up from that first grave and move her," Dean said.

"And a lot of trouble to make sure she was found," Jack said.

Two days later, a news conference was held by the Santa Rosa Police Department. Spokesperson Sgt. Spencer Huberty announced that dental records had verified that the deceased was Dinah Pardini, a former Miss Sonoma County and the socially prominent, fourth wife of Lino Pardini, businessman, attorney, and scion of the Pardini Winery family.

"First of all, our sympathy and condolences to the Pardini family," Huberty said. "DNA tests and a forensic autopsy were performed to determine the cause and manner of death, but official results won't be available for several weeks. But as of now, due to the unusual circumstances of her discovery after a full year of disappearance, the death is deemed suspicious."

"Ya think?" a reporter muttered from the front row.

Huberty glared him down while still talking, "We understand there's a lot of public interest in this case. And FYI, the Pardini family has extended their reward of $50,000 for information in the case."

He stared straight into the television camera. "We want Santa Rosa citizens to know that our number one priority is to find out how and why Mrs. Pardini died. And we won't rest until we do."

# Chapter One

Sixteen Years Later

Santa Rosa, California

Anne McCormack surveyed the living room, casting her eyes from one gilt-framed oil painting to another, taking in the antique red tasseled lampshades, red flocked wallpaper, red floral overstuffed sofa, and the oriental rug woven with every imaginable shade of red. All that exuberant red reminded her of a magazine layout she'd seen featuring the late *Vogue* editor Diana Vreeland's famous New York apartment. Tastefully garish.

The house was one of many Victorian homes lining McDonald Avenue, Santa Rosa's historic "Victorian row." The tree-lined boulevard was the filming location of several Hollywood classics, including the 1943 *Shadow of a Doubt* by Alfred Hitchcock, Disney's 1960 *Pollyanna,* and the nineties camp horror film *Scream.* The Victorian in which Anne was standing was owned by her newest clients, the family of the recently deceased, very wealthy Lily Danielson, who had left behind more treasures and personal effects than her heirs could handle.

Those belongings were why Anne, owner of McCormack Estate Services, was here after eight o'clock on a Sunday night with her teenage assistant, Chloe Grindel. Anne's job was to dispose of everything in the house, one way or another: to assess, catalog, toss out, put up for auction, sell, save for the family, or donate to charities. The executor, the family's lawyer, wanted it all handled ASAP before any more troublesome family fights could break out. *Fine*, Anne thought, the sooner the job was done, the sooner she'd deposit a commission check on the proceeds of any sales.

They were still at the sorting and boxing up stage.

Seven banker's boxes were stacked precariously in the middle of the room, the top ones on the verge of toppling over onto Chloe, who was sitting cross-legged on the floor. Next to her on the rug was an old diary she'd found in the bookcase. Chloe was packing up books—except for the first editions, which would be offered to dealers—and sighing theatrically.

"How are you doing over there?" Anne asked.

"Slow, very slow. I'm not fast like you are," Chloe said, standing up to stretch, raising her arms to the heavens. "But then, you've been doing this for decades…"

"A slight exaggeration," Anne said. In fact, she was fairly new to family estate services. She'd spent most of her twenties as an FBI agent in Sacramento's Violent Crimes division. After six years, she left the Bureau voluntarily, under no cloud (*You did not get fired*, her Uncle Jack, a retired cop would insist). Under no cloud, that is, except the one she conjured up and obsessed over (*But it did get ugly after they discovered I was using their high-security database software to track my ex-husband*, she'd counter).

On the same day she was confronted by her supervisor, she dropped her resignation letter on his desk and walked out the door, vowing that her next career would be a complete 180 from law enforcement. She would follow her passions—researching art and its provenance—and someday be her own boss, health benefits or not. Turns out, those passions were the exact skills required for family estate sales services. And since it was a far cry from crime-fighting, she figured why not do it professionally? For two years, she worked as an assistant to estate services guru Marty Holmes, who became her mentor in the business. His mantra: "Estate sales are *not* garage sales!" The estate sales business, he'd insist, is about helping families dispose of the treasures left behind after a loved one's death and then getting a big fat commission from the sales of said treasures. Period.

CHAPTER ONE

After learning the trade, Anne struck out on her own three years ago. If she'd ever imagined that being a business owner meant naming her own hours and taking long vacations, she was quickly proven wrong. The reality was that when business was good—and it finally was—she ended up working relentlessly long hours. Like tonight.

"After finishing that box, let's call it a night," she said. Chloe had school in the morning.

"Not yet," Chloe pleaded. The girl was always angling for longer hours, arguing "You won't find cheaper or better child labor than me." And Anne almost always relented. She knew that nearly every dollar Chloe earned was being squirreled away into her college fund. Besides, she liked Chloe's company. Chloe was the favorite grandchild of one of Anne's first clients, Claire Murray, whose death two years before had hit the teenager hard. Anne had grown fond of Claire and missed her too, and while she and Chloe worked, they would often swap Claire stories.

But recently, all Chloe wanted to talk about—when not complaining about her mother's strict hours or the unfair soccer coach—was the "Battalion Chief" competition at her high school. Not much had changed about the yearly contest since Anne had participated: The student who searched private homes and collected the most "fire hazard" violation tickets was the winner. Back then, the winning prize was simply being named "Honorary Battalion Chief." But this year, the stakes were high—a $25,000 college scholarship to the winner in each class, donated by a group of wealthy vintners who wanted to encourage fire safety in the wildfire-ravaged Sonoma County.

"I can put it toward any college I want. When I add that to what I'm making working for you and what my parents can chip in, I might get to go to UC Berkeley, Harvard, or California College of the Arts, who knows!"

One of their phones pinged.

"Sky's the limit," Anne agreed, looking down at her phone. Nothing. She hadn't heard from Scott, her boyfriend of three months, since their fight two days before. Nodding toward Chloe's phone on the coffee table, she said, "Bet your mom wants you to come home."

Chloe sauntered over to pick up her phone. Leaning against a wall, she stared intently at the screen—reading the text message, answering it, and reading the response.

"Oh, no," Chloe blurted out. She slowly slid down the wall, crumbling to the hardwood floor. "There goes everything," she said in a low, ominous tone. "Everything I've ever worked for." She set her phone down beside her and hugged her knees to her chest.

Anne bit her lip to keep from smiling. How much work could Chloe have done in her short life? How much did she have to lose? Chloe was a month shy of being sixteen years old, not some frail senior citizen whose life savings were ruthlessly embezzled or whose house was destroyed in a fire without any insurance to cover rebuilding it. But as Anne watched tears well in Chloe's eyes, she knew there was nothing even slightly amusing about whatever was going on. Chloe was heartbroken.

Anne crouched down in front of her. "What do you mean by 'lost everything?' What happened?" she asked in a gentle voice.

Chloe uncovered her eyes, let out a sigh, and pointed to her phone. "That girl. Pam O'Brien. Tomorrow is the last day to hand in our tickets to see who wins the scholarship. She asked me how many I had…."

"And?" Anne prompted.

"I told her I had forty-five, which is way more than anyone else in the class. The nearest kid to me is Justin Frey, and he only has thirty-two. Then Pam texted back, 'Too bad, cause I have fifty.' That's five more than me," Chloe's voice broke. "I never even knew she was *close!*"

Fire hazard violations were hard to come by, as Anne well knew. She remembered having to screw up the courage to knock on the door of a neighbor or acquaintance, then taking a deep breath and asking permission to go poking through their house looking for fire hazards like loose wiring, stacks of newspapers, overloaded electrical outlets, aging space heaters. Most people were good-humored about it, accepted their copies of the tickets, and promised to do better. But others tried to talk her out of the tickets, thinking the violations would be reported to city officials and they'd be fined. That never happened, of course; the fallout would have ended the contest years ago.

"And she tells you this at 8:30 at night…"

"Too late…"

Anne stood up abruptly. "Where's your book of tickets? In your backpack?"

"Yeah. For all the good it does me," Chloe said, giving the bag a shove as if it were to blame for her crushed dreams, the late hour, Pam O'Brien's taunts. Everything.

Anne reached out her hands to the sobbing girl and pulled her to her feet. She grabbed their jackets off the couch and tossed Chloe's to her.

"Get in the car," Anne said.

\* \* \*

Anne started the engine of her fifteen-year-old blue Saab and was amazed, like she was every single day, that it fired right up. Though she'd never admit it to anyone, or actually say it out loud, she'd named the car "True Blue." The Saab had over 275,000 miles on it, and had never left her stranded on the side of the road or cost her any serious repairs. As her mechanic told her, "That car doesn't owe you anything."

"Where are we going first?" Chloe asked, literally bouncing in her seat.

"Did you hit up Betty yet?" Anne asked. Betty Fazio was Chloe's grandmother's best friend and still a close family friend, an honorary aunt.

"I found ten violations at her house."

Anne laughed. "That seems excessive. You only found four at mine."

"I'm sure she planted them for me. Sort of like an Easter egg hunt."

"Then our first stop will be at my aunt and uncle's house," Anne said as she pulled away from the curb. "But before we get there, let your mom know you'll be coming home a little late."

"It might be better coming from you, Anne," Chloe said with a cagey smile.

"Nah…" Anne demurred. She could think of nothing worse than facing the wrath of Chloe's mother, Noreen Grindel, a woman known for a trigger temper and sharp tongue. Though there were hints of a soft heart, it was hidden under layers of attitude. Chloe finally relented and sent her mother a text saying she would be home "REAL soon" and then muted her phone.

Five minutes later, they arrived at the ranch-style home of Jack and Dot McCormack. The curtains were drawn, but the living room lights were on. Before they could knock on the door, Jack swung it wide open. He was in his bright red sweatpants and mustard-stained navy hoodie, with one hand clutching a TV remote. He was clearly settled in for the night.

"I heard your car pull up. I'd recognize that rattle anywhere, Anne. Come on in. You just missed your aunt. She's off helping her sister do God knows what…" He let his sentence trail off as Anne gave him a hug. She apologized for the late hour and explained the emergency.

Nodding at Chloe, Jack said, "I can guarantee that you won't find any violations in here or any room that my wife has dominion over. But my office is a potential firetrap." He pointed to his home office down the hall.

Chloe flipped through her battered Fire Safety Violation pad until she found a blank page. "I know, old school, right?" Chloe said to Anne, who remembered using the same kind when she was in high school. The school must have thousands of them stockpiled in their storage room.

Chloe took off in the direction of Jack's office.

"Thanks for letting us barge in, Uncle Jack," Anne said, dropping onto the couch.

"Anytime. This is the most excitement I've had all day."

"Which means you're not working on any cases right now?" When Jack retired as a police homicide detective twelve years before, he left full-time investigating behind. But periodically, because the county sheriff's and district attorney's offices were short-staffed, he'd fill in for temporary assignments—mostly cold cases, his specialty. Two years ago, Jack convinced Anne to apply for a "special assignment" police badge—which, with her FBI background, wasn't hard to get—so they could work together on a cold case. They'd solved the thirty-year-old murder of a young boy, the son of Claire Murray, Chloe's grandmother. Since then, Anne's crime-fighting career had been largely dormant, but the police chief kept her sworn in and made it clear that she was welcome back on special assignments anytime.

"Nah, where would I find the time to work cases?" They both laughed. His days were mostly spent watching TV, playing an occasional pickle ball game, and napping.

Ten minutes later, Chloe emerged from looking through Jack's office, surrounding rooms, and garage with three ticketed violations. "Thanks, Mr. McCormack," Chloe said.

"My pleasure, young lady." He gave Anne a sideways look and muttered to her, "But you might want to call first next time."

It was 9:20.

"Krista will let us in," Anne said definitively as they climbed back into her car. They headed toward Fountaingrove, one of the town's most affluent neighborhoods, just ten minutes away, which was about as long as it took to get anywhere in Santa Rosa. They drove along winding roads lined with young trees, past Tudor and Spanish-style mansions with gated entrances, and then pulled into the semi-circular stone-paved driveway of Anne's oldest and dearest friend.

\* \* \*

"Do you know what time it is, Anne?" Krista said in mock horror. But after catching sight of Chloe's embarrassed frown, she swiftly added, "Just kidding. Get in here, you two. And close the door; it's chilly out there."

Anne slipped off her jacket and made herself at home, plopping down on the leather sectional while Chloe gave Krista her prepared speech about the contest, what she came to do, and the treachery of Pam O'Brien, who "doesn't even need a scholarship cause she has a big, fat trust fund."

"Have at it, Chloe, but the baby's asleep, so it's best to keep away from the second floor," Krista said, sitting down next to Anne.

"Want my advice?" Anne called out to Chloe, who was halfway down the hall. "The utility room is a disaster. Go there first."

A few minutes later, Chloe was back, clutching her ticket booklet and looking slightly dejected. "I only found two fire hazards, and it's getting late," she said, pointing to the art deco clock above the fireplace. Krista gave an apologetic shrug as she signed the tickets.

It was 9:45.

"Okay, where to now?" Krista hoisted herself off the couch and went to the entry closet. She pulled out a camel's hair wool coat, draping it over her arm. Ready to go.

"You're coming?" Anne asked, though *where* they were going was still uncertain.

"Why not? The baby's sleeping, and Mike's watching football. They won't even know I'm gone. So…where to?"

Anne looked blank, but headed to the door, anyway. As her father had often said when she was a young girl, "Anne's always halfway down the block before she knows where she's going."

"Maybe we could try Brittany, my assistant," Anne said. Chloe nodded vigorously. Then Anne shook her head and said, "Though there's no telling where she's spending the night." Brittany was juggling two boyfriends.

"Or how about Renee and Lino Pardini's house? It's just up the hill," Krista said. "It's a fortress up there, and since you don't know them, you probably won't even get as far as the driveway gate. You'll need me."

"I *do* know him, actually. Lino's given me some job referrals," Anne said. Her best clients these days were coming from recommendations by lawyers, realtors, and morticians. "But I don't know her. What's she like?"

"A gorgeous Texas redhead, smart, dripping with Southern charm. Much, much younger—*wildly* younger—than him. Mid-forties," Krista rattled off. "Well, anyway, I'll smooth the way for you socially, as I've done countless times in the past."

Anne rolled her eyes to the ceiling. There was some truth to that, but Krista's attitude was getting on her nerves.

"And I don't recommend just barging in on them, like you did with me. I'll text—" Krista activated her phone.

"Not so fast," Anne cut in. "Do you really think that's a good idea? She might just ignore the text or make up excuses…"

"Renee's a night owl, and her husband's in his sixties, so he's probably already in bed. It'll just be her." Then Krista tilted her head in thought. "But maybe you're right. Why risk it? Let's just go. And we're taking my car in case she looks out the window."

"And what? If she sees mine, she'll do what...?" Anne broke off, now thoroughly annoyed. "Krista, try to rein in the attitude a little, will you please?"

Anne was in no mood to tolerate her old friend's newly acquired pretensions. They'd known each other too long for these socio-economic shenanigans. Their friendship went back to childhood, back before Krista's designer Gucci bags and three hundred dollar face creams. Back to when they were in sixth grade together and Krista was given free lunches in the cafeteria because the nuns found out that her father's business was going through a rough patch and her mother was juggling two jobs. Anne would always look the other way while an embarrassed Krista slipped the cashier her "No Charge" lunch voucher.

Krista didn't respond for a few seconds. "Okay, sorry. I'm just excited," she said as she ushered them out the front door and locked it behind them. "It's just fun being back in our old Thelma and Louise, partners-in-crime mode again."

"With any luck, we'll wrap up this adventure before Chloe's mom calls the cops to report her as missing."

The trio piled into Krista's luxury all-electric minivan and headed up the hill to the Pardini's house—a hill so steep Anne could feel her ears pop with the elevation change. In the near total darkness, the minivan's headlights illuminated burnt-out, vacant lots on both sides of the road, as well as several houses that were even grander than Krista's, most with four-car garages, private wrought-iron gates, and security call boxes. With few exceptions, most of these were new construction homes, rebuilt after the devastating Tubbs fire in 2017 had wiped out over 1,500 homes in the Fountaingrove area alone.

"Renee's home, like ours, was thankfully spared," Krista told them.

Anne turned toward Chloe in the back seat. "What's your grand total now?" Chloe chewed her lip while methodically recounting her receipts by the light of her phone. "Fifty tickets. All solid," Chloe said, fanning the pad in the air triumphantly. "Better than I thought. I just need one more to win. One more!"

"And maybe a few extra. For safety," Anne said.

The three heads nodded in unison. No one trusted that Pam O'Brien girl.

# Chapter Two

Leaning against her carved marble fireplace mantel, Renee Pardini idly fingered the Murano glass paperweight that she and Lino had brought home from Italy two years before. They visited nearly every year before Covid restrictions kicked in, always making a stop—more of a pilgrimage, really—to the wine growing region of Tuscany, from where her husband's family immigrated in the 1920s.

A few inches from the paperweight was a framed photo of the two of them with their son Josh when he was ten. And next to that, an older photo, one recently added at Lino's insistence, of a happy tableau: two teenage girls throwing their heads back in laughter and hugging a big shaggy mutt of a dog. Renee's stepdaughters. Renee turned the photo toward the wall, making a mental note to turn it back around before heading off to bed. Lino was already upstairs for the night and would never know. *Small pleasures,* she thought.

The sound of the gated entry's call box jolted her back into the moment. Who could possibly be here at this time of night? She briefly considered ignoring it, but what if it was an emergency? She picked up the line and heard the voice of her neighbor from down the street, Krista Hageman. "Sorry for the late hour, but I'm here with my friend Anne McCormack and her friend Chloe. We just need a few minutes of your time."

"Of course, Krista. Come on up," Renee said as she buzzed them in.

Turning around, she was startled to see Lino standing there. He was watching her closely, as if wondering what she was doing in his home. *I live here, believe it or not, and have for fifteen years.* She hid her annoyance with a smile.

"I thought you were in bed," she said.

"I'm watching TV up there. Who was that?"

As she told him of her brief exchange with Krista, she glanced at the mirror above the fireplace, frowned, and quickly ran her fingers through her long auburn curls to make herself more presentable.

"I know Anne McCormack," he said, glancing toward the door. When his eyes were off her, Renee turned the framed photo of her stepdaughters back around. "I've recommended her estate services to some of my clients' families."

*Well, of course, he knows her,* she thought. Didn't Lino know everyone in town? They couldn't go anywhere, not even the grocery store, without running into at least five people he knew. He'd lived his entire sixty-seven years in the area, not counting the years spent in Boston getting his law degree. Plus, the Pardini name was a familiar one, so that accounted for some of it. But more than that, it was Lino's relatable, everyman quality, a favorite uncle essence that swept people up so effortlessly that even if they didn't actually know him, they thought they did.

But lately, that easy charm had turned a bit mercurial, something he switched on and off. A twinkly grin could flatten without much warning, the change so subtle that most people wouldn't notice. But Renee always noticed, and she would calibrate her words and actions to smooth over any situation. Which was one of the many reasons she was his "fifth and *final* wife," as she liked to say.

"I'm going upstairs to change," he said. "Let them know I'll be down to greet them in a few minutes."

"You don't have to, you know…" she began, but he'd already started up the stairs. She knew that when he came back down, he would likely be wearing pressed jeans and a long sleeved blue shirt with a sweater draped casually on his shoulders, as if he were heading out to the country club for a drink with the mayor. He'd make a quick appearance and then excuse himself to go back upstairs and finish watching the football game. If he came down at all.

At the knock on the door, Renee opened it wide and welcomed her visitors inside with an expansive sweep of her arms, as if nothing could have made her happier than to have uninvited guests drop by at almost ten o'clock on a Sunday night.

"Let me take your coats. What'll y'all have to drink? Wine? Hot tea?" she inquired of the two women, then turned to Chloe and said, "Would you like some chocolate milk?"

Chloe declined with thanks, then sped through her spiel about the contest. Renee told Chloe that she could have free run of the house "except for bedrooms." Chloe fairly skipped out of the room and disappeared around the corner to begin her hunt.

"But *we'd* love a drink," Krista said.

When Renee returned with their glasses, the three women settled in front of the burning fire and made the smallest of small talk about each other's health, the gorgeous fall leaves, the new restaurants in town. Krista happened to mention Anne's FBI background, which seemed to fascinate Renee, so that filled up a few more minutes. After a while, Renee said, "Lino wanted to come down and say hello, but he seems to have been detained." Krista gave her a knowing smile. "My husband's been detained with the same damn game for hours."

Chloe appeared suddenly in the doorway. Her blue eyes were wide as she made beckoning motions to Anne. "Can you come with me?" Chloe barely squeaked it out and then turned on her heel. "Excuse me," Anne said and followed her out of the room.

Krista and Renee exchanged confused looks, shrugged, and then went back to discussing the neighborhood's fund raiser for the local food bank.

\* \* \*

"What is it?" Anne asked.

"Just follow."

Anne trailed after Chloe through the kitchen, past the six-burner Wolf range, the freestanding wine cooler, and the Viking commercial-grade refrigerator, to the door leading into the garage. Garages, according to Chloe, were a gold mine for finding fire hazards. At one old bachelor's house, she'd found a rat's nest built with twigs, grass, and other flammable debris—right next to an illegally wired water heater and a dried-up Christmas tree. But should Chloe be rummaging through the Pardini's garage? Technically, it was part of the house, but would Renee have given her permission had she known?

*Too late now*, Anne thought as she entered the four-car garage. Late-model luxury cars—a Mercedes and a BMW—took up half the space. Another two vehicles took up another bay: A vintage pickup truck with a *Pardini Winery* decal on the door was lifted halfway to the ceiling on a single-post car lift; a sleek red convertible was parked underneath it. The remaining space was used for storage.

Chloe went directly to the far end of the garage and stopped in front of a pile of dusty photo albums and old *Town and Country* and *Vogue* magazines. She pointed to two oversized brown manila envelopes lying on top. "I came over to this stack of magazines and photos cause they're fire safety violations. They were pushed up against that big old umbrella." She gestured to a patio umbrella. "It was leaning against the wall, but when I moved the magazines, the umbrella fell to the ground, and that's when I saw what it was covering up...that hole in the wall. See?" She pointed to a rectangular-shaped opening in the drywall.

Someone, it seemed, had methodically cut it to exactly accommodate 15-inch x 20-inch envelopes. "I just reached in and pulled them out...maybe I shouldn't have," Chloe said.

"What am I looking at? Envelopes?" Anne asked.

Chloe picked up the top envelope, which was bulging to the point of bursting, and raised the flap. She pulled out over a dozen thick bundles of twenty-dollar bills wrapped with currency bands and then—from the bottom of the envelope—drew out a long, gleaming strand of what appeared to be real pearls with a blue sapphire clasp. She set the pearls and bundles of cash on top of a plastic storage container next to the pile of magazines.

"And the other envelope has money in it, too! And not just twenties," she said, reaching for it. "There's lots of one-hundred-dollar bundles in this one. And I saw even more envelopes that I didn't grab inside the hole. There must be thousands and thousands of dollars here!" She took a deep, ragged breath and released it. "What should we do?"

"Put everything back. We never saw them."

Chloe tilted her head, clearly perplexed, but she just nodded and started stuffing the money and pearls back inside the envelope. Then Anne abruptly held her hand up.

"Wait a second," she said, reconsidering. Something felt off. Years of collecting evidence, securing crime scenes, and building cases were triggering her cop instincts. Maybe hiding money in the wall of your own home wasn't criminal, but it certainly was strange. She pulled out her phone and took photos of the wall and the contents of the envelopes. Better to record everything than to lose evidence that might mean something later. "Just for safety's sake, because you never know," she said to Chloe. "Now you can put them back where they came from."

"Put what back?" Lino Pardini's silhouette filled the doorframe.

# Chapter Three

The leaf blower was noisily spewing dry maple leaves and a cloud of debris onto the Victorian's front walkway. A gust of northerly wind wasn't helping. "Could you just hold off for a few minutes, please?" Anne shouted to the yard maintenance worker over the din. "I'll be out of your way soon."

Anne was back at work at her client's Victorian house on Monday morning, struggling to carry a bulky oil painting—wrapped in butcher's paper, tied with string, and ready to ship to the auction house—from the house to her car. Her assistant Brittany was inside the house, busy packaging other paintings before taking off for lunch.

"*Apagarla!*" a voice yelled out in Spanish. It was coming from the metallic silver pickup parked in front of the house. There was a *Silver Landscaping* decal on the side door. The leaf blower shut off immediately. Anne called out "Thanks" to the blower operator and waved to the fortyish man in the pickup. She heard the whimpering of a dog coming from the cab of the truck.

"Need some help with that?" the driver asked as he opened the truck door. He was about ten years or so older than she was and wore jeans and a dark T-shirt with a small *Silver Landscaping* logo on it. Without waiting for an answer, he stepped out and sprinted over to Anne with an excited golden retriever at his heel. He relieved her of the package and leaned his tall, lanky frame casually against the side door of her Saab while she opened the trunk.

"I've seen you around here a few times," he said, lifting the painting into the back of the car. "I'm Dave Silver."

"Anne McCormack. I'm working with the family here." She closed the trunk and pointed to the truck decal. "Is that your company?"

"It is." Dave brushed his unruly dark hair off his forehead and reached into his front pocket, pulling out a business card. "Feel free to call anytime," he said with a glimmer in his eyes, "whether you have a yard or not."

Her phone rang. Anne smiled apologetically. He smiled back, then gave her a silent wave and headed off to his truck. She watched his back while she picked up the call.

It was Chloe, out of class for the lunch recess and eager to give Anne the news: She had barely beaten her rival, Pam O'Brien, but beat her she did. "By two fire hazard tickets," Chloe said proudly, "and Pam went totally cray and demanded a recount." But it came out the same: Chloe was officially this year's honorary Battalion Chief and $25,000 scholarship recipient.

"Verbal high-five, girl!" Anne congratulated her.

But there was a catch, Chloe told her. "I never got sign-off signatures from the Pardinis for the three violations because we left there so fast."

"We certainly did," Anne agreed.

"The principal gave me 24 hours to get their signatures, or *else.*"

"Then you better get on it."

"The problem is, I have soccer practice after school, and then we're going to Nana's for dinner tonight. So I was wondering if you could—" Chloe said in a wheedling tone that annoyed Anne to no end but always sucked her in at the same time.

"Okay, okay. I guess we've come this far…" Anne muttered. "Leave the tickets with the secretary in the principal's office, and I'll pick them up in a few minutes. Lucky for you, I'm meeting a client close to the Pardinis' house, so I'll drop by and see if they'll sign them. You owe me, Chloe."

Anne wasn't eager for another visit to the Pardinis' house after last night's "Sunday Night Adventure," as Krista liked to call it. Anne was still processing what Chloe had found in the couple's garage and what it meant. Maybe there was nothing to process, really, nothing unusual about it. Maybe more people than she could dream of were stockpiling thousands of dollars in cash and jewelry inside their garage walls. There was no law against it as far as she knew. Anyone could hide their own money anywhere they wanted: under beds or inside gutted books, vacuum cleaner bag compartments, fake air return grilles, and potholders. Anywhere that their wily, little hoarding minds could think of.

It was odd, that's all. As was Lino's inscrutable, blank face as he watched Chloe hurriedly stuff the cash and pearls back into the envelopes and leave them on top of the plastic container. And when Chloe nervously insisted to him that she hadn't taken any of the money (*I promise! I swear!* she said) Lino just answered in a flat tone, "Of course not," and stood guard by the door until Anne and Chloe left the garage.

More than a little odd.

# Chapter Four

There was a brief period of time, only about an hour, when Renee was still the only person in the world to know.

She sat by his bed for a few minutes, wondering if she should kiss him, maybe on his forehead. Her lipstick left a smudge, and she dabbed most of it off with a tissue. Then she slipped his phone into her pocket and folded his arms over his chest.

*The family needs to be told first,* she thought. Even before calling 911.

Renee was an elder-law attorney's wife—widow, now—so she knew the proper steps to take, and getting a legal pronouncement of death was step one. But she also knew there would be all hell to pay if Lino's family didn't have the chance to say their goodbyes in person—even if it was to a lifeless, cold body lying on a rumpled bed.

So she postponed calling a dispatcher. What could the authorities do to her? Put her in jail?

She headed downstairs to straighten up the living room and then went down the hall into Lino's office to go through his files. The desktop was bare except for a framed family photo, a ceramic pen holder, and his password-protected computer—no files, notebooks, or any kind of business papers. He kept a notebook with a list of his passwords in one of the side drawers, she knew, along with his personal papers. But the drawers were locked, so she went into the garage, where she found a pocketknife and a crowbar. Why not? He'd never know, and it was her property now, anyway.

Afterward, she buzzed open the entry gate and made the calls to the family.

Her first call was to her brother-in-law, Marco, the patriarch of the family now that his and Lino's father had died. Renee would be the executor of Lino's will, but Marco would be the public face of the family and the one the family would lean on.

There was a heavy silence on the line. "Oh Jesus, are you sure?" Marco finally said in a low, ragged voice. "I can't fucking believe this. I talked to him just this morning. We were…what happened?"

She told him Lino had left home around nine o'clock that morning for his regular Monday golf date and lunch with clients. She spent the day at a charity committee meeting and luncheon, and when she came home at three o'clock, she saw his car in the driveway. This was unusual since he always went back to his office after lunch. "When I came into the house, I called out for him, but got no answer, so I went up to his bedroom. He looked like he was sleeping, but when I tried to wake him, he wasn't breathing. His hair was still damp from taking a shower….oh, my God," she managed to say.

All perfectly true, except for the timeline. She'd come home an hour earlier—at two o'clock—and spent that extra time taking care of business. Something Marco didn't need to know.

"What can I do? Anything you need, just tell me," Marco said. Renee asked him to break the news to his sisters and have them spread the word to the rest of the family. She would tell Lino's children. "Of course," he agreed. "Then I'll be right over. Have you called the medics yet? Maybe you should call his lawyer." She assured him that everything was under control.

Her next call was to Jennifer, Lino's thirty-year-old daughter, who never picked up the phone if she knew it was Renee on the line. She felt her jaw tighten as Jennifer's phone rang and rang and then finally gave automated instructions to leave a message. Renee made it brief, "It's an emergency, sweetie. Call me back." The endearment "sweetie" never passed her lips when talking to either of her stepdaughters, so she hoped it would telegraph—even more than the word "emergency"—that the call wasn't to be ignored.

Five minutes later, the phone rang. "Okay, what's up, Renee?"

After an interval of silence, Renee broke the news in a calm, soothing voice. Jennifer said nothing for several seconds, then let out a long howl, a sound so primal and unearthly that it shocked and embarrassed Renee. She hung up the phone and just stared at it. A few minutes later, Jennifer called back, slightly more composed, but her voice was faint and shaky, "Sorry for that. I just can't believe that Daddy…" The grief in Jennifer's voice was palpable.

What was that German word? *Schadenfreude.* That's what Renee felt: that pinprick of cruel pleasure she found in Jennifer's misery. Until she caught herself. When had she become so heartless about those two girls? They'd only been teenagers—fourteen and sixteen—when she first met them, only a month after their mother's body was found. Lino had taken her and his daughters (*My three best girls*, he said) out for a fancy dinner, ordering lobsters for the table. Renee's experience with lobsters was nil, having come from a small Texas town, so she fumbled with the instruments and surreptitiously watched the others to see how it was done.

That drew the attention of the older girl, sixteen-year-old Carrie. "It's almost as if you've never eaten lobster before," she said, disdain dripping from her voice like melted butter off a lobster tail. "Maybe you'd prefer corn fritters."

That evening set the tone of their relationship. Renee did try to make friendly overtures through the years, but the die was cast, the scars from losing their mother too deep. The teens, looking around for a villainess to blame, focused on Renee like a laser beam and never let up. They accused her of stealing their mother's jewelry. They mimicked her soft, lilting Texas drawl, exaggerating it until words like "America" became "Amur-cah" and "thing" became "thang."

After fifteen years of walking on eggshells, being treated with silent contempt and taking it on chin for the sake of her marriage, her heart had hardened. How could it not?

She shook her head to clear those thoughts. Their father had just died, she reminded herself, and that was a profound loss. Soon, she would have to tell Lino's other child, her own sweet, sensitive son, Josh. And how was she going to do that? She couldn't let him walk into this house and be blindsided, not knowing about his father. At this moment he would be at freshman football practice. She decided she had to pick him up at the high school at five o'clock and tell him herself, away from the eyes of the family. Renee ached for her fourteen-year-old son, knowing he would be devastated. Ached more for him than for herself. She wondered when her own grief would kick in. Would it ever? All she felt now was fear and confusion and a steely resolve to get things right, to hold it together.

Jennifer was still talking. "Who will walk me down the aisle when I get married? Someday…"

"I'm so sorry, Jennifer. I know how close you and your father were. Do you want me to call your sister, or do you want to?" Carrie lived with her husband and two children in Florida.

"She'll want to hear it from me. And then I'm coming over. I have to see Daddy."

Renee called no one from her own side of the family. There was no one to call, really, except her semi-estranged sister in Eureka, who derided Renee's lifestyle as "pre-feminist and ostentatious." And a jealous and depressed mother with a drinking problem. *Nope, won't be calling them.* She had friends, thankfully, but she would call them later when she had time to talk—and a glass of wine in her hand.

While Renee waited for the deluge of Lino's family to begin, which she knew would be a nightmare, she went to her computer and wrote a quick obituary—just bullet points, really, listing where he was born, his education, associations, et cetera. Given Lino's prominence, she knew that a full-blown obituary would be written, and these notes would just be used for fact-checking by a reporter. She would leave it to Marco, she decided, to take the call from the reporter, as she would obviously be far too grief-stricken. But, she would tell Marco tearfully, if the reporter wanted a brief comment, she would oblige. She wanted Lino's death to be publicly announced. That way, she wouldn't have to make a million phone calls. She checked her watch. Thankfully, it was still early enough for the obituary to make the next morning's edition. She emailed the note to the obituary desk with an "urgent" in the subject line. One problem averted.

By four o'clock, the family began arriving.

Her brother-in-law was the first to show up. At nearly seventy, Marco was a stockier, more muscular version of his younger brother Lino, with the same gunmetal hair and square-jawed handsomeness. He pulled Renee into a bear hug and asked, "You hanging in there?" She nodded. He nodded back and then made his way upstairs to Lino's bedroom. Five minutes later, Marco's wife, Kay, a tall brunette, arrived. Kay's icy blue eyes darted around the living room and landed on a small framed photo of a young Lino, Marco, and Kay drinking wine outdoors in a vineyard.

Arriving right after Kay was Lino's older cousin, Ada, a short, plump woman wearing a heavy gold cross. Placing a hand on Renee's shoulder, Ada asked her, "What were Lino's last words?" Renee paused a few seconds. "What's for dinner tonight?" was the truth. But that sounded flippant, so she replied, "The last thing he said when he left this morning was, 'I'm looking forward to seeing everyone at Thanksgiving.'"

Ada looked satisfied. "Lino was all about the family. I'm just grateful his parents didn't live to see their son's death," she said, making the sign of the cross. Carlos and Sophia Pardini had died in a car crash just a month before.

Next came Lino's frail, elderly Uncle Cono and his caregiver. Followed by two more female cousins, whom Renee only vaguely remembered having met. And just behind them, Jennifer.

Renee gave each person a hug as they entered and gestured toward the stairway leading to the bedroom. She stayed downstairs, sitting on the couch with her hands folded, giving the family time alone to console each other.

Twenty long minutes went by. *Enough.* Renee stood up, pulled her phone from her jeans pocket, and dialed 911. After filling in the dispatcher, she went upstairs to let the family know that their time with Lino was ending. As she walked down the hallway to the bedroom, she could hear murmuring voices. But all she could make out was a woman's voice, saying, "Quiet. This isn't the time for that."

Stopping in the doorway, Renee glanced past the bed to the family huddled near the window overlooking the back yard. "The medics will be here any minute now," she announced to silence. "You might want to go downstairs soon."

She was turning to leave when a realization hit her: Josh might want to see his father before he was taken away to the mortuary. Or maybe not. Maybe he'd think that was ghoulish and not want to see his father's body at all. She couldn't know for sure, but Josh needed to have the option. Renee gestured to her brother-in-law, who went to her side. "I have to go pick up Josh. Please handle things for a few minutes. I'll be right back. Don't let the medics leave until we come back."

"I'll do what I can."

"Gotta go," she said, turning away.

She went down the stairs and ducked into Lino's office to shut off the computer and collect a few folders, hurrying to finish her tasks. As she closed the office door behind her, she heard sobbing and footsteps trudging down the stairs. Renee waited until the family reached the living room, then peeked around the corner. They were all there except Jennifer, standing around stiffly as if they were part of an honor guard. Waiting in readiness for the moment when the body was brought down the stairs and wheeled out into the ambulance.

But after a few minutes, gathered as they were, with nothing better to do until the medics arrived—and without Lino to temper their hostilities with a cold stare and shake of his head—they started to bicker. In quiet, civil tones at first. "Lino wanted me to have that," a cousin said, gesturing toward a vase. "He said the colors would look nice in my house." Ada disagreed. "It belonged to my mother, so that means it's mine." Renee thought she saw Kay slip a framed photo into her jacket pocket. The family's discussion quickly escalated to include the piano, glassware, the family Bible. Soon, they were interrupting each other, yelling, tossing accusations back and forth. "Promises were made," said the ancient uncle. Whatever *that* means, Renee thought. All those years of her trying to keep the peace. What a joke.

She passed through the living room and went into the kitchen to collect her keys and tote bag. She found her stepdaughter Jennifer there, standing near the kitchen door that led into the garage. With her back to Renee, Jennifer was whispering into her phone. Renee swiftly grabbed her bag off

24

the table and stuffed the folders inside it, then glanced back just as Jennifer disappeared into the garage. Renee had no time to deal with that.

Rushing out the front door, she nearly collided with Marco's two teenage sons who were heading up the walkway. She stopped and locked eyes with them. "Boys, please don't text Josh about this. I'll tell him." They nodded and solemnly agreed.

From the corner of her eye, she spotted a small blue car parked in front of her neighbor's house. A young woman was standing by the passenger side, holding up some kind of booklet and calling out to her. Was that Anne, Krista's friend? The one she'd met last night?

*Was that just last night?*

# Chapter Five

The next morning, Anne stepped out onto the front porch of her Craftsman-style duplex, the cold morning air biting through her sweatshirt as she bent down to pick up the Tuesday edition of the hometown newspaper.

Not many thirty-four-year-olds subscribed to an actual paper-and-ink newspaper anymore, but Anne's father had been an editor for the Pulitzer Prize-winning *Press Democrat*. He died when she was seventeen, before the internet took over and became the preferred way for millennials to get the news. She bucked the trend, in his memory.

She laid the newspaper down on the kitchen table and went about her morning routine: Start the coffee, go out the back door to fill the bird feeder, come back inside to take a shower, pour milk over cereal, pour coffee into a cup. Then she sat down in front of her bowl of shredded wheat and picked up the newspaper.

"Oh, my God," she said aloud. On the front page, just under the fold, in large type, was an obituary with a two-column wide photo of Lino Pardini.

### Lino Pardini, SR lawyer and philanthropist, dies at 67

SANTA ROSA— Angiolino "Lino" Pardini, prominent local estate planning attorney, financier, and philanthropist, died suddenly Monday afternoon in his Fountaingrove home of unknown causes.

"He had a physical just last week and passed it with flying colors," said his wife of 15 years, Renee Pardini. "Lino came home after a late morning round of golf and took a nap, which he never did, and died in his sleep. Probably a heart attack."

"The family is in total shock," said his older brother Marco Pardini, owner of Pardini Winery. "He was the lynchpin of our family and the best man I've ever known."

*So that's what I stumbled onto yesterday.* Anne cringed at how she'd tried to flag down Renee—a woman who had just discovered her dead husband's body—to get her signature on some trivial contest tickets. She kept reading:

Pardini was born in 1954 in Healdsburg to the late Sofia and Carlos Pardini, second-generation vintners and founders of Pardini Winery. An Eagle Scout in his youth, he graduated from Healdsburg High School, graduated from University of California-Berkeley with two business degrees, and obtained his law degree from Harvard Law School.

Pardini began his legal career as a criminal trial attorney and established the law firm of Pardini and Struck in 1985. Former partner Terrance Struck described his colleague as "a model of civility and integrity" who could be an aggressive opponent in the courtroom, "but outside of it, he was known as a big-hearted, easygoing man." In 1995, the firm shifted gears to elder law, specializing in wills, trusts, and probates for a "who's who" among Sonoma County's most prominent families.

"He was fiercely loyal to his elderly clients," Struck said. "Lino treated them like his own family."

After retiring his law practice in 2002, Pardini branched out into providing alternative financial services for his former clients, investing millions through his company, Pardini Financial. "Many senior citizens, including my own parents, are thankful that he did," said James Ballard, mayor of Santa Rosa. "By investing with Lino, they were able to secure their futures by earning larger returns from safe investments."

*Did Aunt Dot take my advice and invest with him?* Anne wondered.

> Among his numerous philanthropic activities, Pardini spear-headed the annual Wine Country Celebrity Charity Golf Tour-nament. Mayor Ballard recalled Pardini as a "larger than life presence" whose personal charm outshone even the celebrities he coaxed into playing. "Without even trying, Lino owned the room."
>
> Pardini founded the Dinah Pardini Scholarship in honor of his fourth wife, whose homicide death in 2004 remains unsolved.
>
> A public celebration of Pardini's life is being planned for later this month. The family will provide details as the event date approaches.

Anne skimmed through the survivors list. She was pretty sure she had seen most of them yesterday out in the front yard, loading their cars with items from the Pardini house after Renee drove off.

She set down the newspaper and wondered if she should send flowers.

*\* \* \**

Anne went to lunch at Nell's Diner on Fourth Street like she did every Tuesday. The downtown restaurant was popular with politicians, attorneys, retailers, anyone who liked a hearty prime rib French dip sandwich or a hamburger with fries, their specialties. The place was packed and noisy, with people standing in line.

But the minute the hostess saw Anne, she was ushered right in. No matter how crowded it was, the booth in the back was always reserved for her and Uncle Jack on Tuesdays. Anne liked to think this preferential treatment had a little something to do with her, but it was clearly all about her uncle. His usual order—the country breakfast—was listed on their menu as the *Handsome Johnny*, which made him a happy man. Nell, the owner, and an old friend, would claim it was actually named after her favorite singer-songwriter, John Prine, but Jack would just wink at her and say, "Sure."

While she waited for her uncle to arrive, Anne settled into the leather booth, her back to the room—her preference so she could concentrate on reading her book instead of being distracted by the restaurant's comings and goings. This was a fortunate choice since Jack insisted on always facing the front door. Like most cops, even retired ones, Jack liked to monitor his surroundings, however benign, because "You can't let 'em get the jump on you." She was content to let him handle the surveillance on the oblivious diners.

A heavy body landed on the other side of the booth, bumping against her back and causing her to look up from her book. From the sound of it, two men were settling into their seats while in the middle of a conversation.

"Makes him sound like a real saint, doesn't it?" a gravelly voice said with a chuckle.

"I remember him when he was on his second marriage, even his first—" The second man interrupted himself to call out a greeting, "Hey, Jack, how 'ya doing?"

"Can't complain." She turned around at the sound of her uncle's voice. He was standing over the neighboring table, shaking hands with the two gray-haired men.

"Did you hear about Lino?" the first man said.

"Yeah, it's all anyone's talking about. Sad news," Jack said, catching Anne's eye. He exchanged a few more pleasantries, then excused himself. "Sorry, fellas, got my niece here with me."

Jack slid into the seat opposite Anne and dropped his phone onto the table. He was wearing loose black jeans and black Nike shoes with orange shoelaces in honor of his beloved SF Giants baseball team. A smudged and stretched-out Grateful Dead T-shirt rounded out his look.

They shared a fist bump, smiled at each other, and then looked down at their menus without a word. Their conversations usually started without social niceties and, when they were on the phone together, ended with one of them hanging up without so much as a "goodbye." A family tradition they both found amusing, but which Aunt Dot railed against as "incredibly rude, and you better not try it" with her.

After their favorite waitress, Kathy, came by and took their order, Jack leaned across the table and gestured with his chin toward the booth behind Anne. "Do you think I look as old as those guys?" he asked in a low, conspiratorial voice.

Jack, in his late sixties, was apparently under the delusion that anyone his own age looked much, much older than he did. As always, Anne shook her head. "No way, they look a good ten years older than you." *What's a niece for?*

Jack nodded. "Yeah. They probably don't exercise."

Anne pulled a newspaper out of her oversized leather handbag and laid in on the table. "Seen this yet?"

"Oh, I saw it, alright."

"I was over at their house yesterday—"

"What?" Jack looked gobsmacked. "Before or after Lino died?"

"It must have been after, but I didn't know he was dead at the time. It was around four-thirty, and I was parked as close to the house as I could get—there must have been five or six cars in front of it. I managed to catch Renee's eye as she was rushing to her car, but she just waved me off, so I—"

"Back up," Jack cut in. "So you saw Renee? What were you doing there, anyway?" Anne filled him in on Chloe's latest contest travails and then went back to describing the scene at the Pardinis' house. "After Renee drove off, I sat in my car checking messages. When I looked up, there were people pouring out of the house, carting out chairs and other stuff, loading up their cars. Then I just drove off. Like I said, I didn't know what was going on."

"Sounds like the minute Renee was out of sight, they helped themselves to whatever they could grab." Jack shook his head.

"'The grubby group.'" Anne nodded. "That's what they're called in law school, according to my lawyer boyfriend Scott. In *my* business, we like to say: 'There's one in every family.' Though usually there's more than one."

Kathy arrived at the table and set down their orders: hamburger and fries for Anne and a country breakfast for Jack. Their usual. "That was fast," Jack said admiringly to Kathy. "I put in the order the minute I saw Anne sit down," she said, walking away.

"So, lawyer boyfriend?" Jack prompted Anne. "Have we met him?"

"Actually, soon to be ex-boyfriend, the way things are going," she said, reaching for the salt and shaking it liberally onto her fries so her uncle, who was on a strict salt-free diet, couldn't steal any. "So on to the next, I guess."

They ate in silence for a few minutes. Anne's love life didn't inspire much discussion now that her ex-husband—the narcissistic, drama-prone Gary—was finally out of the picture. A few men had come and gone during the last few years, but without eliciting any strong feelings on her part—or on theirs' either, apparently. So, things on the romantic front were calm but dull. Scott had been especially dull, she thought. She could predict every word he'd say before it came out of his mouth. She changed the subject.

"Did you know Lino Pardini?"

Jack set his fork down and picked up the newspaper, pointing to the second-to-last paragraph in the obituary. "Did you read this part about his wife Dinah? I picked up the call that reported finding a dead body. My partner Dean and I went to the site and found her. We'd already had a lot of contact with the Pardinis during the year Dinah Pardini was missing. Lino was the first person we interviewed when she disappeared. Very composed, nice enough guy, but he wouldn't take a polygraph test. Though he did pony up a $50,000 reward to anyone with information. Then, after her body was found, he was—again—the first person we talked to."

"It's surprising that the case is still unsolved. After sixteen years?"

"Not so surprising if you saw how little evidence we had to work with. Dinah was totally off the grid for that entire year. No sightings or security camera views. No credit card or cell phone activity. No ransom note. We couldn't trace the limo service or driver."

"What did the autopsy and toxicology reports say?"

"Dinah's remains were pretty much reduced to just bones—there was only a small amount of soft tissue left to do some toxicology tests on. No drugs of any kind—neither prescription, poison, nor illegal—were found," he said. "However, the autopsy did reveal injuries to the small bones of the neck, so the likely cause of death was strangulation."

"No fiber evidence, tape, anything?"

"No, just the purse and her driver's license. Everything was wiped clean of any fingerprints. And the mildewed tarp was untraceable."

"What about motives?"

"The motives are the interesting part," Jack said. "There was a financial motive for Lino: Dinah was insured for a million dollars—"

"—Though arguably," Anne cut in, "in the Pardini world, one million dollars isn't all that much. I'm surprised she wasn't insured for *ten* million. If money was the motive, he would have arranged for a bigger payoff."

"Hmmm, maybe. But money's money. And that brings us to the call that led us to discover the body. We figured it was from someone involved with the murder. Otherwise, how would they know where the body had originally been dumped in order to get it and move it to the fresh grave? And then supposedly 'find' it. It had to have been an inside job. Whoever killed her came up with an elaborate scheme to have her body found."

"Because they needed a declaration of death?"

"Probably. In California, when a person is missing, there's a five-year waiting period until they can be declared dead. That's a long time to wait. Wills are on hold. Life insurance policies can't be cashed in. Remaining spouses can't remarry," Jack said.

"So, suddenly, Mrs. Pardini's body gets conveniently found...."

"Yes, so I ask you, who benefits?"

She just shrugged. "I'm guessing, Lino?"

"Lino, yes, and maybe Renee. He needed Dinah's body found so he could collect on the insurance. But there was also the fact that he and Renee got married seven months after the declaration of death, which makes his marriage to Renee a motive, too. He was the marrying kind."

"And Renee's possible motive? Marriage, also?"

"Let's put it this way: Their son Josh was born eight months after they were married. Maybe she thought marriage was important."

"I'm not buying it. If Renee was so eager to marry Lino, why wait a whole seven months after the declaration of death to do it? Why not get married the next week? The pregnancy is irrelevant, Uncle Jack. She wasn't saying to him, 'Oh Lino, honey, better find the body fast because I'm pregnant!'

Do the math. She didn't get pregnant until *after* the body was found. No, I don't see her involved," Anne said, picking up the last fry and then setting it down uneaten.

Kathy swooped by and dropped the check onto the table.

"Okay, fine…but maybe she *wanted* to get pregnant and wanted to clear the decks first."

Anne just rolled her eyes.

Jack was getting revved up. "Well, that just leads to another bunch of questions…"

And so on. Anne tuned him out, thinking about her afternoon appointment and what she was going to have for dinner. She didn't tune back in until he was winding down: "Who was the guy who placed the call that brought us to her body?" Jack was saying. "Was it the killer? Or someone hired by the killer?"

Anne pushed her empty plate to the side and picked up the newspaper. "Well, you're still working cold cases with the district attorney's office, aren't you? You could get Dinah's case reopened."

Jack threw his napkin down. "Oh, please. There's no new evidence—and the most likely suspect just died. We're just talking here. Shooting the breeze."

"So you think Lino did it."

"Always have. But we didn't have anything on him. Anyway, he certainly went on with his life as if nothing had happened."

"Anyone else have a motive for killing Dinah?" Anne asked, stuffing the newspaper into her purse.

Jack slid out of the booth and stood, hesitating. "Might have been another woman who wanted Dinah out of the way."

"Aside from Renee?"

"Maybe. Lino wasn't the faithful type, even to his mistress. But all we had were suspicions. Just rumors."

"About whom?"

"About someone who had an alibi," he said, waiving the question off as he reached for the check.

Anne didn't even bother making a gratuitous grab for it, thinking, *What's an uncle for?*

# Chapter Six

Wednesday afternoon, Anne waltzed into her office after a morning spent working on the McDonald Avenue estate project.

"Look at you, dressing all 'business lady,'" Brittany said, greeting her with a grin. And that she was: Anne was wearing her white button-down shirt, red lipstick, and black pantsuit for an interview that afternoon.

"Two calls, Anne." Brittany waved the pink "While You Were Out" message slips from her curved reception desk. The reception area was light and airy, banked on both sides by eight-foot-tall windows.

Anne still marveled, but mostly worried, about her new office spaces. Just two months before, she'd made the financially risky move to this ultra-modern, five-story, glass-fronted office building which wrapped around an open-air garden courtyard with water features. Her previous office, where she'd spent two years during the worst of the COVID pandemic, though not an out-and-out dump, was so oppressively small—about five paces long— that there was just enough room to fit a standard-size desk. In fact, it was so claustrophobic she couldn't bear to spend another month there. Even worse, the restroom was located down a long hallway and was shared with the other tenants.

These new accommodations were comparatively grand, with a glassed-in conference room, reception area, private office, kitchenette, and powder room. Parking included. During the pandemic, the trend toward working remotely from home had caused office rental prices to sink to a new low.

It was a bargain, she assured herself.

"Good thing you didn't go straight to your two o'clock appointment because they just cancelled it." Brittany handed Anne the phone messages.

Anne let loose a sigh. *Damn.* "I was looking forward to meeting them." Unlike most business owners, Anne liked the interviewing process. She liked having a look around the prospective clients' houses, hearing the family stories, assuring them that she was the one-stop answer to all their problems, glowing in their blind confidence in her. That was the brief, blissful time before the actual job started, before looming deadlines, grunt work, and the client's inevitable disappointment that their "authentic Tiffany lamp" wasn't so authentic.

"They want you to call and reschedule," Brittany said, going back to her computer. "The second call was from Renee Pardini."

"Seriously? Did she say what she wanted?"

"Just to call her."

\* \* \*

After closing her office door, Anne settled in front of her computer, rescheduled the meeting with the prospective client, and then called Renee.

When Renee didn't pick up, Anne left a message and leaned back in her black swivel chair to wait. After a few minutes of staring at the ceiling, she pushed herself up from the chair and stood in front of the floor-to-ceiling window, gazing down at the blur of red, orange, and russet fall leaves that thickly layered the grounds of the park below.

She sat down at her desk again to wait some more. Wait and wonder why on earth Renee, whose husband had died only forty-eight hours before would be calling her? Help with the estate already? Until she got the answer, she decided she might as well be productive. Maybe straighten her desktop or check for new texts. As she pulled her phone from her handbag, the business card she'd received at her client's house on McDonald fell to the floor. *Silver Landscaping: Let Us Add Polish to Your Yard.* Its owner Dave Silver intrigued her, not in an urgent, can't-stop-thinking-about-him way, but enough to check his Yelp customer ratings while she had time to kill.

She leaned the card in front of her computer and typed his company name into the Google search engine. Up popped his listing with ten reviews, all giving the company five stars. "Real professionals," one customer wrote. Another wrote, "I've known Dave since he won the "Sonoma County Grapevine Pruning Contest, Junior Division" when we were twelve, and he knows more about..." Anne smiled. She Googled the pruning contest and his name. And there he was: a skinny, mischievous-looking kid wearing a baseball cap, dirty jeans, and a tie-dyed T-shirt. All arms and legs and bravado. "I showed up to win,' said Davy Silver, representing Pardini Vineyards and Winery." *Small world.*

She was just about to follow another link when the office line rang. In the front office Brittany picked up the call and was talking loud enough for Anne to catch most of what she said. "Hello, Mrs. Pardini," Brittany said. "Yes, she's here. Just one moment, please." For such a new, expensive building, the walls were criminally thin.

"Got it, Brittany," she called out, then picked up the phone.

"Hi Renee."

"Can you come over?" Renee asked without any preamble. Anne felt herself smiling. *She'd fit right into my family.*

"Is it about those tickets I was waving at you on Monday?" Anne asked.

There was silence on the other end. "I don't know what you're talking about," Renee finally said.

"Nothing, it's nothing, Renee. I'm so sorry for your loss. Of course, I can come when—"

"Right now, if possible," Renee cut in. Anne heard muffled voices in the background.

*Right now? What's the rush?* Anne was taken aback. Estate work usually didn't start until after the funeral.

"Do you mind telling me—"

"I'd rather discuss this in person."

* * *

Anne sent a quick text to Chloe, then swung by the high school to pick up the booklet of contest tickets from the principal's office. The principal had given Chloe a two-week extension due to the "unforeseen circumstances" of Lino Pardini's death. But on the chance that a moment might arise when Anne felt comfortable enough to ask Renee to sign them, she'd have the tickets at the ready. Although etiquette-wise, she wondered, how could there *possibly* be an appropriate moment to badger a newly widowed woman for such a minor thing?

Ten minutes later, Anne parked her car in the street behind two florist vans making deliveries to the Pardinis' house. A black Mercedes and an old tan sedan were parked in the driveway inside the open gate. A stout woman stood guard at the Pardinis' front door, ushering in a heart-shaped standing arrangement of roses from one delivery driver and a mixed autumnal bouquet from the other.

Spotting Anne, the woman gave a short wave. "Are you the memorial service coordinator?" she asked when Anne reached the porch.

"I've got this, Helen," Renee said, stepping out from behind the door. Her auburn hair was pulled back from her face with a black headband, and she had on torn jeans and a leopard print sweater and no makeup, not even lip gloss.

"Thanks for coming on the spur-of-the-moment like this."

"Of course. I was so sorry to hear about Lino," Anne said, entering the living room. The air inside was heavy with the smell of too many flowers. She watched as the housekeeper directed the delivery men on where to place the newest arrangements before she disappeared into the kitchen.

"Thank you. It was quite a shock." Renee sat on the sofa and gestured toward an overstuffed chair. "I won't keep you long."

Sitting down, Anne's left elbow nearly toppled one of the three floral arrangements crowding the side table. She made a quick grab at the vase and righted it. "Beautiful bouquets," she said, scanning the room. They were everywhere. On tabletops, on the fireplace mantel, on the bookshelf, on the coffee table. Massive standing flower arrangements were three-deep on the floor in front of the fireplace. And where there weren't flowers, there were sympathy cards.

"I don't know what to do with them all." Renee sighed and looked around. "I was going to bring them to the memorial service we're holding at Luther Burbank Center and just leave them there, but that's a week away. Take some home with you."

"That's nice of you…" Anne smiled faintly and let her words hang in the air. This wasn't her conversation to lead.

Renee's eyes searched Anne's. "Might as well get to the point," she finally said in a low and controlled voice. "I asked you here to find out what happened last Sunday night. I knew something was wrong when you and the girl came back into the living room with Lino. And you knew it too, the way you hurried out of here. Whatever happened, it upset Lino so much he hardly said another word all evening." She fiddled with her wedding ring. "Then he died the next day."

After a while, she let out a long sigh and leaned forward. "Look, you were an FBI agent. You're a trained observer. Did anything strike you strange about him that night? Did he look sick? Did he say anything?"

Anne hesitated.

"I have a right to know. What happened?"

Anne nodded. "Chloe found envelopes in a hole in your garage wall," she said, reaching inside her purse for her phone. "I took some photos." While she called up the photos, she began describing the scene. How Chloe was looking for fire hazards and saw the stacks of magazines and newspapers and then moved them.

"Take a look." Anne stood up and sat next to Renee on the couch and handed her the phone. "The first photo is the wall…"

"I've never seen that before." Renee swiped left to the next two photos. One showed the two large manila envelopes; the other was of Chloe spreading out some of the bundles of cash on the surface of the plastic container.

"How much money is that?" Renee's eyes narrowed. "Did you count it?"

"There wasn't time. Besides, we didn't want to have anything to do with it. Chloe was getting ready to put the envelopes back where she found them when Lino suddenly came into the garage. He wanted us to leave; that was obvious. So, of course, we did."

"What did he say?"

"Nothing, really. He just stood there, and then he followed us out."

"And you have no idea how much money…"

"No, but there's probably quite a bit more money left inside the hole," Anne said. "Chloe only grabbed two envelopes."

Renee swiped the screen to the next photo. It showed Chloe holding up a long strand of pearls. "She found those, too," Anne said.

"Pearls." Renee's fingers reflexively went to the back of her neck as if she'd find them hanging there. "*My* pearls. Lino told me they were in our deposit box at the bank. For safekeeping, he said," she said in a quiet voice and then lapsed into silence again.

When she finally spoke, it was as if she was talking more to herself than to Anne. "Of course you didn't put the envelopes back in the hiding place. Why would you—not with Lino there. You'd leave them out for him."

Listening to Renee's mutterings, Anne felt like an intruder. Which, in her line of business, was nothing new. She intruded on people's lives and private grief on a daily basis, uncovering their family resentments, greed, and darkest secrets. Pearls taken from Renee? Not the least bit surprising to Anne. Families were always stealing or hiding things from each other in her world—and they always felt justified in doing so, offering up some version of "I earned it" as their excuse. Or "Promises were made." How many times had she heard that one? Delicate family issues needed be handled with tact, Anne knew that very well. But sometimes, it was best to just cut to the chase.

"There's only one thing to do, Renee. Check out the garage. I'll come with you. It'll go faster with the two of us."

Renee nodded, standing up. "Let's go."

"But before we do," Anne said rather sheepishly, "would you mind signing these? I apologize for this, but—" She pulled out the two violation tickets and handed Renee a pen.

"Not a problem." Renee sat back down, took the pen, and signed the tickets. "Now, you have to do me a favor, too," she said with a hint of a smile, "Take some flowers home with you."

CHAPTER SIX

"Deal. Now, let's go to the garage and see what your husband left behind."

# Chapter Seven

O f course, nothing was left behind in the garage. Why would there be? Not when Lino went to all the trouble to hide the money from her in the first place.

He had obviously moved the envelopes, but to where? It couldn't have been far because he stayed home for the rest of the night. Or had he?

Renee thought back to Sunday evening, to the moment Anne and Chloe came back into living room where she was chatting with Krista. Lino was right behind them, a bit of a shock since Renee thought he was still upstairs. "Where have you all been?" she asked Chloe. The girl answered that she'd found some fire hazards, and Anne abruptly added that it was time to go. Lino thanked their guests for coming, turned on the porch light to guide them in the dark, and then waved "goodbye" as they drove off.

It was all very civil, but Lino's face was tight, and his eyes darted from side to side, looking as preoccupied as a cash-strapped roulette player waiting for the next spin. He rebuffed any of her attempts at conversation, not saying a word except to suggest that she should go ahead to bed without him because he felt like reading a book by the fire. She knew him well enough to know that something was off, but she did as he urged and went upstairs. And while she was peacefully sleeping, he'd been down in the garage figuring out a new hiding place.

Perhaps he'd buried the envelopes in the backyard. But she dismissed that thought almost as soon as it came. *Getting his hands dirty wouldn't occur to him.* Or maybe he brought them to his brother Marco's house or to a friend's for hiding. A lot of people owed him, so that wasn't out of the question.

CHAPTER SEVEN

Renee slumped deep into the couch and closed her eyes, overcome by exhaustion. Not just by the last few days of planning Lino's memorial service, fending off well-meaning sympathy calls, and handling the endless arrival of flowers and elaborate trays of food that were now stacked in the refrigerator. She was exhausted by Lino's treachery. And it was only four o'clock in the afternoon. Josh would be coming home from school soon—he was getting a ride from his cousins—and she'd have to rally herself and act as normal as possible for his sake.

Her phone rang; their lawyer's name came up on the caller ID.

She let it go to voicemail. She knew he wanted to discuss the will and trust funds and on and on and on. Always about the money. Maybe the lawyer knew what Lino was up to. Maybe he was in on it. She'd return his call when she was good and ready.

She couldn't remember feeling this caught off guard, this unnerved and angry. The very idea that Lino would betray her by helping himself to *their* money, *their* retirement funds—or at least what little of it could have been considered community property when he was alive—was beyond her. She wracked her brain but couldn't think of any innocent reason for Lino to hide the money. *Upstanding Eagle Scout, my ass*, she thought.

It was ironic that Lino was the one to stash money away; he was the last person in the world with cash flow problems. If anyone should have been hoarding money, it was *her*. And given half a chance, she probably would have—if she had any money to stash. But Lino had a firm hand on the spigot. His accountant deposited her monthly stipend in her separate bank account. She had three credit cards—with strict limits on each—her car, jewelry, and that was about it. Her name wasn't on the title of any of their houses, and Lino held absolute control over their various investments. Lino was a very careful man, just what you would expect from a lawyer with his track record in marriage.

But the money wasn't really the point. God knows they had plenty of it in savings and investments, plus their Fountaingrove home, their beachfront vacation home in Carmel-by-the-Sea, and the ski condo in Aspen, Colorado. Whatever was in those envelopes was a mere pittance.

43

No, the point was that he'd been planning on leaving her, probably for another woman. She had seen the signs and had little doubt. But now it appeared that his plans were much further along than she'd suspected, and like any good boy scout, he was prepared. Worse, he was prepared to take her hard-earned pearls along with him.

* * *

Renee was twenty-seven years old and never married, though not from a lack of offers, when she met Lino in the spring of 2004. Theirs wasn't the kind of serendipitous, meet-cute encounter with destiny that she loved in the movies, but it was a clever one.

She was an assistant to a high-rolling, not altogether honest, real estate developer when she read about a celebrity golfing charity event that was auctioning off an item she couldn't afford to bid on, but desperately wanted: the chance to have lunch with a newly single, thirty-something championship golfer and—in small type—Lino Pardini, a local lawyer and businessman.

The big draw, especially for the town's unattached women, was meant to be the hot young golfer, but Renee's radar told her otherwise. No, the draw for her was Lino Pardini. She'd read up on him, had a good idea of his net worth, and knew he was twenty-two years older than her and in a long-term marriage, his fourth. In fact, she had seen them together at a restaurant; they were both looking vacantly around the room while silently chewing, only showing animation when acquaintances dropped by their table. Renee knew a bored husband when she saw one, and this was a rich, handsome, bored husband. Rich being the siren call.

Renee talked her boss into bidding on the auction. "It'll give you face time with Pardini to pitch the office building investment," she told him. And she would happily come along to "take notes." It worked, and he won.

During lunch at The Parisian hotel, the celebrity golfer's eyes slid right past Renee and landed on the cute busboy pouring water for the table. Which was fine with her, especially since Lino couldn't take his eyes off her. When her boss proposed another business meeting with him, Lino accepted on the condition that she also attend. Although the business deal with her boss never panned out, her love affair with Lino began. Their first date was at a decidedly unglamorous, out-of-the-way bar where they sat in a dark corner, listened to the jukebox, drank some wine, and shot pool. After that, they met every chance they could, mostly at her small apartment or at out-of-town hotels.

For the next five months, she was content to bide her time. But she was careful not to give it too much time. She'd read a few books about enticing a man, like *The Rules*, the best of the bunch in her opinion, but they didn't tell her anything she didn't already know, principally: Don't let a man think you're waiting around with no life and no other offers.

She could have written a few books of her own. Every man she had ever made love with, even if only once, had proposed marriage to her—that's how irresistible men seemed to find her. Which is why she was surprised that it was taking Lino so long to leave his wife. The catalyst for finally putting her foot down was her looming twenty-eight birthday: She adored him, she told him at a tender moment, but she was pushing thirty and wanted children; she was prepared to walk if he didn't leave Dinah. He told her to be patient. They broke up, then got back together, and then broke up again. An emotional roller coaster that continued for another few months.

Her old college friend, Stella, took her out for drinks and tried to set her straight by holding a one-woman intervention. "You don't need this guy to be successful. You can make it on your own," Stella said to her. "It was funny back in college, you acting all Scarlett O'Hara, trying to find a rich husband, but it's 2004, girl, and women don't need men for money and security anymore."

"You've had security all your life," Renee said, "so you just don't get it." It was all well and good, Renee told her, for her and their other Tufts University friends, who were all raised by affluent East Coast parents, not to worry about bearing the weight of poverty and the shame it imprints so heavily on the soul. They weren't raised in the rural, down-on-its-luck town of Cooper—one of the poorest in the whole state of Texas—by a man who burned down his own rundown shack of a house for the insurance money. When the investigator came around asking questions, her father took off the next day, leaving Renee's mother and their two kids—her and her sister—to live in a rented shack with no running water by the side of State Highway 154. With no money for food, rent, or electricity, they got by only with the help of church charities.

"I was the only kid to wear the same raggedy clothes to school every day," Renee said to Stella, "and I got teased mercilessly. We were the poorest of the poor." But Renee was also the only kid in the class to get straight A's all throughout her school years. She was disciplined, smart, and ambitious. As a preteen, she would carry a photo of pop star Madonna in her jeans pocket because the hyper-ambitious Material Girl was someone who knew what she wanted and went after it. Renee received grants and scholarships to Tufts University, earned a business degree, and landed a good job, but her eye was still on the prize. She still wanted in on the glitzy, privileged world of the very rich.

"You're beyond that," her friend assured her.

"Apparently not," Renee answered.

And so the affair with Lino continued on, or by her way of thinking, *dragged* on.

Everything changed later that year, that fall day when Lino's wife, Dinah, disappeared. Simply vanished without a trace. The distraught husband and daughters closed ranks and during the next six months, Renee didn't hear a word from Lino except for one late night call when he told her, "Nothing good will come from you being involved in this, babe. Be patient."

But six months is an impossibly long time for a young woman to be without a man; simply too much to ask, and her patience ran out. So, at precisely the six-month mark, she quietly started seeing other men. One evening, Lino saw her through a restaurant window holding hands across the table with another man. He strode through the near-empty restaurant to their table and, in an epic display of jealousy that she secretly found thrilling, pulled the chair out from under her date, toppling him on the floor. "Stay the hell away from her," Lino growled at him. The next day, Lino showed up at her apartment full of apologies. He draped a Tiffany's turquoise and silver necklace around her neck and promised they would never be apart again.

But that didn't last. After Dinah's body was finally found a year after her disappearance, the police started coming around asking questions again, so Lino kept a low profile until things seemed to cool down. By the following spring, they decided the time was right and were married in the mayor's lush backyard garden with sixty guests in attendance, including his and Dinah's two daughters. Even with the hideously airtight prenup she'd had to sign, Renee always thought of it as the happiest day of her life. A glorious, triumphant day.

She got up off the couch and found herself wandering toward the entry hallway, where their wedding photos were lined up on the wall. Like old books on a bookshelf, she rarely noticed them. Now, facing them, it struck her how remarkably young they both had looked. Lino was fifty-two then, with slightly more hair, dark and curly. She didn't have a wrinkle on her dewy, late-twenties skin, and in every photo, she angled her face to show her good side. She knew all the tricks to being photogenic and hadn't missed a single one that day: Her head was fetchingly tilted, her body turned at a 45-degree angle, and she carried most of her weight on her back leg. She had four bridesmaids, all of whom knew the same tricks and jockeyed to get their own best angles. This made for a slightly ridiculous-looking bride-with-bridesmaids photo, which made her smile, as did Lino's own affectations: a crooked grin and one slightly raised eyebrow. So urbane. *Where were those girls now?* She hadn't heard from any of them for years.

The last photo was the only one that didn't look posed. She and Lino were holding hands, smiling, and gazing at each other under the lattice gazebo in the garden. The moment replayed in her mind: their friends' laughter when she said "I will" a little too fast, the morning sun glinting off their gold rings lying on the satin pillow. She could almost hear Lino's voice as he promised to always love and protect her. This was the one photo worth cherishing. She felt a tear escape from her eye and wiped it away with the back of her hand. Her first real tear since he'd died.

Ultimately, Lino did what he'd promised, at least financially. She hadn't been at all sure it would end up that way. In the days before he died, he had taken to locking himself in his office, talking to his lawyer for hours. He was moody, distant, and spent far too many evenings away from home—all signposts of an affair, the end of their marriage, and an inevitable changing of the will. That piece of paper was the first thing she'd looked for in his desk office the day he died, and she had to pry the drawer open to find it. But surprisingly, he hadn't changed his will. Since his children were already taken care of with trust funds, she was still listed as his sole heir. So now she was a wealthy widow, her assets running in the millions, with three houses and his hefty life insurance policy.

The sound of her phone ringing brought her back to the present. It was their accountant, Burton Zang. First, their lawyer called, now Burt. It was like the two of them were double-teaming her. She put her phone on mute so she wouldn't have to hear him leave a message, boring her ad nauseam about their assets, taxes, leveraging, investments, whatever.

She stepped into the brightly lit kitchen where her housekeeper was tidying up before leaving for the day. "Did that memorial coordinator ever arrive?" Helen asked as she hung a dishtowel to dry on the oven handle.

"No, she rescheduled for tomorrow." Renee put the teakettle under the faucet and gazed out to the backyard, a lush English garden that required three gardeners, coming twice a week, to keep it so wildly natural looking.

"Well, good luck with that, Mrs. Pardini. See you in a few days." Helen shouldered her purse and left by the back door.

While the water was heating, Renee went outside and sat on the carved wooden bench and listened to water gurgling through the three-tiered fountain, her thoughts drifting randomly, but always circling back to the envelopes. There was no denying Lino's deviousness. But what she couldn't figure out was the *why* of it. Why would he need all that cash? It seemed to be some kind of getaway money. But if he was trying to escape her and their life together, he didn't need cash for that. He had access to all the credit cards and ATMs in the world.

Unless he was squirreling it away for his daughters? Is that why Jennifer went to the garage while all the other relatives were gathered in the living room? Had Lino told his daughter where to find the pearls and money—or at least where it *had* been before Sunday night, when he'd been forced to find a new hiding place?

*Oh, Lino, you bastard. What were you up to?*

She heard the kettle whistle and went back inside to fix her tea, distracted and angry. It didn't really matter what he was up to—none of his shenanigans mattered anymore, she thought. And as for those missing pearls and money, she would find them. She had the time; she had the resources. She could hire an investigator if she needed to. It would be a "project," something to devote her energies to. Maybe starting next week after the memorial service, when her new life began.

But right now, with only a few minutes left before she had to go pick up her son at his school, she carried her mug to the dining room table and finally listened to those voice messages.

# Chapter Eight

"This'll be a pretty quick job," Dave Silver said.

He was surveying the minuscule yard in front of Anne's duplex home, a cozy Craftsman bungalow with cedar shingles and dark green trim on the two front doors and the wrap-around porch railing. Dandelion weeds with neon yellow blooms—said to be "so very festive" by her renter in the adjacent unit—dotted the unkept lawn.

This water-thirsty, weed-infested grass had to go, Anne had decided. Along with the half-dead camellia bush and the row of highly flammable juniper bushes that edged the walkway. And since she didn't own a rototiller to unearth it all, nor did she have *any* clue as to how to design an aesthetically pleasing, drought-tolerant yard, she had called *Silver Landscaping*. But not before having an inspector from the city water department come over to measure the lawn to see if she'd get a rebate for tearing it out. They showed up and authorized the project the next morning. She'd taken this Friday afternoon off to meet with Dave and get an idea of how much it would cost to improve this mess of a yard.

"I might have to drag the job out—" he said, glancing up at her with a glimmer in his eye.

Anne raised her eyebrow and gave him a smirky little smile. More coquettish than was her usual style, but wasn't he practically saying he wanted to stretch out the job to spend more time with her?

"—on account of having to fit it around my other existing jobs, Dave said, sliding the words in with a half-smile. "I'll have to work here in fits and starts."

She lowered her brow quickly. She'd misread him. *But who the hell knows anymore?*

"Which should be easy since a few of my other landscaping jobs are in the McDonald neighborhood," he said. Anne's duplex was in Town and Country, a residential area located just blocks from the McDonald Historic District and downtown. The self-contained, village-like neighborhood's well-kept, circa 1950s bungalows formed a horseshoe shape around its very own shopping center with an organic market, small-plates restaurant, fitness center, and post office. All of it within walking distance of her front door. Some might argue, but Anne thought it was the most desirable neighborhood in Santa Rosa.

"So, what do you think should be done here?" she asked, raising her hand to shade her eyes against the sun's late afternoon glare. It was nearing five o'clock.

"Depends on your style, budget and timeframe," he said, bending down to pick a dandelion from between blades of grass. "We can do an English Cottage plan, a minimalist modern, Japanese garden, tropical, my own personal favorite—country rustic—or a Mediterranean design." Dave locked eyes with her and he said with a slight drawl, "You want it, I got it."

*Okay, now he's flirting for sure.* And if he wasn't, then he was the most un-self-aware man over forty she'd come across. She decided to play it safe.

"Not sure…." Which was true. Anne was vacillating between a cottage garden look and Japanese modern. Maybe a fusion of both. She hated gardening and knew nothing about it.

"Got an idea," Dave said. "Let's drive around some neighborhoods and you can point out which yards you like. Then let's go grab a beer at Trudy Lee's. We can talk plants and things."

\* \* \*

An hour later, having driven through some of the best-landscaped neighborhoods in town—pointing out crape myrtle trees, boulder accents, and native ground coverings—they headed to a ramshackle bar on Highway 12 that Dave promised Anne was "the best dive bar" in Sonoma County.

They parked in the gravel parking lot behind Trudy Lee's Bar & Grill and made their way to the front, passing a young couple leaning against the brick building, smoking cigarettes near the entry. Following Dave inside, Anne lingered by an ATM machine next to the coat rack to give herself a moment to check out her surroundings. It was a good-sized crowd for being so early on a Friday evening, fairly noisy and, like most bars, it smelled of stale beer and the second-hand smoke that drifted in from the front door. Patrons crowded in, elbow-to-elbow on bar stools. A red neon sign declared: THIS IS A CASH ONLY ESTABLISHMENT. Above the bar, a stuffed deer head with antlers was staring back at her.

Trudy Lee herself was tending bar. She was a fairly large woman, wearing dark jeans and an unbuttoned plaid flannel shirt over a white T-shirt. She had one of those mouths that curved down even when she was smiling. She gave one of those smiles to Dave and called out with a friendly wave, "Hi there, sweetie!"

Dave waved back and held up two fingers. "Trudy's an old family friend," Dave explained to Anne in a voice loud enough to carry over the din as they weaved their way around servers, customers heading for the bar, and occupied tables. They found a clean table in the center of the room and sat down in the wooden spindle-backed chairs. "I've known Trudy since before I could walk. She lived at the same hippie commune as my folks back in the late 1970s. It was called MoonChild Ranch; maybe you've heard of it?"

"Vaguely, but it was before my time," she said, settling her jacket and purse on the empty chair beside her. "It was on the outskirts of town, right?"

"Yeah, and it's long gone. My old man always said that Trudy Lee was the prettiest girl in the commune, which pissed my mom off no end. Then Dad would say, 'Trudy's dance card was always full.' And then my mom would put it a little differently: She'd say that Trudy slept with every guy in town. She said even Lino Pardini, richest kid in town, was on her 'dance card,' so to speak."

Anne took another look at the woman behind the bar. Mid-sixties at the very least, sad, dark, hooded eyes, long brown hair streaked with strands

52

of gray. Not in any universe could Anne envision Trudy and Lino Pardini being anything other than strangers. And yet Anne could also see the high cheekbones and pert nose that hinted at beauty in her younger days.

"All that was back in the seventies, which was the Wild West, sexually speaking. Back then, Trudy had kind of a cool, hippy chick, young Emmylou Harris look going on. But that was a few heartbreaks ago. Sorry," he said, standing up, "maybe too much information."

"Don't be sorry on my account. The more inappropriate the oversharing, the better I like it."

He nodded and smiled. "I'll go get the beers. Be right back."

While she sat waiting, she took a closer look around at the uneven wide plank floors, knotty pine walls, neon beer signs, low lighting, and cowboy boots on every other customer—even the women, though there weren't many of those. She'd seen plenty of crusty old bars, and this one could be a movie set for a Cohen brothers' modern-day western. She half expected actor Jeff Bridges to walk in the door.

An Art Deco jukebox, standing upright in the corner, caught her eye: a 1947 Wurlitzer "CD bubbler" in mint condition, the kind that went for upwards of five figures at auction. On the wall opposite the front door, a bright blue neon wall clock, over three feet in diameter, was also an expensive collector's item. So there was serious money inside these walls, though not many people other than collectors or estate liquidators would know it.

On his way back to the table, Dave carried a pitcher of beer in one hand and dangled the handles of two mugs in the other. A gruff voice hailed him from across the room. "Dave, *como te va?*" called out a weathered old Hispanic man sitting at a table with two younger men.

"Hey, man, *estoy bien y tu?*" Dave shouted back.

Anne relieved him of the mugs and set them on the table. "Where'd you pick up Spanish?"

Sitting down, Dave began pouring beer into their mugs. "Well, as a kid, I worked in my old man's vineyards with immigrants—in fact, two of those guys, Francisco and Luis, over at that table taught me how to prune." Dave tilted his head toward the men. "Just a minute, Anne," he said, setting the pitcher down. He stood halfway up in his chair and waved toward Trudy. When he caught her eye, he sat back down and mimed drinking from a glass and pointed toward Francisco. Trudy nodded.

"Gracias, *ca*—" Luis, the one with a mole by his eyebrow, yelled out.

"Don't say it, *amigo*!" Dave yelled back with a laugh.

Anne took a sip of beer. "What was that all about?"

"I need to get you a little drunk before I can tell you that story," he said, stretching his legs in front of him.

"I'm working tomorrow at an estate sale, so that might not be happening tonight." Anne grinned and leaned back in the chair, then squirmed against the wooden spindles that were hitting her back wrong. "So tell me your story anyway."

He took a long swallow of beer and set his mug down. "Okay, picture this: a sweet, innocent eleven-year-old kid—"

"You, I take it," she said, rolling up her denim jacket to pad the back of her chair.

"Right, and believe me, there never was a nicer kid. There I was working in the fields at my folks' vineyards alongside a bunch of rowdy guys who spoke only Spanish. Francisco was in charge and spoke a little English, so he bossed me around and had me doing all the grunt work. He'd say, 'Hey, *cabrón*, bring me those other shears.' And '*cabrón*, tie down those vines.' And then, 'Good work, *cabrón*!' The other guys would laugh and slap me on the back. I thought, 'Wow, these guys really like me. I'm their buddy, their *cabrón*.'"

"Their 'jackass' is what you were." Anne laughed. "*That* much Spanish I know."

"Yeah, it took me a while to realize what they were saying," he said with a laugh. "And then it took another few weeks before they'd ask me to sit with them at lunch. But they taught me a lot—about working hard, speaking their language, friendship." He fixed his eyes on her. "Okay, so what about you? What's your story?"

Anne took another taste of beer, gearing up to recite the sanitized, first-

54

date version of her life (*Was this a first date?*) when a plastic bowl of tortilla chips and a plate with four deviled eggs appeared in front of them.

"Trudy thought you looked hungry." The server set down the food and turned away before they could thank him.

"Trudy being here tonight is both a good thing and a bad thing," Dave said. "She's a generous pourer and might even spot you a drink or food every now and then. On the other hand, she might just close the bar early. You never know." He reached for a chip. "Okay, so back to you…"

Anne started her recital by telling him of her roots in Santa Rosa, then lightly glossed over her FBI career and divorce from the psycho Gary (*Most exes are psychos,* he said, grinning), and landed her finish: "So now I'm running my own business. And I own, with the help of the bank, my own house."

He gave a low whistle. "Pretty impressive for a young chick…or lady…"

"Woman," she cut in.

"Of course, woman. Who the hell knows what to say these days? Anyway, I, too, run my own business and own a home with the help of the bank. It's not much to look at, a used mobile home about the size of a two-car garage…but it's mine."

They clinked glasses.

Anne was still on her first beer, Dave on his second, when their conversation turned to families. The Silver family, he told her, had worked at the Pardini Winery, which was located close to the commune, during much of his childhood. Then, after his family was kicked out of the commune when he was eight years old for various offenses (*Dad was a bit of a brawler*), his parents bought some land down the road from the MoonChild Ranch and started growing their own grapes.

She drank some more, though not enough to catch up with Dave, and found herself relaxing, getting lost in his words and falling into his dark brown eyes. *Brooding and soulful,* she thought. A poet's eyes, The kind she was most susceptible to. She liked the way he talked with his hands. The way his braided leather-and-bead wristbands slid up and down his arm as he made his points. His broad, coat hanger shoulders that moved about almost involuntarily, like they had a life of their own. His direct gaze and soft-spoken, slow cadences. She even liked his outdated, brown leather bomber jacket.

"This was back when land prices were relatively cheap," he said. "They were making a pretty decent success of it, selling grapes to local wineries like the Pardini Winery. I wish they'd bought up more of that land."

*Too bad he's so old,* she thought. She had a fairly strict age range for the men she would consider dating: They couldn't be any more than ten years older or ten years younger than herself. Too much of an age gap, and their values, energy levels, and goals might not mesh. This seemed quite reasonable, especially since she'd just recently raised the age limit from a seven-year difference to ten years. Dave had to be at least forty-five, maybe older. But who said anything about dating here, anyway? This was just a business meeting between a yard owner and a landscaper, with drinks.

"Hear that song?" Dave asked. The jukebox was playing "Tangled Up in Blue" by Bob Dylan. "That's how I see my family's connection with the Pardini family. That about sums it up: all tangled up, like a big, twisted ball of rusted-out barbed wire. Intertwined whether we like it or not. The only thing is, we're the only ones who see it—the Pardinis barely notice us. I bet they don't think about us at all. But in the Silver family, that connection's been one of the overriding dramas in our lives."

He told her that his father, Jerry Silver, was a natural born vintner, an innovator who'd shared his unorthodox marketing concepts and grape combining ideas with the Pardini family's oldest son, Marco.

"Marco ran with Dad's ideas. Won some big awards that helped put Sonoma County wines on the map. And just last year, Marco was named a "Wine Country Wine Legend" by a national magazine. And my old man? Maybe he's okay with it, who knows? But he's still working away, selling grapes to wineries instead of running his own winery operations. Still trying to save enough to retire. Then there's me...after school and during summers, I worked in my folks' vineyards, but when it came time to enter a big contest for pruning, my dad made me represent Pardini Winery because they gave us so much business."

Anne knew all about his contest-winning past from Googling him, but he didn't need to know that.

"It's sounding a little like sour grapes, isn't it?" he added with a small chuckle.

Anne rolled her eyes at that. She sat back and watched him, the play of thought in his eyes, the way his face ran through a series of micro expressions, from sheepish embarrassment to delight to irritation.

"But the Pardinis always threw a few crumbs our way," he went on. "During my lost years—"

"Aha! Now we're talking. So, how lost were they?" Anne asked with a sly grin, leaning forward. "Drugs? Prison? Armed robbery? What are we talking here?"

"When I know you better," he said, sidestepping the questions with a grin. "Anyway, the Pardinis kept me afloat, gave me odd jobs to do. Drive here, do that. Back then, I'd do anything for a buck." His tone grew pensive, but then he pulled himself out of it and said, "And after I straightened myself up a while back, they became clients of *Silver Landscaping*. Before he died, Lino was going to front the money for my nursery. But I'm still going through with that. It'll just take a little longer."

From across the room, an outbreak of yelling, swearing, and table pounding was so loud it drowned out their conversation. Looking up, they saw other patrons, pissed off at the interruption, set down their drinks and turn toward the source—a red-faced, barrel-chested man standing up in the back of the room. They tried to out-yell the yeller, but he wasn't through. Shaking his fist toward the water-stained ceiling, he bellowed, "I wish I'd killed that lying son-of-a-bitch when I had a chance! Fucking ruined my life—"

"Hey, keep it down over there!" Trudy thundered, her voice so sharp the guy momentarily stopped yelling, stood stone still, and blinked several times. Then he defiantly pounded the table with his fist one more time and savagely pushed the table over onto its side for good measure, taking two half-full glasses of beer with it.

"Hey asshole, that table better not be broken," Trudy said, making a move to come out from behind the bar to handle things. But by that time, the man had already crumbled back into his seat, deflating into himself. "Oh crap," was the last, very loud thing he said. He sat hunched over, his elbows on his knees and his beefy hands covering his face. Trudy ordered him to set the table right and watched as he slowly, begrudgingly picked it up. After he sat back down again, she walked over and slid into the chair next to him, leaning in while he talked to her quietly. He started sobbing. After a few minutes, she put an arm around his shoulder. The rest of the customers went back to their own business.

"Poor sap." Dave reached for more chips.

"Wonder what that was about…" Anne said.

They both shrugged. Two minutes later, it was all over. Trudy was back behind the bar, and the busboy was mopping up the spilled beer. The jukebox was playing "One," a U2 song from the 1990s.

Dave sang along for a few bars. "One of my favorites."

"Before my time," Anne said, picking up a deviled egg. "You really ought to try one of these. They're pretty good."

"What *isn't* before your time? How old are you anyway?"

"Thirty-four."

He just nodded his head slowly, saying nothing.

Anne polished off the last of her beer and changed the subject. "Well, I look forward to getting your job estimate."

"Right. And let me give you my other cell phone number, the one I always pick up."

"I'll write it on your business card." Anne rifled through her purse and brought it out. "Dave S. Silver, Owner," she read out loud and then idly asked, "What's the "S" in your name stand for?"

"I'll have to know you better for that story, too." He laughed a little, then gently cupped the top of her hand with his. Then quickly withdrew it. "I can't wait to see you again," he said with an almost bashful smile. "I could be over at your house next week. I'll bring my rototiller."

She let out with a laugh. "What a sweet talker."

He grinned. "Guess I'm out of practice, 'cause by my lights, that was a pretty good line." He stood up and yawned. "It's getting late. I'll go settle the tab."

"Let me help with the bill—"

"No thanks. I'm business expensing this. It'll go under 'wining and dining a prospective client.'" He lifted his jacket off the back of the chair and then made his way to the cashier at the bar. He was halfway there when Trudy Lee flagged him down from the other end of the bar. He worked his way over to where she was standing and leaned across the bar to hear what she had to say. Then, they both turned to look at the poor sap who was still slumped down in his chair.

Anne gathered her purse, shrugged on her jacket, and set off toward the front door to wait for Dave.

# Chapter Nine

Anne checked her phone's screen before picking up. It was her Uncle Jack. "Turn on the TV."

"Why?"

"Just do it. Channel 5 news." He hung up.

*Like I have time for these shenanigans*, she thought. The estate sale at the Victorian mansion would start at noon—less than an hour away—and Brittany hadn't shown up yet. Neither had the new sales assistant she'd hired for the weekend. If Chloe weren't off on some high school soccer team weekend, Anne was sure *she* would have shown up on time—early even, like she did. Anne had been working at the house since seven a.m., arranging sales displays and making sure the client's personal items, family photos, and valuables were removed or secured.

Looking out through the rain-splattered, mullioned windows onto McDonald Avenue, Anne counted six cars already lined up at the curb. No doubt most of these early bird shoppers were professional dealers eager to buy and resell anything they found of value at the sale. A little rain wouldn't keep them away. Anne glanced at the wall clock. She still needed to take a final video of the home's contents for reference or evidence in case of disputes between family members, which happened with alarming regularity.

So, no, she didn't have time to sit down and watch TV. But then again, her uncle didn't usually make a big deal over nothing.

She went over to the TV stand where her client's twenty-year-old, twenty-five-inch screen television had a STILL WORKS/MAKE OFFER sign taped to it. After plugging it in and attaching the cable wire, she found the remote laying on top of the coffee table. She sat in a high-back, red velvet Victorian parlor chair marked FOR SALE and clicked onto Channel 5.

A fuzzy image flickered on the screen, gradually clearing to show anchorwoman Tamara Logan, thirtyish with sleek, long dark hair. She was dressed in a sleeveless red top that showed off her toned arms, addressing the camera from the television studio in San Francisco.

"If you're just joining us at News at 11, we're following a breaking story from up north in Santa Rosa that is stunning investors—mostly vulnerable, elderly investors—throughout the Bay Area," Tamara said gravely, reading from a teleprompter.

In the upper right corner of the screen, a square box popped up with a studio portrait of Lino Pardini. The news crawler at the bottom of the screen read: BREAKING NEWS: LATE SANTA ROSA BUSINESSMAN SUSPECTED OF FRAUD."

"Pardini, who died just five days ago, gave all appearances of being a successful businessman, a generous philanthropist, and an upstanding family man. A pillar of his community. But what no one knew while he was alive— not even his family, it's being claimed—is that he was bilking investors in a Ponzi scheme that targeted his clients, along with personal friends and even community leaders. It's rumored that the mayor of Santa Rosa was also taken in," Tamara said with a frown.

"For more on this developing story, we're taking you live to the Pardini house, located in the affluent Fountaingrove neighborhood in north-east Santa Rosa. Reporters and TV vans started showing up there at dawn because of news leaks following an investor meeting held last night. To get ahead of the story, a family representative has called an impromptu news conference. It's set to begin in a few minutes," Tamara said. "Channel 5's own Ted Cameron is on the scene. Ted, I understand that an attorney representing the now defunct Pardini Financial company will be making a statement?"

The camera cut to reporter Ted Cameron, tanned and robust, clutching a microphone in his right hand. He was standing in the middle of a small but agitated crowd of other TV and newspaper reporters and photographers, curious bystanders, neighbors, and irate investors. The sky was thick with gray, threatening clouds.

Ted Cameron touched his left earpiece. "That's right, Tamara, attorney Joel Maroni will be addressing reporters any minute now about this bombshell discovery. As you can see, I'm standing in front of the gated entry of Lino Pardini's palatial estate with a Mercedes-Benz and a late-model BMW sitting in the driveway." The camera lens zoomed through the wrought-iron gate to the luxury cars.

"It appears that while he and his family were living the good life here in this exclusive community of multi-million-dollar homes, his clients were being coldly and systematically wiped out financially, their retirements ravaged," Ted said.

Anne glanced up at the sound of the front door opening. "Sorry I'm late, Anne," Brittany said, lugging in two shopping bags and a large umbrella. "I had to stop by the store and get more stickers, and then I went to the deli to pick up some lunch—"

Anne held up a finger. "Hold on a minute," she said, her eyes locking back onto the TV screen. Brittany shrugged and disappeared into the kitchen without another word.

The doorbell rang. "Britt, would you get that, please? But don't let any shoppers in yet." From the corner of her eye, Anne saw her newly hired sales assistant, Toni, a gregarious matron, walk in the door. Anne gave her a distracted wave. Toni was led away by Brittany to the back bedroom to do some last-minute labeling.

Anne turned back to the screen. Attorney Joel Maroni was stepping up to a makeshift podium; his thin face was grim, his posture ramrod straight. He lifted the microphone and looked out at the reporters.

"Last night we informed investors that Lino Pardini had, for over fifteen years, perpetuated a massive fraud on investors to the tune of about $57 million dollars," Maroni began in a voice so devoid of emotion that he could have been giving a lecture on tax law.

"Just days after Mr. Pardini's death, which was initially presumed to be from a heart attack," the attorney said, "the fraud unraveled when the family learned of problems with the company's finances. We are still learning the extent of those problems with the help of a forensic audit ordered by investigators. What we *do* know is that Pardini was in serious personal debt and had taken out almost all of the equity from this house." He motioned to the family home behind the gate. A light drizzle started to fall, and a few umbrellas popped open in the crowd.

The reporters listened for the next five minutes as Maroni outlined the scope of the fraud. Lino Pardini was "borrowing" about five million dollars per year from investors to keep his personal life afloat, pay old investors, and prop up his business—which included paying salaries for his five-person staff, expenses, and overhead. He paid himself a yearly salary of over $500,000. The police department's Financial Crimes Unit, which investigates corporate malfeasance and elder financial abuse, got involved just prior to Mr. Pardini's death due to several reports from the public, and their investigation was ongoing.

"His public memorial service, scheduled for next week at the Luther Burbank Center for the Arts, has been canceled, and services will be private. I'll take questions now."

Reporters pounced, layering on the questions.

"Who else in the company was involved?"

"Did the firm's accountant know?"

"What about the secretarial staff?"

Maroni answered, "Our current assumption is that Mr. Pardini acted alone."

"How did he lure people in?"

"How high were the returns he promised?"

Maroni said, "He promised investors—and did actually provide—returns of between ten percent and twelve percent a year for years. Even when markets were down."

"How much money was hidden in offshore accounts?"

"So far, forensic accountants have found no links to overseas accounts, but investigations are ongoing because there appears to be money that's unaccounted for."

"How much can investors expect to get back?"

"The Sonoma County Superior Court has appointed a certified public accountant as receiver for the company," Marconi said. "He'll be responsible for finding out how much money is left and then equitably distributing it to investors. Many of these investors have received quarterly payments for years. Those payments will be taken into consideration when calculating their net losses."

"When will the family's assets be liquidated?"

"Are their assets already frozen?"

"Is his wife still living here?"

Maroni's eyes swept over the reporters. "Again, that's up to the receiver. As for the family's living situation, that's a private matter."

He nodded to the reporter from the *Press Democrat*, who asked, "What did you mean when you said, 'his death was initially thought to be from a heart attack?'"

"I spoke out of turn," Maroni said. "That's not my news to give. I believe the medical examiner will be giving a separate statement later this week."

That bit of news brought another barrage of questions.

"Was it suicide?"

"Did he know he was about to get caught?"

"I'm sorry, I can't comment. That's all I have to say for today. Thank you for coming." Joel Maroni stepped away from the podium.

The TV camera panned back to show the tight knot of reporters and captured the sight of two of the reporters being jabbed out of the way by the tip of an umbrella. The weapon was in the gnarled hands of an elderly woman only half their size, who pushed her way to the front.

"Not so fast," the umbrella woman shouted, red-faced with fury. "You were his lawyer. Don't tell me you didn't know what was going on!"

Maroni pivoted sharply and stepped back in front of the podium. "I had absolutely *no* idea," he said in a tight voice. His professional mask dropped, replaced by a reddening face and narrowing eyes. "In fact, I invested my own retirement savings with him, so I'm in the same boat as the other 200 or so investors who trusted him. Including one of his own daughters. And on the day before he died, he was *still* taking money." Joel Maroni was obviously taking it personally. "If Lino Pardini were alive today, he'd be facing fraud charges and, with any justice in the world, he'd be locked up for the rest of his life."

With that, Maroni stepped away from the podium and headed toward his silver Porsche. Meanwhile, one of the iron gates swung open and a black Mercedes sedan inched its way from the driveway of the Pardini house and slowly drove through the crowd. From what little Anne could see, before the car was completely hidden by the crush of reporters, the driver appeared to be a woman. *Was that Renee?*

A burly man, dressed like a golfer in plaid slacks and a green polo shirt, pushed through the human barrier and pounded his fist on the driver side window. "When's his service, Renee? Because I'm gonna be there! I have a few things I'd like to say about your asshole husband."

*Maybe one of the guys Lino golfed with,* Anne guessed. The man was roughly jostled away from the car by the crowd and thrown off-balance, landing on the ground right in front of a surprised Ted Cameron. But the veteran Channel 5 reporter quickly recovered and seized the moment by grabbing the man by the arm and lifting him to his feet. When he was upright, Ted stuck a microphone in his face. "Are you a golfing buddy of Lino Pardini?" he asked.

Looking dazed, the golfer just stared into the camera. "Are we on TV?"

"Were you playing golf with him the day he died?"

"If you can call it that," the golfer said with some of his bluster returning. "He didn't last even one hole. He took a phone call and left the course."

"What was his mood? Did he seem depressed? Agitated?"

"Cool as a cucumber. That guy showed no signs of any stress. And don't call me one of his buddies," he spat out, then turned abruptly away from Ted and disappeared back into the crowd.

The camera followed him for a millisecond, then moved in for a closeup of Ted, who said, "Back to you, Tamara."

Shaking her head sadly, Tamara said into the camera, "For more on the

Lino Pardini scandal—now being called the 'Friends and Family Scam' because of whom he targeted—join us tonight at eight when we'll be talking to the Santa Rosa Police Department's Financial Crimes Unit. And!" she added brightly. "For an in-depth analysis of how Pardini got away with it, be sure to catch us tomorrow on our 'Sunday at Dawn' show when we'll sit down with financial experts who are calling this the 'Bay Area Bombshell.' No weekend off for us, huh, Ted?"

*Geez, pick a catchy handle and go with it,* Anne thought, turning off the television. Brittany came back in the room and pointed to her watch. "Twenty minutes until show time, Boss. Looks like we've got a big crowd out there. Thankfully, the rain has let up."

"Are you okay with manning the cash register today?" Anne asked Brittany.

"Absolutely, you know I love handling money."

"Good. There are plenty of ones and fives in the cash box."

While Brittany would be in charge of the money end of the sale, Anne would be answering questions, gently haggling with customers over prices, and policing the rooms for potential thieves. Toni would greet customers and help them find items.

With ten minutes until the doors opened, Anne recorded the inventory video and then ran through the last-minute chores on automatic pilot—making a sweep of the rooms for readiness and checking that items were marked with prices. But her mind was still on what she'd just seen on TV, the Pardini scandal and all its nasty collateral damage. Maybe Pardini's fraud was behind the incident she witnessed last night in the bar. Maybe that poor sap had just come from the investors' meeting and knew he'd been taken in. While he was crying on Trudy's shoulder, the guy seemed to be venting about whatever it was that had riled him up enough to overturn a table and several beer glasses. And afterward, right before they left, Trudy Lee appeared to be telling Dave something about it. Funny that Dave hadn't told *her*. But she was learning that Dave was a man who could keep a secret.

Anne's phone rang.

"Did you see that?" Uncle Jack asked.

"Hard to believe. Those poor people." She absentmindedly scanned the living room, her eyes drawn to the bookshelf where, among the dozens of books for sale, she saw the diary of the deceased homeowner, the one Chloe had set aside. *What the hell?* She quickly went over and tossed the diary inside her tote purse, which was so large things sometimes got lost inside of it. She would deal with the diary later.

"Did you hear that golfer?" Jack asked. "He upended the whole story about Lino playing nine holes and going to lunch with clients, and then going home. Where *was* Lino all that morning right before he died? If I were a cop on this case—"

She pulled her attention back to her uncle. "Which case? The fraud?"

"No, the suspicious death of Lino Pardini. That's the case I'm interested in. For sure it's not a heart attack, that much the attorney let slip..."

"We don't know that for sure..." she said, tapping her right foot. "And if he didn't die from a heart attack, it was probably just an aneurysm or something. Nothing suspicious. Actually, if it *was* anything out of the ordinary, maybe it was suicide."

"Suicide? A guy like Pardini? No way. All I'm saying is, if I were a cop on this case, I'd be all over that guy, that golfer. Maybe he knows who made the call to Pardini—a call that was apparently so important that he left his buddies in the middle of playing the first hole. We could interview the golfer, then the caller."

"You seem all raring to go, Uncle Jack. You can always nudge the police chief to start investigating and then get hired on."

Jack grunted. "All I'm saying is, something is going on. I can smell it. And the medical examiner's report should have been in by now."

"I'm afraid to ask," she said, pausing a few beats, "but did you and Aunt Dot invest—"

"No, we dodged a bullet there. When Dot told me she wanted to take our money out of our savings and get in on Pardini's investments like some of our friends did, I put my foot down. And do you know how many times I've put my foot down with my wife?"

"Never, that I can remember."

"Never. But like I said to her, I never trusted the guy. With the Pardinis, there's always more to the story than meets the eye."

"Glad to hear it."

The silence from the other end of the line went on so long that Anne wondered if he'd already hung up. But then he said, "But I'd better check with her just to be sure."

Anne turned to see the front door open and heard Toni's hearty greeting, "Welcome, come in!"

"Okay, gotta go. Sale's starting." Anne hung up.

# Chapter Ten

R enee got up in the middle of the night, slipped on her camel coat, poured herself some coffee, and stepped out onto the front porch. The night was still and wicked cold. There wasn't a sound except for the barking of a neighborhood dog. She sat on the hard slate porch stoop, looking out at the empty street, at the stars shining bright above in clusters. Waiting for the dawn yet dreading it.

If she had any kind of luck, any grace from the gods, maybe nothing would happen today. No dying husband, no shocking fraud charges, no wild threats flying her way, no complete and utter destruction of everything she held dear. If she had any luck, her son would stop crying and come out of his room.

*That's all I asked of today*, she thought: nothingness for me and peace for Josh. This idea of a whole day of nothingness, a day of vast, impenetrable stillness, filled her with hope for a brief moment. It was Sunday, after all, a day of rest. But Renee knew better. She could sit here shivering in her wool coat, praying against the dawn for as long as she wanted, but the sun would inevitably come up. The world would start its relentless cycle of activity again, and stuff would happen.

*Stop*, she ordered herself, *stop thinking*. That order had become her new mantra: "No thinking." She supposed a more elegant mantra would be "Let go of thinking," but that took way too much thinking. So she kept it simple. No thinking, not about losing the houses—all three of them—and having to sell off everything inside of them. And no worrying about where she and her son would go or where they would find the money to live on. *Find the*

69

*money.* The thought came out of nowhere and tugged at her. But finding the envelopes of cash that Lino had hidden away—who knows where on their acre of property—seemed like an impossibility, a pipe dream from another lifetime. At least at this moment. She brushed the thought aside.

She had more immediate concerns. The court appointed receiver was practically at her doorstep, gearing up to seize and auction off everything she owned—the paintings, rugs, designer clothes, Louis Vuitton purse, her collection of Chihuly glass sculptures.

She just prayed they wouldn't take away Josh's new bike or, even worse, his PlayStation 5 video game console, his most treasured possession. Lino had spent hours searching online for the popular, almost impossible-to-find console for Josh last Christmas. She remembered asking Lino why he didn't just have his secretary track the PS5 video game console down, and was a bit surprised by his answer: "Look, I can't play touch football or go skiing with Josh, my knees would give out. But I can find him the goddamn console he's got his heart set on."

She had to find someplace to hide the console. Maybe at her nephews' house? Because if she couldn't hide it, Josh could lose all his progress in the video games he was playing—and the boy didn't need any more loss in his life, even if it was only a Fortnite game level.

She glanced up to her left and saw the glare of a car's headlights barreling down the street. It was heading straight toward her house. Then, it skidded to a crawl as it passed her front gate. The window on the passenger side lowered, and the driver leaned across the car seat, flinging an object over the gate. For a millisecond, she feared it was a rock with a nasty note attached to it. It wouldn't be the first this week. Instead, a newspaper landed with a heavy plop onto her driveway. She let out her breath and almost laughed. Just the Sunday newspaper, the fattest news edition of the week. Then she tensed up again. Which meant more news. More fresh hell, in Dorothy Parker's immortal words.

She hugged her knees to her chest. It was only four-thirty a.m., and the sun wouldn't be up for another few hours. She ignored the biting cold and sat for a while longer, remembering how, only a few weeks before, her life was settled and secure. She recalled laughing at a TV comedy about a wealthy family that found itself suddenly flat-broke and was forced to move into a dreary motel out in the boonies. But now it seemed like they were the lucky ones. At least the fictional TV family owned some property and had a roof over their heads.

Any day now, maybe as soon as tomorrow, she feared, the notice to evacuate would arrive, and the locks would be changed on the only home Josh had ever lived in. They literally had nowhere to go, and she didn't dare try her ATM card to pay for a motel room. She couldn't think of anyone they could turn to. The only family she had left were Lino's relatives, but they themselves were reeling with grief and shame. Friends? Too soon to tell. Messages were accumulating on her phone, but she didn't have the heart or the energy to listen to them. She couldn't take the chance of any more hurt right now.

But her brother-in-law might help. *Of course, Marco will help,* she assured herself. Though she wasn't so sure about her sister-in-law.

Pulling a gloved hand out from her coat, she reached for the mug beside her and took one last sip of the lukewarm coffee before standing up. She left the newspaper on the driveway and stepped inside the living room. The stench of dying flowers, their bloated stems floating in rancid water, immediately assaulted her. Those dozens of flower arrangements had been sent by well-meaning friends—or at least they'd been friends a week ago. Who knows how many of them were newly broke thanks to Lino's scams, and newly bitter and angry toward her?

Those stinking flowers had to go.

\* \* \*

Though the drapes were drawn tight, the loosely woven linen fabric couldn't keep the early morning light from slipping into the room. Particles of dust floated around in the streams of sunshine.

Renee had never made it back to bed. She'd made it only as far as the couch, where she turned on the TV to watch a late-night comedy—something about two romance scammers on the prowl for lonely women—hoping for some laughs or at least a bit of distraction, but then she promptly dozed off with the TV still on. The voices and faces of the two actors reached into her dreams, their faces melding into one—which then transformed into the face of Bernie Madoff, the notorious Ponzi schemer who, in turn, morphed into Lino. "Your big mistake was assuming I was an honest man," he said over and over, the words swirling through her brain, getting louder and louder, until she was partially roused out of her sleep.

She found herself curled into a ball on the living room couch. As she cleared the dream from her mind, sounds coming from the TV floated over her and new words wormed their way into her consciousness. They were coming from Tamara Logan, anchorwoman of a Sunday morning talk show and from the two experts in suits she was interviewing. They were pontificating about whatever subjects they were experts on.

Apparently, they were experts on her late husband.

"What was the undoing of Lino Pardini?" Tamara was asking them.

Renee slowly sat up, her eyes at half-mast.

"First of all, his death, obviously." The bar at the bottom of the screen identified the speaker as Thomas Leigh, owner of a forensic accounting firm.

Tamara smirked. "Obviously."

"No, what I meant to say was that his death caused the light to shine on his business," Leigh said. "But to anyone paying attention *before* that, his performance line should have been the tip-off. His clients were making, on average, twelve percent a year with very few down months. And that's just not how the market works. It's very cyclical. It goes up and down. But in Pardini's world, it only went up, with the exception of only about five percent of down months. That's clearly impossible."

"How long could he have kept this up?"

"He was on the verge of getting caught, Tamara. Literally, within days of crashing."

"Was he ever legitimate?"

"Not sure yet. We don't *think* Pardini started out as a crook, but we know it wasn't long before his business moved into the fraud zone."

The accountant continued to lay out Lino's rise and fall: After dissolving his elder-law practice, he started his financial firm and hired a staff at top dollar, positioning himself as the only partner to rake in the profits. But eventually the market went into a severe downturn and those high salaries and the office rent were a money pit. He was tapped out and that was the crossroad. He started subsidizing all those business expenses by fraud.

"And then there were his personal expenditures. All his houses were mortgaged to the hilt. He faced a six-figure credit card debt, and he owed on all his cars.

"Pardini was drowning. Running on fumes," Leigh concluded.

Renee wanted to turn the TV off but couldn't muster the energy to reach for the remote on the coffee table.

"But how did he get away with this for all those years? Surely people aren't that gullible!" Tamara wore an incredulous, who-were-these-idiots look on her face.

He adjusted his glasses and gave a bit of a smirk. "Well, this is a guy you'd never suspect of fraud. Pardini had a patina of authority and respectability. Mind you, I never met the man, but I've seen video and watched his body language. He had a swagger, a glimmer in his eyes. Basically, he charmed them out of their money. And, after all, he was one of the most respected, successful businessmen in the Bay Area. What's not to trust? Besides, people hear what they want to hear."

"This was a classic affinity scam," the woman on Tamara's left threw in. The black bar on the screen identified her as a former federal prosecutor of financial crimes.

Renee's head jerked up.

"What *is* that, exactly?" Tamara asked, leaning in toward her.

*An affinity scam. Of course.* Renee nodded. *Makes sense.* A sudden surge of energy had her scrambling to her feet, bumping her leg on the coffee table. She stood directly in front of the TV and listened with a clenched jaw.

"It's a scam that's run on people similar to oneself," the former prosecutor said. "Pardini was older, the people he preyed on were older. He was educated and so were most of the people he targeted. He was respected in the community. So were many of them. And after being a prominent elder-law attorney for years, he had a built-in clientele of older, vulnerable people. He could just pick them off. It's a tale as old as time."

Renee was now slowly pacing circles around the coffee table, speaking aloud to the TV in a sing-song, sarcastic tone. "Want to know what an affinity scam is? I'll tell you what an affinity scam is," she said, her voice rising. "It's when people feel an affinity for you, and they love you, and they *trust* you, like the fools that we are. And then you turn around and use them in every way you can, for as long as you can!"

She caught sight of herself in the mirror above the fireplace. Her eyes were flashing angrily, and her lips were curled. She stopped. *I'm going fucking crazy*, she thought. *I'm going talking-to-myself, fucking crazy.*

She heard a dry cough and turned around. Her son Josh was standing by the foot of the stairs, just staring at her. His eyes were swollen from crying.

"Who are you talking to?" Josh asked. His tone made clear that he thought she was crazy, too. He was a good-looking kid, lanky and tall for his age, with dark, sleep-tousled hair. He was wearing a faded gray T-shirt and Golden State Warriors pajama bottoms. He moved tentatively into the room.

"No one, it's just the TV."

"Why are you listening to that stuff?" he mumbled. "Does it have to be on? I'm going back upstairs."

He turned back toward the staircase.

"No, stay here," Renee said hurriedly. "I'll turn it off." She clicked the remote and then made a slight move to hug him. Almost imperceptibly, Josh backed away, so she retreated, too.

"Want some breakfast?" she asked. He'd barely eaten all week, just cereal and cookies, as far as she could tell from the trays she'd left outside his bedroom door.

He was looking around the living room and seemed not to have heard what she said.

"Where are all the flowers people sent?" he asked. "They were nice."

She sighed and pointed to the three large, green trash bags leaning against the front door. "I thought they were starting to smell, and besides, the memorial service won't be happening now. At least not the big one."

"Those were Dad's flowers," he said, "not yours." With that, Josh headed back upstairs, leaving Renee to stare after him.

\* \* \*

Later that afternoon, Renee received a call—the third call, actually—from the medical examiner's office. This time, she picked up. It was six days after Lino had died.

"Sorry to disturb you on a Sunday, Mrs. Pardini, but I wanted to give you a heads up before we publicly announce the autopsy results tomorrow," said Louis Robinette, the chief medical examiner of Sonoma County.

According to the preliminary autopsy report, Lino had died, not from a heart attack as she had been led to believe, but most likely from blunt force trauma. "I'll email you a PDF with the report."

She called her brother-in-law Marco with the news.

"The examiner said Lino died from an accidental blow to the head— probably the result of a backward fall onto a hard surface," she told him.

"He must have slipped on the loose bathmat when getting out of the shower," Marco said, "and landed hard on the marble floor. When I was up there I saw a puddle of water on the bathroom floor, so that makes sense."

"That's strange. I don't remember seeing water on the floor."

"Well, I saw it. Anyway, he fell. Hard," Marco said.

She mulled this over for a minute before saying, "The bathmat was out of place, and there was some blood on the pillow, so I guess…but if he fell that hard, how did he make it to the bed?"

"You know Lino, he always minimized injury and pain. He must have dragged himself there. He probably thought he could just sleep it off."

"And instead, he lost consciousness," she agreed.

According to the autopsy report, which she had printed out and was reading to Marco, while Lino was lying flat on the bed, he suffered bleeding in the space around the brain. This caused swelling—swelling that his skull didn't have room to accommodate. That increased pressure resulted in respiratory arrest, and ultimately, death. No foul play appeared likely, she relayed to Marco, however there was still the possibility of drugs or alcohol being involved. A toxicology report could take up to six weeks.

"But what does any of this matter? He's dead. And I'm left with the mess he left behind," she said, letting her bitterness come to the surface for the first time.

Marco let out a ragged breath. "You think you're the only one dealing with the shitshow he left behind?" he said, his voice low and controlled. "The whole family has been getting harassing calls and emails. Our lives are now nothing but fodder for talk shows and social media posts. Hell, two liquor stores in town are pulling our wine label off their shelves. Lino's *ruined* our family name, destroyed everything we've worked for—" Marco let the sentence trail off, and just when she thought he was through, he started up again.

"Thank God, my parents didn't live to see this day. But what I really hate is that our kids have to suffer for his crimes. Do you know what kind of bullying crap is being thrown at them on Snapchat? I can handle the fallout, and you can handle it, but the kids...."

"Well, I could handle it a whole lot better if I had some money. At least you have money to insulate you. You could take your family off to the Bahamas or Hawaii and get away from this town, but Josh and I are stuck here. Our assets are frozen and will be confiscated by the court any minute now..."

Marco erupted. "Is that all you think about, Renee? Goddamn money? Is that what you want from me? Is that why you even bothered to call?"

"There must be some inheritance coming from your parent's estate, Marco," she said, as if not hearing a word he'd said, ignoring everything but her own anguish. "I know Carlos and Sophia only died a month ago in that godawful car accident, but isn't their estate close to being settled? They must have had millions put away in savings. I forget...how much did you pay your parents when you bought out their share of the winery years ago? It was several million, right?"

She was stepping way over the line; she knew that, but these were desperate times. She paused and waited for him to respond, and when he didn't, she plunged ahead.

"And Sofia and Carlos never spent a *dime*. Your parents lived in the first house they ever bought. I haven't heard a word yet about how much Lino was going to inherit."

While still speaking, her mind raced ahead to the most dire and likely outcome: Any money that Lino would have inherited would just go into receivership to pay off his investors. She wouldn't see a dime of it. Unless somehow she could convince Marco to put Lino's share into a secret bank account for her or even give her cash. But given the way he was speaking to her, that didn't seem likely.

"Let me tell you something," Marco started, then paused a few beats. "You know what? I'm not telling you *anything*, except that Lino already got his share. More than his share."

"That can't be true. They never gave us *anything*. They'd never even talk to Lino about money!"

"Lino told you that?" His voice was stiff with rage.

"I know there's money; there has to be." She said, hating the naked desperation in her voice.

"Get a job." He hung up.

\* \* \*

Renee sat down at her computer. She needed to know what Josh was hearing on social media apps like Snapchat and Instagram. She didn't have a Snapchat account, that was for young people mostly, but from what she understood of the instant messaging app, messages stayed up for only a short time before disappearing.

Nor did she have an Instagram account. She could open an account, she supposed, but that still wouldn't get her into Josh's account. She'd have to ask him directly if she wanted any information, and the odds of him giving her any weren't good.

But she did have a Facebook account. She opened it and searched for Josh's page, though she knew he rarely used it. Not there. Thankfully, he'd already deleted it.

Her Facebook page, on the other hand, was blowing up. Forty-two notifications and twenty personal messages awaited her. She closed her eyes tight in dread, and then after a minute, let out a deep breath and clicked on the notification bell.

She only got as far as reading three messages:

"What kind of monster steals from old people?!"

"Bitch, you and your fucked up family can rot in hell..."

"I wish Lino Pardini was alive so I could spit in his face."

*Enough.* For the next five minutes, Renee averted her eyes while she methodically deleted each and every message.

"Please respect our privacy at this difficult time," she typed in, clicked on "post," and closed out.

# Chapter Eleven

K icking off the Sunday night family dinner, Jack brought out a single bottle of wine for the table. A Two-Buck Chuck merlot that Jack and Dot's son Matt gamely pronounced was "better than some of those fancy Pardini wines that I've had." Matt's wife, Lacy, leaned into Anne and whispered, "What? Couldn't they find any screw-top wines to set out?" Anne elbowed her hard. Their hosts were too distracted to notice.

Every month, the family looked forward to Aunt Dot's four-course, gourmet meals. Always comfort food of some kind—beef stroganoff, meatloaf, fried chicken, or such—and always served with sides of garlic mashed potatoes and gravy, whether they were compatible with the main entree or not. Wearing thick oven mitts, Aunt Dot came into the dining room carrying a glass casserole pan straight from the oven. The eight guests looked up expectantly—until they discovered they were being served a burnt cauliflower casserole with bits of celery for color, along with mini store-bought rolls, and thin carrot sticks. They stared moodily at the food. This was a turning out to be a far cry from the group's usual boisterous, laugh-filled gatherings.

Uncle Jack, sitting at the head of the table, spent most of the meal either looking down at his plate or staring sightlessly out the dining room window. Aunt Dot excused herself after one bite and wasn't seen again for the rest of the meal.

It wasn't until after the dishes were cleared and her uncle motioned for Anne to follow him into his home office that her fears were confirmed: Aunt

Dot had invested nearly all their life savings with Lino Pardini.

"She wrote him a check only a month ago, so we never even got one of those quarterly payments. Every dime she invested was lost," Jack said, dropping onto his duct-taped brown leather recliner. Anne sunk down on the plaid couch opposite him and avoided eye contact.

"It took us thirty years to save that money," he said, shaking his head, looking forlorn.

"Maybe some of it can be recovered," Anne said. She desperately hoped so. It was because of her that Dot had invested with Pardini.

"Just pennies on the dollar, they're saying." Jack let out a sigh, leaned back in his recliner, and stared at the acoustic tiles on the ceiling. They were quiet for a moment. "But don't worry about us, Annie," he finally said. "We still have a little savings, and the house is paid for."

Then he gave Anne a sideways look. "But don't mention this to your aunt. She feels bad enough as it is. She knows what she did was..." his voice trailed off.

Anne's guilt wouldn't let her stay quiet any longer. "Uncle Jack, I'm so sorry. This is my fault. I told Aunt Dot about Lino's investments. I said they were a sure thing. I encouraged her."

He stared at Anne for a solid moment, his eyes narrowing in anger. "You did, did you?" he snapped at her. "So, let me understand this...you two hatched up this brilliant plan without giving a goddamn what I thought, even though I'd always made it perfectly clear what I thought—that Lino couldn't be trusted, and certainly not trusted with our hard-earned money." Then, seeing the tears welling in her eyes, his voice softened, "Hey, it's not your fault. You didn't make your aunt do anything. She's a grown woman." He paused, ruminating. "And it could be worse. I've still got my pension. We're not in the poorhouse yet."

* * *

Anne left the house a few minutes later, carrying a container of leftover casserole that Aunt Dot had pushed on her. Pulling out from the curb, she decided to take the long way home, along surface city streets with stop lights at every other block, which added a few minutes and miles to the trip—miles her tired Saab could have done without.

Driving at night usually helped her focus her thoughts and calm her nerves. But tonight, it was having the opposite effect, and she found herself growing angrier by the mile. Not at the slow crawl of traffic or stoplights, but at the hubris and greed of that man, that shyster, Lino Pardini. She fumed. His attitude last week—when she, Chloe, and Krista were at the Pardini house in search of fire hazard violations—had struck her at the time as being odd, but also civilized and patient. After all, they'd intruded on the Pardinis' quiet Sunday evening without giving them any notice and searched through their private property.

But now, his attitude struck her as cold, antisocial, and pathologically arrogant. What a difference a few fraud charges will do for hindsight.

But it was the money Chloe had found inside the garage, not Lino's personality disorders, that Anne couldn't stop thinking about. There were many thousands of dollars in those envelopes—and who knows how much more that Chloe left inside the wall?

Since her quick search with Renee on Wednesday had uncovered nothing in the garage, the money was still unaccounted for—although Anne couldn't know that for sure. Renee was newly broke and motivated, so it's possible she tore the place apart and found the cash. Yet in the wake of all the drama surrounding Lino's death—the reporters swirling around Renee, the lawyers and investors demanding their share, all while taking care of her son—when would Renee have found the time? Anne fervently hoped she hadn't. Because if, by some long shot, the money was still out there, hidden on the property somewhere, unclaimed—and if Anne could somehow find it first—maybe she could return it to investors who had lost so much. First and foremost, her aunt and uncle.

But she would have to gain access to Renee's property first. Another long shot.

Unlocking her front door, Anne entered the kitchen, hoisted her purse off her shoulder, and dropped it with a heavy plop onto the countertop.

She opened the fridge, slid the leftover casserole inside and moved things around, looking for something stronger to drink than iced tea, but only found a half-full bottle of Pardini Winery chardonnay.

While pouring the remaining half of the bottle down the sink (*In pointless protest*, she acknowledged), she glanced over at her purse. Spilling out from the top was Lily Danielson's diary, the one Anne had quickly stashed away during the past weekend's estate sale.

She'd forgotten all about it. Losing track of a client's diary was a serious breach of the most basic of estate services guidelines, essentially Estate Services 101: Secure or remove personal and valuable items—items like family photos, personal papers, materials of a sexual nature, financial records, and firearms—before an estate sale. Diaries and journals were especially sensitive, falling into the category of being so personal they needed to be returned directly and immediately to the executor. They were even too personal for family members to view without the executor's consent. And they were *certainly* too personal to sell to the public.

So why had the diary been left in the bookshelf along with the dozens of Jane Austen, Stephen King, and Nora Roberts novels marked for sale? She thought about calling Chloe to ask her, but Anne could guess her answer: In their mad dash to leave the Victorian house last week to collect more fire hazard violations, Chloe simply shoved the diary back into the bookcase, figuring Anne would see it there later and could decide what to do about it. It was sheer luck that Anne saw it in time.

Anne tossed ice cubes into a tall glass and carried it, along with the diary and a bottle of Bailey's Irish Cream liqueur, to the couch. She poured some Bailey's over the ice cubes, set the bottle on the coffee table, and settled back into the cushions with the diary on her lap.

After months of working at the McDonald Avenue house, Anne felt as if she knew the eighty-five-year-old woman who had lived there. Lily had kept framed photos on every available surface, and in nearly all of them, the petite, homely, vibrant woman was standing in the center of a group of women friends. The estate sale had drawn many of those friends; they purchased small items "to remember our darling Lily by." Anne also knew

Lily had three quarrelsome adult children, was active in the arts and charity work, and had a passion for any and all shades of red. Red chairs, red patterned dinnerware, red purses. Even the cloth cover of her diary was red. Most pages were written in red ink.

Anne took a sip of Bailey's and fanned through the journal, absently looking for any names or dates that popped out at her. Nothing did, so she thumbed near the center of the diary, picked a random page, and started reading.

This was probably inexcusable—this reading of a stranger's private thoughts, Anne supposed. But she blithely brushed off her misgivings, having long ago made peace with this particular vice of hers—this inexhaustible curiosity about people's lives. There were worse character flaws, like meanness, greed, criminal behavior, or addiction, she reasoned. So, as long as sticking her nose into other people's business didn't hurt anyone— and as long as the chances of getting caught doing it were low—she usually gave herself a pass. In fact, she'd found it helpful in her various careers. As an FBI agent, she was driven by her fascination with crime, by what other people did and how they did it. As for her estate services business, the thought of rummaging through the remnants left behind by strangers wasn't everyone's idea of a good time. "I'd rather impale myself on their rusty old garden shears," her friend Krista often said. But Anne never tired of it.

Lily's diary entries were highly sporadic, loosely covering the last two decades of her life. Sometimes, years went by without a single entry.

The page Anne landed on was from mid-August 2004: Lily was dishing about committee members at a planning meeting for the Sonoma Vintage Festival. When Anne turned the page, she found Dinah Pardini's name mentioned as a co-chair, "which is splendid luck since she's such fun and we always work so well together," Lily had written.

Anne did some quick calculations. Back in 2004, Dinah would have been fifty years old and married to Lino for around sixteen years. Lily must have been sixty-seven years old. Yet despite their age difference, it seemed they were good friends and confidants. Lily heard all about Dinah's diets, theories about child raising, and troubles with her sister-in-law Kay. Dinah told Lily that once, while at a charity event, she'd overheard a drunken Kay call out over a bathroom stall door to a friend, "I married the wrong brother. I'm the one who should be with Lino."

*Whoa.* Anne set the diary down, recalling her uncle's remark about rumors of Lino cheating on Dinah with more than one lover. Kay Pardini, possibly? If there had been a flirtation, a romance, between the two of them back then, it must have ended when Renee married Lino.

She picked up the diary again, and as the pages went on, the confidences grew darker. There were references to Dinah being "worried about finances" and Lino's "fury" when she questioned him about it. Two weeks later, Lily wrote, "Dinah is just plain wrong. She must be wrong; it's too crazy. My God. She begged me, 'You cannot tell a soul.' But she needn't worry. I won't tell anyone what she suspects because it's too outlandish. It can't be true. No one does that."

Anne skipped ahead to the weeks just before Dinah disappeared in the fall of 2004 to a passage that read: "Dinah suspects Lino is seeing another woman. I didn't have the heart to tell her that everyone in town has known about that for months."

*Renee? The timing was right.*

"And there's probably more than one," Lily had written.

Another entry, dated two days before Dinah disappeared, read: "I'm frightened for the poor girl. Dinah woke up at two in the morning and looked out the bedroom window. She saw a light sweeping around the back yard, passing over trees and shrubs. Lino was outside in the pitch dark with only a flashlight. Dinah thought he was hiding papers and God knows what else all around the property."

On the following page, there was a primitive map drawn in pencil. Written in its margins were a smattering of random words, like "BBQ," and "hiding places," along with a reference to a bungee cord and a trash bag. Anne tried to make sense of it all.

She flipped to the dates immediately following Dinah's disappearance. A heartbroken Lily wrote about how she, among other family friends, would bring food to Dinah's family, help with the search, post flyers in downtown shops and restaurants, and cooperate with the police when they came with questions. Everyone pitched in. Marco's wife, Kay, practically moved in with Lino and the girls. Lily's entry read, "The last time I talked to Dinah was the night she went missing. Her car was in the shop getting repairs, so I offered her a ride to the dinner, but she said someone was taking her. Why didn't I ask who that someone was?"

A week later, she wrote: "Lino is lying to the officers. He says she ran off with a lover. It's preposterous. It's a stain on her character. Why is he saying that? I can only guess."

There were very few entries until Dinah's body was found. "We all failed her. Those poor young girls, those precious daughters of hers."

Lily didn't write again for years, except for an occasional entry about dinner parties, new exercise plans, lists of household repairs needed, grandchildren, books she read. Her last entry was in late 2020, a year before she died. It was a sad, brief note: "My sweet, handsome husband, the only man I ever loved, passed away tonight from Covid."

Anne set down the diary and finished off her drink. She sat for a while, rattling the ice cubes against the glass, trying to decide what to do with the diary. Maybe her uncle should have it since it mentioned Dinah's disappearance and murder. It didn't seem to contain any new evidence, but it shined a light on a possible motive: Dinah had knowledge of her husband's Ponzi scheme, was distressed about it, and was apparently talking to friends—or at least talking to Lily. Jack could bring it to the attention of the sheriff's office if he thought it might advance the case. But then again, what case would *that* be? A case against Lino? He was dead. Why would anyone care?

No, she wouldn't give it to Jack; the case was stone cold. Nevertheless, out of an abundance of caution, she would pass the information along to her uncle and take photos of the pages.

The diary clearly needed to be returned to the executor. She would drop it off at the lawyer's office tomorrow afternoon.

But first, she needed it as a bargaining chip.

# Chapter Twelve

At seven-thirty the next morning, Anne was standing on Renee Pardini's front porch, pressing her case.

"I don't think you'll be living here much longer, Renee," Anne said, pulling her jacket tight against the morning chill. It would be another warm fall day according to the forecast, but bookending all that lovely seventy-five-degree weather was a cold morning and a cold evening. Just a typical fall day in Northern California.

Anne had been standing there, shivering, carrying on a one-sided conversation for over five minutes. Renee's face had remained impassive all during Anne's warm expressions of sympathy for her latest legal troubles and all throughout the several minutes of persuasive reasoning and logic that followed.

Now Anne was resorting to heavy-handed bluntness. Any longer, and she would start screaming.

When she'd texted Renee last night to say she had something important to discuss, Renee had agreed to meet her. So it wasn't as if this was a surprise visit. But when Renee opened the front door, she just looked at Anne uncertainly, as if trying to place her, as if Anne were delivering an Amazon package she didn't remember ordering—even though only a minute had passed since she'd buzzed open the front gate for her.

"If the money's here on the property, there's only a *very* small window of time left for you to find it." Anne wished she had remembered to bring her fleece gloves. "In fact, I'm surprised they haven't seized the property already." Immediate seizures, Anne went on to explain, were common when there was concern that the owner would go on a selling—or hiding—spree to avoid losing property to the government or to the people suing them.

"Without my help, you probably won't find it in time." Anne studied Renee to see if any of this was sinking in, but Renee's eyes were just blankly looking over Anne's shoulder at nothing in particular. Renee continued standing perfectly still in the doorway, not saying a word, with her left hand clutching the lapels of her blue terry cloth robe to keep it closed. Her right hand was gripping the doorframe, blocking the entrance to the house, whether she meant to or not. Wearing saggy men's pajamas, her face puffy, no makeup, and hair tangled, she looked like hell—or as much like hell as a natural beauty with white, even teeth and glowing translucent skin can look. Renee might be ten years older than her, but Anne was under no illusions about what would happen if the two of them wandered into a party or a bar together: Anne would be pushed to the sidelines, maybe even to the ground, by men making fools of themselves to get to Renee.

Anne shivered and glanced longingly over Renee's shoulder into the heated living room.

Renee followed her gaze and then shook her head suddenly as if to clear it. "Maybe you're right, maybe I'll never find the money," Renee said, her mental fog lifting, "and maybe time *is* running out. But what does this have to do with you?"

"I can help," Anne said.

"Oh, for heaven's...just leave me alone," Renee took a step back and slowly, firmly shut the door in Anne's face.

Anne stood motionless, stunned. "Fine, fine..." she muttered aloud, then turned and headed to her car. But her Irish temper was rising with every step, and she soon found herself doubling back. When she reached the porch, she shouted, loud enough to carry through the door, "Fine, Renee! Good luck with finding it. It's not damn likely!" She stomped away but got only halfway down the driveway when she heard the door creak open again.

"Anne, wait!" Renee swung the door wide. "Don't leave."

Without a word, Anne turned and walked back. When she reached the door, Renee moved aside to let her enter. "I'm sorry about that. I don't know where my head's at these days," Renee said. "Come in."

Anne stepped into the dimly lit living room. It had a closed-in, musty smell. Renee slowly moved about the room, turning on table lamps, but leaving the curtains drawn. There was no sound in the house apart from the hum of the central heating system. Last week's flower arrangements were just a memory.

Renee motioned for Anne to sit on the couch. "You were saying you could help find the money..."

"But it means I'd have to search your property. And I can't do that without your permission."

"No, you can't."

"It's to your advantage. You don't know where to look, and I think I might." Anne pulled out Lily Danielson's diary from inside her purse and held it aloft. "Dinah left a few clues about where it might be."

Renee sat down beside Anne, her tired eyes locked on the diary. "A diary? What could Dinah possibly have to do with this? The woman's been dead for seventeen years," she said with a frown and then shrugged. "But okay, I'm listening."

"Dinah knew Lino's usual hiding places—places we might never think of. She told Lily about watching him hide papers on the property one night. Lily wrote it all down in this diary of hers. There're no guarantees..." Anne paused, looking hard at the distracted woman sitting next to her. A virtual stranger. Maybe partnering up with Renee wasn't the wisest move. But Anne had her own reasons for needing to find the money, and that spurred her on. "But before we look at the diary, here's what I propose."

Anne laid out her plan: They would join forces, search in the yard and garage—the most likely areas according to the information in the diary— then split the money and tell no one. Win-win.

"What about Krista?" Renee asked. "Are you saying you didn't tell her about the money? I like Krista, but if she knows about it, then everyone in town knows."

"Not true," Anne said, a slow burn starting. Krista could dish with the best of them, but if there was one thing she knew about her old friend, it was that she could be trusted to keep a confidence. Guaranteed.

"But even if that was true," Anne said, "it's a non-issue because the subject never came up. Krista doesn't know about any of this."

Renee tilted her head, and Anne could tell she wasn't buying it. But it was true: During the drive back to Krista's house that night, Chloe had monopolized the conversation so thoroughly with excited chatter about how the contest was "in the bag" that neither she nor Krista got a word in edgewise. And during the following days, with all the news of Lino's death and his financial scandal, the money didn't seem important enough to mention. Nor did it seem right to broadcast what Chloe had found in a private residence, particularly since the code of the "Battalion Chief" competition expressly prohibited doing so.

"What about the girl who found the money?" Renee asked.

"Chloe? She's a teenager. She's got too much on her plate to give the money a second thought. She's probably forgotten about it already. Besides, she promised not to tell anyone. And other than her, no one knows. Unless you…"

Renee shook her head. "No. I was thinking of asking my son to help me look, but he's…" She looked toward the stairs and let the sentence drop. Then she sank back into the couch, studying Anne. "Just curious, Anne. I know what I'm going to do with my share." Renee paused, gesturing toward the kitchen. "I'm going to put food on the table for my son and me. I'm going to put a roof over our heads. Pay the heating bill. And I'll need every last dime of that money. But what about you? Is this just a side hustle for you, or what? Or maybe your plan is to play Lady Bountiful and give your share to all those poor investors who are probably richer than you."

Anne felt her jaw tightening. As a matter of fact, yes, that pretty much summed up her plan—to hand over the money to her uncle and other investors. She just hadn't figured out the exact mechanics of how to do it yet. How hard could it be?

"Some of those investors were my own family members, my aunt and uncle, who lost everything—" Anne's tone barely contained her anger.

"I'm sorry about that, I really am," Renee said with a breezy dismissiveness.

"But we *all* got taken in. You can't just go around handing out money. Where would you say you got it? Cause if you tell those people the truth, all hell breaks loose. Because here's the thing: Any money you take from here can probably be traced back to me and Lino. Which means, if they realize that, they'll come after my share, too. So what's your plan if you can't tell them where it came from? Are you thinking about giving it to them anonymously? You can't just deposit cash into their accounts. Banks won't allow that because they'd consider it money laundering. Money has to be accounted for. Will you just leave it on their doorstep and run? You have to be careful here. How can I trust you to be careful?"

"And how can I trust *you*?" Anne shot back. "What's to stop you from calling the police and telling them I'm trespassing onto your property? And then keep whatever we find for yourself."

"Yes, I *could* do that," Renee conceded with a slight sneer. "I could, if I was stupid enough to get the cops involved. They would probably just notify the courts—or the Feds or whatever—and they'd seize all of the cash, and then neither of us would get anything."

The two exchanged a dark look and then nodded simultaneously. They understood each other—they didn't necessarily like or trust each other, but they didn't have to.

"Look, I don't know you, and you don't know me, but we seem to have each other over a barrel. You can't find the money without me, and I can't look for it without you. Maybe we can work together." Anne said.

"We don't even know how much money we're looking for, do we?" Renee asked. "Do you still have those photos you showed me of the money the other day? Maybe we can calculate how much was there. We'd just have to count up the bundles."

"Worth a try." Anne pulled out her phone, called up the photos, and enlarged the one showing Chloe laying out the bundles of cash.

"Each bundle contains one hundred bills of the same denomination. I'm counting thirteen bundles. So that's $26,000 in twenties," Renee said briskly, then caught Anne looking at her with raised eyebrows. "I majored in business with a finance minor." Which raised Anne's eyebrows even higher.

The woman knew her sums, which begged the question: How could Renee have been as ignorant of Lino's financial schemes as she claimed? *Willfully ignorant, at best. At worst, complicit,* she thought.

They looked up at the sharp sound of two beeps of a car horn coming from the street, soon followed by the pounding of footsteps racing down the staircase. "The guys are giving me a ride," Josh called out as he breezed past them with barely a glance. He was dressed like most kids heading out the door to school: black jeans, a T-shirt, sneakers. His knapsack nearly got caught in the door as he was slamming it shut.

"Have a good day—" Renee said a second too late for him to hear. She stood and went over to the drapes, parted them a few inches, and stared out the window. They heard the car door slam shut, and the kids drive away. "Well, I guess that's good," she said, turning to Anne. "At least he's out of his room."

Renee sat back down. "Well, now for the hundred-dollar bills."

Anne enlarged the photo yet again. "Many of the bundles are only partially visible, but I'm guessing there are at least twenty bundles. Which means $200,000."

"And that doesn't factor in whatever was left inside the wall, which had been emptied out by Lino by the time we looked."

"So it could be maybe double that amount."

"Conservatively. After all, it's a big wall," Renee agreed. "This was Lino's 'get out of Dodge' money. He would have to live off of it for the foreseeable future, so I'll bet it's a fortune. He never thought small."

"Like Whitey Bulger. You know, that Boston Irish crime boss," Anne said. "Ever hear of him?"

"Vaguely."

"Before he was caught in 2011, Bulger had been on the run for years along with his girlfriend. He stashed cash inside the walls of their Santa Monica apartment. Over $800,000 was found when he was caught—and that's just what was left after they'd been living off of it for fifteen years. So, who knows how much cash he started with."

"Probably Lino's hero," Renee said ruefully. "So let's ballpark the total at

$400,000."

"That's quite a leap, but okay," Anne said. "Might as well dream. That means we'll each get somewhere around $200,000. Better than a poke in the eye."

"Better than sleeping outside under a park bench," Renee muttered, then shook her head. "No, sorry but that doesn't work. I need a bigger cut. Sixty percent at the very least. This was my money—mine and Lino's—in the first place, and it's on my property." All this talk about money had clearly focused Renee's survival and negotiating skills.

"Well, that's debatable," Anne said, letting a bit of acid drip into her voice. "It really belongs to all those ripped-off investors who…" Anne cut her sentence short. Righteousness wouldn't get her anywhere. Besides, if Renee's story was true, she could be considered one of Lino's victims, too.

"Okay, fine. Sixty-forty split," Anne finally said.

"And, if we find the pearls, they belong to me. Outright."

Anne nodded. "Sure, fine. So, do we have a deal? We search together and split the proceeds? I have a meeting across town, but we can get started after lunch."

Renee hesitated, apparently still mulling it over.

"What's to think over?" Anne said, irritation edging into her voice. "We have to do this while we still have the chance. Tempus fugit. Time waits for no man."

Renee rolled her eyes, then frowned.

"Tick, tock," Anne added, just to be annoying.

"Okay, deal."

"Now all we have to do is find the money." Anne stood up.

"Why not leave the diary here? I can get a head start for us while you're gone."

Anne laughed outright and tucked the diary back into her purse.

# Chapter Thirteen

D ave Silver sat on the curb across the street from Anne's shingle-sided duplex on Winslow Lane. His golden retriever, called 'Trailer' because that's what Dave named every dog he ever owned, was settled down beside him on the sidewalk, tail thumping.

Dave stretched out his long legs for a moment, then drew his knees to his chest and folded his arms around them. He lowered the rim of his baseball cap to shield his eyes from the noonday sun.

Still squinting, Dave studied her yard for a few more minutes. It was divided into two equal parts by a concrete walkway leading to four steps, a wraparound porch, and twin front doors. Easily one of the smallest yards he'd ever been hired to work on, and not much of a challenge.

If he had his druthers, that scraggly, poor excuse of a peach tree, planted just two feet from the walkway, would be dug up and tossed into the compost where it belonged. But preserving the lopsided young tree, which was upright only because of three wooden stakes, was Anne's only condition for his landscape design: The peach tree had to stay. "It was practically the reason why I bought the house in the first place, and it's finally bearing fruit," she'd told him.

He checked his phone for the time. Eleven-fifteen. Fifteen more minutes until his on-site meeting with Anne. She was expecting to see landscape design ideas, a timeline, and a ballpark cost estimate. After she approved the general direction and budget, he would finalize the drawing into a plant-specific landscape design and price it out back at his office.

Dave rummaged through his knapsack, pulled out a graphics drawing tablet and stylus pen, and started sketching. It took him all of ten minutes to come up with a plan. After the lawn was dug up and plastic sheeting laid down, he'd add some drought-tolerant native shrubs in varying sizes: larger ones like blue oat grass would be planted in back and along the sides to frame the yard, and then a few succulents and smaller plants would go in front. He added a brilliant red crepe myrtle tree and a packed earth mound, and then, just as quickly, eliminated them. *Too much.* Instead, he decided, he'd drop a few boulders in strategic places on the mulch ground covering for visual interest until the plants started to grow in.

"What do you think, girl?" He patted Trailer's head, but the dog's attention was on the take-out bag of dim sum next to Dave on the sidewalk. It held an assortment of pork dumplings, steamed BBQ pork buns, and crispy shrimp balls that Dave had picked up from his favorite restaurant for a working lunch with Anne (*Good hot or cold*, he'd told her). Dave moved the bag to his other side.

Dave looked back up at the yard, and while he was trying to decide where to plant some flowering ground cover, a red minivan screeched to a jerky stop right in front of Anne's place. Right in his line of sight. *Well, shit.*

In a blur of motion, a coltish teenager—tall and slender—shot out of the driver's side and barreled up the walkway to Anne's porch. Ringing the bell three times and getting no response, she looked down at her phone, her long, honey blonde hair falling over her eyes, and started texting frantically.

Whoever she was, Dave thought, she looked way too young to be driving that car, especially in her excitable state.

"You looking for Anne?" he called out.

"What?" The girl looked up and around, trying to locate where his voice was coming from.

"I'm over here," he bellowed a bit louder, but didn't move from his curbside seat. "I said, are you looking for Anne McCormack?"

Finally spotting him across the street, she called out, "Yes," and walked across the street toward him, texting away as she went.

"She's not here." Dave said when she stood in front of him. *Yep, too young to drive,* he thought. He looked back down at his tablet and added a few bee-attracting flowering plants to the plan. Lavender and lantana.

"You know Anne? I'm supposed to meet her here," the girl said. Trailer barked out a greeting, and she bent down to pet the dog.

"Me too." Dave set the tablet down and stuck his stylus pen behind his ear. "Any friend of Anne's is a friend of mine. Name's Dave," he said, extending his fist for a bump.

"Chloe." She tapped his fist with her own.

"Might as well sit." He shoved his drawing tablet back into his knapsack and patted the cement curb next to him. "It could be a few minutes."

"What were you drawing there?" She didn't sit and instead pointed to his knapsack.

"See that weed-infected, water-guzzling lawn over there? Anne wants it taken out."

"Oh! You're the guy she hired to do her yard. Right, I see your truck now: *Silver Landscaping*. Well, okay then…" She lowered herself to the curb and sat cross-legged, right next to the take-out bag.

"So, how do you know Anne?"

"She's my employer and friend. Sort of like an aunt, but not. Unless she were to marry one of my uncles someday."

"Any chance of that?"

"No." They sat in silence for a few minutes. She looked down hungrily at the bag of dim sum.

"That your car?" he asked, lifting his chin toward the minivan.

"My mom's."

"Shouldn't you be in school?"

"I'm kind of on the run," she said. She looked down at her phone again.

"On the run?" He smiled at her film noir-like turn of phrase. She sounded like a character straight out of *The Maltese Falcon* or some other hardboiled movie classic.

"What sort of caper are you on?" he asked, mimicking her.

"Huh?" She gave him a blank look, then eventually said, "I just need to get away for a while. The walls are closing in on me. And mom's really cray…" She let the sentence drop. Her right foot was jiggling and her eyes were darting around.

He rubbed his two-day-old beard and gave her a sideways look. Typical teen angst, he decided. He felt a tug of sympathy. He knew something about what drives a kid to want to leave parents and problems behind. He'd run away from home himself a few times. The first time was when he was a tall, skinny thirteen-year-old, after he'd come home from school one day and witnessed his six-month-old puppy—the first "Trailer," given that name because he followed Dave around everywhere—being kicked by his dad all the way from the center of the kitchen to the backyard porch, for no good reason except "the mutt peed on my boots." Dave scooped up the whimpering dog and ran to his mom. He begged her to come with him and leave the son of a bitch, but she just slipped him forty dollars and kissed his forehead. Dave, carrying Trailer in his backpack, rode his bike fourteen miles to Trudy Lee's Bar & Grill and spent the night on Trudy's couch in her apartment above the bar. He heard later that Trudy lit into his dad, telling him that he wouldn't be welcome back in the bar if he "ever harmed a hair on that pup again." He never got a chance; Dave made sure Trailer was never alone with his dad after that.

Then there was the time when he and his friends, just out for a little fun, hot-wired a car from the Walmart parking lot and got pulled over by cops within an hour. That landed him in juvenile detention. And in just those two short weeks, his education got derailed permanently, he befriended a bunch of lost souls who were hard to shake, and he started down a path of drugs and petty crime that ended up becoming a long, fifteen-year fog. Who can afford to waste fifteen years of their life? But that's exactly what he did during what he called his 'dumb ass years'—from his late teens, all through his twenties, and halfway into his thirties.

That sad line from the movie *On the Waterfront* said it all: "I coulda been a contender." Were more woeful words ever spoken? Not a regret he'd wish on anyone.

"I don't know how far along you are on your plan—or if you even have a plan," Dave said, now looking at her full-on, his voice taking on an earnest intensity, "but my advice to you is this: Ditch the car. It's easy to trace, and stealing a car could land you in jail."

Seeing her confused, what-the-hell-are-you-talking-about expression, he realized that he needed to take it down a notch, that he wasn't saying all of this to Chloe so much as to his younger self. It was pure projection. Those years of drugs, dishonor, crippling shame weren't pertinent here—they had nothing to do with this girl. That isn't how this girl's life would unfold.

"I'm just kidding. Your mom won't call the cops. She wouldn't do that to you."

"She would, that's the problem."

They grew silent again. Her phone pinged with an incoming text. She frowned down at it and didn't reply.

He got out his own phone and shot a text to Anne.

Dave: You have a visitor here.

Anne: I know. Keep her company? I'll be there in a second.

He looked off at nothing in particular, racking his brain. He wasn't used to talking to teenage girls.

"So, you got a boyfriend?" he finally asked.

Chloe's eyes widened with something like fear. She slowly inched away from him, her fingers reaching for her backpack, looking ready to bolt.

It took Dave a minute to comprehend what her sudden wariness was about, and when he did, in one fluid movement, he was on his feet and stepping away from her. No point in frightening the girl.

"Relax, kid," he said, stepping back another foot for good measure. "I was just making conversation. I have a stepson around your age, and I was just thinking...not that I'd recommend him...he'd lead you astray...not that you need any help with that..." Dave found himself rambling, digging himself into a deeper hole. He decided to stop talking before she called the cops.

Chloe's grip on her backpack loosened a bit. He sat back down again.

"I'm giving up on boys. I'm sooo done. D-U-N," Chloe said, jutting out her chin. "In fact, I'm done with a lot of things." Then, with a sudden burst of adrenaline, she jumped up off the curb and started looking up and down the street.

"Where's Anne?! I texted her, and she said she was on her way. She should have been here by now!" The words had barely flown from her mouth when they spotted Anne's Saab coming around the corner, heading toward them.

"Thank God," Chloe said.

Anne waved at them through the driver side window, parked her car behind the red minivan, and killed the engine. Before she even had a chance to unbuckle her seatbelt, Chloe was at the driver side door, talking and gesturing broadly through the glass. Anne slowly opened the door and stepped out. For the next few minutes, Chloe stood squarely in front of her, talking non-stop, until Anne drew back slightly and tilted her head in Dave's direction. Holding up her forefinger in Chloe's face, she broke away and walked across the street to where Dave was standing.

"Hi, Dave. I'm so sorry about this. Apparently, Chloe's boyfriend's been seen with another girl, and some pretty blood-curdling acts of revenge are on the table...anyway, is it alright if we meet later?" she asked with a sheepish grin on her face.

A few strands of her sunlit, nut-brown hair fell over her eyes. He raised his hand to brush them off her forehead, but caught himself and ran his hand through his own unruly hair instead, nearly knocking off his cap in the process.

"Later this evening, maybe?"

"Sure, no problem. We can go out to dinner. I'll bring the yard plans with me." He patted his knapsack. "How about Trudy Lee's at seven o'clock?"

"Does she really serve food?"

"For special customers. For us, she will. Best chicken cacciatore in town." Dave opened the pickup's passenger side door and Trailer hopped into the cab.

"Deal. Meet you there at seven," Anne said, then turned back to Chloe and headed toward her house. Before she got halfway across the street, Dave shouted out, "Hey, take the dim sum with you." He twisted the bag opening until it was closed tight and tossed it Anne's way. "Chloe looks hungry."

Anne leaned in for the catch. "Thanks!"

Dave got into the pickup truck and turned around in his seat to look back. Anne's arm was draped around Chloe's shoulder, shepherding the girl into her home. He kept looking at the house long after the front door closed behind them.

By the time he finally turned the key in the ignition, he was feeling an unexpected flare of longing and loneliness. He couldn't remember the last time he'd felt that way when a woman left his sight.

# Chapter Fourteen

Armed with the diary, Anne and Renee started their search that afternoon, thinking it would be something of a breeze—done and dusted in an hour or two, tops.

Lino hadn't had much time that Sunday night to conceal the envelopes of money and pearls, they assured each other, so he probably stuck them someplace temporary. "Someplace easy to get to, figuring he'd move it to a permanent spot when he had the time," Anne said. She slipped off her suit jacket, laid it over the back of an outdoor lounge chair and pushed up the sleeves of her blue silk blouse.

"But time ran out," Renee said in a flat, matter-of-fact tone. She was wearing her version of work clothes: a leopard print tank top, matching drawstring leggings, paper-white sneakers, a bandana tied around her neck. Her cascading auburn curls were barely kept in check by a pair of tortoiseshell barrettes.

It was one o'clock, and already hotter than predicted, eighty-three degrees and rising, and Anne wished she was wearing a sleeveless top like Renee's, though maybe less flashy. But with Chloe tugging at her sleeve back at her house, who had time to change out of her business clothes into something more practical? Anne had barely made it to Renee's house in time, what with comforting the agitated teenager, feeding her lunch, and driving her back home (*Your mom can pick up her car later*, she said). What were the odds that she'd leave here today without thoroughly trashing her good clothes? Not great.

Anne dropped her purse onto the round teak table and lifted out the diary.

Holding it suspended in midair, she hesitated. She couldn't bring herself to place it on the tabletop, grimy with dead leaves and dust. The diary had to be returned by five o'clock that afternoon to the executor, and it had to be returned without any rips, stains, or signs that anyone but Lily had ever looked at it.

"Let me get a towel or something," Renee said, disappearing into the kitchen and coming back a minute later with two placements. Anne laid the diary down and opened it to the page with Lily's rudimentary map.

"According to Lily, she drew this strictly from what Dinah told her and from her own memories of the property, so it's pretty rough." Lily's artistic skills were on par with a four-year-old's, so the Pardini backyard was drawn with wiggly lines and labeled *garden* in red ink. The rectangular-shaped four-car garage was depicted as a plain square box. No attempt had been made to include the house.

The map had three red arrows. Since two of those arrows pointed to the backyard, that's where they started. They made a beeline to the far corner of the yard, to where Lily had drawn an arrow to her stick illustration of a young tree—which they easily recognized as the now-towering Sycamore tree and which Anne declared as being "easily seventy feet high and unclimbable."

Bare of any leaves, all they could see were brittle twigs and branches. "The diary mentioned a bungee cord and plastic bag, but if they'd ever been tossed up there, they're long gone now," Anne said.

One arrow down, two to go.

The next one pointed to a tiny BBQ sketched next to a water fountain. "That was then, and this is now," Renee said, gesturing to a massive, L-shaped outdoor kitchen anchoring the patio, custom-designed with a stainless-steel grill, sink, and dishwasher. They methodically went through every drawer, felt under the venting hood, ran a flashlight over the insides of the dishwasher and fridge, and even unmounted the garbage disposal unit. Nothing.

The third and final arrow led them to the garage. Not to any specific place or item in the garage, just to the whole entirety of its approximately 1,000 square feet of space.

"Not real helpful," groused Renee. "And we need some more light in here." She switched on the overhead lightbulb and pressed the wall button to open the garage doors. The double doors rumbled upward toward the ceiling.

"Maybe Dinah saw Lino enter the garage, but didn't see what he actually did in here," Anne said, looking around to get her bearings. Just like the first time Anne was briefly in the garage, Lino's navy BMW took up a garage bay, and the vintage pickup remained suspended on the lift over the red Miata two-seater convertible. Renee's black Mercedes was out in the driveway. "The money wouldn't be in my car," Renee said ruefully, "Lino wouldn't want me anywhere near it."

Looking directly above her head, Anne spied the most obvious hiding place in the garage: a long plywood shelf that was cantilevered over the entry door. But after climbing a ladder and rummaging through boxes full of Christmas decorations, Anne climbed back down and took another look around. She spotted a dusty old piece-of-crap vacuum cleaner in the corner.

"Why don't you start on Lino's car, and I'll check out that vacuum cleaner."

"Vacuum cleaner? Seriously?" Renee muttered under her breath.

Anne actually had high hopes for the vacuum. The year before, when she was clearing out a client's house for inventory, she'd dragged an old vacuum cleaner out of a closet and removed the dirt-filled brown bag. Inside was a plastic Ziplock bag filled with rolled up twenty-dollar bills secured with rubber bands. "I'm not even going to count it," she told the executor when she called him. There had been over two thousand dollars in that bag.

But that was a luckier day than today. After reaching into the cavity of the vacuum and coming out with nothing but dust and gunk, all she could think was, *Thank God for latex gloves.*

Renee, meanwhile, was busy in the driver's seat of the BMW, checking over the visor and under the mat, reaching behind the seat and under it. Then, she moved to the passenger's side and carried out the same drill. She unlatched the storage compartment between the two seats, but all she pulled out were maps.

"Any luck?" Anne asked, pulling off her gloves. Without being obvious,

Anne was keeping an eye on Renee. What would stop Renee from finding the envelopes and keeping that information to herself? It would be easy for her to just leave the money in its hiding place and retrieve it later when Anne was gone.

"Not yet." Renee got out and opened the trunk. "But there's still the convertible and pickup truck."

"I think I'll check out those paint cans," Anne said, nodding toward a row of old cans lining the garage floor along the back wall.

"Paint cans?" Renee scoffed. "What next, the garden hose?"

Anne ignored her and wasted the next twenty minutes prying open five half-empty paint cans that were tightly sealed with dry, encrusted paint. Lino could have filled the empty cans with cash, put the lids back on, then dripped some paint—paint can dry incredibly fast, she knew—along the rim of the lids to seal them closed again. An ingenious place to hide money, Anne thought. No one would have given the cans a second look.

Too bad Lino hadn't thought of it.

Meanwhile, Renee was busy inspecting the red convertible, starting with the interior and then moving to the mini-sized trunk. That's where the driver's manual and repair records were kept since there was no glove compartment. While Renee was flipping through the manual for cash, Anne headed to a rack on the wall where a wheelbarrow was hung upside down, facing the sheetrock. Maybe Lino stuffed the money in the tray. But after pulling the wheelbarrow away from the wall and checking, she said, "Damn. Nothing, nada."

Anne stood beside Renee as she slammed down the trunk and said, "Same here, zilch. So, is that it? Is that all the diary had to say for itself?"

They went out to the backyard for another look at the sketchy map.

"Maybe we've missed something about that bungee cord," Renee said, pointing to the cramped handwriting along the margins of the map.

"That's possible. Maybe Lily didn't mean the tree at all. Let's see what she actually wrote..." Anne flipped to the bookmarked page. "Here it is: 'Dinah said Lino threw a bungee cord all the way up to the top.'"

"The top, hmmm."

103

"If it wasn't the top of the tree, then the top of what?"

They went back inside the garage and looked up.

\* \* \*

"The bag is full of crap! Nothing but crap," Renee yelled down as she teetered on the ladder, nearly losing her footing while struggling to hold up the black garbage bag.

"Throw it down!" Anne held up her hands for the toss, but when she saw the cloud of dust flying off the plastic, she stepped back and let it land hard on the cement floor. A navy blue knit ski cap partially escaped from the opening at the top of the bag.

After two hours of tearing the garage apart, finding the trash bag was the single *Eureka* moment that could be directly tied to clues in the diary. Lily had written that Dinah saw Lino toss a bungee cord—though where he tossed it, she didn't say—but when they'd looked up toward the rafters, there it was: a black nylon cord with a plastic bag hanging off the other end. It was wrapped around a rafter tie near the garage ceiling, secured with a nail, squeezed behind the rafter tie, and lodged in the corner where the tie met the wall. Almost invisible unless you knew where to look. Maybe it wasn't the same bag—though it easily had sixteen years' worth of dust coating it. And maybe the items inside weren't the same ones that Lino had put there in hiding back then. But it was something, anyway. Maybe it was just crap, as Renee called it, but something.

"I think it's time to regroup," Renee said as she gingerly stepped down the ladder. With the back of her hand, she wiped beads of sweat off her forehead, leaving behind a wet smear of dust. "It's hotter than heck up there. Let's have a drink out on the patio," she said, fanning herself on her way out of the garage.

Anne crouched down and opened the bag. "Okay, I'll be out there in a minute," she called out over her shoulder.

Anne reached into the bag and pulled out an extra-large men's sweatshirt, a color match for the ski cap. There was only one other item inside: a crumpled, brown paper lunch sack containing a flat, business-size envelope and a Ziplock plastic bag covering a compact flip phone with an antenna, the kind she hadn't seen in years.

Anne stared at the items, not knowing exactly what she was looking at, but knowing that she didn't want her fingerprints all over the phone or envelope until she did know. She held the envelope by its edges and flipped it over. On the front, *Find—D* was written in black Sharpie, most likely in Lino's handwriting. Find what? And who—or what—was *D*? The envelope was sealed, and it took all of her self-discipline not to rip it open. Whatever this was all about, this letter and this phone, she had to be careful.

"You're right, Renee, it's crap. Want me to toss it?" she called out.

"Sure, go ahead. Is Diet Coke okay?"

"Yeah. I'll be right there." Anne stuffed the envelope, sweatshirt, and cap back inside the bag and pulled the drawstring closed tight. She lugged the dusty bag to her car in the driveway, popped open the trunk, and tossed it in. But before slamming the trunk shut, a fuzzy, back-of-mind thought suddenly made its way to the front of her mind and stopped her. She was still sworn in as a police officer with powers to collect evidence—if that's what this was—but that didn't mean she could act like the Lone Ranger here.

She pulled out her phone and placed a call to the Police Chief. Luckily, he picked up on the third ring. She filled him in on her findings (*It's probably nothing,* she said). He gave her the go ahead, saying, "Since the owner said you could trash it, you don't need a warrant. Just bring the bag in as soon as possible."

She finished the call, went through the garage, and headed out to the backyard patio, where Renee was waiting at the table with two glasses set in front of her. Anne collapsed in the lounge chair facing her.

"The way I see it," Renee said, sliding a cold drink across the table to Anne, "there's only one place left to look."

"You mean the truck." Anne took a sip of diet soda, then reached back behind her head and, with both hands, lifted her mass of shoulder-length hair off her neck and separated it into three strands. Within seconds, she'd worked her hair into a stubby braid and tied it with a scrunchie she pulled from her purse. "But before we try operating that hydraulic lift, I think I'll take another look at that outdoor kitchen," Anne said.

"You're just stalling…" Renee rolled her cold drink over her forehead.

Anne had to smile; there was some truth to that. The Pardini Winery truck needed to be lowered before it could be searched—and that meant someone had to learn how to make that happen. And that meant reading the operating manual. She couldn't think of anything more tedious than reading directions, unless it was following a recipe with more than four ingredients.

Anne stood up and wandered over to the stone-clad kitchen. She pulled out all the drawers again, looked under the hood again, and then walked around the back and idly ran her fingers over the rough stone. Lifting her hand, she glanced down and noticed a small stain on the porous, light-colored stone. Dried blood? The crimson spot was about the size of a silver-dollar pancake. An even smaller dot of blood had landed on the steel edge of the adjacent grill. *Why didn't I notice these before?* She called out to Renee, "Do you know where this blood came from? At least that's what it looks like."

Renee sauntered over to where Anne was standing. Fanning herself, she looked down. "Never saw it before," she said and turned away, heading back to the table. Anne was just a few steps behind her. "Seriously, no idea," Renee said with a couldn't-care-less expression on her face, sinking into a chair.

Looking down at her watch, Renee frowned. "Well, shoot-fire, I had no idea it was so late. It's coming up on four o'clock, and I have to go pick up Josh at school in a half hour. And we still have to do the truck."

"Before we do, let's sit for a minute. We could both use a breather." Anne dropped into her chair and reached for her drink. "We're worn slap out, as you Texans say," she said, raising her glass to Renee, who just rolled her eyes.

"Okay, but only for a minute," Renee said, her forehead slick with perspiration, "because 'tempus fugit,' as you west coasters like to say. Tick, tock."

The ping of an incoming text made Renee sit up and reach inside her pocket and pull out her phone. She turned to Anne after reading it and said, "Well, this buys us a little time. Turns out I don't have to pick up Josh after all. His cousins want him to spend the night at their house. Which is okay with me, except he doesn't have clean clothes for school tomorrow."

She replied to Josh and, after receiving his answer back, told Anne, "He says they're coming by to pick up some of his stuff. I guess it's good that he'll be with Marco's family. He needs to be with people who love him. Aside from me, that is," she said softly, setting down the phone. Anne watched as Renee's expression slide from melancholy to something like despair and thought, *This will not do.*

"Okay, then!" Anne said, slapping the table with the palm of her hand. "Let's get this truck thing over with. You drive the convertible out of that contraption, and I'll figure out how to do this car lift thing."

Renee, roused out of her doldrums, set off to the kitchen to grab the keys and then headed to the garage to move the car. Meanwhile, Anne, after a mere two minutes of poring over the manual, snapped her fingers and called out, "Aha!" Turns out that lowering the truck was just a matter of pulling down and holding the lock release while pushing the "down" lever.

While the pickup made its smooth, slow descent, the two women stood back to admire the sheen of its emerald-green finish. When it touched the ground, Renee ran her fingers tenderly over the glossy hood. It was even cleaner than the convertible, better cared for, more pristine. "Babied," Renee said definitively. "Lino and Josh babied it shamelessly."

Every month, whether the old truck needed it or not, she told Anne, they drove it to their mechanic in Larkfield-Wikiup, just north of Santa Rosa, for an oil change. On their way home, they'd stop to eat hamburgers at In-N-Out, then pull the truck into the driveway and spend a few hours polishing it up while Lino told Josh stories about how when he was a teenager, he would drive it up and down Fourth Street with his buddies.

"They did a lot of father-son bonding over that truck. Lino promised Josh the pink slip on his sixteenth birthday. Josh was so excited." Tears welled up in Renee's eyes but she blinked them away and squared her shoulders. When she spoke again, her voice had taken on the all-business, time-is-money tone that was like the ringing of a cash register to Anne's ears. "You search the front cab, and I'll take the load bed."

Anne slid onto the vinyl-covered cab bench in front and checked the visors, felt under the seats, and pulled out the ashtray. Renee, meanwhile, went to the rear of the truck, unhitched the tail gate and climbed onto the bed of the truck. She took a screwdriver to the truck bed wheel well, a combination toolbox and tire cover. It popped right off, but nothing was inside that didn't belong there. She picked up a plastic gas can, sloshed it around, opened the cap, and peered inside.

Then, as Renee was putting the gas can back in the corner of the bed, and Anne was checking the inside door panels, they were interrupted by the creaking sound of the entry gate swinging open. A boxy white Jeep Wrangler was driving slowly up the driveway. Anne peeked out of the cab to watch.

"Well, what do you know," Renee said to Anne, nodding toward the SUV. "That's Marco's wife, Kay. Guess she's giving Josh a ride home to pick up his toothbrush." Renee climbed down from the truck bed.

Bringing the Jeep to a stop, Kay stepped out from driver side door and looked over the hood at Anne and Renee. Josh tumbled out of the backseat and broke into a trot, kicking up bits of gravel along the way to the garage. Renee and her sister-in-law stared at each other for a moment, a standoff of sorts, until Renee waved and got a limp wave in return.

Josh came to a skidding stop at the truck in front of his mother. "Mom, what are you doing?"

"Just cleaning out the truck. This is my friend Anne."

"Hi, nice to meet you, Josh—" Anne said, stepping away from the truck and extending her hand.

"Hi," he said without a glance at Anne, who dropped her arm to her side. "It doesn't need cleaning, Mom. Besides, that's my job."

"Don't forget the PS5 console," a teenage boy's voice called from inside the Jeep.

"Gotta go, Mom." Josh turned and disappeared inside the house.

Renee's eyes followed him, then she looked toward Kay's Jeep and made a move to approach her and say hello. But her sister-in-law put a halt to that by abruptly stepping back inside the vehicle and shutting the door.

Renee blew out a ragged breath. Turning to Anne and motioning toward the truck, she said, "Let's wait until they leave." For the next few minutes, Renee looked through an old photo album while Anne feigned interest in Josh's baby pictures.

"Bye, Mom," they heard as Josh dashed past the garage door. He was carrying a bulky cardboard box overflowing with clothes, a video console, sports trophies, his laptop. Way more than the toothbrush and change of clothes he'd need for just one night.

Anne and Renee stood side by side, watching Kay turn the Jeep around in the driveway. As she drove off, Anne saw her bumper sticker: "He who dies with the most toys wins."

Wordlessly, Anne and Renee turned back to the pickup and got to work. Inside the cab, Anne emptied out the glove compartment and pulled up the floor mats. Outside, Renee pulled on gloves and felt around above the wheel wells—all four of them. "Nothing but dirt," she said. Anne got out of the cab to check the narrow sidesteps, found nothing, slammed the driver's door shut, and leaned against it.

"Where haven't we looked?" Anne asked. Her eyes went to the chrome gas cap by the door. In a last-ditch effort, she gave it a turn. "Maybe Lino stuffed some money down the gas tank."

"That's a stretch." Renee hauled herself up onto the tailgate of the truck, tucked her hands under her thighs, and sat with her feet dangling above the ground.

Lifting the gas cap, Anne muttered, "What the heck." She leaned in, took a whiff, and was forced back on her heels by the pungent gas odor. "Not there, that's for sure."

"It's just not here anywhere. Not in this truck, not in this garage, not—" Renee left the sentence hanging.

"But if it's not here, where could it be?" Anne stood facing Renee, hands on hips, not quite ready to admit defeat. "Would he have called someone to help him? Someone he trusted…his brother Marco?

"No." Renee said 'no' the way some might say "oh *hell* to the no."

"Really? Marco called Lino 'the best man he ever knew' in the newspaper obituary, so why wouldn't he help? I'm a little surprised," Anne said, not really surprised at all. Nothing much about family relationships surprised her anymore. Besides, Kay's pointed snub just a few minutes ago signaled that something was obviously off between the two families.

"It's complicated. I'm guessing that was just a PR move. Marco is all about keeping the family name polished up shiny and clean."

"Anyone else? Didn't Lino have a daughter here in town?"

"Jennifer? Lino wouldn't have wanted to put his little princess out. Wouldn't want to worry her pretty little head," Renee said dismissively. Then she stared off into space as if a million thoughts were running through her mind, each vying to pull focus. "I mean, I don't think so…"

"Or maybe someone he worked with?" Anne asked.

"Not his lawyer or former law partner. They'd ask too many questions, and he wouldn't want them involved."

"Maybe a friend…"

"No, I can't think of anyone. He had a lot of acquaintances, but no close friends," Renee said, dismissing the thought. "Maybe his doctor? The landscaper?"

*Dave?* Anne drew in a quick breath. "Who?"

"Dave Silver does our yard. Lino was planning on going into business with him, or maybe he was just going to invest in Dave's new nursery," Renee said, then seemed to reconsider. "But I don't really think so. It was the middle of the night. I don't see Lino calling anyone. And, like you said, he just needed a stop-gap place to hide the money, and he probably thought he had plenty of time. But for all I know, he got in his car that night and drove it to his office." She winced. "Which is now locked. Locked and sealed."

Anne nodded. "A designated crime scene."

Renee dropped down from her perch on the tailgate. "We aren't going to find it, are we?"

Anne's reply was slow in coming. "I really thought the diary would tell us.

I'm sorry it didn't work out."

"Well, I always knew it was a long shot. At least I had a little hope for a while."

Anne looked around. "There must be someplace we haven't thought of...maybe we're missing the obvious," Anne said, though she couldn't think of any nook or cranny they'd missed. And apparently, from the blank expression on Renee's face, neither could she.

It was getting late, and Anne had places to go. Part of her, the skeptical, hard-nosed part, didn't trust Renee to be alone, not if there was any chance of her finding the money while she was gone. But it was unavoidable. What was the alternative? Stay by Renee's side, watching her every move, until U.S. Marshals took over? That could be days, weeks.

Anne went to the backyard to grab her purse and jacket. Entering the garage again, she said, "Listen, Renee, I have to drop the diary off at the executor's office and then I have another meeting, but I can come by afterwards. Maybe around nine this evening?"

"I'll be here." For a brief, unguarded second, Renee's despair was palpable on her face, in her voice, and in the slouch of her body.

"You alright?"

Renee shook her head. "Yeah, I'm fine," she said, straightening up. "Thanks for asking. And I need to apologize for being such a bitch earlier. Believe it or not, I'm not always like this."

"Oh, God, don't worry about it," Anne said with a dismissive wave. "Anyone would feel overwhelmed. You've been through hell and—" Although the word 'survived' was on the tip of her tongue, she had no idea if Renee would, in fact, survive. She was still going through hell, and there didn't appear to be an end in sight. There was still the possibility of homelessness to contend with. "Anyway," she picked up, "it's understandable."

Renee slammed the tailgate shut and walked Anne out through the garage to the driveway. "Well, thanks again." She placed a hand to her chest, then lifted it in a wave, saying, "See you in a few hours."

\* \* \*

Halfway down the hill, Anne passed four dark SUVs caravanning up the steep grade toward the only three houses at the end of the cul-de-sac.

Anne pulled over to the curb and turned around to look back at the slow-moving SUVs. Unmarked. Black. American made. Tinted windows. She'd ridden in enough of those vehicles to know what she was looking at.

She wouldn't be going back to Renee's house later that evening.

The Feds had arrived.

# Chapter Fifteen

Anne only made it as far as the end of Renee's street before pulling over to the curb again. Even from here, at the bottom of the street, the elevation was higher than almost anywhere else in Santa Rosa. Through the windshield, she looked down over golf course fairways, rolling hills, and the city skyline. This was the privileged, million-dollar view that Renee had lived with for the last fifteen years and was losing, along with practically everything else.

Anne trained her eyes straight ahead. She didn't want to get in the middle of a raid, but she also didn't want to abandon Renee, leaving her to contend with that court-ordered nightmare alone. Anne stayed motionless for another minute, considering all the angles. She could turn the car around and drive back up the hill, but what was the point? What could she possibly do or say that would help Renee now? *Not a damn thing.* With the FBI swarming about the property, she'd only be in the way. She considered texting Krista to ask her to keep an eye out for Renee since they lived on the same street, but hesitated. If Renee needed any help, she would reach out. She had a phone. She had lawyers. Family. And closer friends, surely, than her and Krista.

There was nothing, at least for now, for Anne to do.

Besides, she had to take care of her own business right now, and she was running late. She turned the key in the ignition and dropped down the sun visor to block the late afternoon glare. When she caught sight of herself in the mirror on the back of the visor, she groaned and killed the engine. Her hair was still in that tacky makeshift, sweaty braid. And there were unidentifiable smudges on her forehead. She dabbed some water from her drinking bottle onto a tissue to wipe the dirt off her face and ran a comb through her hair. Shrugging at the results, she started the engine, made a right turn, and took off for the law offices of Wilson, Dryer, and Sampson.

\* \* \*

Lily Danielson's executor, Ken Dryer, was flipping through the diary with one hand and gripping and twisting his pen with the other. "Why wasn't this delivered to me sooner? Where was it?" Dryer finally asked from behind his mahogany desk.

"The journal was accidentally misplaced in the bookshelf," Anne said. She then went on to explain how she had only noticed it right before the estate sale started.

He listened to Anne with pursed lips and an occasional nod. "Hmmm. So you found it at the estate sale. That was Saturday. Two days ago," he pointed out.

"Your office was closed over the weekend. And the diary was always someplace safe. I got it here as soon as I could," she said, feeling pleased with herself for sounding so reasonable—and for leaving out the part about Chloe's absentmindedness and her own questionable use of the diary. Things he didn't need to know.

He acknowledged her explanation with another nod, then stared at her in silent judgment. Why was he being so uptight about this anyway, she wondered. It's not as if anyone in Lily's family had even asked about the diary. Dryer's eyes skidded downward toward her chest and lingered there long enough for her to take offense—that is until she looked down and saw what he was staring at. Her beautiful new silk blouse was smudged with three kinds of dirt: grease from the outdoor kitchen on the blouse collar, grime from the table at her waist, and streaks of dust from the bag. None of which would be easy to wash out. She frowned and wondered what else she'd missed.

"Anyway," she said, gathering up her purse, standing up, and backing out of the room, "didn't that estate sale go well? It did, I thought! Lily's family must be very pleased..."

"Un-huh," he said. "Thanks for dropping by."

On her way out of the building, she ducked into the women's restroom in the lobby. With no time to go home and change, Anne just buttoned up her jacket to hide her blouse. She dabbed on some lipstick and cleaned off a dark smudge on her chin that she'd missed. If not entirely presentable, at least she would look like she tried.

* * *

It was after five o'clock when she walked into the police station, dragging the filthy plastic bag behind her. Chief Daniel Russo came out of his office to meet her. Taking possession of the trash bag, he wasted no time in issuing orders for the bag and its contents to be logged in, processed, packaged into marked evidence bags, and signed over to property and evidence personnel.

Now, they were sitting in his office. Chief Russo leaned back in his swivel chair, nearly tipping it over with his bulky, two-hundred-fifty-pound frame. Though Russo's shift was now over, he interlocked his fingers over his chest as if he had all the time in the world.

"Okay, let's go over this again," he said. "You found this bag in the Pardini garage this afternoon?"

Sitting in a hard wooden chair across from him, Anne leaned back too, intent on mirroring his relaxed body language. She'd studied enough about body language at the FBI Academy to carefully monitor her own nonverbal cues. Especially in front of a veteran cop. Especially when she didn't want him to learn too much.

"Yes, it was hidden up near the rafters."

"And from what you said earlier on the phone, the wife was with you, right? I'm surprised she was still living there. It usually doesn't take this long for the Feds to lock down and vacate a house, especially one this high profile."

"The warrant just got executed less than an hour ago." She filled him in on the caravan of SUVs that she'd seen heading toward the house. "But at the time we found the bag, the wife still had possession."

"Okay, back up and start at the beginning. What were you doing snooping around there in the first place?" He said, a snarky smile tugging at the corner of his mouth.

She gave him a weak smile in return. "Renee Pardini lost some pearls, and she thought I could help...it's a long story," she paused, careful not to over-blink. "Anyway, when we found the bag, she looked inside it and saw the old clothes and so on and called it junk. Like I told you. That's when I got her permission to toss it, which meant I could collect it without a warrant. Then I called you."

"And you think the bag contains evidence of what? Pertaining to *what* crime?"

"No idea really, but since it was found on Pardini property, put there by Lino Pardini himself—*hidden* there, to be more precise—it must mean something. My uncle always thought Lino was involved in his wife's murder—"

"Jack and everyone else around here," the chief threw in.

"And since it was possibly hidden around the time of the murder—" Anne cut herself off, but knew it was too late.

"And you know all of this *how*? What makes you think Lino Pardini was even the one who put it up there? And why do you think it was hidden way back—when?—sixteen or so years ago?"

Anne had set her own trap and could see no way out: She had to tell him about the diary. But what the hell—she'd been planning on telling Uncle Jack about it anyway. So, after explaining how she came in possession of the journal through her work, she said, "Lily Danielson's diary ties Lino directly to the bag and the timeline."

The journal, she continued, might also reveal a possible motive for the murder. "Lino's wife was upset about his financial dealings. It's hearsay, of course, since Lily only learned of it through Dinah, but still..."

"I see. If he thought Dinah might go to the authorities about the scam, it could've given him another motive for killing her. In addition to the other

stuff we were already thinking about, like insurance money and a mistress."
Russo paused, collecting his thoughts. "I might call your uncle in on this.
Anything having to do with the Pardini family is right up his alley. He was
one of the officers who found the wife's body and also investigated her
murder. You knew that, right?"

Anne nodded.

"No one's looked at that case in years." He paused for a beat, then leaned
in. "Alright, Anne, I'll call the crime technician and put a rush on this job.
I'm curious to see what we've got here."

"When will the tech be opening the envelope? I'd like to be present."

Chief Russo stood up and walked around his desk toward the door.

"Not sure, but it could be as soon as tomorrow morning. As far as I'm
concerned, you and Jack can be in the evidence room when they examine
the envelope, but that's up to the technician's discretion. As for the clothing,
I'm not ready to have any hairs they find—if they find any, that is—sent
to the lab for DNA yet. They're swamped and cold cases are far from a
priority."

He opened the door for her. "It's a long shot that we'll find anything in
this bag that warrants reopening the murder case, but it can't hurt to look
at it. I'll give you and your uncle a call after I talk to the tech."

# Chapter Sixteen

Dave Silver pulled the bar door open and spotted them at a rear table: two old men deep in conversation. He would have whipped right around and walked back out, but he wasn't fast enough. The wiry one had already looked up.

"Get over here," his dad, Jerry Silver, yelled out in a voice loud enough to carry across the length of the room and over the din, causing patrons to look up from their drinks. Jerry was hunched over a glass of beer, sitting elbow-to-elbow with Marco Pardini.

Dave picked his way through the crush at the front of the bar, pausing now and then to greet a familiar face, until he arrived at his father's table. He was just in time to see Marco stand up and give Jerry a couple of pats on the shoulder.

"Don't forget what I said about the farm truck," Jerry said, looking up from his beer. "It's gotta get sold—that's only right—but it might as well get sold to a Pardini. It might as well go back where it belongs."

Marco nodded and gave Jerry another shoulder pat. "Well, gotta go, Jer," he said, and then turned to Dave. "Dave, good to see you. If you ever get tired of cutting grass, you can always come work for me."

"Later." Dave smiled one of those quick, fast-fading smiles that telegraphed "Hope it's a lot later." He was of the opinion that Marco's rough and jokey, hale-fellow-well-met routine was just a smokescreen, a way to keep people in their place and get them to do what he wanted. Marco's charm had always eluded him.

"Keep me in the loop," Jerry said, motioning for Dave to sit down.

"Will do." Marco drained his beer and gave a little salute. As he was walking out, the crowd gave him a wide berth. Whether this was out of respect because he owned a world class winery and employed a large number of locals—some of whom were in the room—or because they wanted nothing to do with him and his family's financial scandals, was hard to tell. Either way, it didn't seem to faze him.

When Marco reached the door, he called out to Trudy Lee, "Bye, doll." She waved a dirty bar rag at him and went back to her conversation with a regular who was leaning over the bar.

"What was that about?" Dave asked his father. "That 'back to the Pardinis' crap."

"Nothing," Jerry said, giving Marco another wave.

As Marco was stepping outside, he held the door wide open to let a customer walk in. Smiling, Anne McCormack thanked Marco and entered Trudy's bar fifteen minutes late for her appointment.

\* \* \*

Anne scanned the barroom for Dave Silver. She was only a few minutes late—unavoidable, to her mind, because there was no way she'd show up here without first stopping at home to shower and change clothes. Not after the hot and grimy day she'd just had. But in her rush, she forgot to send him a "running late" text. And now, not spotting him in the crowd, she thought maybe he'd given up on her and hightailed it out of there in a snit like some men would have.

But it turns out, no. There he was, standing up and waving to get her attention from across the room. He started making his way toward her, and when halfway there, he signaled toward the bartender and held up two fingers. *Dos Equis*, he mouthed, and the bartender nodded. Anne noticed that he'd shaved off his stubble and was looking the most well-put-together that she'd ever seen him, in dark jeans and a black button-front shirt with rolled-up sleeves.

"Was that Marco Pardini who just held the door for me?" she asked when they came face to face. "I recognize him from newspaper photos."

"Hi to you, too." Dave grinned.

She grinned back. "Hi, sorry. Well, was it?"

"Come and sit down at my dad's table for a minute." He took her lightly by the elbow and led her around several occupied tables to where Jerry was tipping back a beer. "We won't stay long," Dave said under his breath and then raised his voice when they were within earshot of his father. "And yeah, that was Marco. He's a friend of my dad's. Although *why*, I'll never know. Dad, this is—"

"*What* won't you ever know?" asked Jerry, standing up and holding out a chair for Anne. He extended his hand. "I'm Jerry Silver." Wearing a short-sleeved plaid shirt and jeans, he had the same broad shoulders as his son, but on a sinewy frame that was about six inches shorter.

"Anne McCormack," she said, shaking his hand and noting that his grip, like his voice, had a sandy texture.

"Nice to meet you," Jerry said, then turning to Dave, resumed, "Now, I repeat, what were you saying about me?"

"Never mind, Dad."

"Don't *never mind* me. I'm not deaf." Jerry sat back down. "You were saying you don't know why I'm friends with Marco. Well, I'll tell you why—cause we got a lot in common, that's why." He leaned back with his legs stretched out, a relaxed story-telling posture, and held up his hand to count off his fingers. "One," he said, forefinger raised, "we're both great vintners. Best in the county, even the state, probably the entire country." Another finger went up. "Two, we're good family men. Don't roll your eyes, Dave."

"I'm not."

"But mostly," he said, raising a third finger, "it's because of number three: Marco's kid brother, Lino Pardini, didn't just steal *my* money—along with the money of about half the people in this town—"

"You invested with him?" Anne cut in.

Jerry nodded sadly. She noticed that he seemed a little drunk, a little blurry around the edges. He was an everyday kind of man, and if not for his blustery talk, he might go entirely unnoticed in the world. Dave shot her a don't-encourage-him look. She ignored him.

"And Marco did, too?" she persisted.

"No, Marco was too smart. He wanted to keep his finances separate from his brother's. Oh no, it was hella worse than that: Lino stole their *parents'* money. Can you believe that fucking son of a bitch? He went and scammed his own parents!"

"Really?" Anne stared at him with wide eyes and a slackened jaw. She knew from news reports that Lino had also taken money from his own daughter, so she shouldn't have been surprised, but still. "Well, son of a bitch is right." She nodded.

"The parents never told Marco they were investing with Lino. They were the kind of folks who held things close to their chests and did what they wanted. And I guess what they wanted was to support Lino and his bullshit company every time he held out his hand. It wasn't until they died in that car crash that it all came out." Jerry paused for a gulp of beer, then went on, "Marco was going through their financials, trying to sort out their estate so he could divide it up, and that's when he discovered that all their money was tied up with Lino."

"So, Marco was their executor?" Anne asked.

"Yeah, he was the first-born son. That's how Italian families do it. When Marco was trying to sell off investments so he could liquidate the estate, he went to Lino. But Lino wouldn't cash them out. He kept hemming and hawing—and that's when the shit hit the fan."

The server came by with two glasses and a pitcher of beer and set them on the table. Jerry raised a hand. "One more for me, Nick."

When he left, Jerry continued, "Anyway, here's the kicker: Marco found out that Lino not only took millions from them, but he never even paid them one cent in returns. Not even *one* of those ten percent yearly returns went to them in about fifteen years' time. Lino just pocketed their money." Jerry gave out with a low whistle. "Ya gotta admire the balls of that."

"So when was this, this argument between them?"

"Oh man, how would I know? I wasn't privy to that conversation. All I know is that the parents died about a month ago, and Lino died just a week ago today. So it was sometime between all those deaths." Jerry leaned forward. "But boy, was Marco pissed!"

"And you weren't?" Dave asked.

"Sure, I was pissed." Jerry sighed and dropped his eyes to his beer; then he looked back up. "But your mom, now she's the one who really went ballistic. And she blames me. But at least we got some monthly payments over the years, but not at any ten percent return like the press was claiming. More like two percent."

She almost asked him, "Why?" but wasn't interested enough to go down that rabbit hole. Maybe later. Instead, she asked, "Marco told you he was pissed? When was that?"

"The *real* question is why would you invest with Lino in the first place?" Dave threw in.

"Oh, you know, Davy. Damn it. I thought I was doing the smart thing for once in my life." Jerry sucked in his breath.

Anne felt sorry for the man and would have dropped the subject, but for the fact that she wanted her question answered. If Lino's death was no accident—if it was a murder instead, an idea that her uncle kept bandying about—then who better to commit the crime than someone furious about the Ponzi scheme? And that hypothetical someone had obviously known about the fraud before it was revealed to the public.

"When did you find out?"

Jerry clamped his lips together, considering the question. Finally, he said, "After Lino died. When it was all over the newspapers. No, actually, us investors found out the night before the news came out. The lawyers held a meeting to break it to us. Reporters were at the meeting."

"But it wasn't news to Marco. He'd known for a while, obviously. Did he tell you or anyone? Did he report it to the police or SEC?" Anne asked. She knew better than to do this, to pile on the questions. Ask one question at a time; that was her FBI training. Because otherwise, the person could pick and choose which question to answer—and which to ignore. And when that happened, it was impossible to parse out which question was being answered in which way. A tangled mess.

"Huh? Well, aren't you an inquisitive little lady? Are you a reporter or a cop or something?" Jerry looked at her sideways and shook his head.

"As a matter of fact—" Dave started to say more but stopped when Anne placed a death grip on his arm.

"I work in estate services. But my uncle is a cop. Retired, actually," she said, deflecting his question. "Jack McCormack."

"I've heard of him. I think he went to a rival high school. Played football?"

"Not sure." By now, her line of questioning was thoroughly derailed, and it was her own fault. "So, did Marco report—" she started up again, but was interrupted by the arrival of their server, Nick, who set Jerry's beer on the table.

"Can I get you two another?" he asked Anne and Dave, apparently not noticing that their pitcher was still half full. Anne shook her head and took a sip of her beer, wishing it were white wine. *Doesn't anyone in this place drink anything but beer?* She looked around and finally spotted a cocktail, a blue daiquiri with a slice of lime, and it was in front of a redneck biker type. *You never know*, she thought.

"Not yet, thanks," Dave said.

"But maybe we could order some dinner?" Anne looked inquiring at Dave. It was seven-thirty already. Dave nodded.

"I called Trudy earlier…" Dave said to Nick. The waiter assured him that Trudy had ducked upstairs to her apartment and was working on it.

"Thanks for the invite." Jerry winked at Anne. "But I can't stay for dinner."

"Oh, I'm sorry. Why don't you join us?" Anne said.

"Actually, Anne and I have some business to discuss," Dave threw in.

"Nah, don't worry. I was just joking. I gotta get home," he said, but showed no signs of moving. "But your dinner's on me tonight because there's finally something good to celebrate."

"What's that?" Dave asked.

Jerry smirked. "The grieving Pardini widow's worldly possessions have been taken over by the Feds—"

"How did you hear about that?" Anne blurted out.

"Marco just told me. It means we can get some of our money back. They're going to be auctioning off all those cars and fox furs and Rolex watches. And I, for one, can't wait to see that day." He nodded toward Dave and then downed the last of his beer. "Your mom and I will be there with bells on."

"Renee and her son will be left penniless," Anne said, remembering her last glimpse of Renee that afternoon: standing alone in the driveway, waving Anne off, mere minutes away from losing everything. If their search for Lino's envelopes hadn't been such an utter, complete, and dismal failure, Renee would've at least had some cash to start her life over with.

Jerry challenged her sympathy with a scoff. "Cry me a river. She's lucky if she doesn't end up in jail for fraud or tax evasion or something. Don't tell me she wasn't involved," he said with narrowed eyes. Then his face lit up, and he chuckled. "I know. Maybe she can start one of those GoFundMe pages. Or better yet, start looking around for another meal ticket. She's still good-looking enough, still got it going on, from what I've heard."

The three looked up as Nick arrived at the table and placed a basket of French bread, napkins, and silverware in front of Anne and Dave. "I'll be right back with your salads and entrées," he said and left.

"Well, when your food gets here, you better eat fast 'cause there's no telling when Trudy will close down the joint," Jerry said.

Dave tore off a piece of bread and turned to Anne. "He's not kidding. Any minute now, Trudy could signal for the bartender to go over to the jukebox. Then you'll hear some loud groaning because everyone here knows what's coming next—"

"And pretty soon, they'll just give up and leave," Jerry said.

"What are you talking about?" Anne's eyes went from one man to the other.

It all started about fifteen years ago, Jerry explained to Anne, when Trudy's boyfriend, a heavily tattooed, ex-con body builder who wasn't good enough for her, ran off with her best friend. (*Trudy was a hot mess*, he said). Several times a week after that for the next year or so, Trudy would sit in a corner of the bar alone, crying her eyes out, drinking straight bourbon. Playing the same sad love song on the jukebox over and over again.

"Nothing drives out customers faster than seeing a woman drinking and crying," Jerry said. "It's been at least ten years since Trudy's last crying jag, but we all live in fear. We're like Pavlov's dogs on high alert. She pulls it on us a couple of times a week." He laughed.

"Did I hear my name?" They looked up. Trudy Lee was standing over the table.

"Hey, Trudy, sit down," Jerry patted the seat of the chair between him and Dave.

"Can't, it's too busy. And this is a Monday night, for crying out loud. Don't these people have homes to go to? I just came over to say hi," she said, hands on her hips.

"We were just talking about how no one can clear a bar faster than you."

She cracked a smile. "I have my technique down pretty good, don't I?" She turned toward Anne. "The original song was "When I Fell For You.""

"Great song, but Jesus, twenty times in a row?"

"I got sick of it finally, so I changed to "Crying" by Roy Orbison."

"Big mistake." Jerry barked out a laugh. "Who doesn't dig Roy Orbison? No one would leave. They were all waiting for him to hit the high note."

"Scoot over, honey," Trudy said to Dave, sitting between the two men. It was a tight fit, so Dave made room by moving his chair closer to Anne's. "Then, thankfully, my mom reminded me of a 1950s song called "Cry" by Johnny Ray. Pay dirt! He had a real sob in his voice."

"I'm getting depressed just thinking about it." Jerry chuckled.

"I'm Trudy, by the way," she said to Anne, "since neither of these two guys is polite enough to introduce us. You look familiar."

"Anne McCormack. Dave and I were here last Friday."

"Oh, my God, what a night—turned over tables and everything!" Trudy laughed. "I'm going to clean up behind the bar now cause I think it's going to be an early evening." With that, she gave the table a hard smack and pushed herself up out of the chair.

"You're getting old, Trudy," Jerry said. "It's not even nine o'clock, for chrissakes."

"I'll wait until you kids finish your dinner. I cooked you a special dish tonight, and it will be out in a minute. Enjoy," she said and headed back to the bar.

Jerry rose to his feet and yawned. "I'm really leaving this time. You two young people have your own things to talk about."

"Nice meeting you," Anne said.

Dave stood and hugged his dad. "Say hi to Mom."

\* \* \*

"Let's move to a quieter table so we can talk," Dave said, picking his knapsack up off the ground, looking around.

"How about in there?" Anne nodded toward the adjacent room, where a pool table took up most of the space. For once, no one was playing, and the room was empty except for a couple who were arguing quietly in the corner. Anne and Dave gathered up their drinks, cutlery, and breadbasket and claimed a booth, two down from the bickering pair.

"Well, now you've met my dad. He was on his good behavior tonight," Dave said while they were settling into the booth.

"He seems like a real character."

"Oh, he's a character alright. Ask anyone. And he's not the easiest guy to work for. Someday, I'll have to tell you the story about when he had an ex-con working for him."

"Oh, do tell. And *now*, not someday like all your other stories."

"Okay, okay." Dave leaned back, lacing his fingers across his chest. *This might be a long one,* she thought, buttering a piece of bread. "So, he hires this ex-con and works him to death… 'prune this, haul that, clean up that mess.' Basically, the guy was doing the job I'd been doing all my life until I wised up and hauled ass. Anyway, the ex-con leaves work one day and goes straight to the police station and turns himself in for parole violation."

Anne laughed. "Just to get out of working for your dad?"

"Yeah." Dave nodded, laughing. "And it wasn't the dumbest move I've ever heard of."

"Well, your dad can't be all bad. I mean, he's picking up our dinner tab, isn't he?"

"Don't count on it." Dave reached into his knapsack on the cushioned seat and pulled out his drawing tablet and a manila folder.

"Well, you know him better than I do." Anne leaned back with a bemused expression. "But if that's the case, I'm paying my share—"

Dave waved her offer away. "Business expense." He opened a folder on the table and pulled out two pieces of paper. On one was a cost estimate for time and materials; on the other was a list of the drought-tolerant plants he proposed.

"So, do you want to see my artistic vision for your yard first or talk money?"

Anne opted for the vision. For the next ten minutes, they discussed the advantages of one flowering plant over another; the cost differences between redwood bark ground covering, black mulch, and black lava rock; the aesthetics of varying heights and colors (*Can't have too much lavender*, Anne said); and the positioning and number of boulders.

Anne was signing off on the plan and budget with only a few minor changes and vetoes when Nick came to their table holding a bottle of cabernet sauvignon by Pardini Wineries and two wine glasses. "The wine's on the house," Nick said, pouring liberally. They thanked him, and when he left, Anne raised her glass and offered a toast. "To my yard. I love the plan."

"To your yard. I'm glad you like it," Dave said, looking pleased. They clinked glasses. "And here's to us working together." They touched their glasses together again. He leaned back in his chair and took a long sip of wine. "Say what you will about the Pardinis, but they make a good wine."

"They do, indeed," said Nick, who had suddenly reappeared at their table with two steaming plates of chicken cacciatore with pasta. Behind him, a busboy carried a pair of Caesar salads and set them down. Over at the corner booth, the couple waved to Nick and pointed vigorously to Anne's and Dave's food. Nick called out, "Sorry, the kitchen's closed."

Dave picked up his fork and began twirling his pasta onto a spoon, a holdover from his days growing up around old Italians. Anne used the arguably more proper, fork-only method, but lost the high ground by committing a major faux pas: She cut her pasta with a knife and fork beforehand. Dave stopped eating to stare. His mouth was pursed in disbelief as if he'd never seen such appalling table manners. And he'd lived in a hippie commune.

"I'm starving," she said, twirling the short strands. "Chloe ate all the dim sum you gave us for lunch—thank you for that, by the way. You'd have thought she'd be too upset to eat."

"What was going on with her, anyway?" He reached for more grated Parmesan cheese.

"Oh, poor kid. It's her first heartbreak. She saw her boyfriend of two weeks in the mall holding hands with another girl. And not just any girl. Pam O'Brien, her biggest archrival in the world. I told Chloe that I know it's hard, but this wouldn't be the last time she gets her heart broken, which just made her cry harder. Men come and go—"

"You said that? Pretty cynical."

"And I told her that everyone, sooner or later, experiences jealousy and disappointment. Being left by someone is just a part of life."

"That's some hard truth."

"I know. Probably a little harsh, but she might as well hear it now and learn how to handle it. Then, I advised her to stop with the revenge fantasies. I said that while it's fun to think about putting walnuts into Pam's sandwiches cause she's deathly allergic, and doing things like that—"

"Man, she's got to think bigger." Dave grinned.

"Oh, she was thinking bigger, alright. Walnuts were the least of it. I had to talk her down from fake Snapchat posts, hexes, blackmail. Chloe's got a crazy imagination. Anyway, I told her that revenge is best served cold—"

"I never understood that old saying," Dave jumped in, putting his fork down. "What does it even mean? My feeling is that revenge is best served hot when you're good and mad. Otherwise, what's the point?"

"Maybe it means that when it's served hot, there's instant backlash from the person you're trying to get revenge on. And it's better to wait until things have cooled down when they aren't expecting it, and then strike. They won't know what hit them."

Dave laughed. "A diabolical mind."

"Thank you."

"Actually, that's what my ex-wife did. During our rare peaceful periods when we were getting along, she would try to poison me by putting Visine eye drops in my coffee."

Anne burst out laughing. "How'd you find out?"

"I'd start getting sick, vomiting. And there were Visine bottles all over the house. When we finally got divorced, she told me she'd been trying to poison me for years."

Anne's head rolled back in laughter.

"You're the first woman I've ever told that story to who's laughed. It usually gets me a fair amount of sympathy," he said, stifling a smile.

"Sympathy? Ha! It just makes me wonder what you did to deserve it," she said, still chuckling. "Anyway, back to Chloe. I told her to hold her fire. My last piece of advice was for her to ask herself: 'What would Grandma say?' Chloe and her grandmother Claire were very close. That settled her down a bit, and she said, 'Grandma would tell me to hold my head high and act like a lady.'"

Setting her napkin down, she added, "So that's how I left it. Her head was held high when I dropped her off at her house. And tonight, when I got back home after some meetings, her mom's car was gone so they must have driven it home. I haven't heard any more from her."

"Man, glad I'm not her age. All those broken teen dreams," he said, leaning back. "Such a tragic scene."

Anne, taking a sip of wine, fixed her gaze on him. "Chloe mentioned that you tried to fix her up with your stepson," she said with a raised brow.

"Guess I left out a few pieces of my bio last time we talked. So, Nathan is the sixteen-year-old son of my ex-wife. Nice kid, but got some troubles."

Anne leaned in, waiting for more, but he seemed to think the subject was exhausted. "And…" she prompted.

"He lives with her, three towns over. She just got out of rehab again." He set his napkin down, his eyes roaming the room as if casting about for a new subject. All he came up with was, "We can start digging up your lawn next Monday."

"Okay."

Nick came back to pour more wine, but they begged off, and he dropped their check on the corner of the table. "See, what'd I tell you? This didn't go on my old man's tab." Dave dropped cash into the leather check folder. "Ready?"

As they walked toward the door, they waved farewell to Trudy. She waved back from behind the bar and then reached for a bottle of Johnnie Walker Black Label and nodded to Derrick. The bartender slapped down his damp bar rag and headed toward the jukebox. Loud groans could be heard all the way out into the street.

# Chapter Seventeen

The next morning, Anne took the elevator down from her third-story office. She crossed the open-air courtyard to where her uncle was waiting for her, sitting on an ironwork bench, hunched over in front of the sculptured metal water fountain.

She sat down next to him without saying a word. Other than a quick glance her way, Jack didn't acknowledge Anne's presence either. He was too busy staring into the sheets of cascading water, appearing to be mesmerized by the sight and sound of the gurgling water. She touched him on the arm.

"Hi there," she said. "You know, we could have met upstairs in my office."

"I like it out here," Jack said quietly. The soft light from the morning sun was flooding into the garden like misty sprays of pale liquid gold. A slight, cool breeze ruffled what was left of the leaves on the Japanese maple tree to the left of the fountain.

"This is quite a place, Annie. Good for you."

"Well, it's more than I wanted to spend," she said, thinking that was something of an understatement. Back when she signed the six-month lease, part of her rationale was that the splendor of the building would lend her gravitas; it would telegraph success to any prospective clients, broadcasting loud and clear: "Of course, I know what I'm doing. Can't you see that from the gleam of the lobby's marble tile floors?" But the truth was that during these last two months, she rarely brought clients up here. Meetings with clients were mostly held at the family homes where the work was to be done. And unless a few more extremely profitable clients came her way, she might have to leave after the lease expired.

*But, oh my God, I do love it here*, she thought, looking around at the surrounding walls of glass that ran up the ultra-modern, fifty feet high facade. She could see their reflection on a side window—her uncle, slumped over with his arms resting on his knees; and her, sitting ramrod straight with her bulky purse wedged between her feet.

"Everything's more than we want to spend," he said.

She looked over at him. She'd known her uncle since Day One of her life and had seen him in all manner of moods—happy, gleeful, sad, boastful, angry, giddy, bossy, bombastic, affectionate, sarcastic. But this was a new one. Today, his face sagged with a sadness she'd never seen before. She hated that her advice to her aunt contributed to his pain. *Damn Lino.* That thought seemed to be running on a continuous loop in her brain these days.

He glanced over at her and straightened up. "I was surprised to get the call from the Chief this morning when he asked me to join you and the tech in the evidence room. He mentioned the name Pardini, and that always gets my attention. The Chief seemed to think that I already knew what this was all about. I faked it and just said, 'Great. I'll be there.' But as you *well* know," he said, giving Anne a pointed look, "I know nothing about this trash bag. So, fill me in, Anne. What's this about, and where did you get it?"

"I found it at the Pardini house—"

"Why were you at the Pardini house again? Looking for more fire hazard violations for Chloe's contest?" He gave her a wry smile.

Anne hesitated. She had promised Renee that she wouldn't tell anyone about the money Lino had hidden away. But circumstances had changed; there was no money, and the deal was off. So why *not* tell him about it? He'd ask too many questions; that's why, she thought. He would demand to know why she hadn't gone to the police, or, at the very least, gone to him about it.

And, of course, she was right. When Anne was finished relaying the basic story, he started picking it apart.

"So you two were planning to split the money—money that should have gone to the court receiver so he could disperse it to its lawful owners, namely us investors, and not say a word to anyone. Is that right?"

"That's about it," she said, hoping her emphatic tone would derail the conversation. Because really, what more could she say? That she wanted her share of the money to go directly to her uncle and aunt and maybe a few others of her own choosing and not be spread out among some faceless group of anonymous strangers? Or that she struck the deal because she felt sorry for Renee and didn't want her to come away empty-handed? Or that she had been so wrapped up in the adventure of the money chase that it hadn't occurred to her that anything was seriously wrong, legally or otherwise, with this plan?

Well, it *hadn't* occurred to her. Not until this moment, face to face with her uncle.

"But it doesn't matter now." Anne looked away, but felt his eyes on her. "The money wasn't found and calling the Feds wouldn't have made any difference. They wouldn't have been any more successful in finding it than we were."

"You don't know that," he said, his palms raised in exasperation. "And I don't think you're being straight about this."

"Well, like I said, it's all over now." She finally met his gaze. "The money is lost forever, and no one will ever know. It's as if it didn't exist. And something good came of all this: the trash bag. And what's inside it could lead to reopening the murder case of Dinah Pardini," she said, hoping Jack's fascination with that old cold case might divert his attention off of her. "Also, did I tell you? The diary mentioned how Dinah was not happy about Lino's financial dealings, which could have caused arguments. And that could have given him a motive for murdering her. Also, it turns out that Kay might have been Lino's lover at the time of Dinah's death. That gave her a motive to kill Dinah, and if she didn't do it herself, she had the money to hire someone. Motive and opportunity..."

But Jack wasn't biting. "The lost money should be reported."

"There's no point. That would just cause unnecessary problems."

"Well, you're right about that," he said, slowly shaking his head. "If this gets out, you're pretty much screwed. No more police work, and that's the least of it. This was nothing short of an attempted felony. Conspiring to—"

"Well, it *won't* get out. Our little treasure hunt was a bust. It's over. No harm, no foul."

He shook his head. "Don't be so sure it's over. Money has a way of attracting attention. And let's just say that you and Renee, through some miracle, *do* somehow still find the money. There's no stopping her from telling a friend, or admitting it to someone who notices that she's not so poor after all and confronts her. But even if she kept it a secret, sooner or later, someone would figure out where it was coming from. All they'd have to do is pull a single thread, and it all comes unraveled."

Her face reddened, and she averted her eyes again.

"How did you justify this?" he asked. "Finders keepers?"

"I was going to give my share to the investors. I would have found a way to do it carefully."

He just stared at her, unblinking. "Annie, maybe your intentions were good, and knowing you, I don't doubt that, but the money came from Lino, so that means it was stolen money, tainted. Nothing good could come from it. Promise me, if you ever find...look at me."

She raised her head.

"If for any reason you find out where it is, promise you'll report it to the authorities."

Anne leaned over and hugged her uncle, but said nothing. She knew he was right; Jack was always right. He was known as a by-the-book veteran cop who never in his entire thirty years on the police force would have dreamed of skirting the law, at least not in any serious, code-violating way. "The law is a complicated and holy thing," he would often say. And now he was reading her the riot act, laying down that law he loved so much. Laying it down hard.

The trouble was she wasn't sure how she would act if the situation came up again.

"Let's continue this conversation in the car," she said with a long sigh. "They're expecting us at ten."

\* \* \*

To get to the police evidence/property facility, they headed up Highway 101 in Jack's car to the downtown exit and then took surface streets to the police station on Sonoma Avenue. By the time they pulled into the parking lot, the conversation in the car had petered out and left Anne feeling beaten up, defensive, chastised, and more than a little eager to get out of the car.

She slipped her purse strap over her shoulder and pushed the car door open before Jack had even killed the engine. They walked in silence to the property room entrance.

The evidence/property manager met them at the service counter and escorted them to the evidence deposit room, a spare, windowless space with worktables and a pass-through evidence locker built into the wall. This double-sided locker—one side in the deposit room where they stood and the other in the evidence storage room—allowed "bagged and tagged" evidence to be deposited from one side and retrieved from the other.

Somewhere inside that metal wall were the contents of the trash bag that lab technician Carol Simmer would be inspecting this morning in their presence.

"Hi Jack, haven't seen you for a few years." Carol, a smiling, open-faced Black woman in her mid-forties, breezed into the room. She wore red-framed glasses and a white lab coat with blue latex gloves folded over a front pocket. She had the glow of someone entirely happy with her choice of career.

"Hi Carol, thanks for letting us join you. This is my niece, Anne McCormack. She's helping out on special assignment." The two women greeted each other, and then Carol said, as she headed back out the side door, "I have to unlock the locker from the storage room side. You don't need to see the sweatshirt or knit cap, do you?"

"Wouldn't hurt," Jack said.

"Okay, I'll be right back with the goodies," Carol said, putting her gloves on. Anne and her uncle stood silently, staring at the locker until Carol returned a minute later pushing an aluminum utility cart with the packaged contents of the trash bag.

"Okay, let's see what we've got here." Carol set the brown lunch sack and bags of clothing onto the work table. Then, she reached into the sack and withdrew the Ziplock plastic bag containing the flip phone and white business-size envelope with *Find—D* scrawled on the front side.

"'Find—D.' That mean anything to you, Jack? Anne?" Carol asked, holding the envelope up by its edges.

"Possibly." Jack leaned across the table for a better look. Carol slit open the top of the envelope, leaving the full flap area undisturbed for saliva extraction if DNA testing was ever requested.

"The big reveal, as they say on TV." Carol lifted the contents out of the envelope: a nondescript, one-page, one-sided letter. It appeared to have been typed up on a computer and printed out on standard 8.5" x 11" white copy paper. She laid the slightly crumpled letter on the table and rotated it 180 degrees toward Jack and Anne.

Jack lifted his reading glasses off his shirt collar and slipped them on. Standing over the table with his hands clasped behind his back, he started reading the note out loud:

> Do not deviate from this script or you won't get the rest of the money. Don't let them keep you on the phone. Time yourself. Two minutes!

Jack looked up. "Today there's no lag time to trace a call, of course. It's practically instantaneous." The two women nodded, and he went back to reading:

> DS: "I found a big mound of dirt by the side of a road. It's covering up a dead body. There's a handbag there, too. Go to the north edge of town, take the Silverado exit west to Old Corral Road, continue driving until the pavement stops. Once it turns into a dirt road, drive another 600 feet. Stop at three feet from the iron gate leading to someone's private property. The body is on the left side of the road in the vegetation."
> Then HANG UP!

IMPORTANT! When you're done, put THIS phone and THIS note back in THIS bag and leave it in the mailbox where you picked it all up on Reibi Road by 5:30 pm. Then call me from a pay phone. Remember, do everything exactly as written, or you won't get the other $250! If you ever tell the cops you made this call, or try to point the finger at **anyone**, trust me, you and your father will pay.

Jack was rubbing his chin. "This was definitely the phone call we got sixteen years ago when we found Dinah Pardini's body. Back then, the caller threw in stuff like 'hey, man, stop talking' and he told us to hurry before some animals got to the body—which made no sense at all because the body wasn't much more than a skeleton. But other than that, as far as I remember, it's almost word for word."

"So 'find' on the front of the envelope means find the body, right?" Carol asked.

"Yes, find D—as in "find Dinah Pardini's body," Anne said.

"Or, the D could refer to the caller, DS. As in, 'find it, D,'" Jack said.

*DS? Not Dave Silver, surely.* Feeling a bit blindsided, Anne had to turn away to catch her breath. Thinking it over, she quickly brushed away any idea of Dave's involvement. There were a million people with the initials "DS" in the world. Millions. But as she mulled it over a bit more, maybe it wasn't so far-fetched. What did she really know about Dave Silver anyway, other than he knew a lot about decorative plants and old songs and looked good in a leather bomber jacket? Hell, what did anyone really know about anyone else?

"It wouldn't be hard to get the fingerprints off the letter and the flip phone to identify the caller," Jack continued, "who I'm betting has those initials."

"We could get the results back within days," Carol said.

"Wonder why Lino Pardini—it's got to be Lino who wrote this, right?" Anne asked.

Jack nodded.

"—Why would Lino want all of this stuff saved? The phone, this script?"

137

"Blackmail, I'm guessing. Some kind of insurance, maybe?" Jack said. "He needed to have leverage over the guy, this DS. Lino couldn't risk having him go to the police with a tip to collect the reward, which was about $50,000—nothing to sneeze at. Also, Lino couldn't take the chance of this guy having a sudden fit of conscience or having him going around saying anything that could lead back to him. Who knows? But bottom line, he needed the guy to keep his mouth shut."

"So you're saying that after the body was found, Lino would have threatened the caller. Warned him to keep quiet because he had the caller's fingerprints on the phone and the note. And that the fingerprints would tie the caller to the murder," Anne said.

"You can bet that Lino's fingerprints aren't on anything that's here in front of us. Just fingerprints belonging to DS."

"But Lino could never have actually carried out that threat without sinking himself, too. The caller must have known it was a bluff."

"But maybe the caller couldn't be sure. If Pardini hired this guy to kill his wife and then called him a year later to go back and dig up the body, move it, and report it, they were inextricably tied to each other." Jack said. "They were probably threatening each other right and left with exposure. And maybe Lino had something else on the guy. He mentioned a father...."

"Okay, but why would Lino risk keeping the bag on his property?"

Carol held up her gloved hand. "Wait a second. I'm remembering this case now. Wasn't Lino Pardini a strong suspect in the disappearance and murder? Wasn't his property inspected back then? And wouldn't this bag have been found back then?"

"We never got that far," Jack replied. "During the first year, this was just a disappearance. There was no real case against him, so no warrant to search was issued. The bag was probably safely hidden in his garage all during that year. If there even was a bag then."

"Oh, there was a bag, alright. Though obviously not full of these items. Lino used that hiding spot in the garage even *before* Dinah was murdered." Anne said, turning to Carol. "Dinah saw Lino hiding stuff there and told her friend Lily Danielson. That's how we found the trash bag in the first place. It must have been his go-to place to keep things from his wife first, then the cops."

"After the body was found, again, no search," he said. "There wasn't anything new to go on. Just some rumblings from the dead woman's friends about him having an affair. One woman said the wife confided that there was something fishy about Lino's business dealings, so maybe that's why he wanted to shut his wife up. Now, *that* woman we should have listened to!"

"Lily Danielson, no doubt. She was no fan of Lino's," Anne said.

"Anyway, Lino hired the caller sixteen years ago. This evidence," he said, gesturing to the items on the table, "has probably been hanging up there from a rafter tie ever since."

"But back to my original question: why did Lino keep the bag hanging in his garage? Why not bury it or something?" Anne asked. "It could have been found any time during all these years. It would only incriminate him in his wife's murder."

"Maybe Lino was so sure he wouldn't get caught that he took the risk," he said. "God knows the guy was a big taker of risks. He was cocky, and like you said, it wasn't easy to spot in the garage. He didn't think anyone would ever find it. Or maybe he just forgot about it."

Anne took a photo of the letter and looked up to see Carol glancing at the wall clock. "Sorry, we'll get out of your hair soon," Anne said to Carol.

"No, take as long as you need," Carol assured them. "I'm not going anywhere until you're done reviewing the evidence and it's safely back under lock and key." As casual and friendly as her demeanor was, Carol's eyes never left the items on the table. There would be no chain of custody issues while she was in charge.

"One last thing, Carol," Jack said, "could we get some tests on these clothing items? There might be hair follicles."

"Sorry, Jack. The Chief already put DNA testing for them on the back burner."

"I'm not sure there's much point to it anyway, Uncle Jack. What does it matter whose hair is on those clothes? There's no proof they're tied to the murder, or even tied to finding the body. Hell, even if DS's hair is all over them, a smart lawyer could say, 'So what?' Unless there's some kind of proof he was wearing them during a crime—like a security camera photo or something—they have no direct bearing on the case."

"Good point," Jack said. "Okay, only the fingerprints for now. Once we have a match, we'll have a friendly talk with this DS person—if he's still alive—and see about getting this murder case reopened. We can't get Lino, but we can still get his accomplice."

Anne frowned, lost in thought, while Carol beamed. "See, this is why I love my work!" the lab tech said. "Blackmail, threats, murder! Dead bodies! Know what my sister does for a living? She works the cash register at estate sales here in town. Can you imagine doing that for hours on end? My eyes glaze over just thinking about it."

"Well, it takes all kinds," Anne said.

* * *

Jack begged off their usual Tuesday lunch at Nell's Diner, saying, "I just want to go home and take a nap." Anne shot off a text to Brittany to say she was on her way back to the office.

It was closing in on noon by the time Jack dropped Anne off.

Brittany was at her desk, picking at her grande taco salad with a plastic fork and staring at her cell phone. Next to the salad was a small paper bowl filled with tortilla chips, their salty crispness beckoning to Anne, who hadn't eaten since her six-a.m. bowl of cereal.

"Here, have some," Brittany said without looking up, pushing the chips toward Anne. "I knew you'd be hungry, so I picked up some quesadillas for you, too. They're in the fridge. Heat them up in the microwave under a slightly damp paper towel for thirty seconds and not one second longer."

"Brittany, you're getting a big fat raise," Anne said with a grateful sigh. She started off toward the kitchenette, then did a fishhook turn back to her assistant's desk. "That is, when and if we get some more new clients."

"Not today, not yet anyway. But there is some good news: The LA auction house, where you shipped that hideous red screen to be auctioned off for the Danielson estate, just called. They looked it over and think they'll get twice what we expected—can you believe that?" The carved and inlaid mahogany Chinese folding screen, apparently too ornate for the tastes of a twenty-something, was a rare 19th-century treasure. But even so, the estimated auction price was a welcome shock: Anne's sales commission would pay for next month's rent and give her some breathing room.

"Fingers crossed." Anne grabbed her quesadillas from the mini refrigerator and slid them into the microwave, following Brittany's heating directions to the letter. Then she brought her lunch to her desk in the rear office and turned on her computer.

She decided that before pulling together a new client proposal for a family in Healdsburg, she would spend her lunch hour doing what she should have done days ago: a deeper background check on Dave Silver.

She logged onto InstaPeepCheck, an online background-checking service. She paid a monthly fee for the site's access to criminal records, contact information, location, media profiles, and financial records and assets. Though many steps above Googling a name, it was a poor substitute for the high-security databases available to law enforcement. But those databases weren't available to her unless she was working a police case and had prior authorization. Unauthorized use is what landed her in trouble with the FBI and prompted her to resign, and she wasn't going down that rutted road again.

Anne typed in David Silver's name and for the next ten minutes scoured the site. She found no surprises in his basic information: age (48), assets (owner of a mobile home in northwest Santa Rosa), business license (Silver Landscaping) or related people (most with the last name of Silver). His full name was David Sterling Silver. The middle name was apparently his parents' idea of a joke.

Later, when she had time, she would look up his address on Zillow, an online real estate marketing site, and check out photos of the mobile home. She'd also check out a report on a woman named Shannon Turner Silver, one of Dave's personal contacts. *Maybe his ex-wife?*

But first, she needed to delve into the real reason for the search: Dave's criminal background during his self-described "lost years." It turned out he had a lengthy rap sheet dating back to when he was nineteen years old. There were probably earlier offenses, she knew, but juvenile crimes were generally held as confidential except for legal guardians, his attorney, and law enforcement agencies. During his twenties, records from the California Department of Corrections and Rehabilitation showed he was in and out of custody for one drug-related theft or offense after another—cocaine and heroin possession, drug trafficking, multiple burglaries, weapons possession, and a drug DUI. When he was thirty, after repeatedly missing court-ordered drug tests, he was sentenced to a three-year prison stint, but ended up serving only a year at a substance abuse treatment facility and state prison. He got out in 2004, used drugs again, was arrested again, and went back to jail for another year. And so on.

Dave Silver was thirty-four years old when he was finally released from custody for the last time. That was fourteen years ago. Since then, not even a traffic ticket.

*Well, that was depressing,* Anne thought, turning away from her computer. *Lost years, indeed.* She wandered over to the far window overlooking the city park and a playground. Gazing down, she watched as red and gold autumn leaves were whipped to the ground by a sudden gust of wind. Then she caught sight of something she very much needed to see: two young boys jumping up and down on piles of dry leaves. They kicked a few piles onto the walkway just for the fun of making a mess. They were the very picture of joy and innocence.

Dave had been that kind of kid, she thought. "Full of beans," as her father would have said. She went back to the computer and Googled the photo of him winning the Junior Division of the Sonoma County Grapevine Pruning Contest. And there he was, same photo as before: the "in it to win it" kid, skinny as a blade of grass, dark hair poking out of his backwards baseball cap.

*What's left of you, Dave? Is that young boy still in there somewhere?* she wondered, looking at the boy with the wide grin and mouthful of braces. During all those lost and drugged-out years, what had been the toll, the damage, the mark on the soul? *Were parts of you left behind?* And what had he been capable of doing just to survive?

She went over to the window again and looked down at the kids. This time, they were taking turns rolling down a small embankment and landing in clumps of muddy leaves at the bottom. She watched them climb back up the knoll and do it all over again.

Her phone went off, and she crossed to her desk to check the screen: it was Dave Silver. She muted the phone and stared at it while it went to voicemail.

# Chapter Eighteen

"I don't know why Renee didn't just shut down her Facebook page. *Someone* should have shut it down. It's obscene." Krista Hageman handed her phone to Anne and pointed to the screen. "Here's Renee's last post, the one where she asked for people to respect her family's privacy. Big mistake."

Though Anne did have a Facebook page, she wasn't one of Renee's Facebook friends like Krista was, so this was the first time she was seeing these posts.

"Now, scroll down and read her so-called friends' messages. It's like nothing you've ever seen," Krista said, getting up from her seat on the beige sectional couch in her family room. "I'm going to check on dinner." She headed for the adjacent kitchen. "Watch Leo for me."

Hearing his name, Leo flashed a mischievous grin and scrambled off the couch, clearly emboldened by being out of his mother's sight and supervision. When his almost-two-year-old legs touched the ground, he was off, toddling his way to the coffee table where the TV remote control and two half-empty wine glasses were calling to him.

"Hold on, little buster," Anne said, getting to her feet and scooping him up. Balancing him on her left hip, she reached down and grabbed a chewed-up copy of "Llama Lama Red Pajama" off the floor. She sat back down on the couch with Leo on her lap. "Read this while I do some grown-up reading," she told him. Instead, the toddler made a grab for her phone, but she held it away with her left arm. A frustrated Leo squirmed around, but then finally quieted down and started turning—and sometimes ripping—the pages of his favorite book. Anne lifted him off her lap and plopped him down next to her. With Leo preoccupied, she could finally focus on Renee's Facebook page.

She'd read nasty letters in the editorial section of the newspaper, heard righteous rants from talk show commentators, and listened to victims of Pardini's financial scams denounce Lino as the devil, but Renee's post asking for privacy apparently struck a nerve with people, and many of these hundred or so posters were taking rabid hate to a whole new level. It seems their tolerance for the problems of the formerly rich, who had stripped them of their own riches, was at minus zero:

"Are you fucking kidding me?! After your husband destroyed our family?"

"Privacy? You're lucky someone isn't lurking behind every bush. Maybe they are, lol. Look out, bitch."

"We're supposed to feel sorry for YOU?"

But most of the posts were just painfully sad:

"My dad survived the Holocaust, but he didn't survive this."

"Instead of a comfortable retirement, we're now taking renters into our home."

"We took $500k out of our home on a reverse mortgage to invest with him. Maybe that doesn't sound like a lot to you, but it was all we had."

"When my husband, who lost his leg in the Korean War, learned that he lost his life savings because of your husband, he shot himself in the head. Happy now?"

Anne let out a sigh and looked up as Krista came back into the room.

"Dinner's in ten minutes," Krista said, plopping down next to Anne on the couch. Leo, sitting on Anne's other side, tossed his book onto the floor and crawled over Anne's lap to reach his mother's.

"Pretty devastating, aren't they?" Anne said, gesturing toward the phone screen.

"I don't know if Renee has even seen them. At any rate, she hasn't responded to any of this, so probably not,"

"I think you're right. I tried calling her but I just got a message saying 'this line is no longer in service...blah, blah, blah.' Which means her cell phone's not working, and that means she's not seeing Facebook posts on it. And she probably can't see them on her computer either, which—I'd bet anything—has been seized and will be auctioned off along with the rest of her belongings."

"Speaking of auctions," Krista said, ruffling Leo's curly dark hair, "word has it that Mission Farm Winery & Vineyards volunteered their grand banquet room and grounds, which are incredibly spectacular and overlook the vineyards, for the Pardini auction proceedings."

"Are you sure? U.S. Marshals are in charge of these kinds of property seizure auctions, and they always hire Rose Auction House to handle them. Those events are always dull and bare bones and usually held in drafty old community halls."

"Not this time! The owners of Mission Farm Winery pitched the idea to the Feds by telling them that if they're going to auction items in the Sonoma County Wine Country and want it to be a successful event, they need to step it up. Provide a little glitz. You know, take a page from the local charities and hire GiveBig Auctions here in Santa Rosa. That's the only way to bring in the big bidders."

"Mission Farm Winery? They're Pardini Winery's biggest local competitors."

"Kind of nasty, isn't it?" Krista said. "There's a lot of bad blood between the two wineries, and I guess the owners of Mission would like nothing better than to humiliate the Pardini family and make the auction a big hoopla, a gala event. They're also pushing for Sammi Hogan to emcee the affair. She's a speed seller. An item a minute or less."

"I can see the ads for it now: 'Get your piece of the Pardinis.' When's it going to be held?" Anne asked, then raised an eyebrow. "You know, *I* should be the one telling *you* when and where. I'm the one with connections to auction houses because of my business. How do you know these things, Krista?" Anne paused for a few seconds and then added, "Never mind, that's a rhetorical question."

How Krista knew what she knew was something of a mystery, but she always did, and it was always before almost anyone else. It was as though Krista had eyes everywhere, informants everywhere. Anne was used to it.

"It's happening next Saturday. I forget where I heard this…oh, yes, at the committee meeting for the Food Bank auction. Joannie, the chairwoman, got a call from Sammi Hogan, who did our last—"

"Next week? Are you sure? That's fast."

"I know, guess they want to strike while the story's still in the news. Starts around one o'clock, I think."

They were interrupted by the sound of the sliding glass door opening.

"Steaks are ready." Krista's husband, Mike, holding a platter of barbecued filet mignons, stepped inside from the back patio. Leo scrambled off the couch, ran to his father, and wrapped his arms around his legs so tightly that Mike couldn't move. Unruffled, Mike asked, "What are you two talking about?" He handed the platter off to Krista, who was making her way to the kitchen.

"The Pardini auction is in a week," Anne answered him, and then she called to Krista, "Need any help in there?"

"No, just keep my two guys entertained for a couple of minutes."

"I wouldn't mind going to that auction," Mike said to Anne. "I always thought Lino had great taste. Though there's no way I can afford his $100,000 Rolex Monoblocco watch. Maybe a set of golf clubs or one of his miniature sailboats. You know what's a damn shame? They're bound to auction off that old green truck," Mike said as he reached down and picked Leo up. Then he flipped the toddler upside down and swung him in the air by his heels. Leo cackled with delight.

"We used to see that pickup driving up the hill. Lino's teenage son would be sitting behind the wheel with his dad next to him. The kid would be grinding the gears all the way up to their house and driving so slowly—like, I'm not kidding, five miles an hour—that cars would be backed up behind them, honking their horns at them. But those two would just smile and wave at all the neighbors on the street like they were grand marshals leading a parade."

Krista appeared in the kitchen doorway. "Okay, guys, stop the horseplay. Dinner's ready."

"Too bad the kid can't have that truck," Mike said, setting his dizzy son down.

"Still talking about the auction?" Krista asked. She picked Leo up before he could topple over. "I wonder if Renee even knows that it's happening."

"I'm sure her lawyer would have informed her," Mike said.

Krista sighed. "I feel bad that I didn't make an attempt to go over to her house that day—or even call her. I've just been so busy. I haven't seen or talked to her since she got tossed out of her house."

"Me neither," Anne said, following the family into the dining room.

Krista glanced at Anne over her shoulder and said, "Where do you suppose she is?"

# Chapter Nineteen

T*ap-tap-tap.*

Renee Pardini was startled awake. *Where am I?* Touching her face, she felt a tear running down her cheek. She must have been weeping in her dreams.

The rapping was coming from outside the window. She gingerly raised herself into a half-sitting position. The muscles in her lower back were tight and pinched after a night spent lying on top of the jutting seat belt holders in the back seat. The muscles in her neck were too stiff to turn her head directly toward the guy looking in the car window at her. And it was freezing cold.

The man swept the beam of his flashlight over her, and though it blinded her for a second, she was able to get a quick look at him. That's all it took to size him up as an ordinary, pissed-off, fleece-jacket-wearing, paunchy older guy. He wasn't a gang member with tattoos running up and down his neck or, worse, a policeman. Nothing for her to really worry about, so she pulled the wool blanket over her head and tried to will the intruder away. But the tapping started up again, more insistent this time.

*Tap-tap-tap-tap.*

"Hey, get up!" his voice barked.

It wasn't even dawn yet. *Please, please, please go away,* she thought. All she wanted was just one more moment of peace. She'd only slept a couple of hours.

"Lady? You can't stay here." He rapped the end of his flashlight on the side window a few more times. "This isn't some flophouse. This is a nice neighborhood."

The man wouldn't stop talking.

"Okay, okay," she muttered, now fully awake.

"You don't want me to call the cops, do you?" He shut off the flashlight and slowly crouched down so he was eye-level with her. Renee's neck muscles were finally loosened enough so she could face him and see that his watery eyes were looking her up and down. His double chin, covered with mostly gray stubble, was so fleshy he could have hidden a second flashlight in there. Creepier still, his fingers hooked through the two-inch crack in the back window that she'd left open for fresh air. If she had been in the front seat, she would've powered the window up and smashed those stubby, fat fingers until they were broken and bloody.

*Small pleasures,* she thought. And she needed any she could get, even imaginary ones. It had been a rough night.

"There's no law against parking on a city street," Renee said in a low but defiant voice. And it wasn't as if she'd had a choice. Sleeping in her car in a strange neighborhood was a lousy idea, but she'd felt like it was her only option last night. After three nights of couch surfing at her college friend Stella's house, it was clear she couldn't stay there for even one more night—not after Stella's husband tried to join her on the pull-out bed in the den. Renee didn't say a word to Stella about why she had to leave so suddenly, only that her mother in Portland, Oregon, was expecting her, which was a lie, of course. Stella hugged Renee and sent her out the door with all the cash she had in the house, and a day's worth of health bars, a bag of tangerines, and a sixteen-ounce bottle of water.

By the time she'd left Stella's house, the sun was down, and she had no place to go. She ruled out staying with Marco and Kay, who'd always resented her; they didn't want her there, and she'd rather sleep in the car than listen to all the reasons why. She had $350 cash in her purse—the two hundred dollars from Stella and $150 of her own, the sum total of her life savings, as it turned out. She didn't want to waste what little money she had on a hotel room.

In the trunk of the car, there was a Louis Vuitton suitcase filled with all the toiletries and clothes—for both her and Josh—that she could carry out of the house on short notice. Also packed in the trunk was an emergency evacuation box with a pillow, blanket, and first aid kit that her late husband, ever the boy scout, had packed for her last year during the fire season. A banker's box contained birth certificates, papers from Lino's desk, photos, and so on.

Her only plan had been to find a neighborhood on the outskirts of town where no one knew her. She'd driven around aimlessly until she came to this neighborhood, which, in the dark, seemed as good as any—safe and quiet, an older Santa Rosa neighborhood on the northeast side of town where people minded their own business. It would only be for one night, she figured. But now, in the morning light, and with the jaundiced eye of someone who'd spent the last fifteen years in a multi-million-dollar home—and whose pride had just taken a hit—she decided that it was a sketchy, low-class, dirty little street where people got up too early to go to their crummy little jobs and didn't have the decency to mind their own business. *Talk about flop houses.* On the plus side, it was only a couple of miles from Marco's and Kay's house at Pardini Winery, where her son Josh was staying.

"I'm losing my patience," he said. "Now git along with you. I have to go to work, and I'm not leaving here until you're off our street." He tilted his head toward a woman who was scowling at them from the front porch, arms crossed over her sunken chest. "My wife wants you outta here."

Having said his piece, the man straightened up and stepped away from the window, looking her car over, from front bumper to taillights. "Is this yours? A Mercedes? Pretty fancy."

"Of course, it's mine." Her car was the only thing of value that hadn't been on the Feds' forfeiture order. Letting her keep it was apparently a bone the U.S. Attorney's office was willing to toss her way in a compromise deal made by her lawyer.

"Can I see some registration?"

"Are you kidding? For my car? Maybe if you had a warrant, sure. But otherwise, stop harassing me."

She looked him over again. He seemed harmless, so she opened the door and struggled out of the back seat with as much dignity as she could muster. She pulled up the collar on her camel coat and smoothed down her hair. It was time for her to get in gear: she desperately needed a cup of coffee, and, more urgently, she needed to find a bathroom.

Looking over the guy's shoulder toward his plain, paint-chipped, flat-roofed house, she knew that there had to be at least one, maybe even two, functioning toilets inside. But from the looks of the woman glaring at her from the porch, Renee knew she wouldn't be welcome inside. It was occurring to her that this guy's wife was under the illusion that she was better than Renee, more respectable. Renee tilted her head in wonder. *Imagine that.* The idea was so preposterous she couldn't wrap her mind around it. Simply couldn't absorb the thought. And she knew, deep in her bones, that if she ever did, it would be the end of her.

She opened the car's front door and slid into the driver's seat. Rich's Gas & Auto Repair was just a few miles up the road, and she needed gas anyway. As she pulled away from the curb, she heard the guy yell, "Don't come back."

\* \* \*

Renee came out of the mini-mart at Rich's Gas & Auto Repair carrying a container of coffee in one hand and shielding her eyes from the early morning sun with the other. To her left, she could see Troy Canter, son of the owner, duck under a car lift on his way out of the repair shop.

He was heading her way.

"Hey, Mrs. Pardini," the young mechanic called out, wiping his hands on a grease-stained rag. A neck tattoo of a pipe wrench peeked out from the collar of his work shirt. "I thought that was you going into the mini-mart." He stuffed the soiled rag into his pocket.

"Hi Troy, haven't seen you in a while," she said as they walked to her car together. She went around to the driver's side, opened the door, and leaned over the seat to set her drink in the coffee holder.

"Guess it's been about a year since you brought in this Mercedes." He patted the car's hood in a proprietary way. "Now, that pickup truck, on the other hand," he laughed, "was here in the shop all the time. We had a hard time finding things to fix on it. How's the truck doing these—" He trailed off the sentence. "Wait, that came out wrong. I meant to say, how are you and Josh doing? I was really sorry to hear about Mr. Pardini. We all liked him a lot." He gestured toward the two mechanics working under cars in the garage.

"Thanks. Josh is taking it real hard." Renee released the latch to the fuel tank cover and then walked toward the gas pump. As he stood by and watched, she lifted the gas nozzle and put in less than three gallons.

"Don't you want to fill it up?" Troy asked.

*As a matter of fact, I would,* she thought, but said, "I just need ten dollars' worth. I already paid the cashier." She removed the nozzle from the car and slotted it back into the pump.

"Well, okay," he said, giving her an appraising look. "It's none of my business, but this car is a beauty. If you need any cash, you could get a good trade-in price for it. If you're ever interested, let me know. There's a dealership I work with—"

"I'll think about it," she cut him off. Her car was all she had, and she'd have to be down to her last dime, which admittedly could be any day now, before giving it up.

"Same for the truck. I'd be glad to take it off your hands."

"It's being auctioned off along with the other vehicles. And if it wasn't, Josh would get it."

"Huh. Truck's being auctioned off?" Leaning down, he cupped his hands around his face and looked through the car window into the back seat.

"Yes, Troy. Everything except this car, so don't bother inspecting it," she said testily. "And don't ask me when or where the auction is, because I don't know, and I don't care." *Vultures everywhere,* she fumed. She got in the car and shut the door.

"Didn't mean to upset you."

"Don't worry about it." She started the engine. She reminded herself that he was young yet, not even thirty. *Just a baby vulture.*

"You doing okay these days?" Troy asked, apparently not aware the conversation was over.

"Just fine. I've got to go."

# Chapter Twenty

Pulling away from the gas pump, Renee was all too aware that she had nowhere to go and no one to see. Where could she spend the next few punishingly cold and rudderless hours before the confrontation she was dreading that afternoon?

She went over a few options in her head. It was a coin toss.

She could always go to the downtown public library, a safe and warm haven. But she was slightly terrified of all those homeless people, mostly bearded and silent old men, who parked themselves in groups around the library tables, their whole life's belongings held in plastic bags and small shopping carts at their feet. The librarians must be a little frightened, too, because the city hired security guards to keep an eye on them. But it wasn't their actions that worried Renee. What terrified her was the possibility of seeing herself reflected in their faces. That would not do. Besides, the library didn't open until ten o'clock, a good three hours away.

Moving on to other options, she considered seeking out a dark corner at a Starbucks coffee shop in a strip mall. That would be good for a few hours of warmth. On the other hand, the coffee was expensive there, and Starbucks tended to be crowded at this time of morning—and crowds, as she was learning, opened her up to the possibility of having an unfortunate run-in with someone who recognized her.

Yesterday, in line at the Whole Foods grocery store, she'd had one of those run-ins. At the check stand, Renee had just finished unloading a few items onto the conveyor belt when, without thinking, she inserted her debit card into the card swiper for payment like she'd done a thousand times before.

The cashier watched and smirked.

"That card's no good and we all know it, Mrs. Pardini," the cashier said, looking around for agreement from the customers waiting in line. "Now, if you have cash, then fine, but otherwise...." The cashier motioned for a bagger to come over. "Restock these bananas and tampons, will you?" she ordered the teenage bagger, one of Josh's high school friends.

"Hi, Mrs. P.," the boy muttered, looking sheepish.

"Hi, Lucas."

"Are we done here?" The cashier fixed her eyes on Renee.

Renee looked back at her dispassionately, unfazed. It wasn't news to her that people could be rude and cruel, not after the last few days she had just lived through. It was the new normal. But she was hoping that in this era of constantly replenishing viral news, Lino's infamy would have cycled out by now, and people would've turned their short attention spans somewhere else. No such luck, so she kept her guard up.

What she wasn't prepared to handle, what caught her totally off-guard, was what happened as she was leaving the store. With seemingly everyone in the store staring at her, Renee dropped her debit card back into her purse and walked so fast toward the exit that she reached the automatic doors before they could slide open.

"Renee!" a woman's voice behind her called out.

The doors swished open. Renee stepped over the threshold, then she stopped and turned back toward the voice.

It was Lori Paige, an acquaintance who had co-chaired a few society committees with her. "Renee, I'm glad I caught you," the woman said breathlessly when she reached Renee's side. "How are you doing? I tried calling you, but your number—"

"Hi Lori."

"Do you remember last year when we went together to the fund-raising dinner we organized for Sonoma County's at-risk kids?" She started rummaging through her purse.

"Sure, but I'm late and—" Renee gestured toward her car.

"You and Lino paid for our tickets, remember? And I totally forgot to pay you back." Lori drew out her wallet, unzipped the bill storage compartment, and began pulling out money.

"No, I'm sure you did…"

"No, we didn't." Lori was firm about it. "I'm positive we didn't."

*What bullshit,* Renee thought.

Here," Lori said, counting out five twenty-dollar bills and holding them out to Renee. "Here's one hundred dollars for now."

*But what generous and kind bullshit.* So what could Renee do? Call the woman a liar? She took the money.

"I'm so sorry, but it's all the cash I've got on me right now," Lori said as they walked together toward the parking lot. "I'll pay you the remaining four hundred dollars soon. Give me your new address and I'll mail it out this week."

Renee just shook her head. She gave Lori a quick hug, and then they parted company and headed to their respective cars. Standing by her door, Renee zipped up her down jacket and, despite the chill in the air, felt a rush of heat starting from her neck and moving upward to her face. She pressed a hand to one check and then the other. Both were feverish. She wasn't sure what was bringing this on. Embarrassment? Maybe a little. Shame? No, she refused to feel shame. Any disgrace, any shame, in her downfall, was on Lino. She just wasn't feeling it. It wasn't her shame to carry; it was Lino's. His actions, not hers.

But what she did feel, she realized, was humbled, and that was entirely different. She felt humbled by the kindness and empathy of how she was just treated. When she got on her feet again, and she *would* get back on her feet again, she would pay back that kind deed, that mitzvah, and spread around a few other mitzvahs besides. She'd heard somewhere that a single mitzvah buys you two minutes of happiness. It must be true because she couldn't help noticing that Lori had looked rather pleased with herself. Two minutes was a very brief respite from misery—if, in fact, that calculation was in any way true, who knows?—but string together enough good deeds, and it could add up to some needed happiness and peace, she thought. A win-win. Transactional as always.

The blast of a car horn brought Renee back to the moment. Looking in the rearview mirror, she waved to the irate driver stuck behind her at Rich's Auto Repair and pulled into the early morning traffic. One hand was on the wheel, the other reaching inside her tote bag for the plastic-wrapped Danish she'd bought at the mini-mart.

It was only a three-minute drive to the freeway onramp. She'd better decide where she was going.

Maybe she could stroll around inside the enclosed shopping mall, park herself on a bench, and watch teenagers and shoppers go by. Then she remembered that the mall—like the library—wasn't open yet. So that was out. She could just keep driving around in her heated car, but why waste precious gas? Or maybe she could take a short drive to her vacant Fountaingrove home to check the mailbox on the off chance that something had slipped through the mail-stop order. But what if the U.S. Marshal's guards, who were bound to be on duty there, confronted her?

Renee liked concentrating on these small obstacles and worries. It distracted her from the big ones—like what was going to happen when she showed up at Josh's high school around one o'clock that afternoon to sign him out of school. Neither the school nor Josh was expecting her. And he was *not* going to be happy about it.

Her sister Gina, semi-estranged for years, wasn't going to be very happy with her either—not when she found out that Renee, with Josh in tow, was planning to move in with her and stay indefinitely at her tiny house in Eureka. Of course, the reasonable thing to do would be to call Gina first and ask if they could come. But Renee's cell phone hadn't been working for days, not since her credit card was declined for the automatic monthly payment to the mobile provider. But even so, Renee could have used Lino's phone. It was in the glove compartment and still worked; Lino always paid for a year's worth of service in advance, and she kept it charged up. But if Lino's name showed up on the caller ID, her sister would freak out and wouldn't answer the call anyway, Renee reasoned. So calling ahead wasn't really an option, she told herself. Besides, it would be harder for Gina to turn her away if Renee and Josh were literally at her doorstep.

For a woman like Renee, who had spearheaded countless community events, orchestrated her own rise from a poverty-stricken childhood to her place among the county's wealthy and powerful, and whose girlhood heroines were the uber-calculating Scarlett O'Hara and Madonna, these were flimsy plans indeed.

\* \* \*

"What?! Oh my God, no!" Josh was hyperventilating, almost clinging to the wall in the empty school hallway.

"Just get your stuff out of your locker and let's go," Renee said. "It's a three-hour drive, and if we leave now, we can arrive by dark and—"

"Mom! This is so crazy! I don't even have any of my clothes or stuff with me, just my backpack. And I don't even know your sister!" He pressed the palms of his hands back against the cold metal of his locker as if trying to glue them there.

"We need to get out of this town, Josh," she said, lowering her voice to a near whisper. "It's unbearable here. You're being bullied—"

"It's not that bad," he said. "It's not, I swear. And I have friends here. My cousins have my back." He moved away from the wall and looked up and down the corridor. Then his eyes landed solidly on his mother, and the tone of his voice shifted from pleading to verging on defiant. "I'm not leaving with you, Mom. It's just not happening."

Renee felt close to tears, and her breath grew shallow. She was losing her composure just as he was gaining his. "Please, Josh. We can come back to Santa Rosa if it doesn't work out. I promise."

"I don't belong in that stupid Eureka place. I never even heard of it before. I don't know anyone there."

Renee looked up into Josh's unblinking eyes. He must have grown three inches overnight, she thought. As he squared his shoulders and set his jaw, she let out a long, resigned sigh. She knew her boy well enough to know that it was pointless to try to change his mind when he got like this. Renee and Lino had raised him to be independent and make his own decisions, and this was the result. There'd be no budging him.

"I'm sorry, Mom," he said, his hands shoved into his pockets, "but I'm going back into class now, and after school gets out, I'm going to my cousins' house. They want me there."

So that was that. Decided. He wouldn't leave town—and she wouldn't leave town without him. In four short years, he'd be going off to college, and Renee had no intention of relinquishing these few remaining years by letting him live with relatives.

So, now what?

Renee just gave him a quick hug and, without another word, turned to leave.

"Wait, Mom," Josh said. She turned back to face him. "Maybe you could come stay at Uncle Marco's house, too. Aunt Kay will let you. They have eight bedrooms and like a million bathrooms. I'm not even exaggerating. You could have your own room," he said softly. "Or you could stay in the gardener's shed. No one's staying there."

\* \* \*

Josh did the asking.

"I told Aunt Kay it would only be for a few days until you got a job."

They were standing on the porch of the old "gardener's shed," as Josh called it. But Renee was relieved to see it was more than that; it was a cottage-style guesthouse. It was set atop a slight knoll about a hundred yards away from the main Pardini house, accessible by a private dirt road, an off-shoot from the paved road that serviced Marco and Kay's house.

Two rows of olive trees separated the two residences. So, with luck on her side, she wouldn't have to see Kay or Marco at all. They would stay on their side of the trees; she would stay on hers. They might even forget she was staying there, which would be the best-case scenario since it would take more than a few days to land a job, Renee knew. Not to mention the usual two-week wait before getting the first paycheck. And following that, saving up enough for a month's rent on an apartment—or more likely a room in someone's home—that could take another few months. Josh's promise of "only a few days" wasn't in any way realistic, but Renee didn't want to burst his bubble. Josh looked so proud of himself; he'd provided a home for his mother.

Josh turned the key and swung the door open wide for Renee. From the doorway, she could see the entirety of the place—all three hundred or so square feet of it. To her right was a compact U-shaped kitchen. Past the kitchen, in the back corner, was an RV-sized bathroom. Taking up the remaining space—the living area—were pieces of furniture covered with stained white bed sheets. From what Renee could tell by the shapes of the dusty coverings, there were two dining chairs, a twin-sized bed, a dresser, an armchair, and a small round table hiding underneath them.

"Aunt Kay said to tell you not to hang any pictures on the wall. She said they use this place for visitors."

*Not damn likely.* Renee knew full well that Kay would never allow any guests of theirs to stay here. If she and Marco used this guesthouse at all, it was for hired help or any hapless relative they hoped would get the message and hightail it out of there ASAP.

She flipped the wall light switch; the electricity was working. In the kitchen, she turned on the tap. There was running water. She stepped into the windowless bathroom and flushed the toilet; the plumbing was working. A weak spray of water sputtered from the handheld shower head. She saw a bar of soap, toilet paper, and a towel. She lifted the sheet draped over the bed and saw that it was made up with sheets, a blanket, and a pillow. There was a heating thermostat on the wall.

"Did I ever tell you about the house I grew up in?" Renee turned to Josh. "There was no running water, and our bathroom was an outhouse in the backyard. We took showers at our neighbor's house."

"No way."

"This will do just fine, Josh." She kissed him on the cheek. "Thank you."

# Chapter Twenty-One

Anne knew Dave Silver wouldn't be showing up.
He hadn't informed her of it yet, so she did nothing, just waited. Five minutes later, at nine a.m., a text came in.

Dave: I won't be starting on your yard today. Sorry, something came up.

Anne: You okay?

Dave: Fine. Some workers called in sick, and the rototiller got rented out from under me.

Anne slipped on her black blazer and stuffed her laptop computer into her tote purse. She took one last sip of coffee before texting her reply:

Anne: Next week?

Several minutes passed. And then:

Dave: I'll be in touch.

She locked the front door of her house, pulled her Saab out of the garage, and set off for the police station. Traffic was sluggish, exactly the commute-hour gridlock she was expecting on a Monday morning, which is why she'd allowed extra time so she could arrive at least a half hour before the interview started. Instead of parking in the police station lot, she rounded the block and parked her car on the street behind the station.

Dave wouldn't notice her car there.

Anne entered the lobby of the police station with a few minutes to spare before her uncle would be arriving at nine-twenty. She occupied herself by studying the rows of official portraits of Police Chiefs and state governors, past and present, that lined the far side wall until she heard her uncle's familiar voice call out, "Hey, Anne." She turned to see him walking through the heavy glass door with Sgt. Jim Sloan.

There was a spring in Jack's step—probably, she thought, because he liked nothing better than to interrogate suspects. He was dressed nattily in a blue blazer, button-down blue shirt, tan khaki pants, and one of his more subdued black-and-orange SF Giants ties.

"You know Sergeant Sloan, right?" Jack asked.

Anne extended her hand to the tall, slim sergeant. Two years before, Anne, while working on special assignment, and Jim Sloan had solved a homicide case together. Though in truth, Anne thought, *she* had solved the case, and Sloan had just gone along for the ride.

"Hi Jim, it's been a while."

"Good to have you back on board," he said, shaking her hand. "I understand you'll be observing in the next room."

She nodded. "They gave me a choice of watching a live video feed from the other side of the building or watching through one of those one-way mirrors."

"It's old-school, but a lot more entertaining," Jack said, nodding. "I remember once when a detective on the observation side forgot where he was and, like a damn fool, lit up a cigarette. The suspect saw the flame and didn't even bat an eye, just asked if he could borrow a smoke."

"Everyone's seen enough TV crime shows to know that someone's on the other side. It's not really fooling anyone," Sloan said, "and it especially won't fool this guy—Dave Silver's been in and out of custody nearly his entire adult life."

"Did you have a chance to review the files I pulled?" Anne asked them. On Friday, she'd spent two hours at the station running police background investigation software.

"Very helpful," Jack said, slapping a file against his thigh. "I guess we part ways here, Anne, but before we do, any more questions you want me to ask him?"

Anne shook her head. "I'm good."

"Jim will get you set up in the room."

Anne followed Sgt. Sloan down the hall to the observation room where she would sit in the dark, staring through the glass into the interrogation room. The brightly lit interrogation room was hardly more than a box, windowless, sparsely furnished with metal framed, foam padded chairs, two on each side of the six-foot-long stainless-steel table.

Ten minutes later, she watched as Dave Silver was brought in. He was seated at the table and then left alone. She hadn't seen or talked to Dave since last Monday at Trudy Lee's—they'd just swapped texts about scheduling the landscaping job—and he was wearing what appeared to be the same jeans he wore then with a blue crewneck sweater.

Another ten minutes went by, during which Dave shifted in his seat, loosened the muscles of his neck by rolling it from side to side, and cracked his knuckles. His eyes swept the corners of the room as if checking for cameras. He spent a few seconds staring at the reflective glass, straight at Anne.

At the sound of the door opening, Dave jerked his head toward the door. Sloan entered the room with a bland smile, followed by Jack. Dave made a move to stand up.

"Don't get up, Mr. Silver. I'm Detective Sergeant Sloan, and this is my associate."

Dave nodded and sat back down. Sloan and Jack took their seats across the table from him; their backs were to Anne.

"I didn't catch the name," Dave said to Jack.

"Detective Jack McCormack."

Dave smiled faintly. "You're Anne McCormack's uncle, right? She told me you were retired. I wish we were meeting under different circumstances."

Jack smiled back. "I dust myself off for cold cases."

"So this is about a cold case. When I was asked to come in, something was mentioned about the Dinah Pardini case. Is that it?"

"It is." Pleasantries over, Sloan leaned back and let Jack take the lead. For the next few minutes, Jack recited the usual preliminary statements and questions. Jack asked Dave to identify himself (*For the recorded video*, he said). Then he informed Dave, for the record, that he wasn't under arrest, that he could leave at any time, and that, if he didn't want to answer a question, he didn't have to.

"I've looked at your arrest record, Mr. Silver. And in 2004, you were out on probation." Jack looked up from his notes. "Was that here in Santa Rosa?"

"I'd have to think about—"

"You're forty-eight years old now, so you were thirty-one then. Think back. You were still doing drugs then, right?"

Dave grimaced. "I don't see what any of this has to do with me. I hardly knew the woman."

"Well, let's take this step by step. Seventeen years ago, on the night of September 9th, Dinah Pardini got into somebody's car—no one seems to have seen the car—and left her house for a charity event, never to be seen or heard from again. Her husband was out of town, according to hotel receipts. Now, Lino Pardini had all kinds of motives for killing her, or for hiring someone, but we'll get back to that later. Anyway, she disappears. Crickets—until almost exactly one year later when suddenly we get a call about a dead body." Jack leaned in. "Here's where it gets interesting. Tell me if any of this sounds familiar," he said as he dug through his scuffed-up briefcase for the transparent evidence bag containing the *Find—D* letter.

While Jack read the script aloud, Dave was rubbing his chin. Then he dropped both hands to the table and pressed them onto the surface so hard his fingers trembled. From behind the glass, Anne tried sending Dave a message mentally to just sit still. *Stop it. Don't you know they can read every move you make?*

Dave tucked his hands below the table surface, to her relief. Jack finished reading the letter and looked up.

"We found the body, but not much else. And during the last sixteen years, nothing new came to our attention until this letter," Jack said, waving the evidence bag. "And this." He pulled out the old flip-top phone, also packaged in clear plastic. "Both these items were found this week in Lino Pardini's garage, which makes sense because he was behind her death—in some fashion or another. But he didn't do it alone. He had you."

"Had…what?"

"At the very least, he had you to call in the report. Take us through that part first. What happened?"

"I have no memory of anything like that."

"No, of course not." Jack removed his glasses. "So let's talk about Lino Pardini, then. Here's what makes sense: Pardini hired a guy to kill his wife, and then he called that guy a year later and told him to go back and dig up the body, move it, and report it. That guy was you."

*Whoa!* Anne sat forward. What was her uncle up to? He knew Dave's incarceration timeline as well as she did.

Jack leaned back, waiting for a reaction from Dave that didn't come. "We have your fingerprints all over these items. You were the caller. You can't deny *that*, at least."

They sat staring at each other. The ticking clock over the door was the only sound for a full minute. Jack idly tapped his eyeglasses on the table.

"We're still curious about a few things," Jack finally said. "Why move the body from the original grave you put her in? Why not just leave her there and send us to that spot instead?"

"I didn't—" Dave stopped himself.

More silence, then Jack went on, "We're thinking it's because you didn't want us combing the soil for left-behind evidence, clothing scraps, DNA, that kind of thing. Or maybe it's because you buried her so far out in the boonies that no one could 'accidentally find it' like you claimed on your phone call. Talk to us."

Dave took a long breath and looked away.

Jack waited a beat. "And there's another thing we don't understand: There

166

was a $50,000 reward for information about the murder. If you didn't kill her, if you were just some random guy hired to do an odd job, making an innocent call to the cops, why didn't you turn Pardini in and collect the money? That's a hell of a lot more than the $500 or whatever he was paying you. You were an addict with no reliable income. So why not? You could have implicated Pardini and possibly become a rich man. Rich by your standards, anyway."

Jack leaned in. "Well, I'll tell you why not: You were the killer, and Pardini had this letter and this phone," Jack said, holding up the Ziploc bag, "hanging over your head. He probably had more besides. At what point did he start blackmailing you about this?"

Dave listened with a clenched jaw.

"Or were you blackmailing him, too? Maybe during all those years, you got a lot more than the $50,000 reward off of him. I'm guessing you two were so tangled up together, threatening each other back and forth, that it's lucky one of you didn't kill the other."

Jack's eyes were fixed like two lasers on him, and then he leaned back again. "Except, now that I think about it, I might have that all wrong. You don't seem to have a lot of money—after all, you're living in a mobile home parked on your parent's property—so maybe he wasn't a cash cow for you. Also, you and Pardini seemed to be on good terms. At least, from what we've heard, good enough for Lino to consider bankrolling a new business venture for you."

That tidbit had come directly from Anne.

Dave's eyes cut to the one-way mirror.

"So tell us, what was your relationship with Lino Pardini?"

"You tell me. You seem to have all the answers." Dave abruptly stood up, nearly knocking his chair over. Before it hit the ground, he pushed the chair upright and said, "I'm not answering any more questions."

"You haven't even answered *one* yet," Jack said.

Sgt. Sloan casually placed his arm along the back of Jack's chair. "Here's another scenario, Dave," he said in a friendly voice, motioning for Dave to sit back down.

Dave kept standing.

"The way I see it, you were a young man going through some hard times, mixed up, willing to do anything for a buck," Sloan said. "And then this pillar of the community gives you a call—a guy you knew for years. And he asks you for a favor. Just place a call. Simple as that. You respect him. Maybe you couldn't really believe he had anything to do with his wife's murder. At any rate, you needed the money, so you helped him out. And maybe that's as far as your involvement goes, and you had nothing to do with the murder. These past sixteen years, you've straightened out your life and tried to forget it. Your involvement's not so serious, you know? You weren't even an accessory after the fact. At least not knowingly."

Dave shrugged. "I think we're through here," he said, heading for the door.

"A few more questions," Jack called out when Dave opened the door. "How did you kill her, Silver? And what's your father got to do with this?"

Dave stopped in the doorway. He turned around and looked at them, his face wooden. And then, raising the first two fingers of his right hand, said, "Peace out, officers."

\* \* \*

"I didn't even get to ask Silver if he killed Lino," Jack said to Anne. They were standing in the hallway outside the now-deserted interrogation room. Sgt. Sloan had already gone back to his office.

Anne closed her eyes. She felt profoundly tired.

Her uncle hadn't been alone in entertaining the idea that Lino may have been murdered. Several people, his brother Marco included, knew of Lino's Ponzi scheme before it was uncovered and might have had vengeful motives. And there was the blunt-force trauma to the head. The blood on the outdoor kitchen. Good reasons to leave the possibility of homicide wide open until they learned more from the toxicology report.

But right at this moment, after witnessing Dave's grueling and grim interview, Anne didn't have the energy to care.

Her uncle, on the other hand, was energized and just getting started. "I'm thinking that if Dave Silver wasn't involved, then maybe his father, Jerry Silver, was—" he said while they walked to the elevator.

"*Possible* murder, that's all it is. Possible."

"Yeah, well. But like I was saying, maybe Jerry Silver was involved." They stepped into the elevator. "The dad lost money investing with Lino Pardini. Maybe the dad killed Pardini in a fit of rage. Maybe Jerry Silver was the one who killed Dinah Pardini, too. Killed them both."

"Well, it sure wasn't Dave who killed her," she said in a tight voice. "You saw his incarceration timeline. So why accuse him?"

"Just rattling his cage," Jack said, shrugging. "I think I'll pay Jerry Silver a little visit pretty soon. His cage needs to get rattled too, and something *will* shake out. Sooner or later. I can feel it."

The elevator doors opened onto the lobby.

"Wanna go get some coffee and talk about it?"

"I need to get back to my office." Anne turned toward the front exit doors. "See you later."

"Okay," Jack said, watching her leave. "Peace out."

* * *

That evening a visitor dropped by.

Leaning back into the pillows on her couch, Anne was listing possible suspects in Dinah Pardini's murder on a legal pad when she heard the lid of her porch mailbox creak slowly open. Then heard it slam down shut.

She ignored it. It was probably just a neighbor bringing her some mail delivered to their address by mistake, she thought. She continued with her list of suspects, putting Lino at the very top, of course. Then Jerry Silver. Then Marco—though as far as Anne knew, he had no motive for killing his sister-in-law, except maybe to frame his brother out of jealousy over Lino's rumored affair with Kay. Far-fetched, Anne decided. But jealousy is a powerful motivator—which brought her to Kay Pardini, who apparently wanted Dinah out of the way. Kay had attended the charity ball on the night of the murder, so she had an alibi, but she could have hired someone to do the deed. Then Anne added Dave Silver's name just for the satisfaction of crossing it off.

Anne stood and stretched. Finally remembering the mail delivery, curiosity took hold of her, and she went to the front door, turned on the porch light, stepped out, and reached into the mailbox.

The white greeting-card-size envelope had her name scrawled on the front. Inside was the uncashed check she'd made out to "Silver Landscaping," the deposit for landscaping work.

Just that. No note, no reason.

# Chapter Twenty-Two

Dave Silver sat for a long time in the back corner booth, watching as customers straggled out the door and onto the street. It was closing time. The regular closing time, two o'clock in the morning, not the forced early exodus Trudy Lee liked to bring about with sad songs. Dave watched as she stood behind the bar and tipped out the bartender, busboy, and server. Pocketing their cash, they said their goodnights and left by the back door, leaving her alone to turn off the lights and lock up.

Dave walked up to the bar and slid onto a stool.

"So what are you still doing here, Davy?" she said, tenderness in her voice. She looked at him with an appraising eye.

"Do you have any coffee left?"

"I'll heat some up." Trudy turned around to the coffee pot at the far end of the bar, filled a mug with cold coffee, and stuck it into the microwave. "It's not like you to be out this late."

Dave glanced up at her and then broke off eye contact. He concentrated instead on the scarred mahogany bar top, fingering a deep scratch. This was where he always came when he didn't know what else to do. Since he was a child, Trudy had been like an aunt, a mother, a big sister to him—the whole matriarchal support system in one woman. One of the few people in the world he trusted, maybe the only one. When he was battling drugs all those years, she never coddled him; that wasn't her style, but she also never turned him away when he needed a place to crash or a few bucks to get by. In turn, he never did drugs around her, never stole from her, never lied to her, never put her in harm's way. As far as he was concerned, the ground she stood on was sacred. So sacred he didn't feel right about muddying it up with his problems. Trudy liked to tell him that all his bad and horrible days were over, that he had it all together now. So he wasn't inclined to spill his guts about his long and lousy day to the one person who believed in him. He didn't want to burden—or worse, disillusion—her. He just wanted to be in her company.

After a moment of silence between them, time she spent watching him, and he spent fiddling with a salt shaker, the microwave timer went off. Trudy took out the mug and set it in front of him. "Black, right?"

He nodded.

"Well, if you're not going to talk, I will," said Trudy. "I was getting ready to call you anyway. I have a favor to ask of you."

"Name it."

"I need a drink first." She pulled a bottle of Jack Daniels down off the shelf and poured herself a shot. A few whiskey droplets sloshed over the rim. "Here's the thing: I need you to attend that auction next Saturday."

"The Pardini auction? Sure, but why?"

"There's something there that I need to get. I promised someone. But the problem is, I have to go out of town next week for a family funeral—my father's brother just died."

"Sorry about that."

"Well, he was ninety-four."

Dave nodded.

"The funeral's being held on Saturday morning, so there's no way I can be back here in time for the auction," she said. "Anyway, it's important that I send someone to represent me. You're the only person in town I trust enough."

"Represent you how? And who did you promise?"

"I'm not really free to get into all the particulars of it, but he gave me the cash to buy something. And if there's any money left over after buying it, I'll split it with you. But if we don't win the bid, which is unlikely, the entire amount goes somewhere else. No money for either of us. Which is fine with me. But I'm telling you just so you know. I can't say much more than that."

He gave her a sideways look. It wasn't like Trudy to be so evasive. Usually, she was unapologetically blunt and tended to blurt things out, take it or leave it. Something was wrong here, he thought.

"Okay, what's this about, Trudy? And who is *he*?"

"I can't tell you everything because some of it's confidential and involves innocent people. And, by the way, what I'm saying to you right now has to stay confidential, too."

"Okay."

"But I can tell you this, the important part," she said, draining her glass. "It was Lino Pardini who asked me. He came here the day he died."

"You're kidding." He raised his eyebrows. "You might have been the last person to see him alive."

"Could be. It was around noon on Monday and he just showed up at the door. Everyone knows I don't open up until one, so I was alone in here, setting up for the day. Man, he looked about ten years older," she said. "His face looked gray, and he was unsteady on his feet. He was doing that rocking from side-to-side thing, like elephants do—like he was trying to keep his balance. I'm telling you, he did *not* look healthy. I wasn't surprised that he had a heart attack a few hours later. Not surprised at all." She shook her head at the memory.

"Then he started saying a lot of crazy stuff. Saying 'shit's coming down.' He never used words like that. I asked him what he was talking about...I mean, at the time, we didn't know about the Ponzi scheme. All he kept saying was that everything he owned would be sold off and that he was running out of time. I told him to calm down, that he looked like hell. Have some coffee. He asked for a shot of Jack Daniels instead. He was breathing really heavy. Kept saying that his house, his cars, his jewelry—everything was going, he said. He knew it. Then he pulled out a thick envelope filled with cash—I'm talking thousands of dollars—and just dropped it on the bar and told me he needed a favor. He wanted me to bid on something at the auction. We talked about it a while, and then he got up, saying he had to get back, like he had an appointment or something. And he was gone. Just as fast as he came."

"Bid on what?" Dave asked, a sneer in his voice. "And why? I'll bet Lino was just trying to launder money through you. Have a little something to sell after he got busted by the Feds, so he'd have access to money."

Dave's bitter tone seemed to catch Trudy off guard. She searched his face a moment, then turned away to heat up more coffee for him. Dave stared past her shoulder to the glowing, back-lit liqueur bottles lining the shelves behind the bar. He was having a hard time remembering why he'd ever thought of Lino as a friend. But the truth was, he had counted him among his friends as recently as two weeks before. But all that chummy back and forth of the last few years—the offer to finance his nursery, Lino's hiring Dave's landscaping firm for his properties—was fading away in the present-day danger of his criminal exposure because of the bastard. Things had been so good lately that he'd let himself get lulled into thinking that maybe it had never happened. But now it was all piling back onto him, like some delayed mudslide or avalanche. Landing on him long after the storm had supposedly cleared. All that remained of his relationship with Lino was bile and regret.

"I can't just walk into that auction with a wad of cash. Everyone knows I don't have that kind of money. They're going to want to know where I got it."

"If anyone asks, just tell them the truth. Say you're doing it for me. I don't care who knows. I run a cash-only business, and no one would bat an eye."

Not even a blink. Her business was prosperous, and it seemed she never spent a dime, certainly not on bar renovations, so it was widely believed that Trudy was loaded. Not only loaded, but since she was never seen inside banks, she must have huge piles of cash—in small denominations—stashed somewhere on the bar property. Probably upstairs in her apartment. Hidden in old shoes or, they often speculated, stacked in Tupperware in the freezer. *Frozen assets,* they'd laugh. It must be unnerving, Dave supposed, for her to know how many people were thinking about her money. Probably that's why she kept a handgun upstairs, or so she said.

174

"Okay, but I don't like the sound of this, Trudy, and I have some advice for you," he said, leaning forward. "Don't have anything to do with Pardini and his schemes, dead or alive. You don't need to keep some promise to him. He's dead. Two weeks dead, and he's still having people do his bidding." Dave fairly spat out the words. "And what are you supposed to do with whatever the hell it is he wanted you to bid on? It sounds shady. And you know why? Because it is shady."

"Before I owned this bar I was broke," she said quietly, "It was Lino who staked me to the down payment. I paid back within a few years, but he was there when I needed him."

"Ancient history. Take it from me, nothing good can come from getting involved."

"This is different, Dave. It's complicated, and this is a good thing. Whatever happened bad between you and him is in the past, right? That's ancient history, too. And you've gone on with your life," Trudy said, coming around the bar to sit on the stool next to him. "Over and done with. The past is the past. It doesn't own you, Davy."

*Maybe it does, maybe it doesn't*, he thought, replaying the morning's grilling at the police station. *But shame owns me, and that's a fact.*

He finally met her eyes. When he spoke again, his tone was softer. "Okay, I'll do it. Not because Lino asked for it. Not because of some fucking, last minute, manipulative dying request he wrangled out of you. Fuck Lino. And fuck his so-called 'good thing.' And not because of any money that might be left over from the bid, which probably won't be much anyway, but even if it is, anything coming from Pardini has a stink to it." He stopped, looking off into the middle distance.

Trudy waited him out.

"The only reason I'll do it," he said after a moment, "is because I owe you. You were the only one who visited me at the treatment facility and state prison that year. Remember that? Not even my mother made that eight-hour round trip to Corcoran. And I don't forget."

Trudy rested her hand on Dave's.

"That gives you license to ask me to do anything," he went on. "Within reason, anyway. I'm trusting you that this *is* within reason, and I won't land in jail."

"Thanks, Dave." She gave his hand a light squeeze. "Someday, I'll tell you all about it..."

"The less I know about Pardini the better, is my feeling. So, what's the plan?"

The front door swung open, letting in a bitter cold wind along with a wiry old man apparently too drunk to know it was closing time.

"Can anyone join this party?" Jerry Silver bellowed, clearly deep into that sloppy, gregarious stage of inebriation. He flung his arms out wide as if to embrace the world, then made his way toward his son and Trudy at the bar. At the last second, he made an unexpected detour and collapsed into the nearest chair instead.

Dave let out with a low groan that only Trudy seemed to notice.

"Party's over, Dad," Dave said. Then he leaned across the bar toward Trudy and in a near whisper, said, "I'll call you tomorrow."

She nodded.

"Party's just getting started!" Jerry said, pounding the table.

"Sorry, Jerry, it's closing time. I was just getting ready to lock up." Trudy flicked a light switch on and off to make her point.

"At least give me one for the road, Trudy. I'm begging you!" Jerry said, winking at her and pounding the table so hard the saltshaker nearly toppled over. "Show some mercy, Trudster." If he thought using an affectionate nickname would get him anywhere, he was mistaken. She blithely cleared the coffee mug and shot glass off the bar and wiped it down one last time.

"Hey, Trudy, did we ever hook up back in the day?" He winked again.

"Sweet Jesus," Trudy said, setting the rag down. "Get him out of here, Dave."

Dave went over to Jerry. "Come on, get up. I'm driving you home, Dad." He turned to Trudy. "You don't mind if we leave his car in the parking lot, do you?"

"No problem."

Jerry pulled himself out of the chair with a little assist from his son and puffed out his bony chest. "Later, Trudy, you hard-hearted wench."

"Later, you two."

Jerry slung his arm around Dave's shoulder and leaned all of his weight, no more than a hundred-fifty pounds, against his son for balance. Together, they headed for the door. "How're things going, Davy boy?"

"Been better," Dave said, pushing the door open for his father. A rush of cold, dry wind blew into them and slammed the door shut the second they'd passed through. October was known as the fire season in Sonoma County, and everyone actively hated the wind. The smallest gust could whip up the smallest embers into an out-of-control firestorm within minutes. The wind blew Dave's jacket wide open, so he cursed it and stepped away from his father so he could pull his zipper up. "Wish it would rain one of these days," Dave said, looking up at the clear, starry night sky. Jerry looked to be in danger of being blown sideways, so Dave grabbed onto his elbow and steered him to the truck.

Opening the passenger side, Dave added, as if an afterthought, "Just a heads up, Dad—I think you'll be hearing from some detectives soon."

\* \* \*

After that bit of information, Jerry Silver found himself sobering up faster than he would have liked. Not fast enough that he could drive himself home, but fast enough that he could put two thoughts together.

Neither of those thoughts concerned Dave or any trouble he might be in. Jerry had stopped worrying about his son a long time ago. While Dave was in his free-fall from drugs, which went on for years, there was nothing he could do to help, so why bother worrying? These days Dave could handle himself. Again, no point in worrying.

No, Jerry's first thought was: *Why? Why would a cop want to talk to a fine, upstanding citizen such as myself?* He chuckled softly.

Dave gave him a sideways look and asked, "What's so funny?"

"Nothing." They lapsed into silence.

Jerry's second thought, darker, was along the lines of: *Dave's been talking to cops and my name came up in those discussions.* Putting those two thoughts together, he finally came up with something to say.

"Should I be worried?"

"I don't know, should you?" Dave shot back.

"Well, should I?" Jerry persisted.

"They're asking about Dinah Pardini's murder."

"Man," Jerry said, shaking his head slowly, "that was what—twenty years ago? Shit. They're reopening that old investigation?"

"I don't see how they can. They don't have anything." Dave squeezed and released the steering wheel and then did it again. His large red knuckles were turning white.

Another period of silence followed. The only sounds inside the truck were coming from the heater and the wind howling outside the window.

They were halfway home. It was a fourteen-mile drive from Trudy's bar to where they lived on the same piece of property, Jerry's property—or what was left of it. Only about fifteen acres now. He and his wife Carol had started Silver Family Vineyards, a small wine grape growing operation, in the 1980s with about a hundred acres of planted chardonnay and pinot noir vines. Cool-climate grapes, best grown on the west side of Highway 101, closer to coastal breezes.

Wineries vied for their yield, especially the pinot noir grapes, a tricky fruit to grow. Jerry liked to call himself a simple "fruit farmer" because he liked how it made him sound humble, which he wasn't, not by a long shot. He knew he was respected, even esteemed in the vintner community, as a "pinot pioneer."

But he was starting to think that last month's harvest would be his last.

Decades of low-profit margins, unreliable weather, too many regulations, and a lack of skilled labor and housing in Sonoma County had taken their toll. The Silver Family Vineyards was down to its last, heavily mortgaged acres. The chardonnay acres had been the first to be sold because, as Jerry never tired of saying, "Any fool can grow chardonnay." He held onto his remaining block of prized pinot vines, but he was on the verge of selling even those. He was pushing seventy, he needed the money—especially with his retirement funds taking a nosedive thanks to Lino Pardini—and he had a bad case of owner fatigue. He was just plain tired of the day-to-day grind of running the operation.

Like many fathers, Jerry had pinned his hopes on having his son take over, but Dave was a contrarian, and there was no telling him anything. Maybe Dave had had enough of working in the vineyard fields as a kid. And now, it seemed, he wanted to start his own plant nursery and grow shrubs and pansies and other crap. Which pissed Jerry off so bad he wouldn't let Dave use any of the family land for his new business.

Jerry could sell it all tomorrow—plenty of big wineries, Pardini Winery included, would love to increase their holdings with the last of his premium land—and he wouldn't look back. All he wanted were a few acres of vines surrounding his house and the small piece of land where Dave parked his mobile home.

Jerry turned toward the passenger side window, looking out into the darkness. The sun wouldn't be up for a few hours, and there was nothing to see, not even a faint outline of the rows upon rows of grapevines that he knew they were passing. Some of those grapevines—not his, it goes without saying—were a sloppy, badly tended mess: errant sprouts at the plant base. Excess canes shooting out into the rows. It would have hurt his eyes and heart to see them, so it was just as well it was pitch black outside. Pruning season was coming up. Maybe those lame-ass amateur growers would do better this year, but he doubted it.

Jerry turned away from the window. Fixating on grapevines was just a mental stalling tactic, good for a while, but the problem with the cops wasn't going away. He finally looked over at Dave and said, "You're saying there's no new evidence? They must have something."

"They've got something, but nothing that concerns you." Dave paused a few beats, then went on, "If they call you in, just keep quiet and let them run their mouths. One detective is really jacked up about this. Name's McCormack. Don't let him rile you up."

"That name's familiar." Jerry furrowed his brow in thought, then snapped his fingers. "He's related to that Anne chick. Your new girlfriend, right?"

"Not my girlfriend." Dave's tone was flat.

"Don't be so damn touchy. You're always so damn touchy," Jerry said, shaking his head, sinking deep into that tired, melancholy stage of inebriation. "It's like I can't say anything to you."

Dave didn't say a word. He made a slight right turn onto his parent's private road. His truck bounced along the rocky dirt surface, which was doing his suspension system no favors. He parked near the wrap-around porch of the narrow, old Victorian farmhouse and cut the engine.

Jerry looked up at his house. No lights were on. His wife knew better than to wait up for him. She didn't care enough to bother anyway, he thought. He couldn't even make her jealous anymore. Theirs was just one of those marriages that goes on and on and on, and no one really knows why.

"Well, thanks for the ride," Jerry said. But he made no move to get out.

"Okay, Dad, say hi to Mom for me," Dave said, like he always did in parting. Then he reached an arm across his father's skinny chest and opened the passenger side door for him. Jerry slid off the cab bench and made his slow, wobbly way up toward the porch, trying his best to walk straight and keep his dignity.

# Chapter Twenty-Three

"Ladies and gentlemen, get your paddles up and your bids in, and get ready to buy the car of your dreams!" called out Sammi Hogan, emcee and auctioneer for the Pardini auction. "Opener for this sweet 2019 Miata convertible is $15,000...now $20,000...any more? Are you going to do it, sir? Bam! That's $25,000 to you, sir."

Sammi Hogan did her trademark shimmy shoulder shake and two-handed celebratory fist pumps. "That's what we're talking about! And there are more ride-of-your-life vehicles coming up a little later."

It was one-thirty on a sunny mid-autumn afternoon, just a half hour into the auction, and already Sammi had wheedled almost a half-million dollars from the well-heeled crowd inside the grand banquet room of Mission Farm Winery & Vineyards. A projection screen, which spanned half the length of the back wall, was set up behind the podium. The words ASSETS FORMERLY BELONGING TO LINO PARDINI were splashed across the top of the screen. With all the proceeds going to the victims of the Pardini Ponzi scheme, there was a win-win, party-like vibe in the room.

Anne and Krista had seats together on the center aisle in the middle of the room. Every few minutes, they had to squeeze their knees to the side to let people stumble over them to get to their seats. All of the seats had been reserved, and only a few of the hundreds of chairs—elegant gold Chiavari banquet chairs with thick black cushions—were still empty.

"I think I'm underdressed for the room," Anne said, looking around the grand banquet room.

"You look fine," Krista said, giving her the once-over. "Nothing wrong with wearing nice jeans on a Saturday afternoon. It's the room that's over the top."

Their seats were facing the elaborately carved mahogany podium on the raised stage. The vast room was lit from the mirrored ceiling by a dozen three-tiered Italian chandeliers trimmed with Swarovski crystal drops. Along one side wall, a long banquet table was draped in starched white tablecloths and laden with silver platters and chafing dishes. Waiters in black tie were serving up hors d'oeuvres catered by Le Jardin, the chicest restaurant in town. Along the opposite wall, a phone table was manned by representatives of off-site bidders.

Anne and Krista sat with their paddles placed firmly face down in their laps while some high-end items, like diamond bracelets, season tickets to the San Francisco 49ers, and antiques, went for top dollar. Bidders vied for Lino's Rolex watch, a gift from Renee, which ultimately fetched $58,000. An original 1969 *Peanuts* Sunday comic strip, hand-drawn and signed by Santa Rosa's own Charles Schulz, went through dozens of escalating bids. According to the program caption, Schulz had donated the Sunday strip for a charity auction where Lino purchased it for $800 in the late eighties.

"$62,000, amazing," Anne said when the final bid came in. "Prices for an original Schulz have soared over the years, but even so..."

Kristi shrugged. "Well, it's a Charles Schulz." Enough said. The fabled cartoonist, a longtime Santa Rosa resident, had been a beloved and generous citizen of the community before his death in 2000.

Though the pricey items were going fast, it was the "vanity crap," as Krista called it—the customized pens, monogrammed Post-it notes, autographed photos of Lino with his arm around celebrities—that got the crowd most excited. A pair of black velveteen slippers embroidered with Lino's initials went for $4,000.

Kristi went back to studying her auction program, then abruptly stopped to point to an item. "Hey, get a load of this," she said, poking Anne in the ribs. "Lot 52 in the program."

Anne paged through her thick auction program with its over one hundred and fifty items until she found the lot Krista was referring to: a container of

Lino's boxer shorts and socks.

"I might have to get that for Mike. He can always use more boxers." Krista said as she glanced over her shoulder. "Oh look, the Channel 5 TV news crew is here, and they're talking to Ben and Camille Gleason. You know, the winery owners."

Anne didn't know any such thing, but she twisted around toward the back of the room. Television reporter Tamara Logan held a microphone in front of a tall, weathered-looking man with a military bearing wearing a tux. Next to him was a much younger woman, apparently his wife, wearing a full-length gown. They were in their glory, smiling and gesturing like game show hosts toward the long banquet table along the back wall of the room, where bartenders were pouring complimentary glasses of Mission Farm wine for a long line of attendees. A familiar face passed behind them, then ducked out of camera range.

"Well, look at that!" Krista said. "Marco Pardini is here."

"Seriously? You'd think he'd stay far away from this scene."

"I've heard he wants to buy up anything having to do with the Pardini winery," Krista said. "He plans to display some in the winery showroom. Like Francis Ford Coppola did at his winery." The Coppola winery in nearby Geyserville, just north of Santa Rosa, showcased a pool, vineyards, bocce courts, an Italian restaurant, and a gallery displaying movie memorabilia, including Oscars he won for *The Godfather* movies. The original Tucker automobile from the movie *Tucker: The Man and His Dreams* rotated on a motorized turntable in the gallery.

"What next?" the pert auctioneer called out, pointing to the image of Renee's engagement ring on the screen. "Lot 45, a five-carat center diamond ring to die for. Yes, this is Mrs. Pardini's personal engagement ring! This exquisite ring's two side diamonds bring its total weight to seven carats. Remember, all proceeds go to a worthy cause—to all those poor, disabused investors. And I know there are quite a few of you in the room here this afternoon!" Cheers mixed with boos went up in the packed room. "So dig deep into your pockets!" Sammi said.

"Well, what do you know! The Shermans are here," Krista said, waving across the room to a young couple holding a squirming toddler. "I have to go over and say hello to them. You should mingle, too, Anne. You might meet some new clients here. I'll be right back."

Left alone, Anne studied the room a bit more. Anything to avoid mingling, an activity that ranked at the bottom of her list of favorite things to do, right down there with reading how-to manuals.

Across the room she spotted two people she actually knew, so she did some waving of her own. Chloe Murray grinned broadly at Anne, giving her a two-handed wave. Chloe was sitting with her Aunt Joanne. Anne hadn't seen Joanne in two years, not since she helped solve a case that resulted in murder charges being filed by the DA's office against Joanne's brother. As far as Anne knew, he was still living abroad in Sarajevo, safely out of U.S. law enforcement's reach. During one of Anne and Krista's late-night, rambling, wine-fueled conversations, Krista declared that the accused murderer was "kind of hot" and proposed that they take a girls' trip overseas to visit him. "You could do worse," Krista told Anne, who said, "He's wanted for murder," to which Krista said defensively, "But not convicted." To which Anne countered, "Only because he fled the country." But Krista had the last word, "Every relationship has its roadblocks."

Chloe never mentioned her fugitive uncle, and if the family held any grudges against Anne for her part in the charges, it wasn't apparent from Joanne's cheery wave from across the room. Unfortunately, Joanne was doing her waving with her numbered paddle and inadvertently placed a bid on Renee's ring.

"This sparkler is now $400,000..." the auctioneer called out, nodding at Joanne. With wide eyes, Joanne mouthed the words, "Oh shit!'

Lucky for her, Sammi spied another upraised paddle. "And now $425,000, come on, folks..." Joanne pantomimed wiping her brow in a "phew, dodged a bullet there" gesture. Laughing, Anne watched as Joanne sunk down into her chair in relief. Anne then turned her gaze toward the room again in search of Krista, who was still chatting away with the Shermans. She knew Krista wouldn't be coming back to her seat for a while.

As Anne was casually looking toward the hors d'oeuvres table along the far wall to see if the line had gotten any shorter so she could grab a plate, a tall man in a brown leather jacket standing in the back of the room caught her eye. He was looking down at his program, absently slapping an auction paddle against his leg.

*Dave Silver? Why on earth would Dave be at this high-end auction,* she wondered. And as a registered bidder, no less. As far as she knew, he didn't have a lot of money to throw around, and besides, this just didn't seem to be his kind of scene. But then again, everyone else in town seemed to be here, so why not him?

Dave looked up, and their eyes connected for a split second. Then he blinked quickly and looked away.

A phone went off, making her jump. Hers. *Oh damn, forgot to mute it.*

"Please, people! Your phones need to be off," admonished Sammi from the stage, shaking her blonde bob. "Now, where were we? Now $485,000? Yes sir, now $485,000…"

Anne quickly yanked her purse off the floor, rummaged around inside it, and pulled out her phone. Just as she was about to disconnect the call, a name flashed on the screen.

*Lino Pardini? The very dead Lino Pardini?*

The phone slipped from her fingers, but she managed to catch it before it hit the floor. Clutching it tightly, she leapt out of her seat and scanned the room for the nearest exit. This was one call Anne wasn't going to miss. And she needed to be outside to take it.

She saw an exit sign over the side door to her right. What was the fastest way to get there? She could walk up the aisle and cross in front of Sammi on the stage, but that was out of the question. She didn't need any more public scolding from Sammi. Walking all the way to the back of the room, and then crossing over to the side wall, would take too long. So, the quickest route was straight down her row. She hit the green *Accept* button and took off, clambering over the legs and feet of at least ten seated people, saying "excuse me" every few feet until she made it to the end of the row.

"Hello?" she whispered into the phone as she turned toward the side door. "Who is this?"

"Me, Anne. It's Renee."

"Renee?! The caller ID says Lino. What the hell!"

"Never mind about that. Are you at the auction?"

"Yes, where are—"

"Thank God! They're about to arrest my boy!"

"Josh? What—"

"You've got to help! Go outside to where our vehicles are parked—you know, the ones they're going to auction off? That's where they've got him! He stole the pickup truck—the one he thinks belongs to him—out of the vehicle impound area about fifteen minutes ago. He drove it right out of the lot and took it for a joyride. What the hell?! He had a key, but still..." There was a tinge of panic in her voice, and her words were cutting out.

"What? I can hardly hear you, Renee. Are you in a car?"

"Yes, I'm almost there. Two....to..." Renee's voice kept cutting in and out.

Though she was hearing more static than recognizable words, Anne kept the phone to her ear anyway, speed walking toward the exit, which luckily was the one nearest to the impound area. But when she got within a few feet of the double doorway, she found herself blocked from going any farther by a tight knot of people who were standing around on the threshold, gawking at something that was going on in the parking lot outside. Anne overheard snatches of conversation about "a hoodlum in a hoodie."

Squeezing herself between two waiters in black tie, Anne stretched up to her toes and peered over a woman's shoulder. But she still couldn't see Renee's son. Coming up from behind her, a TV cameraman was barking out orders for them all to "Move aside, people." And, for some reason, probably having to do with the power and aura of the media, the crowd actually parted for him. Anne followed quickly in his wake, but only got another few feet before the mob closed in again, leaving her a good five feet from the open door.

Still stuck inside.

"....and how did Josh get past the security guard, anyway?! What's wrong with guards these days?" Renee's voice finally picked up again. "So then he was driving in the truck—though he couldn't have gotten far since he can

186

hardly grind his way out of first gear—and he called me, all proud of himself, and I told him in *no uncertain terms* to hightail it back to the auction parking lot and return the pickup before they noticed it was gone. I'm pulling up right now. Oh my God—"

Anne could hear the slamming of a car door through the phone and then a gruff voice in the background saying, "Ma'am, is this your son? He's committed a felony and…"

"What's happening, Renee?"

"Anne!" Renee's voice was now loud and clear. "The security guard is trying to arrest him now! Where are you? Bring your badge!"

*My badge? What for?* Anne could hear low, steady chants of "Lock him up!" coming through the phone—the same chanting that was going on, louder, all around Anne inside the auction room.

"Hurry!" Renee hung up.

* * *

There was no hurrying to be done, not while this mob blocked the doorway and kept her from reaching Josh and Renee out in the parking lot. Granted, it was a small, well dressed and well-to-do mob, but nevertheless.

*Bam-bam-bam.* The auctioneer's gavel pounded on the podium. "Outside, people! Take it outside! We have an auction going on here!' Sammi ordered briskly. "Close those doors. Please. Now. Thank you!"

That was Anne's cue to drop all niceties and elbow her way to the doorway in earnest (*Watch it, lady,* a guy said). While fumbling in her bag for her police badge, she carved a one-person path through the crowd. She barely made it to the other side of the double doors before they were slammed shut behind her.

Out in the sunlight, just a few feet straight ahead of her was a dark-haired uniformed security guard. His left hand was resting on a two-way radio, while his other hand was covering handcuffs that dangled from his duty belt. Standing easy with his legs spread shoulder width apart, the guard was staring down a squirmy, defiant looking Josh and ordering Renee to get out of his way while he did his job.

Renee wasn't budging from her son's side.

Anne reached them just as the guard was barking out, "You better cooperate, lady, or I'm gonna call for back up, and you're going in, too." He unfastened the handcuffs from his belt and dangled them from his fingertips. Josh jammed his hands into the pockets of his black sweatshirt.

"Can I help?" Anne cut in, stepping forward. Her police badge was still palmed in her hand, and she was ready to whip it out if things got any worse for Josh. Nothing, she knew, tamped down a security guard's sense of authority faster than someone with real police powers. But for now, she would just wait and see.

The guard barely looked at her. "I don't see how, lady, so step back," he said, taking Josh by the arm. "Both of you ladies, move on back." The guard looked familiar, but she couldn't quite place him.

While they were arguing back and forth, with Renee pleading her son's case (*He was only gone for ten minutes!*), a sudden movement caught Anne's eye. She turned toward the back entrance of the building and saw Dave Silver jogging over to them. Was that a baby carrier strapped on his chest? Could be, for all she *really* knew about him.

Dave was waving and smiling, but not at her.

"Angel, my man, what's going on here?" Dave called out to the security guard.

Turning toward Dave, the guard broke into a big grin that made him look years younger. That's when Anne remembered where she'd seen him before—at Trudy Lee's bar two weeks ago. He was one of Dave's friends from his younger years, working in the vineyards.

"Hey, *cabrón!*" the guard hollered back. He loosened his grip on Josh.

"Who you calling *cabrón?*" When Dave got alongside the guard, he gave him a hearty slap on the back. He slid off one of the shoulder straps of the leather knapsack, letting it dangle by his side. No baby, then.

"Hey, I'm in the middle of something here, *amigo*, but let's get a beer tonight."

"Sounds good, but listen," Dave said, taking Angel's arm and pulling him aside. "I know this kid…"

The two of them set off walking toward where the Pardini Winery truck was parked near the entrance. Coming to a stop by the chain link fence, they stood facing each other, talking and gesturing, out of hearing distance.

Renee and Anne just stared at each other for a few beats, both a bit shell-shocked. Josh looked like he was ready to bolt. When he started to make a move, Renee reached out her arm to block him. "You're not going anywhere, young man."

"I'm just getting my bike!" Josh exclaimed, pointing to a blue mountain bike lying on the ground. It was partially hidden in the weeds along the far fence, obviously dumped there in favor of a joyride in the pickup.

"Okay, but come right back."

Anne looped her arm through Renee's. "Now tell me what happened here."

Renee let out a breath, keeping her eye on Josh. "Okay, but you won't believe this. Josh rode his bike all the way here—which is at least ten miles and includes a highway overpass. And he got inside the secured area—who the hell knows how? But he can climb anything, so I don't know why I'm surprised. Anyway, he gets in here, starts up the pickup, and drives it out of here, slick as you please! The guard musta been looking the other way."

"And he must have left the gate unlocked, too—" Anne threw in.

"Then Josh calls me and tells me he got his truck back—like this is something he thinks I'd be proud of. Well, I had a total come-apart and told him to bring it back NOW, or I'd tan his hide. But he wasn't fast enough. The guard was already waiting for him." Renee paused, darted her eyes around, and then forged ahead, letting her Texas flag fly, "And, well, shoot-fire, y'all never heard such a ruckus…."

Anne looked at Renee, really looked, for the first time that afternoon. Her hair was slightly greasy and tangled. Her darting, wild eyes were visible beneath the sunglasses. No makeup, not even lipstick. A coffee stain on the front of her camel coat. A total come-apart indeed.

"Oh no," Renee groaned. "The television cameras are pointed right at us. Just what we need." Anne looked over her shoulder. The Channel 5 cameraman, standing about fifteen feet away from them, was indeed pointing his lens their way.

"I've got to get out of here," Renee said, an expression of panic crossing her face.

"Just keep your back to him."

That's what they were doing when they heard reporter Tamara Logan, who seemed to have appeared out of nowhere, call out to the cameraman, "Forget about those two for now, Tom. Get all of *that*." Tamara gestured loosely in the direction of the security guard, Dave, and Josh. "I'll do some voice-over. Then, count of ten, close-up on me."

Tamara raised her mic for the voice-over, while the cameraman took a few more steps back and panned wider to encompass the rest of the action: the security guard talking to Dave, the vintage Pardini pickup truck, Josh jerking up his hoodie and tramping through the weeds toward his bike. Then Tom spun around to get a sweeping shot of the fifty or so people who were emptying out of the auction room; they were gathering in a knot to see what all the commotion was about.

"Let's get out of the line of sight," Anne said to Renee. The pickup truck was still over by the entrance gate, but the other two vehicles—the just-sold Miata convertible and Lino's navy BMW—were parked next to each other in the showcase area. "Over there." Anne pointed to the BMW. "Let's go!" While the crowd's attention was on the TV crew, they made a dash for the driver's side of the BMW—the side farthest away from the camera and action—and ducked for cover below the window.

They could hear what Tamara, in an excited, news-flash voice, was saying in voiceover: "We have some breaking news here at Mission Farm Winery. The auction appears to have been hijacked—and by none other than Lino Pardini's widow Renee and her teenage son."

Still off camera, Tamara gave her long, black hair a quick fluffing up. The cameraman pointed a finger at her.

Time for her close-up.

"That's right," Tamara said, staring into the camera. "Young Josh Pardini allegedly broke into the impound area where the vehicles are being stored for auction and took one of them...the old truck...by force just a few minutes ago. It seems the Pardini family isn't about to let their personal belongings be auctioned off today."

Tamara gave the cameraman an *over-there* nod in Angel's direction, indicating where the next shot should come from. He pointed the lens at the security guard, picking up Angel's movements as he left Dave's side and headed to where Josh was standing alone by his bike.

"Yes, and as you can see," Tamara continued, "the security guard is advancing on the teen right now. I do believe Josh Pardini is about to be arrested. Except...wait a moment...the guard is putting away the handcuffs. There seems to be some delay." The reporter looked confused. "The security guard now appears to be putting his arm around the suspect."

For five full seconds, an eternity of dead air in broadcast time, Tamara said nothing, then finally, "So while they're talking about...whatever...let's see if we can get a statement from the boy's mother, Mrs. Pardini." Tamara sidled over to the cameraman and mouthed, "Where is she?" After a quick scan, he zoomed over to where Renee's head was peering out from behind the BMW.

Tamara called out, "Mrs. Pardini! Can you answer a few questions?"

Renee quickly ducked back down.

Tamara was striding in Renee's direction, rapidly closing in, when suddenly Angel appeared, coming from her right side. He stepped between her and the BMW, his bear-like frame blocking the reporter's view of Renee and Anne.

"There's nothing to see here!" Angel said, holding up his hand. "Just a minor disturbance. Nothing to be concerned about. Nada." Meanwhile, Dave and Josh made their way over to the passenger side of the BMW. They leaned against the car door while Angel took the heat.

"Officer, what is going on here?" Tamara asked.

"Just a little misunderstanding." Angel looked directly into the camera with a flat smile pasted on his face. "A teenage prank, I'm afraid. That's all." Then he looked past Tamara to the crowd gathered behind her. "Now, folks, I hear there's an auction going on inside. I suggest you all go back into the ballroom before everything gets sold off."

He motioned for them to move along. A long minute went by before the crowd started to lose interest and slowly headed back inside. They were reluctantly followed by Tamera and the cameraman.

After a moment, Renee peered over the roof of the car again. As she watched the slow-moving crowd funnel through the doorway into the ballroom, a look of bewilderment came over her face. She poked Anne in the arm.

"See that?" Renee said, grabbing Anne by the elbow and hauling her to her feet.

"What?" All Anne could see, except for the backs of the departing crowd, were two young men wearing ball caps who were bringing up the rear. As they shuffled to the door, they looked over their shoulders every now and then toward the two women.

"Those two. They're Lino's mechanics. Troy and another guy from the Rich's Auto Repair shop." Renee tilted her head. "Wonder what they're doing here. Strange."

# Chapter Twenty-Four

"Hand over the keys, young man."

Josh had a death grip on the truck keys, holding them behind his back, out of the guard's reach. His face was blank.

"Now!" Angel wasn't in the mood for attitude from a teenager whose ass he had just saved. The TV cameras were gone, and "happy time" was over.

"Okay! But on one condition—"

"You're in no position to be bargaining here, kid."

"Okay, but shit, officer! All I want is a photo of me and my truck. Just one photo!"

"Oh, for chrissakes," the guard grumbled, and then to Dave, who was standing next to him, "Do you believe this shit? I'm the only guard on duty here today cause this is supposed to be an easy detail. Broad daylight, fancy crowd. And then I get *this* kid."

Dave nodded sympathetically.

Angel went on, "I need to get this pickup back inside the showcase area ASAP, or it's my job. I've covered for this kid long enough."

"But what can it hurt, Angel?" Dave said, shrugging. "Just let him have one photo. It'll only take a second."

Angel grunted, thinking it over. "Okay, okay!" he finally said and then began clapping his hands together. "But hurry up, you people! One photo. That's it."

Anne watched as Renee fished through her tote bag—a bag even more voluminous than her own—and pulled out Lino's phone. Renee entered the passcode and motioned for her son to get in front of the pickup. "Go, Josh,

193

be fast about it." Josh pushed off his hoodie, ran his hand through his hair, and jogged over to the pickup.

"And I want some photos on my phone, too, Mom. It's in my pack," he said, pointing to his knapsack by his bike.

"No time!" Angel barked, his arms crossed over his chest. "Take the photo now or never."

"Alright, alright, but I want my mom in the picture, too. Mom!"

The guard threw up his hands.

Renee, not looking too happy about these developments either, handed the phone off to Anne and hastened to Josh's side. They quickly arranged themselves in front of the truck: Renee forcing a grin and Josh flashing a cocky Clyde Barrow-style smile, resting one foot on the stainless-steel stepside, his left arm draped jauntily around his mother's shoulder.

Anne backed away just far enough to get both of them—along with the full length of the pickup truck—in the frame. She snapped a couple of shots. "Got it!"

"Let's see!" Josh said, starting to trot over to her.

"Hey, stop right there!" the guard said, blocking his path. "Gimme the keys, kid."

Frowning, Josh stopped just a few inches short of the guard. He pulled out his key ring from his pocket, ceremoniously unhooked a key, and handed it over.

"And you're going to pay for that busted padlock, too."

"You broke the padlock, Josh?" Renee asked, her eyes widening.

"Yeah, he busted the padlock!" Angel said, pocketing the key. "You think I'd leave the gate wide open? No way." Angel glared at Josh. "Now get your bike and get out of here, kid, before I change my mind."

While Josh set off for his bike, the guard turned to Renee and Anne and pointed to Dave Silver's back. "You can thank your amigo over there for getting him off."

Dave was already halfway out of the compound area, making his way back to the auction in the banquet room. *Fleeing the scene*, Anne thought.

"If Dave Silver hadn't come along and vouched for your son, I would've called the cops, or gotten some help from those U.S. Marshals inside the auction," Angel said, then looked intently at Renee. "Mrs. Pardini, I don't want to tell you how to raise your kid, but he's got a wild streak in him as wide as—"

"I know, I know," Renee said with a weary sigh, extending her hand. "But thank you, officer."

"Name's Angel." He shook her hand, and then reached out and shook Anne's too. "Excuse me, but I've got to go and return the pickup to its rightful parking spot."

Angel headed off but didn't get far before he was almost sideswiped by Josh, who careened past him on his bike. "Slow down, kid!" But Josh didn't even bother glancing his way. He just kept riding, and when he reached his mother and Anne, he skidded to a dust-spewing stop and jumped off his mountain bike. He dropped it to the ground.

"Okay, let's see the photos!" Josh said. He yanked off his backpack and tossed it on top of the bike. Poking out from the open zipper of the backpack was a red-handled steel bolt cutter.

"A bolt cutter?" Anne asked, pointing to the backpack. "Wow, you really came prepared, didn't you?"

"Josh! Are you kidding me? Where did you get those?" Renee demanded.

"From Uncle Marco's garage. I had to get inside the security fence," Josh said in a matter-of-fact tone, looking in the direction of the phone in Anne's hand. "Okay, let me see the photos now," he said, but then quickly added, "please," with a glance to his mother. But Renee wasn't so easily assuaged.

"You're not seeing anything until I have a word with you first." Renee jutted her chin to her Mercedes which, in her rush to rescue Josh, was parked haphazardly, taking up two spaces in the customer parking area. "Over there."

While they were off to the side having a parenting moment, Anne opened the photo gallery icon on Lino's phone. She was surprised to see only three images stored in the phone; Anne had thousands on hers, a virtual checkerboard of photo thumbnails. The last two photos were the ones she'd just taken. They showed Renee looking strained, and Josh looking totally

195

relaxed, leaning against the pickup. One blurry, one not.

The only other image in the gallery was a closeup of Lino Pardini.

Just staring back at her.

*  *  *

*What the hell is this?*

It looked like a mug shot. A sad image of a tired old man facing the music. It looked like Whitey Bulger, the Boston Irish crime boss, the last time he was caught.

If this was merely a photo of Lino looking sick and terrible, it wouldn't be especially interesting. But this was a video, most likely made by Lino himself, and according to the running time stamp in the bottom right corner, it was five minutes and change in length.

Five minutes is a long time to stare into a camera and talk. Then again, there was no end to the subjects he could go on about, Anne thought. His financial crimes, for starters. Maybe he was confessing to it all—how he did it and why he did it, and who else was involved. Maybe he'd name some co-conspirators. Maybe he would even apologize to the victims whose lives he ruined. What else? There was a slim chance he would talk about his fourth wife's murder and his part in it. He might even reveal where he hid the money that she and Renee had spent hours searching the Pardini property for. It could be any or all of those things—or something else entirely.

But why talk at all? That was the question. Why unburden himself now? She couldn't think of any good reason. If he'd known that he was just a few hours away from dying, he might have felt free to confess to his crimes and set the record straight, figuring he wouldn't have to live with any consequences of his actions. So why not? But he *didn't* know he was dying. As far as he knew, he had years to live. No, this was to be his getaway video, a final statement to anyone who was interested. Lino probably had big plans for a new life—along with a new identity, passport, and enough cash for years. A comfortable life that was far away from this mess he'd created for Renee and his children. But the more Anne thought about it, the less that storyline added up. Lino didn't look like a man who was setting off for an adventure. He looked scared and sick. And if he was a runner, then he was a rare one—most of them didn't care enough about the people they left behind to bother setting the record straight. So again, why the video?

Anne needed time alone with the recording, but that would have to wait: Josh was just a few feet away, and he was casting furtive glances at her and the phone, while half-listening to his mother. The kid was itching to see his photos, and Anne would never get rid of him until he did.

So she'd have to look at the recording later. The file was too large to email to herself, so she tapped the share icon and AirDropped the video to her phone. She had no legal right to copy anything off Lino's phone: the phone and its contents belonged to Renee, and Anne didn't even have the right to watch the video without Renee's permission. She knew all of that, but decided she'd worry about the legalities later. She couldn't risk Renee keeping this to herself. Or worse, deleting the video. Of course, if Renee had wanted this video destroyed, wouldn't she have done that already?

Unless, of course, she didn't even know of its existence.

Josh and Renee were heading her way, so she shook off those thoughts and concentrated on pulling up the photos of them by the pickup. She tapped on the non-blurry one, placed two fingers on the screen, and pressed them outward to enlarge the image.

"Only one photo came out," Anne said when they reached her. "The other one was out of focus." She held the phone out in front of her so they could see.

Renee gave it only a brief glance. "Nice."

"Sweet," Josh said. "I like it. Let me send it to my phone."

Josh made a quick grab for the phone, but Anne held fast. The last thing she wanted was for Josh to play around with the phone and see his father's image. If he did, Josh would never give it back—and she couldn't let that happen. Because now that the phone was unlocked—and would stay unlocked for as long as she kept it active—Anne had no intention of handing the phone over without checking out a few things first. Like the list of Lino's last calls, for instance. The ones he received right before he died. Plus, his text messages.

Emails. History of online activity. She needed more time with the phone.

"I'll send it to your phone," Anne said in a tone that left no room for argument. "What's your number?" His expressions swung from puzzled to defiant to resigned, all within seconds. "It's in Dad's contact list," Josh said, shrugging.

While Anne was forwarding the photo, she started walking briskly to the banquet room. Josh stayed behind, looking down at his phone, waiting. But Renee followed her.

"I'm going back into the auction. There are a few things I want to bid on," Anne called out to Renee over her shoulder, slipping the phone into her purse while she walked. "And my friend Krista is still inside."

Renee stopped when she got within a few yards of the side entrance. "I can't go in there." Renee's voice rose a few octaves. "I can't be seen in there."

"That's fine," Anne said, not breaking stride. "I'll call you later and tell you how it went."

"No, wait, my phone!"

But Anne was already inside. Leaving Renee out in the cold.

# Chapter Twenty-Five

Two minutes later in the auction ballroom, Sammi Hogan was standing behind the podium gazing down at a sea of eager faces. All those truck-stealing shenanigans out in the parking lot were now just a distant memory, and she was firmly back in charge of the auction, busy wrapping up a sale. One of the last of the day.

"Do we have another bid? You can do it, sir…yes, sold! Thank you, sir!" Another shoulder shimmy shake for the high bidder of a Yuan Dynasty vase.

Standing near the back of the room, Dave Silver was waiting for lot 152 to be called, and according to the program, it was coming up fast.

"Now we have Lino Pardini's very own private car, a navy blue 2021 BMW 7 Series Sedan." Sammi pointed to its glitzy image on the projection screen and went on to describe its plush leather interior, horsepower, sleek design, and low mileage.

*Nice car*, Dave supposed, but not what he was here for. So, while the bidding went back and forth on the BMW, Dave spent those minutes glancing around the room. Marco Pardini was standing directly across the room. Six rows up, Dave spotted Anne McCormack, now back at her seat on the center aisle, talking to Krista Hageman, a nice lady, one of his customers. He watched as the women stood and embraced. Then Krista took off down the aisle, smiling and waving to people she knew on her way toward the exit.

He glanced back at Anne. She was seated again and looking down at her phone.

Dave turned back to his program and reread the notes describing lot 152 for what felt like the umpteenth time. He glanced over in Anne's direction again. Still looking down at her phone, scrolling away. A few more seconds went by, then she reached into her purse and fished out a second phone. Holding it above the phone lying in her lap, she appeared to be taking photos. Which was pretty odd, he thought. Why not just take a screenshot of whatever was on the screen in her lap and forward it to the other phone? Hell, why take any photos of another phone at all?

*Bam.* With a pound of the gavel, Lino's BMW was sold.

Onward.

"For the last item of the day, Lot 152, I'm coming down into the audience. Don't worry, I've changed out of my heels," Sammi said, laughing. "This is the truck that all the fuss was about outside."

She hitched a thumb over her shoulder, pointing to the overhead screen. Projected there was a three-quarter view of the vintage Pardini Winery pickup truck. Bright green and shiny, spotlessly clean, showroom ready. The chrome-finished stepsides and hubcaps gleamed. Any scratches or dents it might have amassed during the last sixty-plus years had been popped out, smoothed over, painted, and polished.

Dave's moment had come.

He rested a clammy palm over his brown leather knapsack. Inside the main pouch was stashed more money than he'd ever seen before in his life. Hundreds of one-hundred-dollar bills, flattened and stuffed inside business-size envelopes. Stacked one on top of the other, they had the thickness of two bricks. This was many thousands of dollars in cash, and it was making him properly nervous. He could have locked the money up inside his truck cab, but trucks can be broken into, especially an older one like his. No, he wasn't about to let this kind of money out of his sight, which is why he'd packed it all in his knapsack and wore the straps backwards so the money would be right in front of him. Like a baby carrier. Hands free. He felt conspicuous and slightly ridiculous. A few people gave him funny looks after they tried to sneak a peek at the baby that wasn't there. But that's the way it goes.

"This is the original 1956 pickup truck owned by Carlos Pardini, founder of Pardini Winery. A classic Chevy 3100 Stepside pickup, beautifully maintained…." Sammi continued giving the full rundown, then added, "But before we start the bids, just a few housekeeping notes."

Dave groaned inwardly. This auction couldn't be over fast enough for him. If it weren't for Trudy wanting that damn truck—correction, if not for Lino wanting that damn truck—he'd be home watching the 49ers game, a cold beer in hand. Why Lino wanted it was still a mystery that Dave hadn't been able to worm out of Trudy. All he knew was that if he won the bid, he'd bring the pickup truck to Trudy and let her deal with it. Done, except for splitting any leftover money with her. And if he was outbid—though he couldn't imagine anyone else spending more than Trudy on that relic with its clunky, three-on-the-tree manual transmission—then he would bring all the cash back to Trudy.

If things went smoothly, he'd be back home within an hour or so, he assured himself.

"For anyone interested in the seven-bedroom Pardini mansion in Fountaingrove: it will be auctioned off separately," Sammi said. While she continued on about the house, Dave tuned her out until she said, "Now, back to this rare, vintage pickup. It's selling at no reserve, which means that regardless of how low the final bid is, this beauty will be sold today. And remember, it's not just any ol' pickup. It's a classic Tri-Five Chevy truck. So, $20,000? Sounds like a good number to me. If it sounds like a good number to you, raise your paddle."

Four paddles shot up.

"Lookie right here, I've got $20,000," the auctioneer said, pointing to the young man in a "Rich's" ball cap who'd just won the first bid. Sammi then took off, prowling up and down the aisle, alert to the slightest twitch of a paddle. She picked up a few more bids. "Now $25,000…here we go. Who wants the classic pickup truck? $30,000…now $35,000. Everyone, it seems!"

Clearly pleased, she practically skipped from one end of the room to the other, pointing at one bidder and then at the next. Marco Pardini's paddle went up for a bid of $50,000. Dave quickly upped it to $55,000. Marco glared at Dave and raised his paddle. Dave glared right back and outbid him again. *Too bad, Marco.* But then it was Marco's turn again. Then the young man in the "Rich's" cap, who looked like he didn't have a pot to piss in, drove it up to $65,000.

"Okay, this is going to take forever!" Sammi laughed. "Let's increase the increments to $25,000 a bid and see who's really serious. Do I get $80,000...yes, $105,000..."

One minute and several bids later, Sammi called out, "Going once, going twice...fair warning!" She held back the gavel for a few seconds, looking to the audience, then looking toward the phone table for any last bids.

"Sold to the gentleman in the back for $155,000!" Down went the gavel, and Sammi gave the crowd one last shimmy shake.

"Okay, then. All done," she said. "Thank you, lovely people, for coming today. Please make your payments and take delivery of your winnings by five o'clock tonight."

# Chapter Twenty-Six

I t was late afternoon by the time Anne made her way out of the auction room. One of the last to leave, she hesitated on the threshold as a few stragglers brushed past her. She was in no hurry to step out into the chill air.

Anne was looking toward the horizon, at the winery's rows of vines that were still clinging to a few rust-color leaves, when a thought crossed her mind—what if Lino's video hadn't fully downloaded onto her phone? *Ridiculous*, she thought. But she pulled out her phone and checked it anyway.

*It didn't go through, what the...*

She checked the AirDrop file transfer app on Lino's phone. No wonder the file didn't go through: Someone had turned AirDrop off. *Who does that?* The same guy who doesn't take or store any photos; the same one who doesn't know much about apps, so he turns them off willy-nilly. *That's who*, she thought.

Anne needed just a little more time with Lino's phone. Just two minutes would be all it would take to get into his system's preferences settings, turn the AirDrop app back on, and try again.

She heard a car door slam.

Renee stepped out of her car and headed toward Anne.

"You're still here?" Anne called out, irritation creeping into her voice. She dropped Lino's phone back in her bag. Right next to her own.

"I waited for you so I could get my phone back." Reaching Anne's side, Renee seemed a little annoyed, too. She pulled up the collar of her camel coat against the cold.

Her time was up, Anne knew, and she had a choice to make: Either hand over Lino's phone to Renee and say nothing about the video—which would put Anne's chances of viewing it at around zero—or tell Renee about it, which would give her only slightly better odds.

"I'm not leaving without it," Renee said, leveling her eyes at Anne.

Though Anne nodded reasonably and pulled the phone out of her bag, she kept a tight grip on it while saying, "Listen, there's something you need to know, Renee."

"Yes?"

"But first, where's Josh?" Anne was stalling, and not smoothly.

Renee looked at her sideways, on to her. "He got a ride home with his uncle. They took his bike, too." She cocked a brow. "So, what do I need to know?"

"Well, there's a video on the phone. It's five minutes long. Have you seen it already?" Anne asked, all wide-eyed innocence.

"A video? Of what?" Renee looked like she was in shock. "No, I never looked at his photos. He never took photos that I know of, so I never even thought of checking. What's the date stamp on it?" Renee held her hand out for the phone. "Let me see."

Anne, ignoring the outstretched hand, called up the video. Renee planted her hands on her hips, but then dropped them and went to Anne's side to look at the still image of Lino.

"It says October 18," Anne said.

"The day he died. My God." Renee's voice faltered. "You haven't seen the video yet, have you?"

"No." Of course, if she'd had some wireless earbuds with her when she was sitting in the auction room while Renee stood outside, Anne would have played the video right then and there with no qualms at all. It was just bad luck that she'd forgotten to toss them into her purse that morning.

"Should we look at it now?" Anne's finger hovered over the play arrow.

Renee looked around the parking lot. A few people were still milling about. "Not here," she said and then abruptly snatched the phone away from Anne.

Anne just raised her hands in silent, unconditional surrender, watching as Renee slipped it into her coat pocket.

"Come over to my place," Renee said. "Follow me in your car."

"Okay."

"I don't want to watch it alone."

# Chapter Twenty-Seven

Renee couldn't put her finger on the moment she'd first started thinking of Anne as a friend.

There were moments during their search for Lino's money when they would finish each other's sentences and laugh at things that were so dark and inappropriate no one else would find them funny. But there were also moments of wariness and mistrust, not unlike what had just happened when Anne tried to pull a fast one by bringing Lino's phone inside the auction room. But then, that could just mean that Anne didn't fully trust *her* with the phone either. Fair enough. So, given all that mistrust and skittishness, perhaps "friend" was too strong a word. Maybe "ally" was more like it. They'd certainly been allies when they'd searched for Lino's hidden money; they had a common goal, struck a deal, acted in good faith, and each kept their parts of the bargain.

But friend or ally, what did it really matter? Renee desperately needed a friend right now, but she'd take what she could get. Ally was better than nothing, especially since nothing was pretty much what she had these days. The simple truth was that Renee couldn't be alone with this video. Not after fifteen years of living with Lino, having to constantly be on guard for any curveball he might throw her way. She wasn't sure she could handle any more of his nasty surprises. Not without having someone by her side. So yes, she would take an ally and be grateful for her.

Renee stepped into the guesthouse, switched on the lights, and tossed her coat across the twin-size bed in the back corner. She turned on the heat and sat on the bed, waiting. After five minutes, she went to the window and peered through a break in the curtains. What was taking Anne so long? Anne's car had been right behind hers when she'd veered onto the road for the Pardini property.

Renee opened the door, glanced to her right, and saw Anne walking up the dirt road with her phone pressed to her ear. "Okay, see you in a few," Anne was saying into the phone.

"What happened?" Renee called out after Anne got off the call.

"Flat tire. I just called my emergency roadside service, and one of their service trucks is in the neighborhood, so he'll be here within twenty minutes," Anne said as she reached Renee's side. "Or so they say."

"Well, sorry about that. It's these damn rutted-out roads." Renee swung the door wide and motioned for Anne to enter. "I've made some coffee," she said, heading into the kitchen. "Can I get you a cup or anything? Though the truth is, there's not much of "anything" in the cupboard except for cereal and coffee. I wish I could offer you something stronger."

"No, coffee's perfect." Anne peeled off her white jeans jacket while looking around the guesthouse.

Renee, stepping back into the room, followed Anne's gaze and saw the cottage through her eyes. It wasn't much to look at—certainly not compared to her last residence, the gated house in the hills overlooking a golf course and the city skyline. There was no fireplace with a carved marble mantle. No six-burner Wolf range nor commercial-grade Viking refrigerator. No radiant floor heating in the bathrooms. No housekeeper.

There wasn't even a couch for them to share while they watched the video. The two wooden chairs pushed together would have to do.

Anne apparently had the same idea. "Why don't we move the chairs side by side and sit at this table?" she said, already busy sliding the chairs into place.

"I'll get the coffee," Renee said. "Sorry, it'll have to be black. No cream or sugar in the house." She'd been to the grocery store just once since moving in here last week, picking up just the bare minimum—bread, fruit, frozen dinners, soup, coffee, milk, cereal—and begrudging every dollar. If she didn't find an income source soon, the Mercedes would have to go. She'd made a few calls to set up job interviews, but after giving her name, there was suddenly "no time on the calendar" for a meeting.

"Black's good," Anne said and hung her jacket on the back of a chair.

In the kitchen, Renee poured two cups and carried them to the table with shaky hands. Then she retrieved the phone from her coat on the bed. "I guess we might as well get started," she said. She dropped into the chair beside Anne and handed her the phone. "You do it."

Anne tapped the photo gallery icon. Up came the still image of Lino looking old and drained of color. They stared at it together for a minute until Anne asked, "Ready?"

Renee nodded. Anne pressed 'play', and they watched, transfixed, as the ghost-like image of Lino came to life again, blinking and talking a little too slowly and carefully.

"My name is Angiolino Pardini. But I'm known as Lino. My company is Pardini Financial," Lino raised his chin at that, a bit of residual pride. Then he sighed deeply and let his head drop, seeming to shrink into himself. He lifted his head again and continued, "Renee, I hope you'll be the one—"

"Stop, go back." Renee took a long, deep breath. "I wasn't concentrating. Start at the beginning again, please."

"Sure." Anne hit the replay button, and they began again, playing it for a few seconds until they caught up to the part where he was rubbing his eyes and saying, "...you'll be the one to find this recording, and you'll find me too. Unless Helen does, though I told her to go home early. I'm sorry, Renee, but I know you can handle it. I need to say some things and I don't have long. If you don't already know, you will soon...there were some irregularities regarding my financial dealings. I needed to borrow money from my investors to pay our bills and keep the business afloat. When I started, I had every intention of paying it back. I didn't plan to do anything illegal, but one time led to another time. It started out manageable and small, back before Dinah died. She found out. After that, it just snowballed. It wasn't hard to get new clients. The more successful you look, the easier it is to get people to hand you money. But, like I said, it got out of control. The market tanked more than once over the years...2008 was a bitch. Like quicksand. As hard as I tried, I couldn't fix it. I could never catch up."

"Where is he?" Anne stopped the recording to ask.

"In the upstairs bedroom. At the desk by the bed."

Anne hit the play button again. Lino was rubbing his forehead, then the corners of his eyes with both hands. "Things were crashing down and I made some plans to leave, I almost left a few weeks ago, but I couldn't do it. I kept hoping, thinking if I waited just a little while...but now I know...after that call I got this morning from...let's just say, an unsatisfied customer was reporting me...I know it's over. No one else was involved in this. Not my lawyer, not anyone in my family, not my accountant. They thought I was some kind of financial genius and trusted me. My secretary Rosemary...she suspected a few years ago, so I gave her a raise. But she didn't know for sure, so leave her alone. We all know where this is leading. The house is gone, Renee. It's been mortgaged to the hilt; all the houses are gone. I stopped paying our life insurance premiums months ago. I could never bring myself to tell you. No money, no savings. Nothing. I'm sorry, but you came into the marriage with nothing and got a free ride for all those years, so it's not like you really lost anything...."

He was taking shallow breaths, and with every exhale, he seemed to grow smaller, like a balloon losing air. "We've lost everything," he continued, "and the Feds will try to bring charges against me. I can't let that happen. I can't watch the FBI come into our home and go through our things. Then, the fingerprints, mugshot, cable TV. I can't go to prison. I can't live that way, Renee. That's not how I end.

"So, about two hours ago, I took hydrocodone with some Ativans on top. Three pills each. Some Jack Daniels." Droplets of sweat trailed from his forehead down to his ears. The gray curls at his neck were glistening. His hair had been damp, Renee recalled, when she found his dead body; she had assumed it was from taking a shower. Now she knew the real cause: a fatal cocktail of drugs and alcohol.

"I'll send a copy of this to my attorney Joel Maroni when I'm done here. Joel, show this to the police or anyone you think needs to see it. Except the media. Don't let them see this."

His breathing wasn't coming easy, but he went on, "There's more. Tell my daughters...tell Carrie and Jennifer that I'm sorry. Tell them that no matter what anyone says, I didn't have anything to do with their mother's death. But the truth is, I know more about it than I've told anyone before, and I want to set some things straight. The night Dinah died, I was out of town and couldn't go to the charity dinner with her, so I hired a man, someone Dinah and I both knew, to pick her up in a limo and drive her there. As a special treat. I told him to make a stop on the way to the dinner, to go into the Safeway market and pick up a corsage that I'd ordered in the floral department. I wanted to surprise Dinah with her favorite, a gardenia corsage. But the driver was...oh god, so stupid. He left the key in the ignition, and while he was in the store, someone got into the car. Her killer got in. And the killer just drove off with her. Or that's the story the driver gave. But he could have made it up. Maybe he was the killer. Anyway, that's all I know."

His shoulders rose in helplessness. Looking off in the middle distance, he continued, "But I couldn't tell the detectives any of this because they'd come after me. They'd think I set it up somehow. That I killed the mother of my children. And the driver I hired, he never said anything either because...well, he'd be a fool to..."

Lino took another shallow breath, then rested his head in his hands. Looking up again, he spoke slowly and deliberately, his words stretching out in a soft, tired slur. "Renee, I can't make this up to you, I know that. But please forgive me and remember the good times. Would you do that for me?" He picked up his head and looked directly into the camera. "Please, think back to our first date, what we did, and where we went that evening. Remember? Go back there, relive that date, everything from how we drove, to where we ate. Do it exactly the way we did that first night. Talk to the owner of that place. Just remind the owner who you are, and then drive to where we had our first honeymoon night. The lodge. Take the same road. You must do this. For the good memories. And bring Josh."

Lino closed his eyes for a full minute, then jerked himself upright. "And Joel, take care of my family. Take my son Josh to a baseball game..." Another long pause followed. "I'm going to finish this later."

The screen went dark.

* * *

They held their silence, waiting, as if the recording would start up again.

Renee finally said, "Is that all?"

"He never finished it," Anne said, still staring at the screen.

Renee stood up, motionless for a moment. Then she started pacing the tiny space. "Lino must have gotten up from the desk and gone into the bathroom, at least I think he did—he must have—because he slipped and fell. The medical examiner said he died from blunt force trauma to the back of his head, and of course, there was that spot of blood on the pillow that I found," Renee muttered, as if thinking out loud, narrating a movie replaying in her head.

"But now we know it was suicide," Anne said. "With pills. Ordinary anxiety pills and pain killers, plus some booze on top."

"Yes, but the fall couldn't have helped."

"No, of course not—" Anne stopped short when a realization hit her. "Renee, Lino died before he could finish this, and that means he never sent this video to Joel Maroni, his lawyer, like he was planning to. No one's seen this but us."

Renee looked blankly at Anne. She stopped pacing.

"We need to send it to Maroni or to the police, or both. This should be entered into evidence," Anne said as she tapped into the phone settings and turned on the AirDrop file transfer app. "But first, I'm sending this to my own phone, okay?"

"Sure, I guess," Renee said distractingly while dragging her chair to a spot across the table from Anne. She slumped into the chair. "I can't believe he took his own life. That's the last thing I thought he'd do." Setting her elbows on the table, she cupped her head in her hands.

Anne, meanwhile, was quickly sending the video to her own phone before Renee could change her mind. "But why do you need it?" Renee asked

211

suddenly, looking up. But it was too late, the file was already on its way. "And why would anyone else need to see this? What do you mean by 'entered into evidence?' Evidence of what?"

"Well, first of all, this is Lino's testimony—his admission—about the Ponzi scheme," Anne said. "It might clear up some questions about having co-conspirators. Or at least it gives Lino's version of the events. Then there's Dinah's murder. That case is cold, but it's not entirely closed, and I know my uncle Jack would like to hear what Lino had to say. And then, of course, there's the cause of death. Suicide."

"No, I don't want that part going into evidence. Not suicide. My father took his own life, and it was devastating. I don't want his children to know." Renee's voice faltered. "No, I don't want Josh to think his father left him on purpose."

"It'll come out in the toxicology report anyway. And that could be released any day now."

Renee looked sad and defeated. "Okay, whatever. But I'll tell them myself. I'll tell Josh and Lino's daughters. I don't want them reading or hearing about this somewhere else."

"Of course not," Anne said, concern in her voice. She paused just long enough to show her sympathy before diving into another subject. "I was surprised that Lino didn't mention all those thousands of dollars he hid. The envelopes? You would think he'd want you to have that money." Anne paused again, another thought occurring to her. "Though maybe he didn't mention it because he was afraid someone other than you would find his body...and would then watch the video since the phone was right there by the bed. If he'd given instructions about where to find the money, that person would've scooped it up and kept it—or else hand it over to the U.S. Marshals."

"That's possible. On the video Lino said he told our housekeeper to go home early," Renee said, "but he couldn't be sure that she wasn't still hanging around downstairs. Helen had full run of the house and came and went as she pleased. And if she'd found his body instead of me..."

"She would have called the authorities, who would have confiscated the money."

"And then there's Josh," Renee said. "Sometimes, he would come home early from school. There was *that* horrible possibility."

"So maybe that's the upshot: Lino couldn't be sure you would be the one to find him and the phone," Anne said. "Which means that Lino couldn't just come right out and say where the stolen money was. Too many people would have their hands out. But why didn't he just call you? Have a private conversation with you?"

"He did call. I was at a committee meeting, but I picked up the call. His voice was breaking up, so I told him I'd call him back. I hung up. I didn't call him back. And he didn't call again either. And no texts..."

They lapsed into another silence, each lost in her own thoughts.

Anne's thoughts went back to her brief moments alone with Lino's phone. While sitting in the auction room, she'd pulled up the text messages he sent the night before he died. The last one was a cryptic message to his daughter Jennifer, instructing her to "check the place where you kept your dolls." So maybe Lino didn't mention those envelopes in the video because he had already given the money away.

Renee's thoughts, it turned out, were of a more personal nature.

"He never said he loved us," she said, breaking the silence. "Did you notice that?"

# Chapter Twenty-Eight

Trailer was as good as her name. If Dave took a few steps, Trailer took a few steps. If Dave stopped, the dog pulled up right at his heel. If Dave smiled, Trailer thumped her tail. And if, like now, Dave stood on his porch and looked off at a rectangular garden patch set back fifty yards or so from his mobile home, then Trailer looked at it too, sniffing at the air, waiting for Dave's next move.

It would be evening soon, and Dave needed to get going. He hefted his leather knapsack off the ground, slung one of the straps over his shoulder, and locked the front door. He turned around and stood motionless for a few seconds.

Sometimes, when Dave was taking too long, just standing around and thinking, like now, Trailer would break character and take the lead. The aging golden retriever could anticipate where Dave would go next, and so she lumbered down the porch steps and headed toward the truck, which was parked steps from their single-wide mobile home. When she got to the closed door on the driver's side, Trailer stopped and sat, waiting patiently while Dave let his eyes wander back to the rock-lined dirt patch.

It was still slightly concave after all these years, but not enough for anyone else to notice. Every spring, bunches of daffodils and African irises would pop up through the dirt. But now, deep into late fall, there was nothing to see except dormant, woody ground cover, dry, matted leaf mold, and fallen twigs from the sycamore tree.

Trudy would be back from her uncle's funeral by now, Dave figured, and he'd have to tell her about the auction results. He wanted to give her the news in person, before the Saturday night crowd descended on the bar. It was news that Trudy wasn't going to like hearing: Once the bidding for the pickup truck went over $90,000, Dave was out of the running. The rangy young guy wearing the "Rich's" logo on his baseball cap folded soon after. Which left the last two bidders—Marco Pardini and the phone bidder—to battle it out to the finish. Out of curiosity, Dave had stayed around to watch.

He sent Trudy a quick text to make sure she was back at the bar. She replied, "Yep." He joined Trailer by the pickup, opened the door, and tossed his knapsack onto the floor of the cab. Trailer hopped in. Dave backed up the truck, turned it around, and took off toward the main road.

\* \* \*

Jerry Silver was speed walking down the road in front of his house as fast he could without actually breaking into a run.

"Dave!" he called out when he was within twenty feet of Dave's truck, which was slowly nearing the junction where Dave's dirt road met his parents' dirt road.

"Hey, Dave!" he shouted again, louder. The truck squealed to a stop, kicking up a few brown clouds of dust in its wake.

Coming up behind the truck, Jerry walked to Dave's window, coughing from the dust flurries that Dave had, in his opinion, deliberately kicked up. Dave could have just as easily rolled the truck to a gentle stop. Jerry pasted on a smile.

"You didn't make it to the auction," Dave said.

"Nah, I needed a nap, and your mom's having a bad day. So, tell me, did they rake in a lot of money for us victims?"

"A fair amount."

"How about for those vehicles? Who got the farm truck?"

"Marco did, but he had a lot of competition."

Jerry tilted his head back and barked out a short laugh. When he noticed Dave looking at him with tight lips, Jerry asked, "What's wrong with that? It's back with the Pardinis where it belongs. And there'll be money in my pocket from the sale. Where's the truck now?"

Dave started up the engine. "Don't know, but probably at Marco's house. Gotta go."

"Where to?"

"Trudy's."

"Want some company?"

"Maybe you should stay home with Mom."

"She won't know if I'm home or not. And by tomorrow, she won't remember." Jerry was having to keep an eye on her these days. She was picking up strange habits. Like writing in her journal until all hours of the night, writing all kinds of bat-shit crazy things. Lately, he'd seen her putting letters in the mailbox and would have to intercept them before the mail carrier came. But Jerry had his business to run and couldn't be checking the mailbox every day. He wasn't too worried, though, because mostly she got the addresses wrong, or forgot to put stamps on the envelopes. Once she even forgot the envelope—so they weren't going anywhere.

"She's getting bad, you know. She's not the same person."

"I know."

"She's saying things, off-the wall things," Jerry said, shaking his head. "She's having false memories."

"Is that what you call them?"

"Well, anyway," Jerry said, glancing back up at the house. He slapped the side of Dave's truck. "Say hi to Trudy for me."

"Say hi to Mom."

Jerry watched him drive off, then dug out his phone from his pocket and sent a text.

# Chapter Twenty-Nine

From outside Renee's house, just beyond the double rows of olive trees, a horn went off—three fast beeps that startled Renee and Anne into looking toward the front window. The next thing they heard was the low rumbling of a truck driving along the road leading to Marco's house. It was accompanied by raucous laughter and shouts of "woo-hoo!"

"Sounds like a party's going on over there," Anne said. "Did I tell you that Marco won the bid for the pickup? Maybe that's what all the hoopla's about."

"Better him than a stranger, I guess."

Just then, the horn beeps got faster and sharper, taking on a staccato rhythm—almost drowning out the yelling and carryings on, which seemed to be taking a nasty turn. Voices were shouting over each other. "Shut up, you moron!" and "Hell, no!" were the only words they could make out for sure, but there was no denying the anger behind them.

"Hope Josh isn't in the middle of all that," Renee said, frowning. After a few seconds, when the commotion had died down a bit, the two women shared a questioning look and then went back to hashing over the video they had just seen. Lino's rambling explanation about his financial crimes and his justifications for doing what he did—and why—had left them both cold.

"Why would he make such a nasty remark, saying that I 'got a free ride for all those years, so what do I have to complain about now?' Swear to God, if I'm ever tempted to cry over that man again, all I'll have to do is remember those words. That'll keep my mascara from running. I never really saw the arrogance until now," Renee said, shaking her head. "Well, maybe I saw it, but I just couldn't afford to face it."

"What was all that about your first date? It was like Lino was talking in code. Like he didn't want anyone else to understand. Me, for example, I have no idea if he wanted you to visit the place, or was just being romantic—"

"Oh, please. Lino wasn't that romantic. No, he meant it literally, and he wants me to actually go there, and I think it's plain weird."

"But go where? Do you remember what you did that night?"

"Like it was yesterday. But the date wasn't much, really," Renee said with a dismissive wave. "We just went to a funky little western-style bar. Lino said he wanted me to see the 'real him,' as he put it, and so we got into the Pardini Winery pickup and drove out to Trudy Lee's Bar & Grill."

"I've been there a few times. It's just east of town on Highway 12."

"That's the one. We just had hamburgers and a few drinks. Shot a game of pool. And that's about it. I think the reason he took me to Trudy's was because it's a little outside of town, and his friends and business associates wouldn't see him there. He was still married to Dinah at the time, you know. We never went back there, in all the years we were married."

"Didn't he date Trudy Lee back in high school? I remember hearing something like that."

Renee scoffed. "*That* woman? Not likely. Is she saying that?"

Before Anne could reply, a new outburst of swearing and angry shouting interrupted them. It was a fierce renewal of the fighting from before, only now it was closer to the front door. Then, just as the racket was building to a crescendo, the sound of approaching footsteps got the women to their feet. Before they reached the window, the door flew open.

"Mom!" Josh yelled, bursting into the room. His eyes were wild, and his whole body seemed to vibrate with anger. "I'm staying here tonight! I'll sleep on the floor. I don't care!" He tossed a sleeping bag and his knapsack onto the floor in the center of the room, where they landed with a thud, causing Anne and Renee to back up a few steps.

"They're over there celebrating buying my truck at the auction. *My* truck." He was gesticulating wildly, and his face was twisted in fury. "My cousins say it belongs to *them* now. Can you believe that? That's cray."

"Calm down, honey," Renee said. "It can't be that bad."

"Yeah, it is. We got into a big fight. Look at this." He poked a finger through a fresh rip in his black hooded sweatshirt. "Ryan tore it. Then Uncle Marco told me the truck was going on display at the winery. He's going to put it on one of those motorized disc things, so it goes around and around, like it's a toy or something. And then, when I said that it was mine, he said it wasn't. He said I was lucky they let me stay there, and I should act more grateful." Josh paused, and when he started up again, both his face and tone had downshifted from anger to hurt. "But I do act grateful, Mom. I don't know why they're acting like this. And it *is* my truck. Dad always said…"

The boy looked close to tears. Renee made a move to comfort him, but he turned away, saying, "I've gotta use the bathroom."

As they watched him disappear around the corner, Renee looked close to tears herself. Only after hearing the bathroom door click shut, when they were sure he was out of hearing range, did the women start speaking again.

"Poor kid," Anne said in a low voice.

"It's been weeks of Josh crying. And when he's not crying, he's acting out. I feel so awful for him, and it'll only get worse when he learns what his father did."

"I should leave you two alone," Anne said, checking the time on her phone. "I'll wait outside for the tire service guy." She picked up her coffee cup and set it in the kitchen sink. "He should have been here by now."

"Before you go, remember what we were talking about before?" Renee asked. She brought her own cup to the sink and stood beside Anne, rinsing both cups and setting them on the dish rack.

"You mean about going to see Trudy? For God knows what possible reason…"

"And making a pure fool of myself, besides," Renee said.

"Well, I wouldn't worry about that. There's nothing Trudy hasn't seen before, and she doesn't seem like the judgmental type," Anne said.

"I might do it tomorrow. Will you come with me?"

Anne hesitated, so Renee continued, "Lino's video has me running all over the place—all the way from Trudy's to the honeymoon hotel in Calistoga, and I could use the company. But if you're busy, no problem." She shrugged her shoulders. "Maybe I won't go. It seems so pointless. Except it was Lino's last wish." She shrugged again.

"Mom?" Josh appeared from around the corner. They hadn't heard the bathroom door open. "What are you guys talking about? There's a video of Dad?" His eyes darted from his mother to Anne and back to Renee again.

"Oh, Josh." Renee shot Anne an imploring look, a pleading for some kind of rescue. But she was clearly looking to the wrong person. Anne was out of her depth and knew nothing about mother/son relationships, Renee realized. All Anne could offer was a helpless shrug while looking longingly at her jacket lying on the bed.

"Yes," Renee finally said to Josh. "Your father left us a message. We just found it…"

"What kind of message?" he asked in a low, choked voice.

Renee avoided his eyes.

"Mom? What did he say?"

"Nothing much. He just talked about his business and things," Renee stuttered, her eyes darting around the room as if looking for a new subject. "Are you really staying here tonight? You can take the bed and I'll sleep on the floor in the sleeping bag. Maybe we can get pizza for dinner…"

"I want to see it."

"I don't think so, sweetheart," Renee said quietly and reached out and lightly touched his shoulder. "There are some things on the recording that are for grown-ups only." But as she was looking into his dark, intelligent eyes, so like his father's, she found herself pulling back, reconsidering.

"Alright, Josh, if you really want to, I won't stop you," she said as she watched Anne duck out the front door. "But you need to know a few things first."

* * *

Josh didn't speak when the video ended. Not for a good five minutes. He just left the phone on the small table and moved to the armchair where he sat hunched over, looking down at his folded hands.

After a while, Renee went over to him and perched on the padded armrest. She put an arm around his shoulder. "I'm so sorry, Josh. Are you okay?" Though the video had lasted mere minutes, Renee knew how profound an impact it would have on him. She worried that she'd made the wrong decision in letting him watch his father at his lowest point, struggling and near death. Perhaps Josh was too young. But he would have found out sooner or later, she told herself, once the final results of the autopsy came out. So maybe it was better to hear it directly from his father? But how could that be better? He would never be able to erase that image from his mind.

She watched helplessly as tears trailed down Josh's cheek. She couldn't second guess herself now. It was done. Josh wiped them roughly away with the palm of his hand and blew out a long breath. "Yeah, I'll be okay." His voice was thick with grief.

She nodded but knew it would never be okay. Her own father had taken his life when she was ten, a few years after he left the family to fend for themselves in a rented dump on the side of a Texas highway. Her father always liked his money to come easy. So he got involved in a get-rich scheme in Oklahoma that turned criminal. He shot himself before the trial.

Not so very different from Lino. Lino's crimes were more upscale than her father's, more newsworthy, but it was essentially the same story: a father taking the easy way out, leaving a damaged family behind, broke, and practically homeless. So she knew that devastation, but she never thought she'd have to see her own child live through it.

# Chapter Thirty

Fifteen minutes had passed. Anne had spent ten of those minutes waiting in her car for the mechanic to show up to fix her tire. She probably could have fixed it herself, but why have an AAA card if you don't use it? When the white truck rolled up, Anne ventured from the warm comfort of her car and spent another few minutes standing around outside, a chill wind whipping through her hair, while the young mechanic jacked up the car, removed the flat tire, and replaced it with her spare. All in under five minutes (*A personal best*, he told her). She signed the paperwork and waved goodbye as he backed down the road, driving in reverse all the way out to the main road, a good quarter of a mile.

Anne knocked tentatively on Renee's door.

"Anne? Come in," Renee called out.

"Sorry to bother you," Anne said from the threshold, looking from Renee to her son. They were sitting at the small formica-top table. Josh was fidgeting in his seat and idly tossing the dark-screened phone from one hand to the other. The mood in the room was grim.

"The mechanic just finished up, so I'll be taking off now. Just thought I'd say goodbye."

"Come in for a few minutes," Renee said, gesturing her into the room.

Anne took a step inside and shut the door, all the while keeping one hand on the doorknob. Feeling like an intruder, she didn't want to stay long. Hello and goodbye. She smiled at the unsmiling Josh. He nodded back, then dropped his eyes and went back to fiddling with the phone.

"Like we were talking about before, Anne, I'm going to Trudy Lee's Bar—"

Renee said.

Josh's head jerked up quickly. He cut her off, "Not without me, you're not—" He set the phone down.

His words hung in the air while Renee leveled her eyes at him for a full five seconds. Then she acknowledged his words with a nod and continued, "Okay, fine. Josh and I are going to Trudy's tomorrow. Have you given any more thought about coming along?"

"I'm not sure if tomorrow really works," Anne said, thinking it over. It wasn't that she wasn't up for an adventure; it was just that her entire Sunday, the first one in months that wasn't devoted to an estate sale, was already mapped out. She planned on spending it catching up on business. She needed to go over invoices, pay bills, price out art pieces, and on and on. "I'm pretty busy, sorry, but..."

"That's okay. Tomorrow's no good anyway," Josh said. "We can't wait until tomorrow. Dad gave all those instructions on the day he died, almost three weeks ago. That's a lot of time we've already wasted. Maybe we're already too late..."

"Too late for what?"

"I don't know, Mom, all I know is we have to go now. And it's only four-thirty. It's still light outside."

"He has a point," Renee said slowly, turning toward Anne. "I mean, it wouldn't hurt to get it over with."

"Well, I guess...yeah, why not?" It was a Saturday night, and it wasn't as if she had a hot date lined up. It beat pizza on the couch. Besides, she'd already come this far with Renee. And she had to admit she was curious about whatever Trudy would have to say about all of this. If anything. "Okay, I'm in."

"We'll take my car," Renee said.

"We need to take the pickup—" Josh said.

"No, we don't. There's no reason why—" Renee said.

"Dad said to do everything *exactly* like you did that first night."

"I don't think it makes *any* difference what we drive."

"No, Mom!" Josh said, sounding like his hyper, animated teenage self for the first time since seeing the video. "We have to do it just like Dad said. Dad was always very specific. He meant what he said. You told me that you and Dad drove the pickup that night, right? And he said on the video to relive that day *exactly*, starting with how you drove there. And that means he said to drive the truck. I can borrow it—"

"Borrow it?" Renee's brows shot up.

"Sure! They'll never know it's gone. Uncle Marco and Aunt Kay have already started drinking, and my cousins won't notice anything cause they're probably playing video games upstairs. And it's parked right out in front of the house. Easy. They don't even need to give me a key." Josh pulled out a key from his jeans and held it aloft. "See? Got one." He looked proud of himself for outfoxing the security guard by withholding one of his truck keys.

"You can't do that, Josh. You've been in enough trouble for one day."

"Right," Anne agreed in a firm voice. "No so-called 'borrowing.' You need their permission." But while speaking those law-abiding words, what was really running through her mind was: If Josh were to go over to his uncle's house and stay there long enough to ask for permission—say, about five minutes—and then came back here with the truck...well, who's to say for certain he didn't get their consent? Not her. There was plenty of plausible deniability in that kind of time-lapse.

It worked for her.

"Okay, okay," Josh muttered. "I'll ask them. I'll be right back. Gonna go over and ask for permission."

Was it Anne's imagination, or did he wink at her on his way to the door? As if he considered them partners in crime, both of them in on the joke. Anne found herself biting her lip to keep back a smile. He wasn't, apparently, someone who was opposed to bending the law a little, a trait he shared with Anne. Although it was a trait she was starting to get a little concerned about. Her relationship with the law, never as firmly straight-arrow as her Uncle Jack's, was fast becoming a little too casual. She should probably be more careful about the kind of company she was keeping, she mused as she watched Josh step through the door and give her a "thumbs up" as he closed it behind him.

* * *

The cab bench of the pickup was just long enough for the three of them. Josh was sitting behind the wheel, grinding along down the dirt road, slow and loud.

"Why is he even driving?" Anne asked incredulously, looking at Renee, who was sitting scrunched up in the middle.

"No reason that I can see," Renee offered.

"Because I'm the one with the key, that's why!" Josh answered, his brow furrowed in concentration as he shifted from first gear to second gear. Then back to first. Up to second. Then back down to first again, until Anne couldn't take it anymore.

"Pull over, Josh. I'm begging you," Anne said. It wasn't just the slowness that was getting to her; it was the growling, metallic, skin-crawling, godawful noise of the grinding gears. It was a wonder Marco and his family didn't come out screaming from their house and discover that their pickup was driving off. Maybe it wasn't as ear-splitting as all that, but in this enclosed space, she felt like she was sitting next to a speaker at a heavy metal concert.

"No way. I'm doing good."

Anne groaned. "No, you are *not*. First of all, you don't even have a driver's license. How would you like it if a cop pulled you over?" Anne said while simultaneously realizing that she was, for all intents and purposes, still a cop herself. "But the worst part is, your driving sucks," Anne continued. "You don't have the hang of shifting. The clutch is there for a reason. Pull over—"

"*Now!*" Renee jumped in.

"*Now,*" Anne echoed.

"Like you could do better? Girls can't drive a stick shift. My dad taught me—" But Josh's airy bravado sprung a leak when he glanced over and registered the dark look on his mother's face.

225

"Are you kidding, Joshua Angiolino? Pull over now," Renee ordered in her mom-voice, "or your hide's going to be tanned, and I don't care how big you think you are." Doubtless an empty threat, but Anne liked her spirit and nodded vigorously in support.

"Okay, okay," he muttered.

"And apologize to Anne for your smart-alecky tone of voice."

"Actually, it was the comment about women drivers that really offended—" Anne threw in.

"Sorry." Josh muttered, but even so, his grip on the steering wheel remained rock solid.

"You have to the count of three..." Renee said sharply. That did it. Something about that age-old threat—used by every mother, everywhere— struck a neuron in the primitive back part of his brain. He swerved to the side of the road, narrowly avoiding the ditch, and slammed on the brakes. The truck shuddered to a stop.

Anne jumped out of the cab, rounded the front of the truck, and hopped into the driver seat while Josh and Renee slid over. And with that, Anne's participation level shifted from "going along for the ride of it" to taking over and leading the charge.

It was an eight-mile drive along winding roads to Trudy Lee's Bar & Grill, but once they reached the end of the dirt road on the Pardini property and finally hit the smooth pavement on Thomas Lake Harris Drive, it was fairly easy going. The plan was to steer clear of the major highways, thus avoiding detection (*Not that we stole the truck, 'cause we didn't,* Josh said) and take the back roads to the more rural Highway 12. Turning left onto Fountaingrove Parkway, they traveled along the lush, oak tree-lined boulevard through the neighborhood's hills and valleys. As they neared the turn-off for the street where the family had lived only weeks before, Anne noticed Renee gently patting Josh's knee.

Anne pulled her eyes forward. "This truck runs pretty good, considering its age. A little trouble on the hills, but not bad," she said, smoothly shifting the gears. The old engine was practically purring, as if in thanks for the change in drivers. Anne's father had taught her how to drive a stick when she was a teen, and though she hadn't handled one in years, it was one of those handy life skills—like typing, picking a lock, and tailing an ex-lover—that never goes away. "And we have a lot of gas," Anne said, looking at the needle on the fuel gauge.

"Dad always kept it full. And the oil's good, too. We had it changed at Rich's Auto Shop all the time," Josh said with a hint of pride. "Every month."

"No kidding? The guy who just changed my tire came in a tow truck with Rich's logo on the side of it. Small world." Anne signaled and turned right onto Middle Rincon Road. "We'll be at Trudy's in less than ten minutes."

"What if she isn't there? Maybe we should have called first," Renee said.

"And said what, exactly?" Anne asked. "No, if she's not there—or doesn't know anything—we'll just turn around and go back home. Or head on out to the honeymoon hotel in Calistoga."

"We don't have any idea in hell what we're supposed to do at that hotel," Renee said. "I'm counting on Trudy to tell us. But what if she just stares at us?"

"You've met her, right?" Anne asked.

"Just that once—the night we went to the bar on our first date. It was the first and only time Lino ever spoke of Trudy." Renee went on to say how Lino mentioned that they'd gone to high school together, and after that, he went his way—off to Harvard and law school—and she went and lived in a commune. But he always respected how she ran her own business and how she never took crap from anyone. She was "no bull shit," according to Lino.

"I don't think he ever saw her again, but who knows..." Renee said. "I obviously knew nothing about that man."

"We're coming up on Highway 12 now," Anne said, glancing at the rearview mirror. Traffic was light. The only car in front of her was two hundred feet ahead, and the only vehicle behind her was a white Ford truck. Though it was a few car lengths back, she never liked being anywhere near big-tired, high-riding white trucks with massive chrome grilles. In her experience, they tended to have aggressive, road-raging drivers behind the wheel. When they weren't cutting her off, they were on her bumper, tailgating so menacingly she'd have to pull over and let them pass. Maybe her prejudice was largely unfounded. Maybe it didn't apply to most of those drivers. Nevertheless, she felt her stomach tighten.

Anne signaled for a left turn and, when the traffic light turned green, swung onto the two-lane, rural Highway 12. She glanced in the rearview mirror again. The white truck was speeding up to make the light with them. Then it slowed way down again, drifting back.

"Keep your eyes on the road, Anne," Josh snickered, "or I'll have to take over. Right, Mom?" Renee didn't reply at first, her eyes following Anne's gaze at the mirror. "Right," she said distractedly to Josh. Renee twisted around in her seat to get a look at the road behind them. Josh looked back, too. Driving behind the slow-moving white truck, an impatient sedan laid on the horn and passed it on the right, zipping into position behind the Pardini pickup.

Anne and her passengers drove in silence for the next few miles.

Trudy Lee's Bar & Grill loomed ahead on the left, near the corner of the highway and a quiet residential side road to the west. The bar was buffered from the side road by a tall hedge and a vacant lot. Anne slowed. The TRUDY LEE'S BAR & GRILL red neon sign was on. The brick-sided building was set back from the highway, fronted by a short row of parking spots. Two gravel-surfaced alleyways, one on each side of the building, led to the parking lot in back.

Anne flipped on the turn signal. Waiting for an opening in the oncoming traffic, she scanned the bar's facade. It was lit up with a sagging string of white Christmas lights that were hanging like a limp clothesline across the top of the porch. A neon Budweiser beer sign glowed in the window.

She noticed the tailgate of a familiar truck in the front parking area: Dave Silver's silver-colored work pickup was slotted in at an angle near the end of the row. From this direction, she couldn't tell if Dave was inside the cab or not, but she saw the shaggy head of his golden retriever poking through the open crack in the passenger window. She found herself running her fingers through her hair.

Anne pulled her eyes back to the oncoming highway traffic, caught an opening in the flow, turned left, and swung into the left alleyway alongside the bar. Inching the truck along the gravel road toward the back parking lot, she took another look in the rearview mirror.

The big white truck was gone. She let out a breath she didn't know she was holding.

# Chapter Thirty-One

"Is it just me, or is it strange that Dave Silver's here?" Renee asked as they made their way along the side of the building to the front of Trudy's. The gravel-and-dirt driveway was uneven and hard to walk on.

"If he hadn't arrived here before we did, I'd swear he was following us. That's twice in one day he's shown up," Anne said, giving a hard pull to the front door. She moved aside so Renee could go in ahead of her. "Your show, Renee." Josh walked in after his mother.

Before stepping inside, Anne looked over to where Dave's pickup was still parked. He was standing beside the open, driver side door with his back to her. She looked away and entered the bar behind Josh.

As their eyes adjusted to the low light, they spotted Trudy Lee sitting on a stool, facing in their direction. She was languidly leaning her back against the bartop, one arm draped along its surface. It was early by bar standards, only five o'clock, and the place was empty of patrons except for the two men shooting pool in the adjacent game room. The bartender was behind the bar, stocking bottles onto shelves. Josh, his first time in a bar, was taking in everything, from the stuffed deer head with antlers above the bar to the glowing Wurlitzer jukebox.

"Well, that was fast," Trudy called out, regarding them carefully.

"What was fast?" Renee stepped forward. "You were expecting us? I'm Renee Pardini, by the way. And this is my son Josh and my friend Anne."

"Anne and I have met." Trudy and Anne smiled politely at each other. Trudy motioned to a table in the middle of the room. "Of course, I know who you are, Renee."

"Hope it's alright if my son stays," Renee said. "We won't be here long. As far as I know, anyway."

"Sure, minors are okay here. We're licensed to serve food." Trudy gave Josh the once-over. "You look hungry. How about a turkey sandwich? Kitchen's closed, but we can make a sandwich up for you easy enough." He nodded vigorously and said, "And a can of Red Bull, please."

"Anything for you, ladies? Wine? Beer?"

"White wine," they both said.

"Go give our orders to Derrick," Trudy said to Josh, motioning to the bar, "and tell him it's on the house." Josh went off to the bar.

Once the three women were alone, Renee leaned forward in her seat. "So, I'm not sure where to start," she said slowly, placing her hands flat on the table. "I don't think we've seen each other in fifteen years, Trudy. But you said you were expecting us?"

"I wasn't expecting to see you tonight, but sometime soon. Your husband told me you'd be coming by. And he said if I didn't hear from you, I was to give you a call."

"When did he say all of this?" Renee asked. "It must have been right before he died. He left me a message—very cryptic—to come here, and I'm not sure why, or what it means."

"The very same day. Lino came here just hours before he died." Trudy shook her head at the memory. "He wasn't looking well, so I'm not surprised he had a heart attack."

"It wasn't a heart attack," Renee cut in.

"No? What was it?"

"A fall," Renee said. Anne shot a puzzled look at Renee.

"A fall," Trudy repeated slowly. "Huh. Well, I'm sorry for your loss."

Renee nodded. The drone of a football game on the overhead flat-screen television and the crack of a pool ball sounded in the background. Josh was sitting on a bar stool, his eyes locked onto the screen.

Trudy continued, "I hadn't seen your husband in a couple of years, and then when he shows up here, he was acting...well, not like himself...and he says he needs a favor. I said, 'Maybe, what is it?' Then he says, 'No maybes about it.'" She shook her head at the memory. "As you know, Lino didn't talk like that. Usually, he was all finesse and charm. And it just hit me the wrong way. It ruffled my feathers. So I said, 'What do you mean, I *have* to?' And he says, 'Unless you want me to sic the IRS on you.' I laughed in his face at that, because if there's one thing I never do, it's mess with the IRS. I run a cash business, sure, but I pay my taxes. I plan on getting my fair share of Social Security payments someday, so…but that's neither here nor there."

Derrick appeared at the table and set down the three glasses of wine. Josh was right behind him. He dropped into a chair next to his mother and opened a bag of chips.

Trudy broke off the conversation, raising her brows and tilting her head toward Josh.

"It's okay," Renee said. "Go on."

"Anyway, it made me wonder—why was he threatening me? It wasn't like him. I told him to cut the crap. Then he told me his plan—that he wanted me to buy the Pardini pickup truck at the auction. I said, 'What auction? What the hell are you talking about?' I was mystified by the whole thing. Why buy a truck that he already owned? It didn't make sense."

"He knew everything was falling apart."

"Yes, I know that *now*, of course. I told him I didn't want to get involved in this imaginary auction of his. I said to him, 'Do it yourself, Lino.' He said to just trust him." Trudy took a sip of wine. "He was such a mess, stumbling all over his words. I felt sorry for him and tried to calm him down, and said, 'Sure, why not?' Then he said…" Trudy abruptly went silent. Her eyes darted from Renee to Anne to Josh and then back again.

"Maybe it's better if some things stay confidential," Trudy eventually said, leveling her eyes at Renee. "Just between you and me."

"No, it's alright. Like I said, you can talk in front of Anne and Josh."

Trudy looked doubtful. "Maybe it's okay for you, but not for me."

A shout from Derrick behind the bar interrupted them. "Your sandwich is ready, kid." Josh jumped up.

Trudy kept her eyes on Renee, then gestured to the back door and abruptly stood up.

# CHAPTER THIRTY-ONE

"Come with me to my apartment upstairs—alone—and we'll finish this discussion."

\* \* \*

A dog was barking outside. It could've been any dog, but Anne was sure it was Trailer. Which could only mean, if she was right, that Dave was still somewhere outside.

Since she had nothing else to do now that Renee was off with Trudy and Josh was wolfing down his sandwich at the bar, Anne decided to go outside to investigate. This was as good a time as any to find out why Dave was here at Trudy's bar. Why he went to the auction with all that money. And why he was ignoring her. Although, in truth, she already knew the answer to that—her connection with the cold case investigation—and there wasn't much she could do about it.

Pushing open the heavy door, she stepped outside and heard a blast of angry shouts and loud groans coming from behind the building. The barking was getting louder, more frantic. She saw that Dave's truck was no longer in the front parking space, but she would swear it was his voice yelling, "Get away from there!"

Rushing down the porch steps, Anne was heading toward the noise when she was blindsided on her left side by a man in a ski mask, who hurtled past her and toppled her to the ground. She was halfway to standing up again, gasping for air, when she heard more footsteps advancing from the back parking lot. Another guy, this one with a black cap and a yellow bandana around his mouth and nose, was sprinting toward her. He deliberately veered in her direction so he could knock into her. She saw him coming, as if in slow motion, but couldn't duck out of his way fast enough. The impact was so hard her purse flew off her shoulder, and she dropped back down onto the gravel-and-dirt surface. This guy—bandana or no bandana—she got a decent look at.

Wiping loose bits of gravel from her cheek and the palms of her hands, Anne scrambled to her feet. She brushed grit off her white jacket and picked up her purse, wishing to God she had her handgun inside it. She stumbled off in the direction where the two men were heading—south along the tall hedge that lined the driveway. She got halfway down the driveway when she dimly realized the pointlessness of the chase. She slowed to a walk. What would she do if she caught them? Drag them to the police station? What was their crime? Bumping into her?

But there was no catching them, anyway. They were in the wind, already rounding the corner toward the side road and disappearing from view behind the hedges. But if she couldn't catch them, at least she wanted to see what they were up to. Anne spied a break in the hedge and tried wedging her hands through the dense foliage. Her plan was to pull it apart enough to see the vacant lot on the other side—and then beyond that, to the side road. That's where they were headed, and she guessed they had a getaway vehicle parked and waiting there. These weren't two regular guys from the neighborhood out for a stroll. They were masked, and masked men don't run around without a car.

The woody, closely spaced shrubs weren't giving way. After a few seconds, she heard the faint gunning of an engine, and then the sounds of tires peeling out came from the direction of the side road. So, they apparently *did* have a vehicle waiting for them, and they were using it. And she was too late to see or do anything about it.

Just then, another engine revved up behind her. A horn blasted two warning beeps. Spinning around, she saw the front end of Dave's pickup barreling toward her, its tires crunching the gravel. She flattened herself against the hedge. With Dave behind the wheel, the vehicle passed by with a *whoosh*, kicking up gravel and dirt, spraying it out into the air. Much of that debris landed on her head and jacket. As she tried dusting it off, Dave's truck sped to the road's end, slowing down for a fraction of a second before making a hard right turn onto the highway. He peeled off into traffic.

The bar's porch was only a few yards away, calling to her like a mirage in the desert. She needed to sit. Catch her breath. As she was willing herself across the alleyway, she suddenly remembered the scuffle behind the bar. Going against everything she felt like doing, she turned and walked to the back parking lot to check out the damage.

Aside from two sedans and an SUV parked at the far end, the Pardini truck had the parking lot to itself. If the pickup had been any part of the scuffle, it didn't show. It was as shiny green and pristine as it had been during the auction. Anne tried the door handle on the driver's side. The door swung wide open. Not good. She had locked up the pickup when she parked it there. And there was something else: Right behind the front tire, someone had dropped a ratchet wrench in the gravel.

*What went on here?* Whatever it was, she'd think about it later. In the meantime, she figured there was no harm in preserving any possible fingerprints on the wrench. She picked it up, careful to touch only the bottom of the handle, and lowered it onto the load bed.

When she finally made it back to the front of the bar, she dropped onto the bottom porch step. Folding her arms around her knees, she closed her eyes and focused on steadying her heartbeat. The bar door opened behind her. It was one of the pool-playing customers. She moved over a few inches, barely giving him enough room to squeeze down the steps. She pulled out her phone, her hands still shaking with adrenaline. She was about to text Dave a "What the F?" message—which he wouldn't answer anytime soon, she knew, because he was obviously in hot pursuit—when the bar door opened again.

Out stepped Josh and Renee. Josh bounded down the porch steps, taking them two at a time, while Renee stood perfectly still on the porch. Cradling her bulky purse to her chest, she breathed in the clean, cool air and looked out over the horizon.

"Beautiful day, isn't it? Ready to go home?" Renee asked, her beatific smile glowing with the light of a thousand burning candles. She took another deep, cleansing breath.

Anne stared up at Renee in wonder.

This was a new, unrecognizable Renee. Everything about her radiated serenity, lightness, and Zen-like well-being. Anne didn't know this Renee. She was so unrecognizable that Anne nearly forgot where she was and why the palms of her hands were stinging and the sleeve of her jacket was torn.

Josh wasn't so easily swept away. "We're not going home, Mom! Not home!" he said, bouncing up and down on his toes. "We need to go to Calistoga and complete our mission. Dad said—"

"Oh, alright," Renee said airily. "But let's stop for dinner on the way; what do y'all say? There's a nice restaurant near Calistoga I've been wanting to try." Renee squinted into the fading sunlight. She dropped her heavy purse to the ground, unzipped it, pulled out her sunglasses, slipped them on, and then zipped the purse closed again. All the while, smiling serenely.

Anne watched her closely.

"Renee, what happened in there?" Anne asked. "What did Trudy tell you?"

"We had a nice talk. She told me that Lino begged her to bid on the Pardini Winery pickup," Renee said and then turned to her son. "Your father wanted you to have it, Josh. He knew how much it meant to you. Trudy couldn't go to the auction herself, so she gave the money to Dave Silver so he could bid on it for her. Her own money. Can you imagine that?"

"No, I can't," Anne said pointedly. "Why would she do that?"

"Out of kindness, I suppose." Renee finally stepped off the porch and stood next to Josh and put her arm around his shoulder.

"Kindness? Really? Dave had over eighty thousand dollars in cash on him to bid with. That's a whole new level of kindness going on there," Anne said. "There's something you're not telling me, Renee. It's not adding up."

"Well, I suppose Trudy felt bad that Josh and I were suddenly penniless after Lino's shameless stealing—" She cut herself off after a glance at Josh's stricken expression.

"Anyway," Renee continued, "she knew Lino's last wish was for Josh to get the truck, so she kindly put up her own money. Although none of it matters now: Dave lost the bid, Trudy got her money back…that's why Dave was here, to return the money. And even though the truck went to Marco, I'm sure he'll let Josh drive it once in a…"

"So you're saying that Lino sent us here to pick up the truck from Trudy after she won it at the auction? Okay, but then why did he tell you to *drive* the truck here? You couldn't have driven it here if it was supposed to already *be* here in her possession after buying it…so confusing. Explain that."

"He wasn't thinking straight…and he didn't actually say to drive the *truck*, just to *drive* here. All that "drive the truck" stuff was Josh's interpretation."

"He said to do exactly—" Josh started.

"Anyway," Renee said, stopping his words with a wave of her hand, "Lino wanted us to come here. That's the point."

Anne scoffed. "For a whole lot of nothing, apparently."

"Oh, I don't know," Renee said, "I had a nice moment with Trudy."

Anne rolled her eyes.

Renee shrugged lightly. Then she took a close look at Anne, who was still slumped against the stair railing, finally noticing her flushed, sweaty face and dusty clothes.

"You okay?" Renee asked, leaning down and plucking some hedge debris out of Anne's hair.

# Chapter Thirty-Two

"Shall we go?" Renee started walking to the back parking lot. Anne and Josh trailed after her. They climbed into the pickup and assumed their former positions: Anne at the wheel, Josh by the window, and Renee in the middle, tightly lodging Anne's purse and her own between her feet.

"Let's decide where we're going first. No point getting halfway down the road before we know where we're going," Anne said, channeling her father. She slid the key into the ignition. "Back to your house? Or on to the honeymoon hotel in Calistoga?"

"I vote for Calistoga," Josh said. "How far is it?"

"It's less than a half-hour away. So, I guess, why not?" Anne asked, turning to Renee. "Did Trudy give you any hints about that leg of our journey? Did Lino clue her in?"

Renee shook her head.

"Maybe we can talk to the hotel owner and see if Lino left a note for you at the desk or something," Anne said.

"Not a bad thought."

Anne pulled out her phone. "But first…" she said while typing in a quick message, "I have to send a text to Dave."

Anne: Catch them?

Without waiting for a reply, which she wasn't counting on getting anyway, Anne dropped the phone into her purse. Even if Dave messaged her back, her phone would be out of cell tower range once they started climbing up Calistoga Road. She fired up the engine, shifted the truck into reverse, and maneuvered out of the parking lot.

Two minutes later, the trio were heading north on Calistoga Road, a serpentine, two-lane country road that twisted and turned all the way to the town of Calistoga. There and back, it was going to be twenty-six miles of bare-knuckle driving. She'd be navigating hills, sharp blind curves, deep ravines, busted guardrails, and—more treacherously— oncoming cars intent on straightening out the curve by cheating the double yellow lines and veering into her lane.

"So, Anne, do you want to tell us why your white jean jacket suddenly looks like a used coffee filter? What went on outside the bar?" Renee asked.

With her eyes glued to the road, Anne gave them a blow-by-blow of the action: the dog barking; the shouting and arguing; the first masked man running past her and knocking her over; the second man running past her and knocking her over; the two of them sprinting to the getaway vehicle and driving off; Dave giving chase; the unlocked doors and the left-behind wench.

"Sick, real robbers!" Josh said.

"They broke into the truck?" Renee said, alarm in her voice.

"I wish you'd come and gotten me," Josh said, "I could have caught them."

"Fingers crossed, we'll never see those creeps again." Anne glanced at her side mirror and thought she saw a big white truck, maybe four cars back, but couldn't be sure. Probably just her imagination. Focus, she told herself. She'd drive into a ditch if she kept looking back.

Ahead was another road sign with a black arrow and a speed warning: 15 M.P.H. Anne slowed down fast and turned the wheel hard to the right to make the curve. When the road straightened out, she snuck another look back. Now, the truck was just three cars behind them. She'd swear it was the same white Ford truck that had followed them to Trudy's bar, carrying the same two guys who knocked her over and ran.

Another curve came up, and then another. Ancient oak trees and moss-covered boulders lined the road, which became narrower with each mile they drove beyond the Santa Rosa city limits. There was no shoulder along the side of the road, just a steep drop into a rocky ravine.

It was dangerous to keep looking back in the mirror. Anne didn't want to alarm Josh and Renee, but she needed some help here. "Josh, do me a favor and keep an eye on that white truck back there."

Josh twisted to look through the window behind his head. "Why am I looking at it?" he asked, but quickly caught on. "How long has it been there?"

"A while."

Josh kept staring out the back window. They were starting up a long, steep incline, and all the way up the hill, the engine grumbled at the strain. Anne dropped gears and maintained a steady, agonizingly slow pace.

"The truck's moved up a space," Josh said. "Can you gun it?"

"No, can't go any faster," Anne said, shooting a glance at the side mirror. The road thankfully was beginning a winding descent. Curve after hairpin curve, Josh gave them the same update: "It's still there." After a few miles, the white truck started hanging back a bit and Josh stopped repeating himself, and they fell into a tense silence.

Anne eventually broke the quiet. "It's funny, but the fuel gauge needle hasn't moved. Not even a bit, and it's been driven a lot today."

Josh turned around, facing front, and said, "That's cause the gas gauge is broken, and it's always stuck on full. Dad was going to get it fixed on our next service at Rich's. But don't worry, it's probably pretty full. And anyway, we carry extra gas in a can, just in case. It's right there," Josh said, twisting in his seat to look into the truck's load bed. "See, it's right there in corner..." he stopped himself and, with surprise in his voice, said, "The truck's gone!"

"Did you see it turn off?" Renee asked

"No, but it must have happened while I was looking away—like for five seconds. Weird."

"I don't remember passing any side roads," Anne said.

"Maybe it just parked in a turnout area?" Renee said.

"I haven't seen one for miles."

"Well, it's gone, anyway," Renee said, letting out a long breath, "so that's a relief."

\* \* \*

Up ahead loomed the steepest hill on Calistoga Road. At its very peak was a sharp bend. A blind curve.

The Pardini Winery pickup was laboring mightily to get up the hill. It would have come to a complete stop in the road, or even rolled back down the hill, without Anne's constant gear shifting and on-and-off acceleration. Maintaining a steady fifteen miles per hour required an ungodly amount of concentration, and the tension was making itself felt in Anne's neck muscles. The dense shrubbery and trees lining the road on both sides were making her feel hemmed-in and claustrophobic.

Also, she was hungry and tired.

"Maybe we should just turn around here," she muttered.

"Won't get any argument from me," Renee said. "I've had enough of this adventure."

But Josh, apparently, hadn't. "No way. We're already halfway to Calistoga. There's no turning back now. If you're tired of driving, Anne, I'll take over."

Anne and Renee groaned in unison.

"I could drive, I suppose," Renee said with a slight roll of her shoulder.

"You can drive stick? Why didn't you tell me?" Anne asked.

Renee hadn't told her, she explained, because—while she could work a manual transmission and had since girlhood—she simply "chose not to." Except in an emergency. If there'd been a shoulder on the road, Anne would've swerved into it and hopped out and traded places with Renee so fast she wouldn't have known what happened. But there was no turnout, nothing ahead but an ever-narrowing road and a steep hill to climb.

*So, onward,* Anne thought.

Nearing the peak, she caught sight of sudden movement in the vegetation on the right side of the road, about forty feet ahead. "A lot of deer in these—"

Just then, two dark-clothed men stepped out from the thickets. Both masked. They planted themselves directly in the path of the pickup, blocking the road like they owned it.

There was no way forward on the road, except to go around them or through them. And the truck didn't have the engine power to do either. Pure reflex, pure animal instinct, had Anne slamming on the brakes to avoid hitting them. But her instincts had betrayed her—she'd played right into their hands. Now, the pickup was immobile.

The men stood stock-still, shoulder to shoulder. The shortish, reedy one was dressed from head to toe in black. His face and hair were completely hidden by a ski mask, so it was impossible to guess his age until Anne noticed the skin on his left hand. Red, wrinkled, veiny. His gnarled ring finger bore a wedding band. His right hand was shoved inside his jacket pocket.

The other guy was taller, with dark hair sticking out of a baseball cap. The yellow bandana tied around his head couldn't hide the mole on his eyebrow. "Step out of the truck!" he ordered. Anne had seen that mole and heard that voice before—his name, too, but it hadn't stuck. If she was right, this wasn't going to go well.

The ski mask guy didn't say anything, just lifted the hand inside his jacket pocket and pointed it at them. A gun? That's what he wanted them to think. But if it was really a gun, why not just pull it out?

Then, the taller guy pulled out a semiautomatic—a real one—from his back waistband and aimed the gun two-handed, shoulder high, at their windshield.

"Lock the doors! Duck down!" Anne ordered.

"Those are the robbers!" Josh said, barely above a whisper. His eyes wide. "Like back at the bar, right, Anne? Same ones?"

"Yes. And they're the same ones who were just following us in the white truck. Renee, take out my phone and start filming this."

"But we're out of cell phone range," Renee protested.

"Doesn't matter, Mom, the camera will still work. I'll do it. I'll use my phone."

"No! Use mine," Anne insisted. The video might be needed as evidence, and she wanted control over it. Josh reached into Anne's purse. Anne gave him the phone passcode, saying, "Just be careful they don't see you doing it."

"How'd they get ahead of us?" Renee asked.

"Maybe they turned off and found a shortcut." Anne eased her foot off the brake, thinking that their best bet would be to roll back and make a sloppy U-turn and haul ass out of there. But the men were advancing on them too fast. Now, they were only twenty feet away, blocking any room for her to maneuver in. She could just ease off the breaks and let the pickup roll back down the hill. Hell, it would probably roll faster than those guys could run after it.

But the bandana-wearing guy was still aiming the gun and getting closer, now within fifteen feet. "We're not playing! Get out now and make it fast!" he ordered again. Now, within ten feet.

"Not a damn chance," Renee said in a near whisper to Anne. "We're not leaving this truck. I'll die first." She had a death grip on her purse.

"Leave the truck!" he yelled. "Then start walking back down the hill. You won't get hurt if you get out now!" He motioned with the gun.

Loud, agitated barking erupted from the high bushes to the right.

The two men stopped cold, their heads snapping toward the sound. The taller guy pointed his gun into the bushes and fired off a shot. Then another. A mournful howl, then a whimper, cut through the air.

*Trailer?* Anne felt helpless. Without her handgun, she wasn't a player here.

"Let's go help," Josh said.

"No, we're staying in the truck," Anne said. "Keep filming."

The next sound was a rustling, as if someone was trampling through thick brush. A second later, another shot was fired. This time, the gunfire wasn't coming from the masked men in the road. It was coming from the bushes to the right, and it was aimed at the ground the two men were standing on. The bullet hit the road squarely between them, so laser-focused it only grazed the tip of one of their leather boots.

A warning shot. The men froze for a millisecond, then jumped back and away from each other. Their eyes raked over the bushes. The shorter, older guy yelled out, *Vamos!*" to his partner, then spun around and took off up the steep hill. The younger man ran after him, overtaking him within seconds.

They disappeared behind the curve in the road.

Anne heard more barking coming from the right and saw the second shooter walking out of the dense brushes. Relief flooded over her. Dave

Silver navigated his way down the uneven grassy slope. Trailer wasn't far behind him, hopping through high grasses and bushes like a rabbit, barking all the way.

Anne scrambled out of the pickup. "We thought he hit your dog," she called out as she headed up the slope toward Dave. He was walking to meet her, his rifle hanging down by his side.

"No, that gun didn't have any reach," he said when they met. "It just scared her."

Josh hopped from the truck and jogged toward them. Renee didn't budge from the pickup.

"Let's go after them!" Josh said.

"Too dangerous," Anne said. "But don't worry, they're not getting away with anything. We know who they are." Anne and Dave darted sidelong glances at each other. Something was going on behind his eyes, she thought. Dread? Maybe. Wariness, for sure. Was she wrong in thinking that he knew, too? Dave looked away.

"So, who are they?" Josh asked, leaning down and rubbing behind Trailer's ears. The dog was still shaking. "At first, I thought they were the guys from Rich's Auto because they were at the auction, and Troy likes the pickup and has a white truck. But then I thought, no way. Troy's my friend."

"I'm not totally sure," Anne said, hedging a bit and glancing at Dave. She searched her brain for the name of the bandana-wearing guy. It escaped her. "But we're going to the police station now. We'll show them the video you took and let them handle it."

Then it came to her: Luis.

Dave kept his eyes on the crest of the hill. "I'll get my truck and be back in a few minutes. I'll follow you to the station in Santa Rosa. Meanwhile, take this rifle, just in case they come back." He held out his Nosler hunting rifle to Anne. "You know how to use it, right?" Anne nodded.

"I'll take that," Renee called out from inside the truck.

Anne's brow went up. "You know how to shoot a rifle?"

"I'm from Texas. What do *you* think?"

That got a half-smile from Dave. Anne watched as he walked to the Pardini pickup and passed the rifle through the open window to Renee—but not to the new, serene Renee, who it seemed, had vanished. But to an even newer, badass Renee. A ready-to-do-battle Renee.

Dave was heading back across the street toward the bushes, through to where his truck was parked on the service road, when Anne called out to him, "Before you go, will you tell me something?"

Dave turned back slowly. When he reached her side, she said, "We're a long way from Trudy's Bar. How did you find us here?"

"Some other time," he said impatiently, his voice flat.

"How about now?" she insisted. "You show up like a—well," but her words failed her, and she asked herself again what he was hiding.

"Yeah, well, I saved your ass, didn't I?" he said, apparently not in the mood to banter. "So...you're welcome."

"We would have survived," she said. Even to her own ears, that sounded like empty, childish petulance, so she added, "But thank you." She didn't want to think of what would have happened if Dave hadn't shown up. She and Josh would have gotten out of the truck, but Renee wasn't going anywhere, and that could have led to real violence.

"I'm sure you would have," he said, now with an edge in his voice. "Anyway, after the two guys ran off from Trudy's bar, they got into the white truck, doubled back, and parked out of sight on the other side of the highway. I parked far enough away so they didn't see me. After you left Trudy's, they started following you again. And here I am." He took a small ironic bow, making her smile, but only slightly.

Tracking them on Calistoga Road was trickier, harder to do without being seen, Dave told her. The white truck eventually went off-road through a clearing in the landscape. The clearing widened into a dirt path, which led to a service road—a shortcut to the top curve on Calistoga Road. The two men parked just below the hill crest, walked through the brush, and waited for the Pardini pickup. Dave parked out of sight.

"They knew your truck would struggle up the hill. It was easy for them to just step out onto the road and overtake you," Dave said, lifting his eyes to her. "It's an old trick. Right out of the "Gentleman Bandit" playbook. I just

245

shadowed them."

Meeting his gaze, she said, "Thanks is too small of a word. I mean it." Then she looked away, realizing what he must be seeing: her flushed cheeks, running mascara, the flyaway hair falling over her eyes.

His expression softened, and with a faint smile, he said, "You're kind of a mess, do you know that?" He raised his hand and brushed a few strands of tangled hair off her forehead. A tiny piece of gravel fell out. They both laughed. Then she climbed in the pickup, and Dave patted the door, saying, "I'll be right back. Don't take off for the police station until I return."

"We'll be waiting for you. By the way, who's the Gentleman Bandit?" Anne asked.

"That's a story for another time." *Another time. Well, good,* she thought.

Ten minutes later, the two trucks were on their way. For the next seven, mostly downhill miles, they drove uneventfully back to civilization. Back into cell phone range. The mood in the pickup lightened. Nerves calmed. Renee even loosened her grip on the rifle. There was talk about ordering take-out for dinner back at Renee's house. And talk about inviting Dave (*A cool guy,* Josh said) in for a few pieces of pepperoni pizza and a beer.

Then, the engine noises began. The coughing, low whining, sputtering. There were intermittent power surges, but no real power when Anne needed it for acceleration. The truck was clearly shutting down. Running on fumes alone. No question about it: They were out of gas on the side of a country road.

With the steering wheel vibrating under her hands, Anne brought the pickup to a rolling stop in a turnout and set the brake. Dave pulled up behind her.

*What the hell else could happen today?*

# Chapter Thirty-Three

While Josh hopped onto the bed of the pickup, grabbed the orange plastic gas can, and handed it down to Dave, Anne was leaning on the driver side door, watching. *Let men be men,* was her feeling. Let them knock themselves out. She'd seen enough action for one day. She checked the time on her phone. How could it only be six o'clock? She glanced inside the truck. Renee still had the rifle across her lap, the two purses clamped tight between her feet, her eyes trained straight ahead.

Dave set the gas can down on the ground, right below the chrome gas cap on the driver's side. Anne moved over a few inches to give him some room while he was unscrewing the round cap. Josh hopped down from the truck bed and sidled up to him.

"That's not where the gas goes," Josh said.

Dave leaned over and took a whiff. "Sure smells like gasoline to me."

"Of course, it's gas," Anne chimed in. "When your mom and I were searching for...never mind. But I smelled gas there, too."

"Nah, that's just a wine bottle full of gasoline placed in the fuel filler neck. Me and Dad thought that up as a joke. Come back here and I'll show you where you really fill up the tank." He led Dave and Anne to the back of the truck and pointed to the area below the closed tailgate. They saw nothing unusual, just four round, red taillights in a row. Two on either side of the license plate.

"See this? Dad had these two fake lights put in next to the existing lights. They don't work, but they look like regular round taillights. This one," he said, unscrewing the one to the right of the license plate, "is where you pump the gas in."

Josh went on to say how his father had the gas tank moved from behind the front seat, the usual place for trucks of this vintage, to under the load bed because "Dad was sick of the smelly gas fumes in the cab and also, he wanted a bigger tank.

"Look down here." They crouched down, three abreast. What they saw, between the wheel wells—and above the wheel axles and exhaust—was a fuel tank mounted to the frame of the truck.

While Anne was watching Josh pour gas from the orange can into the fake tail light/real pump, a thought tugged at her.

"So if there's no gas stored in the old fuel tank behind the seat in the cab," Anne asked, "what *is* stored in there?"

\* \* \*

"Anyone can do it," Josh said. "The guys at Rich's Auto showed me how. There are only four bolts holding the seat in place. All it takes is a wrench." He made a move toward the ratchet wrench laying on the truck's load bed, the one Anne had found in the dirt in the parking lot.

"Don't touch that!" Anne said.

"Okay, okay!" Josh raised his hands in surrender.

"That needs to go in my purse." Anne retrieved her purse from Renee, who was finally out of the truck and watching from the sidelines.

Dave found the truck's toolbox. "There's probably a ratchet wrench in here."

Once they started, it took Dave and Josh less than five minutes to pop the seat off. They set it on the ground in front of the pickup. With the seat removed, the old fuel tank was exposed. It was about four feet long and eight inches thick and was bolted and strapped to the cab of the truck. Black nubby carpet material covered it.

Dave stepped back. "Taking this tank out will be a bitch. The top and bottom halves of these tanks are welded together. Breaking the welding seal will be a bitch. I'm not sure it's worth—"

"I'll take off the carpet," Josh said.

"Okay, I'll see if I brought my cordless circular saw."

# Chapter Thirty-Four

While Dave went to his truck to look for his saw and Anne wandered off to check her phone, Renee and Josh stayed inside the cab. Sitting in the tight floor space in front of the fuel tank, Josh was cross-legged, and Renee sat with her knees drawn to one side, as they contemplated the black carpet covering the fuel tank.

"It's just spray glued on," he said, unfolding his legs to get on his knees. "Watch this." After a few yanks, the rectangle metal box was revealed.

"That's strange…" Renee pointed to a metal latch protruding from the front of the tank. It was a pulling mechanism for a slider that ran half the length of the tank. Like a sliding glass door. It gave an opening to the insides of the metal tank.

"Oh yeah, I remember now. Dad said he hired a metal guy to install the slider so he'd have easy access to inside the tank," he said. "But he never said why."

Josh reached for the latch. "Let's slide it open."

But Renee's reach was faster. She pulled his hand back.

"Don't open it. Let's stop for a minute," Renee said. Josh stopped. "I need to think." Josh nodded and turned sideways so his legs dangled out of the passenger door.

Renee sat still, deep in thought. What had Lino been up to? What kind of convoluted Gordian knot of a plan had he conjured up? It took her barely a moment to untangle the knots and see how Lino's video message had, step by step, led them to this very moment: He sent her to Trudy's Bar. Next, he wanted her to drive to the Calistoga honeymoon hotel in the Pardini pickup

250

truck. And next, he wanted her to run out of gas along the way. That was the whole point. He'd left the gas tank practically empty, and he'd picked Calistoga Road because it was a long and lonely stretch of road, not heavily traveled, not overrun with Good Samaritans who would stop and interfere. He wanted Josh to be there with Renee because Josh knew all about the new gas tank being in the back. And Lino knew that that piece of knowledge would make her wonder what was hidden in the original tank. Josh would pop off the seat, and they would find the money he had stashed away for them.

For *them*, she thought. For her and Josh. But if Lino had wanted her to have the money, why not just hide it in the glove compartment of her car? Maybe because on the night before he died, he was still planning on taking off and needed that money. He went to a lot of trouble to hide it—taking the seat out, covering the tank with carpet, popping the seat back in—and by the time his plans had changed, and he knew it was over, he was too exhausted to move it. Who knows what was in his mind? He did try to call her, she remembered, but she had brushed him off. Nevertheless, ultimately, he led her to the money.

"But it's not our money to keep," she said to herself, barely above a whisper. And she kept repeating that, softly, "It's not our money, it's not..."

But if the money wasn't theirs to keep, what was she to do? How could she salvage the situation and turn it to her advantage? She needed a plan. Gazing out the back truck window to where Dave and Anne were talking, she began conjuring up her own knot of a plan. Image by image, it came into focus: police, camera lights, her stepdaughter Jennifer, the mayor, her friend Lori Paige. It was audacious, given her fall from grace, but it had to be. Faint heart never won anything. No phoenix ever rose from the ashes without boldness. Meekness would never give Renee and Josh their lives back.

She could make this work.

Josh's voice jolted her out of her thoughts. "Mom, what are you talking about? What do you mean, it's not our money? So, are you saying there's money in the tank?" He crouched down in front of the tank opening.

"I'm sure of it."

"Then it *is* ours, Mom!" Josh made a move for the latch.

"No. Don't even touch it." Her hand blocked the opening. "It's money your father took from people."

"Can't we keep some of it?"

"It needs to go to the police. They'll decide where it goes."

"But we don't have any money," Josh said, looking worried. "How about if we give *most* of it to the police? They'll never know."

She turned to face him, then took him firmly by the shoulders. "That would be stealing." Her eyes bore into his. "You and me? We're not thieves, Josh. Never were, never will be." She loosened her grip. "Don't worry about money. I'll sell the car or trade it in or something. Let me do the worrying."

She reached for the door handle. "But for right now, let's get out of the truck."

With that, they climbed out and stood by the side door. Holding her purse tightly against her hip with her left arm, Renee waved her right hand wildly in the air.

"Anne! Dave!" she yelled, "Come here!"

# Chapter Thirty-Five

The four of them stared at the metal gas tank. No one even blinked. "Jesus," someone finally said.

Crammed up tight against the open sliding door were stacks and stacks of one-hundred dollar bills wrapped with currency bands. Some of the bundles were even bulging out from the opening. There was no way of telling how many more were stuffed into the far reaches of the tank's interior. They could be looking at hundreds of thousands of dollars.

Anne, Dave, and Renee were outside of the truck, looking in. Josh was crouched in front of the box. "How much do you think is in there?" he asked. "Should we pull it out and count it?"

"No point in that," Anne said firmly, motioning for Josh to climb out. "We're bringing it in. Every last dollar bill of it, understand? Untouched by any one of us. I'll call the police station and tell them we're on our way."

While Anne brought out her phone, took photos of the money, and then dialed the station, Josh turned to his mother and asked, "Why is *Anne* the boss all of a sudden? It isn't even her truck."

Renee nodded toward Anne. "Because Anne's a police officer, and she wants to do things the right way. And I agree," she said. Which drew a surprised look from Anne. She was expecting more of a fight from Renee. Where was the woman who'd negotiated her down to a sixty-forty split less than two weeks ago? Here, instead, was the voice of reason itself. Which was a relief because Anne was too tired to fight—though fight she would, because the situation held no ambiguity. There was only the law.

Anne's call went through to the watch commander, the after-hours officer in charge, but she was put on hold. "Renee, while I'm talking to the police, why don't you call your lawyer and let him know what's going on. Attorneys don't like to be surprised. It's Joel Maroni, right?"

"Yes, he represents everyone in the family,"

"Even Marco and the Pardini Winery business?"

"Yes."

"Then the sooner Maroni gets involved, the better," Anne said. "Ask him to meet us outside the police station—before we surrender the money. He can coordinate with the police and Feds. That way, there's no question about where the money came from and how much was found."

Renee nodded again, reached into her purse, and took out her phone. Anne was still on hold. "After I alert the station," Anne said, "I'll call my uncle and see if he can meet us there. Hope we can get everyone together. It won't be easy on a Saturday night."

Renee held up Lino's phone. "Lino's name's on the caller ID. That'll get Joel's attention."

The attorney picked up on the second ring. "Joel? It's me, Renee. Sorry to bother you, but I've got an emergency." Renee turned her back and wandered off out of earshot.

Anne was still standing guard over the fuel tank, still waiting for the watch commander to pick up again. She looked over at Dave. He was standing on the opposite side of the truck, leaning against the passenger door, his back to her. He hadn't spoken a word since they'd found the money.

"You're coming into the station with us, right, Dave?"

They looked at each other across the front cab through half-open windows. "No, I'll put the seat back in and follow you there," he said. "Make sure you get there safe. Then I'm taking off. Trailer needs to be fed."

"But we'll need you there. Not to sort out the money business—that's just a matter of handing it over and signing off on it. All that red tape. But those two robbers—we need to get them identified and arrested. We'll need your statement."

"You don't need me. You've got the video—though I don't know what good that's going to do. And you've got the ratchet wrench—which may or may not have fingerprints on it. Even if it does, that wouldn't prove anything. And who cares anyway?"

"It was an attempted robbery, Dave. An *armed* robbery."

He shook his head slowly.

"They had a gun pointed at us. That's a felony."

He said nothing.

"And don't tell me you didn't recognize Luis! I only met him that one time at the bar, and I made him."

Still nothing from him.

"Your pal Luis shot at your dog! He shot at *you!*"

"Drop it, will you?"

"And who was that older, skinnier masked guy? I can only guess."

Without another word, Dave went around to the front of the truck, picked up the vinyl-covered seat, hauled it inside, and bolted it in place in front of the fuel tank. Anne had a few more things to say but didn't. She just watched as he picked up his rifle from the floor, slammed the door closed, and set off for his truck where Trailer was waiting.

"Like I said, I'll follow you there," he called out over his shoulder.

She watched his back. Then her phone came alive again. "This is Lieutenant James, what can I do for you?"

\* \* \*

It was twilight, nearing eight o'clock, by the time they arrived at the Santa Rosa police station on Sonoma Avenue. The sun was low in the sky, fiery with streaks of purples and burnt oranges. Floodlights lit up the parking lot in front of the low-slung, clay-colored public building.

"They're already here," Anne said, slipping the Pardini truck into the spot nearest the front door. Dave parked a few slots down and killed his lights.

Everyone had shown up. Joel Maroni, the Pardinis' attorney, and Jack McCormack were waiting under the metal awning at the entrance. Anne, Renee and Josh joined them. A minute later, Lieutenant James walked out of the building. And a minute after that, two officers came out of the building,

255

which seemed to be Dave's cue to clear out. He backed his truck out of the lot and drove off.

While the officers climbed into the pickup and removed the bench seat and gas tank, Anne relayed the saga—the robbers, the video Josh took, the empty gas tank, the found money, and Anne's suspicions about the two masked men.

"The video and wrench need to go into evidence," Lt. James said. "And we'll get arrest warrants going."

"Marco will say it's his truck, and that means it's his money," Renee said.

"He can say that all he wants," Jack said, "but the money can be traced back to Lino—and that means Marco doesn't have a prayer of getting it."

"I've already told him," attorney Maroni said. Then he turned to Josh. "But it *is* his truck, Josh, and he wants it back."

"As soon as we're done here—and as soon as the seat gets put back—we'll drive it back," Renee assured him.

They watched as the officers, without removing the money, carried the tank inside the station to have it logged in and processed. It would soon be in the custody of U.S. Marshals.

Anne stepped away from the group and motioned for her uncle to join her. "Uncle Jack," she said when he was at her side, "there's another video you need to see."

# Chapter Thirty-Six

His father's truck was out front. Dave Silver knocked on the door of the old Victorian farmhouse. He looked through the stained-glass panel and saw his mother, still in her robe, shuffling to the door.

When she cracked it open, he asked, "Dad here?"

"No hello for me?" She frowned, then motioned for him to enter. "No, he isn't."

She hadn't allowed him into the house for weeks. He almost tripped over the boxes piled up near the doorway. He didn't ask.

"His truck's here," he said. "Are you sure he's not home?" Sometimes she forgot.

"He went with Luis. They had big plans for today. They thought I didn't hear them talking about them, but I did." She looked pleased with herself.

"What kind of plans?"

"About getting money in an old farm truck. Your dad said it was at Marco's house." She hesitated. "I think so, anyway. I know they were bringing disguises like they were kids playing cops and robbers. Ha! What fools."

"How'd they know that?"

"Huh?

"The money they were looking for...how'd they know it was in the truck?"

His mother looked down at the worn Oriental runner under her feet, as if the answer could be found among the loose threads. "I think Luis said...he built a sliding door for Lino? But that doesn't make sense. Luis isn't a door guy. He works at a metal shop."

"Dad might get arrested, Mom. Be prepared."

"But that was so long ago. And I explained all of that."

"What are you talking about?"

"My letter."

\* \* \*

Jack flicked on the overhead lights. "Jim won't mind if we take over his office," he said, plopping down in the swivel chair behind Sgt. Sloan's desk. He motioned Anne toward the blue guest chair opposite him. "He's probably home watching *Saturday Night Wrestling*," he said as he dropped a brown leather folder onto the desktop.

"You have a video of Lino Pardini to show me?" Jack pulled a plastic encased note card out of his folder.

Anne nodded. "Certainly do. Renee and I pulled this off his phone earlier today." She called up the five-minute video recording of Lino's last few moments on earth. "It'll explain a lot about why we were on that joyride. And it'll answer your questions about his death. Maybe about Dinah's death, too, if he can be believed." She slid the phone toward him.

"Okay. Trade." He pushed the note card across the desk.

"What's this?"

"Just read it."

Jack put in his earbuds and silently watched the video—stopping and rewinding every few minutes—while Anne read the note. It was a vague, disjointed letter written in loopy handwriting.

> Police. Don't talk to my son again. I know everything, not him. I followed Jerry that night to catch him meeting one of his girlfriends. He drove Lino's wife to a grocery store, and he went in. She sat in the back seat like he was her servant. A man gets in the limo and drives it away. I saw everything that happened! I know who the killer is! Jerry comes out with flowers in his hand. Black limo gone. I honked and told Jerry to get in my car. We

drove home. We couldn't talk to police. Now I can. Dave wasn't there, so stop asking him! Carol Silver

Jack's phone went off. He looked at the caller ID, paused the video, and put up a finger. *One moment.* "It's Lt. James," he said to Anne as he accepted the call. "Hi, Otto." He listened for a moment, then said, "Pulled them in, huh? That was fast. My niece and I look forward to talking to him."

He finished the call and turned to Anne. "You free tomorrow morning? Want to sit in on an interview with one of those masked robbers?"

# Chapter Thirty-Seven

Sitting in a prison-issue metal chair, with her uncle beside her, Anne looked across the stainless-steel table at Jerry Silver, unshaven, watery-eyed, and fidgety. The interrogation room at the Sonoma County detention facility wasn't much different from the one Jerry's son Dave had sat in less than a week before. Stark and windowless.

"Long time no see," Jerry smirked at Anne.

She just shrugged, tired of him already.

"Thanks for joining us so bright and early on a Sunday morning, Mr. Silver," Jack said. "As we discussed with your lawyer, this interview has nothing to do with yesterday's robbery escapade—"

"The *armed* robbery escapade. A felony," Anne cut in, baiting him. Her uncle shot her a dark look.

"I didn't have a gun, and, hell, I wasn't even there. That's all my lawyer will let me say."

"The other suspect, Luis, *did* have a gun, and by law, that's the same as you holding it yourself. All of this is only alleged, of course," Anne said.

"Like I said, that's not why we're here," Jack cut in. "Other officers are handling the robbery."

"So why are you here? I mean, I know why *I'm* here— for a change of scenery."

"We're here to talk about a cold case you may have information on. The Dinah Pardini murder."

"What? Aren't you tired of that by now?" Jerry locked his fingers behind his head, then he leaned back while he listened to Jack recite the usual

260

preliminary statements and questions. Jerry identified himself for the recorded video and then heard that he wasn't a suspect and didn't have to answer any question he didn't want to.

"So let's start. Lino Pardini made a video before he died." Jack let that sink in for a few beats, then continued. "And he told us all about it. All about how he innocently hired a driver for Dinah, ordered a corsage, and then—poof!—never saw her again. We think you were that driver."

"I didn't drive anyone—"

"That's not what your wife says."

"You talked to Carol?" He sat up slowly.

"The police department got a letter a few days ago."

Jerry quietly groaned.

Jack slid the letter across the table to Jerry. Skimming it quickly, he pushed it back at Jack, saying, "Don't try..."

"Lino's recorded statement and your wife's letter have led us to some conclusions. Here's what we're thinking," Jack said. "You got hired to drive the limo. Your wife was a jealous woman. She saw you sneaking off and meeting Dinah. So when you went into the store, Carol got into the limo and drove it away and killed her. Carol confessed to you, so you and she buried the body, probably on your own property. Lino suspected *you* of killing Dinah—after all, he'd hired you that night. After a year goes by, he wants the body found, so he makes you a deal: Move Dinah's body somewhere it can be found easily and call the police. He pays you money to make sure it happens. Sounds good to you because you didn't want the body in your own back yard, anyway. You might want to sell the land someday. You got Dave to help. Lino wanted it moved cause he wanted closure for his family. It all makes sense. Way we see it, you, Lino, Dave, and your wife were all in on this together."

"Not true."

"Are you saying it wasn't your wife who killed her?"

"Not saying anything. Leave me and my family alone."

"Then tell us your side. Put it to rest. Because unless we learn different about that night, Lino will have the last word, and your family will be aggressively investigated. And with all the trouble you're already in, they don't need that," Jack said.

Jerry smiled faintly, but his fingers betrayed his nervousness: he rubbed them against each other like a fly planning its way out of a trap.

"What do you have to lose?" Anne asked. "You're going down for armed robbery for nine years or so anyway. Might as well talk and save your family."

They gave him another full minute, then he started to speak. "Lino planned everything. Two weeks before Dinah disappeared, he asked me to dig a grave on my property. Big enough for a large dog, he said. His daughters' dog was sick, and he was going to shoot it and bury it there so his daughters wouldn't see it. I gave Dave fifty dollars to dig the grave. Lino wanted it close to the main road for some reason. But Dave was a drugged-out mess back then, and he dug the grave close to his own trailer. It was an empty hole when Dave went to jail. When he came back home two weeks later, it was filled up."

Jerry stared down at the table, his words slowing to a stop. Anne gave him some motivation to keep talking: "Lino says he suspected the driver— you—of killing her."

"He always was a liar," Jerry said, sitting up. "Lino hired me to pick her up and take her to a fancy dinner. But I was supposed to stop at Safeway and pick up a corsage. Lino told me to leave the keys in the ignition so the heater would stay on. When I came out, the limo is gone. No trace of it. Then I hear a horn, and it's my wife. She's in the parking lot. She says let's leave 'cause Lino just drove off in the limo while I was in the store. Lino! So, I was relieved. I thought Dinah was safe. But later, when I heard she was missing, I called him, saying what the fuck? He said it wasn't him who drove off. He said Carol was mistaken. He said to be quiet, or I'd be suspected."

Jerry rubbed his face. "It was easier to just believe him. Then he bought us some investment stocks. That was the first real money me and Carol ever had. I let it all slide, practically forgot about it—until a year later when he told me to dig up the body. The body? Jesus. He'd dumped her body on my land. The hole Dave had dug was covered with dirt, but I just thought it was the dog. I told Lino, no fucking way! He must have gotten someone else to do it, cause next thing I knew, behind my back, he got Dave involved."

"Did Dave dig up the body and move it?" Jack asked.

Jerry nodded sadly. "Yeah, I think so."

"No, he didn't." Anne looked down at her notes, the tight timeline retrieved from police software. "He couldn't have. He was in the county jail. He'd been there for over a year. He'd started his sentence a week before Dinah Pardini was killed. And he was there until his release on September 19, 2005, at three o'clock. Two hours after his release, at five o'clock, the call was made to the police telling them where to find the body. It's entirely possible Dave made that call. It's likely, in fact. But as far as digging up her body and digging a new grave, the timing's off: he couldn't have driven from jail to your property, dug up the body, and carted it to the new location—all in less than two hours. So that means he didn't dig up her body. Someone else did. And trying to pin it on your son isn't your best look."

"Was that you?" Jack asked.

Jerry bristled. "No way. I'm not talking anymore. Unless we can arrange for a leniency deal on the robbery charge." Anne had wondered how long it would take before he thought of that.

"That's possible, if you feel you have more to say that will interest the DA. In the meantime, how much did Carol know?" Jack asked.

"She saw Lino get into that limo, like I said. She knew Lino had killed his wife. I didn't want to believe her. In fact, I *didn't* believe her until Lino told me where Dinah's body was buried. All these years since, we kept his secrets. Bound up and tangled in his lies and secrets. We never even talked about it among ourselves. And what did it get us? He scams us out of our investments."

"What does Dave know?" Anne asked.

Jerry looked defeated. "Dave knows he dug a hole, the first grave. And then he made a call to the cops. Me and my wife never said anything to him about Lino probably killing her. Dave knows there are secrets, but he never asked. Maybe he knows more. But, like I said, we don't really talk."

"So, what's your thinking, now?" Anne asked. "Pass the ketchup, please."

Anne and Jack had come straight from their interview with Jerry Silver to the nearly empty Nell's Diner, not a place that catered to the traditional Sunday brunch crowd.

"You still think Lino was murdered?" Anne teased her uncle. Jack had seen Lino's video, heard from Lino's own mouth about the drugs, saw the glazed look in his eyes, the sweat on his brow. Yet even so, he was finding Lino's suicide hard to believe. "We won't know for sure until the toxicology report comes in," Jack said, sliding the ketchup her way.

"Oh, please. Of course, it was drugs. Not from a fall, not from some mysterious killer. Case closed."

Jack held a piece of buttered toast aloft. "I never thought a guy like that would take his own life. It just goes to show: You can bet on horses, but you can't bet on people."

"One case closed, and as for the other case, the attempted robbery yesterday, we aren't involved because it's not a cold case," Anne said.

"Right, not our problem."

"Though I *am* looking forward to testifying at the trial," Anne pounded the ketchup bottle. A red puddle landed on her fries.

"But the cold case of Dinah Pardini's murder—that *is* our problem," Jack said.

"Not mine, I'm not convinced there's a 'there there' and I won't accept an assignment to work on that case. There's no new evidence, just Lino's word against the Silvers.' And Lino's dead, so it's just their word. Carol Silver says she saw Lino get into the limo and drive off, and I believe her. It's a dead end. Seems like Jerry and Dave Silver just got tangled up in Lino's mess."

Jack nodded. "There's no going after Lino. The DA's office wouldn't waste their resources going after any of them for accessory to a murder that can't be proved. I'd still like to know who else was working with Lino. I can't see him digging up her body and moving it. Maybe someday we'll find out, but not now."

"Well, it wasn't Kay Pardini," Anne said and laughed at the thought of the matron wielding a shovel. "She was in Europe during that body-moving escapade. Both families—the Silvers and Pardinis—will be happy to leave the case alone."

They ate in silence for a few minutes.

"Something's been on my mind," Jack set down his fork. "Remember when we talked about what you would do if you ever found the money Lino hid? You wouldn't promise me that you'd turn it over to the authorities. I was worried about you."

"I know."

"So when you hauled all the money in yesterday, I was relieved. You did the right thing. It was a good move."

"There were really no other moves, Uncle Jack. Believe it or not, I listened to you. The things you said about a slippery slope..."

Jack gave her a sideways, I-can't-believe-what-I'm-hearing look. "Just for that, I'm paying for lunch...or brunch, or whatever this is called."

"Oh, I wouldn't hear of it." They both smiled, then Anne said, "I just wish Renee and Josh didn't have to live off the charity of Marco, although..." Anne let the sentence fade as she recalled the bulging purse that Renee had clung to for dear life in the truck.

"She's a smart woman, and she'll figure out how to play the cards she was dealt," Jack said.

"You're right. In fact, if I was someone who bet on people, I'd bet on Renee Pardini."

# Chapter Thirty-Eight

Renee kept reading:

Always write your name on the bottom of your Tupperware when bringing food to a party; your wealthy beau will think it's adorable that you're so thrifty.

*Sweet Jesus.* Renee shook her head at her younger self's list of advice on landing a rich husband. The "Tupperware" part was okay, but the rest? If that's the way she was thinking back then, no wonder she landed in the mess she's in now.

She was flipping through the old notebook that she'd started ten years before when she was considering writing a how-to dating book along the lines of *The Rules.* But the book idea faded fast because, one: Writing is hard. Two: She didn't need the money since she and Lino were rolling in it. And three: She didn't want Lino to think she'd manipulated him into marrying her.

But Lino wasn't around anymore, and life had changed. From the moment she'd carried her bulky purse out of Trudy's Bar & Grill two weeks before, she had a cache of money, which she justified keeping by thinking of it as her rightful community property, money she'd earned and not part of Lino's sheisty schemes. A wobbly justification—one that took a lot of mental gymnastics to arrive at—but she was sticking to it.

At any rate, the money presented a dilemma because she couldn't spend it without raising red flags. People would wonder how she could suddenly afford to move out of the guest cottage—which she and Josh were doing next week—and move into a two-bedroom apartment within Josh's school district. To avoid questions, she had traded in her beloved Mercedes in for an old Camry, which gave her an influx of cash she could account for. That money, added to what she carried out of Trudy's bar, was a good start, a cushion, but she couldn't live on it forever. She still needed a job or a money stream—which is why, when her friend Stella called yesterday with an idea, she listened. In college, Stella never approved of Renee's husband hunting tactics, but now she encouraged her to take another pass at the *How to Marry the Really Rich* guide. "But instead of a book, start a YouTube channel," Stella said. "You know more about attracting men than anyone I know. Monetize yourself!"

Renee did the calculations: For every 1,000 views of her YouTube channel, she'd make about twenty dollars. Paltry. But as the widow of the disgraced Lino Pardini, she had some notoriety, a "brand" some might call it, and that would draw viewers and quickly grow her platform. Some of those YouTubers made serious money.

For five minutes, she sat at the small table, pen in hand, and tried channeling her inner Helen Gurley Brown for fortune-hunting advice. She came up with nothing better than "Take up sailing." Because the truth was, since she was fourteen, she'd never had to think about how to attract a man. Even now, in her mid-forties, it was a rare man she couldn't land with minimal effort. Her attorney, Joel Maroni? It'd be easy. Marco? His wife Kay wouldn't know what hit her. Renee's hold over men had little to do with rules and strategies. It sprang from some sort of alchemy of lucky genetics, men's subconscious, and hormones. Part beauty, part sexual allure/skill. Beyond that, it was an ineffable, mysterious power that couldn't be taught.

But that didn't mean she shouldn't try. So she tried for another five long minutes. Maybe she'd do better if…if what? She couldn't even finish the thought. She put the pen down. *Good God, this is boring,* she thought. Boring and ridiculous. What does any of this have to do with anything that's real? What's this have to do with her life right now? With making a place for herself and Josh in the community again? With giving him his pride back?

And hers, too.

Nothing.

Renee crumpled the paper and started another list: Next Steps. She would get a real job, she wrote, one that made use of her degree in business. Then, she would contact the Women's Financial Abuse Council and join its team of volunteers who were using their financial skills to thwart scammers and help victims. Volunteering there might flip the public's perception of her from being an accomplice to being a victim, one who survived her victimhood. A fighter on the side of righting wrongs. And by righting those wrongs, she would be doing good deeds—those mitzvahs she'd vowed to do. A win-win.

But before all of that, she needed to call the mayor's office to finalize plans for next week's awards ceremony honoring outstanding high school students. She'd engineered every detail of the event—from its concept to the venue, including the list of students who would be on the stage. Marco and her friend Lori Paige had lent their social clout to the project, which is the only reason it got off the ground.

But off the ground, it was: This very public ceremony would be the biggest, showiest, most foundational piece of her plan.

# Chapter Thirty-Nine

There was only one reason the Channel 5 news cameras, along with second-tier reporter Nick King, bothered to show up for the first annual "Leaders of Tomorrow" award ceremony in Santa Rosa: The public remained fascinated by any news having to do with the Pardini family.

Three weeks had gone by since the attempted hijacking, during which time Jerry Silver and Luis Ramirez had been released on bail and were now awaiting trial. It was six weeks since Lino Pardini's financial crimes came to light, and the court-appointed receiver was busy distributing the proceeds from Lino's and Renee's seized property, including the nearly $500,000 found in the pickup, to victims of the Ponzi scheme. Sixteen years had passed since Dinah Pardini's body was found. Dave Silver voluntarily made a statement about the call he had made. No charges were filed.

"Today's event highlights the personal side of the Pardini saga," Nick King said. "We're here in the gallery of the Pardini Winery, where the 1956 pickup truck holds pride of place in the center of the room."

The truck was slowly revolving around on a motorized disc; camera lights glinting off its polished green paint job and chrome surfaces. In front of it were eight nervous high school students holding up their various civic awards.

Eight miles away at Trudy Lee's Bar & Grill, Anne and Trudy were sitting side by side on bar stools, sharing a basket of chips and salsa and staring up at the flat-screen television. Trudy had invited Anne over to get her professional opinion about how much she could get for her Wurlitzer jukebox. "About $15,000," Anne said. Trudy looked disappointed and said, "Guess I'll keep it," and turned back to the TV screen.

"There's Chloe, my assistant," Anne said, pointing to the teen, who was proudly holding her Battalion Chef badge waist-high for the cameras. Standing next to her was Josh Pardini, fidgeting and bouncing on his toes.

"We'll be right back with the major presentations of the day," the reporter said. A commercial came on, and Trudy turned the volume down.

"I've been wondering about something, Trudy," Anne said, reaching for a chip. "Maybe you can clear it up. So…Dave shows up at the auction with $90,000 of yours, according to the story Renee's been handing me—and I'm sure it's the same story Dave would hand me, too, if he was talking to me," Anne smiled ruefully. "The story is that the money came from your own pocket, donated out of the goodness and kindness of your heart…"

"Is that so hard to believe?"

"Frankly, yes. Because I think the $90,000 was part of Lino's stash, a fraction of it. He used that money to bid on the truck for Renee, so she could find and keep the big money. Which unfortunately for her, didn't happen, but that's beside the point. So, here's my question: Lino trusted you with the money. You gave it to Dave…"

Trudy got up and walked around to the other side of the bar. Anne took that to mean that Trudy wanted the subject changed, but Anne continued with her musings, not losing a beat. "Where was I? Oh yes, all that money that Lino put aside for bidding on the truck…$90,000, am I right? Lino handed you all that money so the truck could go to Renee…"

Trudy picked up the bar rag, took a desultory swipe at the bartop, and then shrugged. Said nothing. Just continued wiping the same water spot over and over, not looking at Anne.

"All that money should have been turned over to the U.S. Marshals," Anne went on. "It should have been put into the kitty along with all the rest of the money they're collecting for Lino's ripped off investors. But instead, Renee has it. Not that she doesn't need it, I'm just…"

"What money?" Trudy leaned against the back counter and leveled her eyes at Anne. "I don't know anything about any $90,000." She folded her arms across her chest.

Anne held her gaze. What money, indeed? Who can prove it even existed? No one seems to be thinking about it. No one had asked about it, anyway. And if they did, Dave could just tell the truth: Trudy gave it to him for bidding. Everyone knew Trudy had money, so what's the problem? No one gave a damn about the $90,000. It was small potatoes, and all the focus was on the $500,000—the real money—that the Feds had collected from the gas tank. And they had collected every last dime of it.

Anne made a decision. "Me neither, Trudy. I know nothing," she said with a faint smile. "And I'm pretty sure Dave knows nothing, too. And Renee most *certainly* knows nothing."

"And really, when you think about it," Trudy said, a philosophical lilt in her voice as she reached back and pulled a bottle of Johnnie Walker Black Label down from the back-lit shelf, "who really knows anything about anything these days?"

Anne nodded genially. "Not me. I know nothing."

Trudy set out two shot glasses and gave each one a healthy pour.

"A toast, then," Trudy said, sliding a glass across the scarred wood in Anne's direction, "to being a couple of know-nothings." They clinked shot glasses and sipped their whiskey. Anne shuddered a bit at the taste but knocked back the rest, anyway.

Commercial over, Trudy raised the volume. Mayor James Ballard was shaking hands with Josh.

"So, young man, in recognition of your honesty, unselfishness, and commitment to strong community and family values, it's my pleasure to award you with this year's 'Honesty and Integrity Award.'" He smiled broadly at the assembled press and handed the framed certificate to Josh, who took it with shaking hands. Wearing a tie and a size-too-small suit and looking nervous, Josh moved closer to the microphone. He coughed into his fist and said, "I just have a few words to say, if that's okay." He looked over at the mayor for permission. The mayor nodded. "Of course, son."

"We—my mom and me—turned over the money we found because my dad always wanted me to do the right thing. I know he would have wanted people to have their money back." He looked near tears. "He didn't mean to hurt anybody."

Josh stepped away from the microphone and stood between his mother and Dave Silver. *Why is Dave there?* Anne wondered. Probably because Josh wanted him there; Dave had come to their rescue and Josh looked up to him. Also standing with them was Renee's stepdaughter, Jennifer, wearing a familiar strand of pearls with a blue sapphire clasp. Anne saw Renee glance at the pearls and then smile at Jennifer. Some kind of reconciliation had occurred. *Well, what do you know?*

"If I may say a few words..." Marco Pardini stepped up to the microphone. "I'd just like to say something about this young man here, my nephew. Josh has made the Pardini family proud. His selfless actions give honor back to the Pardini name."

"My mom is really the one—" Josh threw in.

"Yes, of course," Marco said.

Anne and Trudy exchanged looks. Renee's part in recovering the money was common knowledge, but as the widow of the town's villain, her image wasn't as appealing as that of the brave young son. Their focus went back to the screen.

"Not liking *that*," Trudy murmured.

"What?" All Anne could see was the teenager, grinning proudly and standing between his mother and Dave Silver. His arms were slung over their shoulders.

"Looks a little cozy, is all I'm saying. Like a regular little family."

"Dave and Renee and Josh?" Anne watched as Josh slipped away from them to talk to Chloe and the other students. That left Renee and Dave alone together, laughing and chatting.

Trudy watched Anne watching them.

"Want to know what I think?" Trudy asked, aiming a forefinger at Anne.

"Do tell."

"It's none of my business, but I think you have only a short, short window of opportunity here. Renee is a powerful force. I know we were joking about not knowing anything, but there's one thing I *do* know: If you're waiting around to find someone better than Dave Silver, your grapes will die on the vine before it happens. Shrivel into tiny raisins."

Anne rolled her eyes.

"Seriously, I know of no one better. Besides being a good and decent man, he has another quality: You never know what he's going to say or do, which is no small thing in the long run. You'll never be bored. I'm not saying he's perfect—"

"He has quite a past."

"Oh, please, honey," Trudy exhaled an exasperated breath and put her hands on her hips, "Who doesn't? Who worth a goddamn doesn't?"

# Chapter Forty

Dave Silver hitched a booted foot onto the lowest rung of the split rail fence and looked out at the grassy, rectangular patch of land across the side street from Trudy's bar.

It was about ten fenced-in acres, stretching north from Highway 12, with no landscaping of any kind to disturb the terrain. No berry bushes, no flowering shrubs, no volunteer trees. With the exception of weeds and an ancient oak tree in the center, nothing to distract from the sheer possibilities of the land.

Trudy crossed the road, weaving behind and between cars, and came up beside him. Her arms rested on the top railing. Looking straight ahead, she said, "Sorry about your dad and Luis. Your dad can be a damn fool sometimes, but I never figured him for someone who'd wave around a gun. What the hell was he thinking?"

"Thinking about money, of course. He figured Lino stashed money in the truck, and he was right. But Luis was the one who forged that metal slider on the old fuel tank and told Dad about it. Luis was the one with the gun—"

"Your friend since childhood. I don't know how many times Luis has been in my bar, friendly as can be." Trudy shook her head at the vagaries of mankind. "But, giving him the benefit of the doubt, maybe he didn't know it was you and Trailer in the bushes. Anyway, those two were lucky you showed up. You saved them from getting in deeper. Saved them from hurting someone."

Her words hung in the air. The muffled drone of Highway 12 traffic was coming from just beyond the row of cypress trees. Dave's eyes roved the property north to south, east to west. He could smell the rich, dark soil.

"Pretty piece of land," he said after a moment.

"It looks the same as the day I bought it," she said.

He looked at her sideways.

"Don't look so surprised. I had to put my money into something, and land's the best investment there is. Someday, I'll think of something to do with it."

"Ever consider selling it? It'd be a good place for a nursery. Can't beat the location. Everyone in town passes along Highway 12. I might be…"

"I'm not sure about selling. But I might consider a partnership, if you're up for it."

"What kind?"

"The kind where I own the land, and that's the extent of it."

They fell quiet for a few seconds, then she said, "I'm serious about this. You can use the land rent-free and run the nursery any way you please. There's room for your mobile home back there in the corner, see?" With his father possibly headed for a long prison sentence and his mother moving to a memory care facility, the Silver Vineyards property was being sold to a neighboring winery. Dave needed to move. He was ready for a change, anyway. Past ready.

"That's very generous of you, Trudy, but I can afford to lease it."

"I know, but here's the thing: I have no children, Davy. And no nieces, no nephews. You're kind of 'it.' You're going to inherit my property and savings someday. Not soon, but someday. Half of my holdings, anyway," she said. "Fair warning, you won't be getting the bar—that goes to Derrick for services rendered." A pause. "Don't smirk at me, Dave."

"I'm not." He smiled faintly.

"What I meant was that he's bartended for me for over twenty years, and he's earned it."

Dave left that comment alone.

"If you change your mind about starting the nursery business, I have another idea. I've always wanted to get back to the land," she said with a soft laugh. "Start up a commune with some like-minded—"

"No commune, Trudy. That's where I put my foot down."

They both smiled at that. "No commune, fine," Trudy said.

\* \* \*

Dave was sitting on the curb across the street from Anne's duplex. Anne was standing next to him. Both were surveying her small yard. Landscaping-wise and otherwise, they were starting over.

"Now I'm leaning toward a minimalist look." Anne narrowed her eyes, as if conjuring up a vision. "A few tasteful grassy things, some flowering red whatevers."

"Which means the peach tree *really* has to go." He stretched out his legs and reached into his knapsack for his graphics drawing tablet.

"Not a chance. By the way, sorry I was late. I was seeing a new client, packing things up for auction, bringing a housewarming gift over to Renee's new apartment. All that and, of course, trying to figure out what to wear." She was dressed in her usual jeans and black tee.

He nodded, looking her up and down. "I agonized over what I'd wear, too. I tried on a few shirts, but decided to go with this one," he said with a half-smile, pulling at the collar of his black button-front shirt. "We got along so well the last time I was wearing it."

She sat down next to him, close.

"So, are you seeing anyone?" he asked in an off-hand way, squinting against the noonday sun.

"No. You?"

"I'm working on it."

"So, how's it going?"

He let out a short laugh. He leaned sideways into her, bumping her shoulder with his. "You tell me."

"Pretty well, I'd say. A little slow, but getting there. Why don't we discuss it inside." Anne stood up. "I have a peach pie I made in the kitchen...actually, that's a lie. I gave some peaches to my Aunt Dot last summer and she made the pie. From scratch. But I did wrap it up in foil and label it and put it in my freezer, and then I took it out this morning and set it on the counter to defrost."

Dave laughed, getting to his feet. "I like a woman who knows her way around a kitchen."

Trailer followed them across the street to the front door.

"Sit, girl. I'll just be a few minutes," he said as Anne opened the door.

Trailer looked from Dave to Anne. Then looked back to Dave again. Then she laid down on the porch and put her head on her paws. Anticipating a long, long nap.

# A Note from the Author

Those familiar with Santa Rosa will notice I've taken liberties with geography and have inserted hills and streets where none exist. Restaurants, wineries, police facilities, and other institutions have been altered or invented to suit the story and should therefore be regarded as entirely fictitious.

# Acknowledgments

Thank you to Shawn Reilly Simmons, Deb Well, and Verena Rose of Level Best Books for making *Running on Empty* a reality. Thanks also to those who read and/or edited the early versions and gave me honest feedback: Kristen Weber, Allie Yohn, and Virginia Adams. I'm indebted to David Samuel Levinson, a brilliant editor, for suggesting ways to deepen the suspense and sharpen characterizations. Much gratitude, too, to Harriette Wasserman Sackler for her many insights and encouragement.

Much like watching a game of *Jeopardy*, writing reveals to me how little I know about so many things. Many thanks to those who patiently answered questions about the law, drugs, video games, the FBI, Spanish, construction, and wine making: Mike McCaskill, Nicole Tierheimer, George Fong, Kenny Sanford, Jack Kane, Connell Kane, John Kane, Bob Priestley, and Clark and Bonny Lystra of Betty Ann Vineyard. Very special thanks to my neighbor Charles Sardina, a self-described "car guy," for his generous sharing of ideas and knowledge. And thank you, John Leach, retired homicide detective and co-grandparent, for once again graciously answering all my police-related questions. Any and all mistakes are mine.

Finally, but not least, thank you to friends and family who passed along story ideas (whether they intended to or not) and provided much-welcomed support: Tina Fruiht Bacon, Katie Torgerson, Sharon Kane, Pauline Bartholomew, Margaret Visek, Bailey Kane, Randy Grenier, and Ray Kuhn. To Harley Tierheimer, best son in the entire world, thanks for lending the name of your first dog, Trailer, for the story. And of course, thanks to my husband Allen Sanford, who made his dashing appearance in my life wearing a brown leather bomber jacket, for his patience, love, and understanding, and for watching *Jeopardy* with me.

# About the Author

Karin Fitz Sanford, a former advertising copywriter, was born in New York but grew up in Northern California's Wine Country, the setting for her *Wine Country Cold Case* series. Having run her own award-winning ad agency for over twenty-five years, she is a member of Sisters in Crime and lives in Northern California with her husband.

SOCIAL MEDIA HANDLES:
  Facebook: Karin Fitzgerald Sanford
  Instagram: karinfitz8

AUTHOR WEBSITE:
  FitzSanford.com

# Also by Karin Fitz Sanford

*The Last Thing Claire Wanted*: A Wine Country Cold Case

Printed in the USA
CPSIA information can be obtained
at www.ICGtesting.com
LVHW090744110724
785130LV00001B/46